# The First Pharaoh

Lester Picker

Copyright © 2012 Lester Picker

All rights reserved.

ISBN-10: 1479202304
ISBN-13: 978-1479202300

# Dedication

For Leslie, my Neith-Hotep

| | |
|---|---|
| Dedication | iii |
| Acknowledgements | vii |
| Book I - Anhotek | 11 |

  Scroll One
    Under The Wings of Horus .......................................... 15
  Scroll Two
    The Scorpion's Sting .................................................... 29
  Scroll Three
    Tremors ........................................................................ 51
  Scroll Four
    Questions ..................................................................... 63
  Scroll Five
    A Severe Remedy ......................................................... 79
  Scroll Six
    The Vision .................................................................... 91
  Scroll Seven
    Ra's Glory .................................................................. 109
  Scroll Eight
    Mother Nile ............................................................... 125
  Scroll Nine
    Light of God .............................................................. 141
  Scroll Ten
    Crossing The Line ..................................................... 155
  Scroll Eleven
    Turmoil ...................................................................... 169
  Scroll Twelve
    Traitor In Our midst ................................................. 183

Book II - Narmer .................................................................. 199
   Scroll Thirteen
      Ascension ................................................................ 203
   Scroll Fourteen
      Unification .............................................................. 219
   Scroll Fifteen
      The Palette .............................................................. 241
   Scroll Sixteen
      Immersion ............................................................... 259
   Scroll Seventeen
      An Uneasy Alliance ................................................ 277
   Scroll Eighteen
      I Whispered Her Name ......................................... 291
   Scroll Nineteen
      Ma'at ....................................................................... 313
   Scroll Twenty
      Desert Wisdom ...................................................... 333
   Scroll Twenty-One
      A Sweet Drop Of Rain .......................................... 351
   Scroll Twenty-Two
      My Son .................................................................... 375
   Scroll Twenty-Three
      The Scorpion Returns ........................................... 393
   Scroll Twenty-Four
      The Lesson ............................................................. 417
   Scroll Twenty-Five
      Horus ...................................................................... 437
   Scroll Twenty-Six
      For But One Moment… ........................................ 449

Afterward ............................................................................ 453

The First Pharaoh Reader's Guide ..................................... 455

About The Author .............................................................. 459

# ACKNOWLEDGEMENTS

Trite as it sounds, I could not have written this book without the wisdom and time of many generous people. I would like to acknowledge some of them here.

Dr. Gunter Dreyer of the German Archaeological Institute, patiently spent many hours with me in Cairo and Berlin, by email and on the telephone, answering my questions and tutoring me about life in Narmer's time.

Dr. Toby Wilkinson of Christ's College, Cambridge University, gave me fresh perspectives on early dynastic life and patiently answered my questions. He shared my enthusiasm for this project, for which I will be always grateful. His book, Early Dynastic Egypt (Routledge, 1999) is a wonderful, readable resource for those people serious about Egyptian civilization at the time of Narmer.

Abdel Zaher Sulimaan, my Bedouin guide, patiently taught me about life in Egypt's eastern desert and, more importantly, about life. Dr. Zawi Hawass, head of the Egyptian government's archaeological program, without whose dedication and passion for his country's ancient past much of the archaeological work that led to my writing this book would not have been possible.

I also acknowledge the contribution to this work of Egyptologists Dr. Betsy Bryan (The Johns Hopkins

University), Dr. Renee Friedman (The Hierakonpolis Society), Dr. Richard Jasnow (The Johns Hopkins University), Ethan Watrall (then a doctoral student at University of Indiana), and their many colleagues who spent time with me explaining aspects of early dynastic Egypt. These dedicated scientists toil, often in obscurity and always under trying conditions, to uncover our past so that we can understand ourselves better.

William Cates, John Hurley, Jay Magenheim, Randy Richie and Joel Rosenberg, Dave Jaffe, Sherif Osman, and Scott Brown, my men's teams, have collectively supported my vision, kept me on track and knocked-me-up-side-of-the-head when needed, usually regularly. I owe them a huge debt of gratitude but, of course, not as large as they owe me.

Special thanks to Cathy Cohen, my able assistant at the inception of this project and Lu Maistros, my extraordinary research assistant, who is now off doing her own writing. Terry Sexton, my Tuesday-mornings-with-Terry writing companion, brainstorming partner, and personal editor. I can't wait to celebrate publication of your books!

As with any work of historical fiction, there may be numerous fabrications and embellishments in this story, although I suspect that there may not have needed to be had we known more about the actual facts of Narmer's life. However, to the extent that there are historical inaccuracies in this work, I take full responsibility for them.

Finally, and most importantly, I thank my incredible wife, Leslie, without whose abiding love and unconditional support I could never have written this book. She is the love of my life (and my first-line editor).

*Concerning Egypt I will now speak at length, because nowhere are there so many marvelous things, nor in the whole world beside are there to be seen so many works of unspeakable greatness.*

- Herodotus

# BOOK I - ANHOTEK

*That I am dead when you read these words is of no consequence. That I once walked the Two Lands of my beloved Kem, served my King and wrote this account of his life is all that matters. I birthed his mortal flesh from his mother's womb, I changed his swaddling clothes, I traveled with him to all reaches of our lands and beyond. Future generations will revere him as a God-King and I, above all others, would agree.*

*These words I swear in Ra's name to be a true account of my beloved King's life. Read them that you shall know how Kem achieved its own greatness. Read them and you shall know the story of how the son of Ra walked the Two Lands, loved its people and fought its enemies, both within and without.*

*I am Anhotek, Chief Scribe and Shaman of King Narmer, Beloved of Horus, Unifier of Upper and Lower Kem, Ruler of the Lands of the Lotus and Papyrus.*

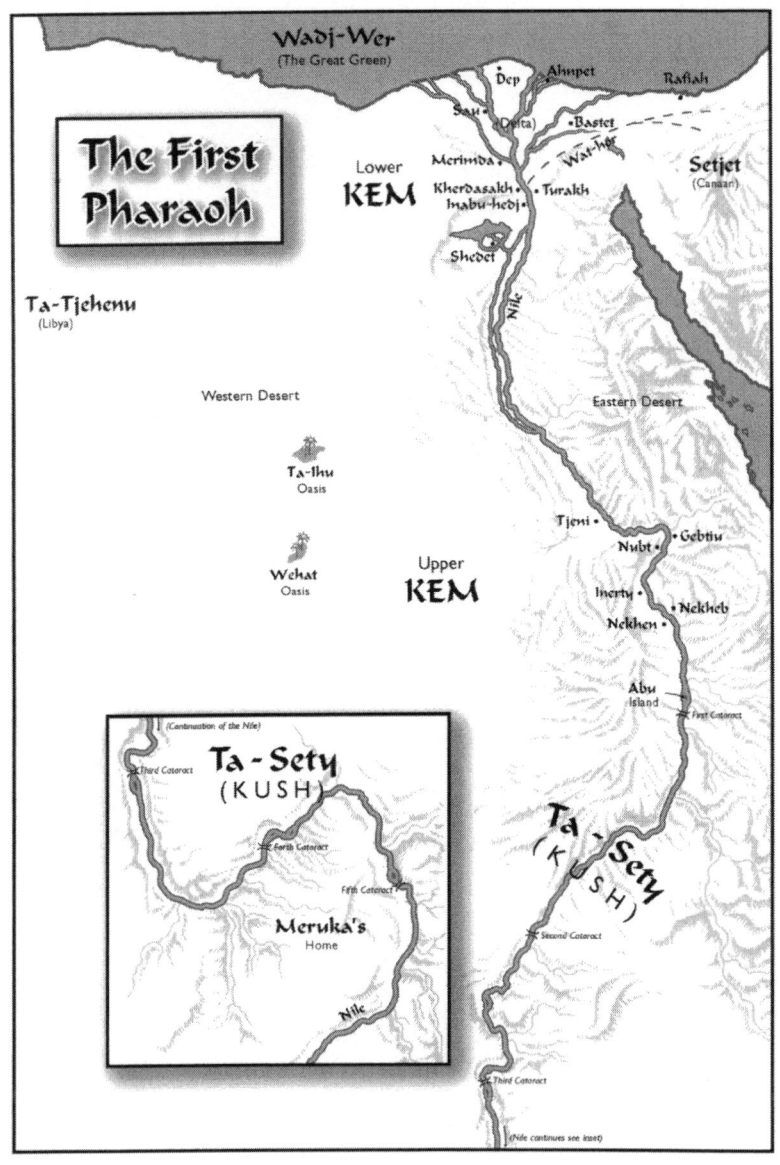

# SCROLL ONE

## *Under The Wings of Horus*

  The bright afternoon sun changed color slowly, now taking on a reddish hue, not a favorable sign from the gods. I tried to think what it was we might have done that had angered Ra, but my weary mind swam in a fog, so that I felt like a blind beggar on the streets of Tjeni. I was exhausted, standing by the bed of the Queen, watching the great orb of Ra descend under the portico, between two square mud brick columns in the courtyard. It had been almost two days since the Queen started labor and her strength was waning. With her tiny stature and frail nature it was a miracle that she had lasted this long.

  Servants, dressed alike in coarse white linen robes that draped their ankles, scurried barefoot around the Queen's quarters like bees in a hive. One of them brought water to the Queen's bedside, while two others changed the fine linen sheets upon which she lay. The water-bearer wiped the sweat from the Queen's naked body.

  A young girl, not yet ten years judging by her unformed breasts, carried pomegranates, dates and figs to refresh the bowls of fruits and nuts that were carefully arranged on long, brightly painted wooden tables around the periphery of the spacious birth pavilion. Like all children, she wore her single, pleated braid down the side of her head. The rest of her head was shaved clean.

The dry afternoon winds blew freely through the gardens, lightly rustling the dark green columbine leaves that spiraled around each of the pavilion's many columns.

Despite my weariness, I marveled at how ordered, how divinely ordained was life in our beloved Upper Kem, Land of the Lotus. Each servant knew precisely what her role was, no more, but also no less. It was the natural order of things, ma'at, a perfect balance that kept chaos and the forces of evil at bay. I felt a certain sense of pride, even at a desperate time like this, for I, Anhotek, Chief Scribe, Horus priest and shaman to the royal court of King Scorpion, was in no small measure responsible for maintaining that balance.

The Queen had slept for but a few moments between contractions. Now she began to stir, as another wave of pain began its climb to an inevitable crescendo. I rushed over and took her hand.

"Is it time, yet?" she moaned, so weakly I had to bend nearer to hear her words. Her soft, unblemished skin was again soaked in perspiration. I mopped her brow and neck with a clean cloth, taking care not to disturb the gold amulet necklace of the frog god, Heket, who protected her during her labor. Her hair was still tightly bound in tiny braids and beads atop her head, but strands had come loose and lay twisted on her pillow, coated with the scented fat that I had poured on her head at the beginning of her labor as part of the ritual to Hathor.

"Soon, my dear Neith-hotpu," I whispered in her ear. "Very soon."

But, the Queen hardly heard me. Her mind was numbed with fatigue and she hardly stirred in the birthing bed, despite the pain. "How long has it been, Anhotek? It seems like an eternity already."

I breathed deeply, fighting back my tears, and took the Queen's tiny hand in my own, massaging it gently with my fingertips.

"My sweet lotus, it takes time to create things great and wonderful," I whispered. "It is like Upper Kem itself. The gods took a long, long time to birth it from Mother Nile so they could give it as a gift to our people." Her brow relaxed as she listened to my voice. "You are birthing a son... a mighty prince. Your ka and the King's created him and he will follow your mighty husband and lead our land to even more greatness."

Neith-hotpu's eyes closed. "Anhotek, do you still believe it will be a boy?"

I gazed at her body before answering. It distressed me to no end to see her breaths coming in short gasps. I put my hand on her abdomen and felt the muscles tensed with pain, then smoothed a palm over my forehead, as if to erase its creases from the Queen's view.

"Oh, my lovely Queen, ruler of Upper Kem, of this I am sure. You will bear a son. There is no mistaking the color your urine turns the emmer wheat. And he will be a great and mighty warrior." I patted her abdomen gently. "But now you must rest to save your strength." I pointed to the amulet on her neck. "Even Heket needs your help."

"It will be yet a little while before the young prince is ready to face the world. Perhaps he waits for his father to return from battle." The Queen just stared at me vacantly. I shivered at what I saw behind her eyes and I quickly whispered a prayer to Hathor, goddess of women in childbirth.

"My hand is upon you and your baby, Queen Neith-hotpu, beloved of Upper Kem. May Hathor bring the sweet north wind to hasten the delivery of the Prince and may the seal of Hathor be your protection." Seven times did I repeat this chant, which may only be offered by a Horus priest to a woman in childbirth.

Neith-hotpu closed her eyes. My body slouched with fatigue. I had not slept for at least a day and I began to worry that my judgment would be affected by my exhaustion. But, there could be no mistaking the signs the last time I had examined the Queen, hardly an hour ago.

She had not dilated beyond the width of my two fingers and both baby and mother were in distress. It was a breach birth, of that I was sure. I had inserted my fingers to feel for tiny toes or even, Ra forbid, the baby's soft backside. But in all my years ministering at dozens of births I had never encountered a baby positioned as precipitously as was this one.

While the Queen's servants watched nervously from various corners of the room, I placed four curved ivory magic wands, one at each corner of the Queen's bed, their ninety-degree bends defining the edges of a rectangle that enclosed her in a magical protective space. Each of the servants that were allowed to touch the Queen was careful not to disturb them. But, as the day wore on, it was obvious to me that another powerful magic was at work in the Queen's birthing, a power from the other world that far exceeded my own.

I opened a drawer of my cedar herbal chest and removed two small clay jars. I had known for hours that something was wrong, but in my weariness I had hoped against hope that natural events would speed the labor, as I had seen happen so many times before. I had no choice now but to act and to ready myself for the worst.

I opened the clay jars and out wafted pungent aromas. The herbs they contained I had gathered myself, from as far away as the sandy shores of the Great Green and the sheer cliffs of Upper Kush.

I motioned to Neith-hotpu's head mistress to bring my mortars and pestles. The woman returned in less than two minutes. Her ashen face radiated the fear that all the Queen's servants had for her very life. Their love for her was as real as the danger they all knew she now faced. Every woman in the room had seen friends and relatives die in childbirth. Such was the burden from the gods that women shouldered, although I hardly understood why they so willingly did so.

Steadying my hands, I made a paste of the fenugreek seeds with my mortar and pestle and heated it over a candle until it turned a dark brown. Then I added an equal measure of honey and stirred until the mixture was consistent.

I opened another container, this one smelling of fir resin, which I had extracted myself from tree chips I had the King's traders import from lands far away, near Canaan. Soaked for months in the fermented juices of thyme and other plants, the thick fluid prevented wounds from festering. I added a few drops of the resin to the concoction in the bowl, watching them diffuse through the paste. Satisfied, I took out yet another jar from my cedar chest and added a pinch of incense to the mixture.

Working quickly, so the magic of the medicine would not dissipate, I ground the bulbs of three scallions in a clean pestle and emptied the contents of the pestle into the mixture. Reaching to my side, I opened a jar of dark barley beer, ladled out several drops and mixed all the ingredients together, adding a few sprigs of powdered juniper leaves to thicken it.

The women murmured in assent as I worked, shaking their heads or pointing toward me and whispering. I formed the doughy mixture into a tube, as long and as wide as two of my fingers, then lifted it from the bowl, amidst a rising crescendo of whispers. I looked with annoyance at the head mistress, instantly silencing her. She raised and lowered her hands and all the women in the room quieted, some holding their hands over their mouths as if, in their excitement and anxiety, it was the only way they could contain themselves.

I cocked my head toward the exit and the older woman instructed all the others to leave the room. When the last of the Queen's hand maidens passed through the portico, the woman walked to my side.

"Hemamiya," I whispered, "I must hurry this labor. Talk to your mistress, while I examine her." Hemamiya nodded knowingly, her lips tightly closed. She had lost her youngest daughter in childbirth not more than four years ago. I knew she understood the gravity of the situation.

While Hemamiya sat on the edge of the bed, speaking soothingly and wiping the Queen's brow, I worked quickly. I held my hand on the Queen's abdomen, waiting for the contraction to peak, then lifted the sheet guarding the

Queen's modesty. I lifted her knees and spread her legs, feeling no resistance whatsoever. I marveled, yet again, at how tiny her body was, even with her abdomen so distended. I had seen countless births in my thirty-five long years, and dozens more in women from neighboring lands. And, while the babies were invariably similar in size, the women, most decidedly, were not. Kemian women were by far the smallest, and the birth process was far from kind to them. In villages throughout Upper Kem it was not uncommon to lose half its women to childbirth, a problem that vexed me to no end. For without our women, where was our hope for the future?

I checked to see how dilated the opening to the womb was, then I gently inserted the suppository, molding it under and around the opening to her womb. I would give the suppository an hour to work its magic.

I grabbed the bowl of medicine and added several more drops of moringa oil, then carried it over to the Queen's side. "Here, Hemamiya," I said, placing it in her outstretched hands. "Rub this oil carefully over the Queen's abdomen... down here," I said, pointing to my own pubic bone. "Rub gently for fifteen minutes, then come get me... and be sure she drinks plenty of water. Mother Nile must do her part, too." I turned around, stooped with fatigue, and added. "I... I will be in my quarters, mixing up some potions."

Once in my quarters, I lay down on my bed. It was a simple wooden bench, darkly stained, but intricately caned with rushes harvested from Mother Nile. On top of the caning rested a thick mattress made of coarse linen stuffed with goat hair, now fluffed up by the servants. I tried to go over a mental list of items I would need for the actual birth, but in seconds I was asleep, besieged by frightening dreams of swimming against Mother Nile's current. All around me demons slithered easily through the waters.

"Anhotek! Anhotek, wake up!" Hemamiya was holding my shoulders and shaking me. "The Queen... she needs you! Anhotek, get up!"

"What? How...ummm...how long have I slept?" I

asked, swinging my legs over the bed and already thinking through what tools and herbals I might need.

"I'm not sure. Perhaps thirty minutes, perhaps an hour... come quickly!" Her eyes were wide with fear. "The Queen is bleeding badly. She..."

But I had already picked up my surgical bag and was through the doorway leading to the Queen's chambers. I ran down the brick causeway, silently cursing Hemamiya for not waking me in fifteen minutes, then realizing I should never have left the Queen's side after ministering such a powerful medicine. The air was dry and hot and I felt dehydrated. But, my own needs would have to wait.

I surveyed the scene as soon as I entered the Queen's chamber. The women parted. Neith-hotpu's bed glistened crimson. A stack of blood-stained sheets lay in a heap nearby. The servants stood around, some crying, some consoling their peers, no one knowing what to do. Hemamiya pointed with her fingers and immediately two young girls grabbed the bloody sheets and ran from the room.

"Hemamiya," I said. "Choose two of your most trustworthy women to assist us... ones that have borne children themselves. Get the rest of them out of here!" I turned toward the Queen, then back again to Hemamiya. "One more thing you must do yourself, Hemamiya. Go to the head guard and have him cordon off the Queen's compound. No one is to be allowed to enter. I want no one within earshot." The poor woman's face was contorted in pain as if she, herself, had been skewered by an enemy's blade. But, I, too felt skewered by the same blade, for I loved the Queen as surely as if she were my own flesh and blood.

"But, isn't there...?"

"Every second you waste is a second I cannot spend saving the Queen's life," I lied. "Go!"

As Hemamiya raced out, whispering orders for all to leave except for two of her charges, I threw the sheet off Neith-hotpu's pale body. She lay still, her legs straight on the bed, despite the birth process having begun.

I grabbed the Queen and hoisted her up on her pillows. Then I placed a straw-filled matt under the Queen's buttocks. I positioned one woman on each side and had them hold the Queen's knees bent up toward her chest. I quickly coated my hands with juniper juice.

Opening my surgical bag, I removed the wood birth canal openers my mentor Sisi, a Ta-Sety shaman, had given me. These openers had no equal in all of Kem, such are the healing arts of the Ta-Setians. Yet, I had to carve and sand the wood pieces for use in the smaller birth canals of Kemian women. I inserted the longer wooden blades into Neith-hotpu's birth canal and spread them apart, holding them open with a wooden dowel, then quickly wrapped the attached piece of rawhide above the dowel.

With the opener in place, I immediately saw that the suppository I had placed in the Queen's birth canal had worked, perhaps even too well. The Queen's womb was fully open, but the baby's breech position had begun to tear the opening. Blood spurted from several torn arteries. The baby's head was still not visible.

I inserted both my hands into the canal and tried to ascertain the baby's position. The women holding the Queen's knees were white with fear. The baby's head was bent backward at the neck, its chin caught on the inside of the pubic bone. The more the Queen's womb contracted, the greater the risk of breaking its neck. If I did not act immediately, both mother and baby would surely die.

Hemamiya had been standing behind me throughout, watching, and talking softly to calm the Queen's young handmaidens. She handed me a towel soaked in juniper juice. I cleaned my hands and instructed the two women to lower the Queen's knees. I motioned to Hemamiya to follow me.

Out of earshot of the two maidservants, I turned toward Hemamiya. "May the gods have mercy on us, dear Hemamiya. There is no choice to what I must do… and quickly, too." Tears ran down her cheeks.

"But, we are two of us used to doing what we must do." I glanced at the Queen and took a deep breath. "The baby is stuck. They will both die if we wait any longer. As is, I don't know what damage has been done to the new prince."

"She is so young," Hemamiya sobbed, protesting for both of us.

Only last year Hemamiya and I had been present at the blessing for the Queen's first flow of menstrual blood. "Yes, fourteen years... much too young."

We stood in silence for a moment, as the two women stared at us. "They will be of little use to us now. The two of us can handle what needs to be done. Dismiss them while I make ready."

Hemamiya gently ushered them out of the room, as I took my place by the side of the Queen's bed. Hemamiya soon joined me. As I removed various surgical tools from my bag, she placed them neatly on a wooden tray. I silently offered a prayer to Horus and Osiris.

"Hemamiya, set up a stand of water and a cloth to wash off the Prince once he emerges. Once I sedate the Queen, we have but a few moments to complete this or..." I did not need to finish my statement. The two of us worked as if in a trance, shutting out the unthinkable for as long as possible.

"She is sedated now. She will feel no pain, Hemamiya... that I promise you."

I passed my hands over the Queen's body three times, while Hemamiya covered her eyes. "Ra, father of the sky and Upper Kem, we have done our best to prepare our Queen for life in the hereafter, even though she leaves us in the ascending years of life. She has been a good daughter, a good wife to King Scorpion, and a fair and just Queen. Her heart is light. She has worked hard to bear a son for the King. Please judge her with compassion and sail with her on the heavenly boat to your palace in the Western sky. Please make it so."

Hemamiya looked up at me, her face flushed. "Hemamiya, you will need to draw upon all your strength for what I am about to do." She stared straight back into my ka.

"I am ready." I placed my finest flint knife on the Queen's abdomen and traced my path with the handle. "I will make a cut from here to here. There will be much blood and it will look very bad," I whispered, hardly believing I was speaking such words. "If necessary look away, but you must hold the skin firmly on your side and pull it gently toward you as I cut." Tears steadily fell from Hemamiya's cheeks onto the bed sheet, but she held herself from sobbing fully.

"Do you understand?" She only nodded. "I am depending on you to do this, Hemamiya, or I may cut through her womb and cut the baby, too."

"You need not worry," Hemamiya said.

I closed my eyes in prayer for a moment to ask the gods to guide my hands, and to beg their forgiveness if I did not succeed. Then I made an arcing cut from just above and to the side of the Queen's navel, down toward her pubic bone and then back up the other side. I attached the three copper hooks of the retractor to the flesh near the lowest point of the arc, each hook with a rawhide cord attached. Still fixated on my cut, I handed the cords to Hemamiya and reminded her to pull back gently. I heard a muffled moan rise from deep in her throat and looked up to see her nose and eyes running freely now.

With the top layer of skin peeled back, the Queen's swollen womb was clearly visible. I picked up a smaller flint knife and carefully cut into the base of the Queen's womb. The sweat from my dripping brow stung my eyes. Blood quickly obscured my view. We mopped it away with rags from the pile Hemamiya had stacked by the bed. After what seemed like an eternity, the walls of the womb began to part and I could see strands of dark, matted hair. My heart quickened.

Placing my left hand into the womb to protect the baby's head and upper trunk, my right hand traced the blade along the baby's body, until the cut was large enough to free him. I put down the knife. Holding the baby under his arms, I pulled him firmly from the Queen's limp body into Ra's light and placed him on the bed sheet.

Next, I tied the umbilical cord with a thin piece of goat rawhide a few finger widths from the baby's abdomen and tied it off again, a few finger widths away, then cut between them with a special, engraved flint knife that I had commissioned for the birth. As I turned the baby over onto my left hand, I noticed that Hemamiya stood rigidly, still holding the retractors.

"Hemamiya," I whispered. "Hemamiya... let go the cords." She registered no recognition, looking as if she were following the Queen into the netherworld.

"Hemamiya," I said again, louder. "Help me with the Prince. Quickly now!"

At that, Hemamiya looked up at me with such dark, blank eyes, my blood ran cold. She dropped the laces as one might discard the pit of a date. Like the spirit of the dead, she shuffled a few feet down the bed, opposite to where I held the baby. She knows the Queen's ka has left her body, I thought, and like the dutiful servant she is, hers has departed, too. My heart pained at the thought.

But for the moment my attention was focused on the lifeless baby perched face down in my hand. His neck was bent back from the strain he had endured in the womb. His color was of such a deep blue, I feared that he was stillborn. I gently probed the baby's mouth and throat, checking for the mucous plug. With my right, I gave a series of light chops between the baby's shoulder blades. But even after repeating the entire procedure more forcefully, the Prince lay limp in my hand. I desperately tried to think of what I might do next.

Behind the Queen's bed, the sky was aflame with Ra's departure, small clouds mottling the sky as if it were the underside of Horus' outstretched falcon wings. Despite the pain in my heart, I took this as a strong omen, a sign that the Prince would be protected by Horus. I held his tiny body high in the air.

"Horus!" I called out with all my strength. "I, Anhotek of Nekhen, priest of your temple, beseech you in your holy name. I have delivered the Prince from the darkness of the womb into the light of Ra. Beat your golden wings that they may blow the breath of life into the Prince... so that he may lead your people to greatness." My words snapped Hemamiya out of her trance and she looked aghast at the Prince's lifeless body. "I swear by your holy power, Horus, that if you choose to give him life, I will serve him faithfully until my dying breath."

For what seemed like an eternity I held the lifeless child in my hands above my head. A vision entered my heart in that moment, a vision that it was not I, but Anubis who held him, weighing his heart in the underworld, as if he had already lived his life. I had no sensation of the Prince's weight at all. He felt lighter than a feather.

And then the Prince sputtered and coughed and my vision of Anubis dissipated. Yet, he did not cry. Not once. Just as suddenly, I felt his full weight and murmured my thanks to Anubis for releasing his ka so that it could unite with his body. I hugged the Prince close to my chest, once again humbled by the magic that Horus flowed through me so that I might heal others.

"Good, little Prince," I sighed, my shoulders slumped over and my arms suddenly unable to hold him anymore. "Today we shall announce to the world your arrival on the wings of Horus." I offered the baby to the comfort of Hemamiya's embrace. She stood wide-eyed, disbelieving all she had just witnessed. It would be but a few hours before the entire court knew of my actions.

"Here, dear Hemamiya, faithful servant of your mistress, Queen Neith-hotpu. You have borne witness to the power of Horus of Nekhen. Take the Prince, heir to the throne of Scorpion. Clean him up well, for soon he will be the object of all Upper Kem's attention."

Shaken by the Queen's death and the spectacle of what she had just witnessed, Hemamiya slowly turned to grab a linen sheet, spread it on the bed and laid the baby on it.

With my heart heavier than I had ever before known, I gazed at the Queen's face, now colorless, but still beautiful at the end of her greatest ordeal. I could feel Hemamiya's eyes upon me as I checked the Queen's vital signs again, to be certain she was dead.

"I must prepare the Queen's body for the afterlife. Send a messenger to King Scorpion with this news." Hemamiya glanced at me, as if to protest, but I did not want to entertain yet another of her diatribes against the King and his mistreatment of her beloved Queen. I ignored the curse she made under her breath.

I carefully removed the entire placenta and umbilical cord, washed them, and laid them out on a linen sheet, to be dried and saved in an alabaster jar so that, at his own death, the Prince's ka would be complete in the underworld. I then performed the priestly blessing over the Queen's body. I felt her ka still hovering close by and stood silently with it for a moment or two before ending my prayers and releasing it on its journey.

"It is done," I said above the baby's whimpering. Hemamiya cradled the baby in her arms, rocking it gently back and forth, looking as if she were in a trance. "The Queen has begun her journey to the next world. May the gods grant her a quick journey and … and an eternity of happiness." The tears flowed down my cheeks.

Hemamiya could no longer contain herself. She quickly handed the baby to me and began to wail, an upwelling of emotion from deep in her soul, a soulful ululation of grief and anger. At that moment I felt a violent shaking begin in the arm that held the Prince and extend to my chest. At first I thought this shaking a result of my fatigue. Then I looked down at the tiny baby, the future King of Upper Kem, and felt I might become sick. The Prince had turned purplish-blue. Only the whites of his eyes were visible. He frothed at the mouth and his limbs twitched wildly.

And so it was, on that day, Horus changed the Prince's destiny and in so doing changed mine and that of all Kem.

# SCROLL TWO

## *The Scorpion's Sting*

It had been two weeks, perhaps even three, since I had written a papyrus, so absorbed was I in the affairs of the court during King Scorpion's absence. As a Horus priest I was one of perhaps only a hundred in the entire land knowledgeable in the picture words and my habit was to write down important events that had occurred each week or new medical information I had recently acquired. I took this duty seriously, for writing is nothing less than creating order from the chaos that surrounds us.

The past few weeks had not been good ones. The Prince had been continuously ill with a malaise that I found frustratingly difficult to treat. King Scorpion had not yet seen his son, distracted as he was by the wars with Lower Kem that had kept him away from Tjeni since the Prince's birth. This I considered a fortunate gift from the gods.

The baby's present illness caused me great concern. I needed new approaches for his condition. Each time he had a fever, the shakes would follow. The birthwort preparation I had been using was no longer as effective, despite my administration of increasingly larger doses, which I feared to continue. If we were fortunate enough to notice his symptoms before the shakes began, we would rush him to the vapor tent I had constructed in his room. There I would burn a few hemp leaves to calm him, but that often put him into a stupor that lasted much of the day.

So much of the vision that the gods had visited upon me for Kem's future rested with the Prince's well-being. I packed a papyrus scroll and writing implements into my goat leather carrying bag, adjusted the gold amulet around my neck and straightened my gold armband, embossed with Scorpion's royal seal. I tightened my loincloth, satisfied that my abdomen was still trim, then started out the door.

We had arrived the night before in Nekhen, having sailed and rowed upstream from Tjeni, and set up camp on a plateau overlooking the city. The day's heat was already searing. As I exited my tent, I gazed with pride down at the city, the largest in Upper Kem. It was covered in a haze of desert dust and smoke from the fires of hundreds of hearths and fine pottery kilns. Below me more than fifty thousand people worked and lived. Having traveled north to The Great Green and as far south as the forests of Ta-Sety and east and west across both great deserts, I knew how blessed Kem truly was. The life-giving Mother Nile nourished our land and the weather was predictable, just as the gods willed it. We had the luxury of devoting ourselves to noble pursuits that allowed us to grow and prosper.

On a low-lying rocky ridge, stretching for more than a thousand cubits, pottery kilns were crowded together, taking advantage of the gentle winds that continuously blew down the valley. The very constancy of the winds allowed the potters of Nekhen to fire their kilns hotter than at any other site in Kem, making their thin, elegant pottery the most valued in our land and in those of our neighbors. The swamp-dwellers of Lower Kem tried to imitate our delicate style, but their clumsy attempts always met with laughable failure.

I had planned to spend the day in prayer at the Temple of Horus, where the incantations I put on papyrus would invoke Horus' holy blessings. I walked down to the city and in a few minutes, I was strolling through the narrow dirt alleys of my boyhood home. Life teemed around me. Goats rummaged through piles of refuse and small flocks of chickens scattered as I walked along the packed earth and sand walkways. The thick smell of people living close together, of sweat and cooking, of decaying refuse and perfumes, and of the yeasty aromas of Nekhen's many breweries filled my nostrils.

On either side of me walls made from Mother Nile's mud and fortified with dried reeds and rushes, loomed above my head. Each passing breeze caused the dried flower heads to flutter gently together. The altogether pleasant sound brought back memories of my youth, of guiding my sister and my twin younger brothers down the narrow alleys on our way to the market to barter my father's spices and goods for foods for the evening meal. I would stand in the shade at the edge of the market, holding tight to the hands of my siblings, watching mothers scolding their children. Even now I wonder how differently my life might have turned out had my own mother not died during the birth of my youngest brothers. If my mother had been there to console him, would my father still have given me over to the service of Horus when my two brothers drowned? Certainly I could not complain about my position in life, nor the many blessings the gods had sent me. I felt proud of what I had so far accomplished in this life. But, still, I wondered what might have been.

The alleyways curved in patterns both random and familiar. Nekhen had grown considerably since my youth. The greatest city in Upper Kem had evolved into neighborhoods where people of the lowliest means could see their neighbors living under better circumstances and strive for better themselves. Throughout most of Upper and Lower Kem, farmers and peasants lived under the most difficult of circumstances. But, in Nekhen, Tjeni, Nubt and a sprinkling of other cities along the Nile, trade had created a large middle class with both leisure time and excess money beyond their immediate needs. Many families rose to nobility and were able to afford luxuries like mud-brick mastaba tombs with intricate and colorful wall paintings inside.

As I approached the Temple, the Head Priest, dressed only in a white loincloth, greeted me warmly and escorted me to a private chamber within the Temple sanctuary. Throughout that day I fasted and meditated and wrote, often distracted by my worries about Scorpion's court. The King was due back soon to the palace. My spies reported that Scorpion's disposition had soured of late. He drank continuously, not the refined wines from Canaan, but the course barley beer of the lowest classes of Kem. I had often prayed that Scorpion would rise to the occasion of his kingship and become the unifying force that would benefit the Two Lands. But I had long ago accepted my disappointment, that his weaknesses far overpowered his strengths. Rather than developing a far-reaching vision for our lands, he blinded himself with short-sighted actions.

I meditated and prayed over the circumstances of the Prince's birth, which the entire Horus priesthood believed to be extraordinary beyond imagining. There were signs within signs that pointed to greatness for the Prince and for Kem, protected as he was by Horus' presence. But that protection also came at great peril, for the gods, seeking to achieve balance, would undoubtedly place many obstacles in our paths.

My own visions for a united Kem were intertwined with the Prince's destiny. I saw with excitement that the notes I had just scrawled formed a pattern, a sketchy plan, a way to explain to Scorpion the significance of the Prince's birth in achieving the gods' vision. With my hopes renewed, with Horus' presence infusing my ka with strength, we sailed back to Tjeni that very evening and by the time Ra's disk was high in the heavens on the third day we tied up to the King's docks. The Royal compound was a hive of activity. Scorpion had arrived, much earlier than I had expected. My heart skipped a beat. I walked through the gate of the outer walls. A group of army officers stood together, talking amongst themselves animatedly.

"Praise be to Anhotek!" one of the men said aloud and

each of the others joined in a chorus of greetings.

"May the gods bless you, Kagemni," I called out to the Chief General of Scorpion's army, who stood a head taller than the other men. "Welcome home. Welcome all of you!" I said, holding my staff high and spreading my arms to include all the officers. "May the gods continue to protect you and to always return you here to your loved ones."

Kagemni left the officers and rushed toward me. We stared at each other for a long moment. He smelled of sweat and dust.

"I... I don't know what to say," Kagemni started, agitated. "I tried to dissuade him, but..."

"What are you talking about?"

Kagemni opened his eyes wide in amazement. "You... you do not know?" Then he took my arm in his huge hand. "Scorpion pushed us hard, like... like he was possessed. I'm covered with dust and dung." Indeed, sand dust adhered to every inch of Kagemni's sculpted body, tiny grains visible even in the crow's feet of his eyes.

"Anhotek, I do not know what has come over Scorpion. He has been so despondent and so damned miserable to live with lately. He..."

"Kagemni, we do not have much time."

"Right," Kagemni said, taking a breath. "Here it is, then. The King has confided in me. He is to be married again." At that very moment I felt as if I had been hit by a mace. For Scorpion to consider such a significant undertaking without consulting me first was unthinkable. There were matters of state to consider, religious rituals, feasts to plan and favors to dispense.

"I can see you are shocked. Perhaps we should..."

"No, tell me the rest... quickly."

"Under torture, a tribal chief in Lower Kem told us that gold and silver from King W'ash himself fueled these wars... the swine!" he said, spitting on the ground. "We mobilized to attack Dep. Then... I'm not even certain how it happened... I mean, it happened so fast. This Ihy, he... he arrived from King W'ash, with a royal escort and proposed to Scorpion a marriage to Mersyankh, W'ash's cousin."

"Who is this Ihy?"

"A shaman of some sort in W'ash's Royal Court. Beyond that I do not know."

"A shaman?"

"An emissary in this case, but my sources claim he is a powerful shaman, a magician of the old rites." Kagemni paused to look around. "I will tell you this, Anhotek. His eyes are evil, as if Anubis himself stares out through them from the underworld. I do not like him one bit."

My mind raced. I had heard of a powerful shaman in the Delta who still practiced the ancient dark magic, but I had dismissed the rumors as legends that the people of Lower Kem still clung to in order to elevate their lowly status.

"Scorpion is convinced this marriage will end the cursed wars with Lower Kem. They came back with us to Tjeni. Ihy is with Scorpion now."

"Kagemni," I whispered, "what is happening might be of great peril to us all... to the King, to our great land, to our people." I paused, weighing my words.

"I know how loyal you are to Scorpion. You know I would never ask you to compromise your friendship." Kagemni stared hard into my eyes.

"Say no more. I am with you on this, Anhotek. I fear the worst, but... what can we do?"

"For now, just gather as much information as you can about this Ihy and about... about... what is her name again?"

"Mersyankh. She is beautiful beyond words. Once Scorpion saw her, he fell under her spell."

"Squeeze Ihy's escorts for all the information you can. Send out your spies. I'll do the same with my priests." I took a moment to think through my strategy. "And, be sure to keep in close touch with me, as I will do with you. Every piece of information is important."

"I'll do it, Anhotek. But, it is a fine line I..."

"Nothing more need be said, Kagemni. I understand." I placed my hand on his chest. "May the gods always protect you."

No more than fifty cubits separated the outer courtyard from Scorpion's living quarters. I walked slowly, breathing in with one step, out with another, feeling Ra's powerful rays warming my body, energizing my ka. The bustle of the soldiers and servants faded into the distance.

I approached the twin columns of the King's quarters, hewn from two immense trunks of Lebanon cedar to clearly delineate the area from the rest of the Royal compound. The columns were intricately carved by one of the finest tradesmen in Tjeni. The twin horns of a huge rhinoceros was mounted near the top of the columns.

I passed through the entranceway, where the brickwork on the floor was arranged and colored in the shape of a scorpion ready to strike, its tail and stinger held high. The two guards on duty bowed as I passed. In a few steps more I was through the outer edge of the courtyard, which was densely planted in palms and native flowers, as much to muffle voices as to decorate the quarters. I, myself, had supervised the plantings to provide insulation from sound and prying eyes, so that the King and I could discuss sensitive matters.

Scorpion's chambers were in the center of the courtyard, tightly built of double-walled mud bricks, interspersed with large, rectangular openings that allowed whatever breezes were available to flow freely. At the top of the walls, notches were carved for the roofing poles. On top of the poles, palm thatch provided shade from the searing desert heat.

The chambers were in complete disarray. Along one wall, Scorpion's leather armor lay scattered about, as if he had walked in, disrobed and left them where they fell. A young aide sat on a wooden bench, quietly cleaning the King's thick leather breastplate. War booty was stacked in every corner and along the remaining walls. A group of men I did not recognize were talking in one corner. Despite the airy room, the stench of sweat, unclean bodies and foul breath assaulted my senses. King Scorpion sat slumped in a chair. His eyes glowered above a week's worth of stubble, accentuating his scarred cheeks, made gaunt by the deprivations of war. He looked like he had been to the underworld and back.

"Ah, I have just sent my runner to get you," Scorpion called to me as I removed my goat hide bag and lay my staff upon it. "There are some people I wish you to meet, my dear teacher." Scorpion started to stand up, already wobbly from the beer. Four alabaster beer jugs stood on the table.

I scanned the room, my senses fine tuned, the hairs on my body feeling prickly. My gaze immediately fell on the man who must be Ihy, and a profound disquiet overcame me. The shaman was perhaps a head taller than was I, but also younger and somewhat thinner. He wore a lion's skin across his chest, pinned to his loincloth in the front and back with fish bones. His long, black hair hung behind him unadorned, tied simply with a piece of twine. His face was dark and pockmarked, the wide swath of his black eyebrows accentuating his brooding look.

"Please, stay seated, King Scorpion." Ihy strode across the room. "There is no need to introduce the great Anhotek," He stopped a pace in front of me, crossed his arms, then opened them wide and bowed deeply, holding his hands at knee level in a gesture of respect. "Your reputation is great throughout the land, Anhotek, advisor to the nobles, shaman to King Scorpion himself. I am honored to meet you."

Ihy's eyes pierced to my core. I felt skewered from within by a dagger. Yet, outwardly he revealed no sign of malice. I prayed that the chill that ran through me would not betray my fears. This man was clearly announcing his powers to someone who would understand them. I nodded my head slightly.

"I am honored to meet a shaman from the House of Dep," I replied. I noticed the slightest twitch of a smirk in the corner of Ihy's lips.

"Now that the pleasantries are out of the way," Scorpion continued, oblivious to the nuances in our exchange, "would you like to lift a cup with us?"

I initially thought to refuse. "Yes, a quick drink, then.

There is still much to do today."

"Forget your other duties, Anhotek. There is business here to discuss." Scorpion thumped the beer urn down on the table, as if to emphasize his command. "As for the rest of you" - he waved his hand- "leave our guest alone with me and Anhotek. Send in Kagemni."

Scorpion stood, dressed in a dirty, coarse linen loincloth. His muscled torso was riddled with battle scars, some healed in raised welts, nearly every one personally treated by me. One wound, near his lower abdomen, was recent and still oozed. Scorpion winced in pain and I rushed toward him.

"No!" Scorpion held up his hand as if to keep me at a distance. "It's just a small stab wound. Since we were away, Ihy treated it." He fell onto a large cushioned bench with a groan. I did my best to hide my discontent at the thought of another healer administering to Scorpion.

"Anhotek, Ihy has made a proposal to us... a way out of a long-standing dilemma that we have faced." Scorpion gulped his beer and placed his cup on the heavy wooden table next to him. "Explain, Ihy."

"Certainly." Ihy strode to the table, in a smooth motion that nearly made him appear to have floated. His grace triggered a pang of envy in me.

"After lengthy discussions with my King... and with yours," Ihy said, "I have proposed... I should say my King has proposed a marriage between the Houses of Upper and Lower Kem." He waited for my reaction. I looked at Scorpion. Silence hung heavy in the air.

"It makes good sense to me," Scorpion said, breaking the silence.

"Good!" I replied as nonchalantly as I could muster. "Then by the will of the gods, do it!" I turned lazily and walked toward the entranceway, bending to pick up my collecting bag and staff. I saw Ihy turn to look at Scorpion, who was transfixed by my movements.

"As I said, I have many things of importance to yet do today. I beg your leave, King Scorpion."

Scorpion stood and held his chair to steady himself.

"Wait, Anhotek! We are asking your opinion in this matter."

"Did you say 'we,' Scorpion?" I gave my former student a disapproving look.

"I... I meant that... what I mean is that..."

"Because, as everyone in Upper Kem knows, I am the advisor only to Scorpion, Ruler of the Land of the Lotus." Scorpion struggled to decipher my veiled message.

"Perhaps I should go," Ihy said. "I am fatigued from the journey and there are things that you and your shaman must discuss... privately. King Scorpion?"

"Yes... yes," Scorpion muttered, pushing his white alabaster drinking cup aside. "We... we will meet in the morning. There is always much to do when I have been away."

At that very moment, Kagemni entered, his lips distorted into a shape of embarrassment and containment that I had seen on his face only rarely. "Scorpion, I... the woman... Mersyankh asks your permission to enter."

Before Scorpion could even respond, Mersyankh strode through the archway, smiling, with three of her attendants. The effect on Scorpion was immediate. He tried to reach for his tunic, but it was too late. Mersyankh ignored the gesture and walked to his side.

I was taken off guard. Mersyankh was strikingly beautiful. Her facial features were so fine, they appeared to have been chiseled from stone by an artisan. The kohl around her eyes was deftly applied and the combination of her jewels and her fine linen gown made her look resplendent. But, it was the way she carried herself, head held high, her posture erect that commanded our attention.

Scorpion, obviously embarrassed by his haggard appearance, looked desperately at me. "Allow me to introduce myself, fair noblewoman. I am Anhotek, Chief Scribe and shaman of King Scorpion's Royal Court." I nodded my head in her direction. She eyed me from toe to head.

"Ah, yes. I believe I have heard of you," she said dismissively, her eyes cold, before turning her back to me and facing toward Scorpion. I noticed Ihy wince. For a few moments, the only sounds in the room were of Mersyankh whispering earnestly to Scorpion. Kagemni and I exchanged glances.

"And, how is the Prince?" Scorpion suddenly asked.

"He is fine now," I lied. "The birth was long and difficult. But, the boy is strong, born of yours and the Queen's stock," I said pointedly. "He is quite handsome. He will endure."

Mersyankh screwed up her brow. "Endure? That is an odd word."

"I suppose it is. The child of such a difficult birth experiences a conflict between wanting to stay with its dead mother and its natural desire to survive on its own. The child's ka is strong."

"And the Seven Hathors?" Scorpion asked warily.

I recalled the ritual over which I had presided, exactly one week after the Prince's birth, although now it seemed like another lifetime. "Hathor's visit was... it was the most profound visit the priests at the Temple of Horus have ever witnessed," I answered. "And their memories go back hundreds of years.

"The Chief Priest blessed the child under Horus' watchful eyes and we could immediately feel Hathor's presence. It was wondrous, Scorpion. Her seven voices echoed in harmony. They told of the Prince's ascendancy to the throne, of how he was destined to honor you, to provision your tomb with gifts so bounteous you would lack for nothing in the afterlife. And they told of how he would vanquish the warlords of... ummm... of Ta-Tjehenu and Ta-Sety." I thought it best to avoid any reference to the common warlords of Lower Kem. "He will complete the work you have begun."

"What you describe is indeed a powerful vision," Ihy said, turning first to Scorpion, then to Mersyankh. "Was that all they revealed?" Ihy had either read my innermost thoughts, a disturbing notion or, even worse, he had already been successful in bribing a Horus priest.

My breath returned to me slowly. "No... no, that was not all," I said, looking deep into Scorpion's eyes. "They also said that his ka was destined to struggle throughout his life… to… to do battle with demons here." The veins in Scorpion's forearms pulsed from gripping the arms of the chair so hard.

"But in the end, the Seven Hathors saw that he would emerge victorious over his enemies and that his reign would be a great one."

Scorpion was lost in thought for several moments. "Bring him to me," he said, looking up at Mersyankh, who nodded her head. "I wish to see him with my own eyes… to hold the future King."

"He naps now," I protested. But Scorpion was not to be denied, and so I left to gather the baby.

"Hemamiya!" I shouted as soon as I entered the Prince's small quarters. "Quickly, we must ready the Prince for the King."

Panic was written all over Hemamiya's face. "But, he might… "

"I know, I know," I said, dismissing her half-formed objection, "but Scorpion is determined." I fumbled through my bag of medicinals and retrieved a small jar.

"Bring me some red wine. I'll mix a potion and feed it to the little one. He will sleep well enough."

I mixed several strands of birthwort root with wine, honey and ripe dates. Hemamiya fed the Prince quickly.

"We're lucky he's hungry," Hemamiya remarked. "Shall I take him to the wet nurse before we go?"

"Yes, do it. And swath him tightly. We don't want…"

"I understand," Hemamiya said before leaving.

When we entered the King's quarters with the Prince's entourage, Scorpion was sitting at his table with Mersyankh. Ihy stood behind them. Next to Scorpion, Kagemni stood, his body tense. He glanced toward the table, where a fresh pitcher of beer stood, so that I knew which of Scorpion's demons I would need to battle.

"My guests, in the capable hands of Hemamiya is the future wearer of the White Crown of Upper Kem," Scorpion announced. In his drunkenness he slurred his words.

Scorpion sauntered unsteadily toward Hemamiya and the wet nurse and leaned close to them. Hemamiya winced from smelling the mixture of cheap beer and strong sweat that emanated from Scorpion's body. "Missed me that much, dear Hemamiya?" Scorpion whispered, not a hand's width from her face. She dropped her eyes and held out the baby toward him.

"Is this a baby or a mummified dog, woman?" Scorpion scolded, taking the child from her. "You have wrapped him so tightly, he will suffocate!"

Hemamiya shot a look at me. "What do you say, Anhotek?" Scorpion asked, turning toward me. I gave a little laugh.

"My King, your reputation as a warrior is well deserved. Your skills as a nurse maid, on the other hand, leave much to be desired." At that Mersyankh tittered, but Scorpion glared at me.

"He's right, Scorpion," Kagemni yelled across the room, smiling. "You'd change a bloody battle dressing better than a baby's swaddling cloth!"

As the snickering subsided, Scorpion stole a look at the baby, sleeping peacefully in his arms. "By the gods, he does have a pleasing appearance," he declared, dipping his arm down to show the baby's face to Mersyankh, Ihy and Kagemni.

Kagemni moved forward to get a better view of the sleeping baby. "He is handsome looking," he said. "Have you decided on a name, Scorpion?"

"No, I have not decided it," he said hesitantly.

"And what do you say, wise counsel?" Kagemni asked me.

I related to them the story of the Prince's birth under the dappled wings of Horus. "The omen would suggest that his name be either S'ab, for the dappled underside of Horus' wings or else Meni, for the enduring one. The priests at the Temple of Horus in Nekhen were unaware of the exact day of the Prince's birth, yet they had recorded the same dappled skies in their scrolls that evening as a strong omen. Horus' hawk presence portends a strong future."

Scorpion considered my reasoning silently, looking from me to the baby, then to Mersyankh. "What name appeals to you?" he asked Mersyankh.

She looked from Scorpion to the floor, an ingratiating look that seemed entirely inconsistent with her ba. "I... I have no experience with names for Upper Kem," she offered sincerely. "Neither sits comfortably with me." As Scorpion turned away from her toward Kagemni, she lifted her eyes just enough to coldly gaze at me.

"And you, my trusted friend?"

"The name Meni appeals to me," Kagemni carefully responded. "It shows strength and power and... and destiny."

"I will consider your suggestions, then," Scorpion said with authority. "I will announce my decision soon." He walked with the baby toward the table.

"Does he ever wake up?" he asked, flopping into the chair. "He sleeps so peacefully." He began to unwrap the colorful swaddling clothes, much to Hemamiya's dismay. As he did so she started toward the table, but my raised hand stopped her.

When the baby was exposed, Scorpion called out in alarm. "Come here, Anhotek. Look how thin he is. Do you not agree, Mersyankh?"

Mersyankh leaned over and peeked at the baby. "He does look underfed, yes," she responded, "as if he does not thrive."

I walked behind the King, feeling uneasy. "All babies lose weight after birth. His birth was difficult, so he must catch up even more."

"Is the wet nurse well suited for him? Does he suckle soundly?"

"She has nursed more than a dozen healthy children of wealthy families." With that I motioned for the wet nurse to come closer. She trembled, but at my hand gesture she removed her double-wrapped linen halter and revealed her swollen breasts. Both nipples leaked milk.

"Look, her breasts are engorged beyond measure," I pointed out. "The baby suckles to his heart's content."

Apparently satisfied, Scorpion called to Hemamiya. "Come here, Hemamiya. Wrap him again, but not so tightly this time." As he handed the infant to Hemamiya, he looked down to see him moving. "Look! He is waking," Scorpion said excitedly. "The Prince opens his eyes to see his father." Deftly, Hemamiya wrapped the cloth around the baby, then swept him into her arms.

"Not so quick, woman!" Scorpion shouted. "Give him here one last time." Hemamiya held out the wriggling baby to Scorpion.

"Do you wish to hold him?" Scorpion asked Mersyankh. She shot a panicked glance at Ihy.

"I... he is not my son. I am not sure..." she objected. But Scorpion, may the gods hold his memory dear, naively held out the Prince to her. "But, as his future step-mother I suppose I should become familiar with him."

Once the Prince was settled in her arm, Scorpion raised a finger toward his son's cheek. The Prince's eyes became vacant. Scorpion's finger stopped in mid gesture, his face mirroring his confusion, but he continued to stare at the baby, silent, as if transfixed by a terrible spell, a spell that was reflected in the faces of Mersyankh and Ihy.

Scorpion looked from the Prince to me pleadingly, before he returned his morbid gaze to his heir. I watched the tragedy unfold before my eyes. Mersyankh's arm began to jerk, then shake. The pair looked down again, as if in a nightmare, to see the baby's skin take on a sickening, pale cast. The Prince shook violently against his wrappings, throwing his head back, spittle forming on his lips. He wet his swaddling cloth. Stunned, Mersyankh cried out, nearly throwing the baby from her bejeweled arms.

"By the gods! What... what is happening to him? What..."

But before she could utter another word, I removed the baby from her grasp and Kagemni rushed to the King's side, easing him to a chair. I handed the baby to Hemamiya and rummaged through my medical box to administer more birthwort to the Prince.

"In Ra's name, Anhotek, what is happening?" Scorpion

shouted. Kagemni stood with his hand on the King's shoulder. Both were as pale as spirits from the netherworld. Ihy moved to Mersyankh's side to steady her. I heard Scorpion's shout, but medicating the Prince was my more immediate task. "Anhotek, answer me!"

I spun on my heels, but immediately thought better of embarrassing a drunken Scorpion in front of his intended wife. Instead, I only glared at him, but with the same penetrating look I had controlled him with since I became his tutor when he was but twelve years old. With the baby finally asleep, I turned back toward the King, who was sitting stiffly in the deathly silent room.

"With your intended wife here to bear witness, Scorpion, I tell you the Prince is normal in all ways, save that he does have shakes. Yet…"

Scorpion's head was cocked to the side, trying to comprehend through his alcohol-clouded mind. "What… what are these shakes?" He looked as if he were about to be sick.

"They are not common, to be sure." Although I had hoped for more ideal circumstances to explain the Prince's illness to Scorpion, perhaps the presence of his officers might be of some good.

"In the eastern lands they call it the sacred illness, since it seems to favor those who are of Royal birth. The Horus priests believe that the shakes are a gift from the gods, as if the gods themselves are sending the person a sacred message. They last only a minute or two, then the person is quiet. They sometimes have a vision while they are shaking, or even before they start shaking, which the priests feel is an omen, more powerful even than dreams. People with the sacred illness are highly revered, Scorpion."

Scorpion looked toward Mersyankh and Ihy then hung his head in his hands. Hemamiya and a few of Neith-hotpu's servants waited by the entrance, anxious to take their leave. The wet nurse shook in fear.

After a moment, Scorpion stood up, breathing in deeply to control the pain in his side. His muscles rippled from the tension in his body. "Leave, all of you!" he shouted.

Hemamiya and the Prince's entourage nearly tripped over themselves running out of the King's chambers.

"You, too, my dear," Scorpion added. Ihy quickly grabbed Mersyankh's arm, then bowed to both Scorpion and me and escorted her out the door.

"Anhotek, you and Kagemni stay." With the room now empty save for the three of us, Scorpion slumped in his chair. "I am... " he started to say, his face suddenly composed. His command of his faculties, even with the wine still coursing through his body, frightened me. "I feel as if Horus has sucked the life spirit out of me."

"Scorpion, I implore... " I began.

"No, Anhotek, you will not use your fine words against me!" he raged. "I have heard the tale of the Prince's birth, of how your... your magic snatched him back from his journey to the afterlife. Perhaps you should not have meddled in the affairs of the gods." The poisons oozed from Scorpion's wounded soul. "Perhaps he was meant to journey with his mother!"

Scorpion perched at the edge of the table. "From now on you will be Counsel to the Prince. Instruct him in the ways of the world, in the ways of the Royal Court. Tend to his spiritual development and to his medical needs. Use Hemamiya and... and the rest of the Queen's servants to aide you."

I was shocked by Scorpion's reaction. He sat rigidly, unsure of his own pronouncements. "And, you, Kagemni. Have the wet nurse killed!" Scorpion watched the shock spread over his friend's face. "Immediately, before this night is out!"

"But, Scorpion," I protested, stepping forward toward him. "The Prince's illness is not her fault. He... he improves every day. She sustains him."

Scorpion stood up, a full head taller than me and raised his hand to stop me from approaching him. It was a moment I shall never forget, as when a father finally comes to realize that his son has grown to complete independence and that the relationship will never again be the same. Scorpion opened his mouth as if to explain his action to me, but turned instead to Kagemni. "And you, Kagemni, what do you say? Give me your valued counsel," he said pointedly.

Kagemni forced his gaze to stay upon the King. "I will do as you command, Scorpion... now, as always." With that he placed his right forearm roughly across his chest to salute his King. "I... I can see your point. If a hand becomes putrid from a battle wound we cut off the damned arm to prevent death. But... but in this matter, I would follow Anhotek's advice. He is the most powerful shaman in all Kem." Kagemni knew instantly he had spoken too much. He did not have to wait long for Scorpion's rejoinder.

"Oh, yes, powerful, indeed," Scorpion answered so softly, we simultaneously turned our heads to hear him. Suddenly, Scorpion spun around to face Kagemni, his finger pointing directly at my face.

"Why hasn't mighty Anhotek used his power to heal the Prince from these... these cursed shakes?" Kagemni shifted uncomfortably. Scorpion sat down, exhausted and for a moment no one spoke. "Well, Anhotek, do you have an answer?"

It was futile to explain anything to Scorpion at this moment. But, to not answer him would be to court his ire, already inflamed by alcohol and disappointment.

"It boils down to one matter, King Scorpion, Wearer of the White Crown, ruler of all Upper Kem," I answered very deliberately, giving him time to assume his role as leader. "Queen Neith-hotpu was too young and too small to carry a baby to birth. When you first saw her in Nekhen, I thought... we all thought she was the most beautiful young woman we had ever seen, her slender body, her beautiful face, her gentle manner. But, when you asked my opinion about placing your seed in her, I told you that she needed another two years for her body to ripen. She had barely started her monthly cycle."

Scorpion started to rise in protest. "And," I continued, "your side of the family has large men, such as yourself. Your own mother, Scorpion... your own mother died weeks after your birth." With that, I walked to the nearest bench and sat down heavily.

"When I had to cut the Queen to save the baby, a part of my ka was surely ripped from my own body and now accompanies her on her journey through the underworld. I... I have... not been the same since. Every night when I awake to pace my quarters, I think, 'What could you have done differently, Anhotek? How could you have saved your beloved Queen?' And, I swear by Ra that I do not have an answer that satisfies me, let alone you, Scorpion. I tried everything I could, but in the end... in the end... it was not good enough." We each stared at the floor, pondering our own roles in the Queen's life and death.

"You did your best," Scorpion finally said. "You know that my strengths are on the battlefield, not in diplomacy." I acknowledged Scorpion's gesture to me with a nod of my head.

"Ignore my instructions about the wet nurse," he said, turning first to Kagemni. "But, be forewarned," he added. "If the child worsens, I will hold her responsible. Watch her carefully, Anhotek. Evil magic may lurk about."

I put down my staff, pulled a chair opposite Scorpion and sat down. I drew a deep, relaxing breath, planting the seed for Scorpion to do the same, which he soon did.

"Well, what do you think of Mersyankh?" Scorpion asked.

"On the face of it, the marriage makes sense," I offered, sidestepping my true impressions of Mersyankh.

"But?"

"We know nothing of this Ihy, and little of your future bride, although some of the things I do know about him I am hesitant to repeat without confirmation from others I trust." Soon enough I would need to deal with why my network of informers had not gathered even a rumor of such monumental plans. "We also do not know what the Royal family in Dep believes they will gain from the alliance, other than stopping our superior forces from defeating them."

"So, what do you recommend?" Scorpion pressed,

pouring himself a cup of water from the intricately carved alabaster pitcher. He quaffed its entire contents in one gulp.

"Give us some time to gather more information. I will personally see to it that my informants…"

"Spies, Anhotek. Why not call them what they are?"

"Some are indeed spies, Scorpion. But fewer than you might imagine. Much information can be gathered by more subtle means, subtleties that are best left to my guidance."

"As opposed to my brutish mentality?" Scorpion laughed sarcastically.

"A man needs to hone his strengths and gather about him those whom he can trust to fortify his weaknesses. On the battlefield I would be useless as a swordsman. In matters of administration and statecraft you rely on my strengths. The gods have provided many opportunities in our Land to use our gifts to keep ma'at strong."

Scorpion fingered the smoothly carved surface of his water cup. "What you think of this Ihy? He is quite something, is he not?"

I read Scorpion's body and there seemed to be no subterfuge present. That meant that Ihy had already made headway with him. It felt like I was fording Mother Nile, balanced on the tops of a few small rocks, with flood waters raging all around me.

"He possesses powerful magic," I said, choosing my words carefully.

"So I have heard," Scorpion replied. "I have not had occasion to see it as of yet, but I have heard that his people shake in fear of it."

"And that is the very problem with powerful magic, Scorpion. Sometimes a person has no idea it is being worked, while all along the spider weaves its web, ensnaring its unsuspecting victim."

Scorpion stared at me. His eyes followed the crook of my nose upward, studying the deeply etched lines of my forehead.

"What are you saying, Anhotek? That I am under some sort of spell?"

"Perhaps," I whispered with such solemnity it made the

hairs of Scorpion's arms stand on end. "And, as it has always been, the victim is the last one to know it." We sat thus in silence for many minutes, listening to the sounds of the servants preparing the evening meal.

"Scorpion," I interrupted softly, "we must deal with the matter of the Prince's name. Until the Naming ceremony his ka will not settle in his body. We have waited far too long already."

"Were Horus' wings truly spread at the Prince's birth?"

"Without a doubt, Scorpion. It was a powerful omen. As surely as I sit here now, the beat of Horus' wings breathed life into the infant."

"So I have heard. And you, Kagemni?"

Kagemni considered my words. "To deny such an omen could unleash a damned disaster on us."

"Fine, then. Since Horus willed him to survive, we will call him Meni, the enduring one," Scorpion said in his most officious tone. "Meni," he repeated. "Make it so, Anhotek."

"I will, by your authority," I answered.

"I am tired beyond measure," Scorpion sighed. "Kagemni, take your leave and get some well deserved rest."

As soon as Kagemni left, Scorpion turned to me. "You probably think poorly of me this minute, old teacher. But, the boy's condition, frankly... it sickens me," he said, turning away from me. "I wish it weren't so, but these shakes... I... I have seen them on the battlefield when a man's head is bashed with a mace. It appalls me above all other wounds. A... a powerful man, a worthy opponent, lying there helpless, staring at the sky as if he cannot see, all his limbs shaking, until..."

"Scorpion, people react differently to illness. The gods have given us shamans the ability to treat torments of the body that others cannot bear to witness. Do not feel shame in this. No one but the two of us shall ever know how you presently feel.

"The boy will improve," I added. "You will have occasion to be proud of him as the years go by."

Scorpion slowly turned his head toward me. There are

times when the evening desert winds blow so cold they chill a man's very soul. That is how I felt when Scorpion looked at me then, as if his cold stare confirmed the lie that we both knew I had just told.

# SCROLL THREE

*Tremors*

The warm, gentle breezes that swept down the river valley caressed my skin. The sails of our boats billowed until, like the stomach of a man at the end of a great feast, they ballooned greatly and could fit no more. We had been sailing downriver for four days in two large reed boats from Scorpion's fleet, moving gracefully amidst the rhythmic groans of the ropes pulling against the reed bundles and the periodic thump of our sails filling with wind.

My dutiful, if dimwitted assistants sat on either side of me, their fine linen tunics belying their common origins. All seemed right in the Two Lands, everything balanced, ma'at strong. Mother Nile flowed endlessly to The Great Green, while Ra beamed down upon us. Both elemental forces brought good fortune to our land. I felt as happy as I could ever hope to be.

The greenery of Mother Nile's reeds and rushes, and the fields of barley and emmer wheat far beyond them, passed by along the banks. The endless cycle of the seasons forced its rhythm upon the people in this borderland between Upper and Lower Kem. I watched for telltale signs of discontent among the poor farmers, as they toiled at the difficult tasks that sustained them.

The pungent mix of desert dust, manure from the fields, and the smells of the mighty river itself hung in the air, thick enough to see, so that each syrupy breath was full of promise and peril. Periodically a farmer, or a group of women washing clothes, would catch sight of our boat, flying King Scorpion's pennant, and wave to us. They strained to see if they might catch a glimpse of royalty. They only saw an old shaman, surrounded by two young boys and a filthy captain. Our companion boat held a troop of tired soldiers.

"Do you have the medicines?" I asked dark-skinned Panehsy, who sat on his haunches, his pronounced bodily odors wafting up when the wind chanced to cast in my direction.

"They are safe, Anhotek," he responded, while patting the large leather bag that hung down from his bony shoulder. "Safe as they were when you asked an hour ago."

I was amused by the boy's impertinent response, although I dared not show it, for he was surely simple enough to misinterpret a kind gesture. But I did notice that Surero, my second assistant and of late Panehsy's partner in crime, shot a sideways glance at him and tried to suppress a giggle. Being a dwarf, Surero's laugh had a throaty, high-pitched sound. I rapped my staff lightly on the side of Surero's head, which put a quick end to their belief that they had bested me. Over the years of instructing young men, I found it often effective for the offender to watch the effect of his thoughtless actions on his accomplices. In that manner the wayward youth has two opportunities to gain the moral I wish to teach; once by having him witness my punishment of his friend and yet again when his friend later repays him his debt.

At the point where a small tributary fanned out from the river's main channel, the head of a mother hippopotamus surfaced, its bulbous eyes watching us warily. A calf floated close by its side. I muttered a silent prayer, cursing one of the many forces of chaos that stood at the edge of ma'at, constantly threatening us. How often had I been summoned to the river's edge to minister to a child who had come between a mother and her calf as they grazed on land near the shore? In another moment the winds carried us safely past them, praised be Ra.

So far the collecting trip for medicines that I might employ to alleviate the Prince's illness had been disappointing, despite the pitiful herbs that Panehsy carried in his bag. Crushed ibex horns! Dried crocodile dung mixed with fly excrement! It amazed me how backward some of our own shamans and healers were.

At my command, the captain sailed directly to the Delta lands, where Mother Nile splits into five rivers before branching out further like a fan to distribute its life sustaining waters to the marshland and its people until it, and we riding its life force, reached Wadj-wer, The Great Green. From there I planned for us to sail east, hugging the coast of Wadj-wer for several more days, to reach the land where I hoped to finally find the medicines I needed to treat the young Prince Meni, may his name be blessed by the gods.

We were north of Dashur, still far from where the Nile splits and two full days journey south of the coastal city of Dep, the capital of Lower Kem, when Surero pointed to a procession of large boats rowing against the current on the far side of the river. The boats were made entirely of wood, a precious commodity in Upper Kem. But the people of the marshlands imported wood regularly from Satjet and Babylon. The bare masts and the oars protruding from the decks gave the impression of a group of malnourished men, their ribs protruding from hunger. From high up on their masts flew a banner with the image of the sacred bull, the emblem of the King of Dep.

Set upon the deck of the middle boat was a Royal carrying chair. From the attendants milling around the curtained chair, I felt certain that I was witnessing Mersyankh's wedding procession south to Scorpion's palace in Tjeni. I had prayed to the gods that they might see fit to delay her arrival.

Even from across the river, we could hear the sounds of the beatmaster urging the rowers on, raining curses on them that would have embarrassed Anubis. A man mounted on the bow of the lead boat yelled ahead to clear the way of fishermen and ferryboats. I was left with the terrible feeling of helplessness that most of my countrymen must feel every day of their existence, the inability to gauge the direction of things, to detect undercurrents and then to control them to achieve one's goals.

Soon, the procession was but a tiny speck, like toy boats that we used to play with as carefree boys growing up at the river's edge in Nekhen. Then we rounded a bend in the river and the procession disappeared from view and with that an unease began to grow in my stomach, so deep it made me taste bitter bile. Here I was, drifting further and further away from Tjeni, from the whirling dust storm that had become the Royal court, while Mersyankh and Ihy, those evil forces from the underworld, may their names be cursed, hastened back to Tjeni. Yet, there was nothing I could do. The future of Kem depended on the Prince surviving his childhood.

Another group of farmers had stopped to wave at our small procession and it was then that I noticed a slightly built man who watched us from behind the group at the shore. He did not wave, but stared for the briefest of moments, then continued on in the same direction as our boat. Under other circumstances it would not have attracted my attention, but he walked with a pronounced limp. My mind searched for a reason for its discomfort and it was then that I realized I had seen him a full day past, near a town we had stopped at to provision our boats. I remembered that he squatted on a hill overlooking Mother Nile and when he stood to walk away, he stumbled slightly, attracting my attention.

I looked down to see both Panehsy and Surero staring at me expectantly. "What?" I asked, snapping back to the unfortunate reality of having to care for these two misfits, born with dung between their toes.

"I just wished you to know that I still had the

medicines," Panehsy said with a straight face. His comment hung in the air for a full moment, before I realized what he had said. His subtle humor was more of a surprise to me than his disrespect. By then he had started to giggle. I rapped him, too, a good solid blow to the side of his head, but he was quick enough to partially block it with his hand, a happenstance that did not displease me. At his core, he was a good boy, with solid values taught him by his poor farmer parents. He would get my point. If there was one thing I would not tolerate, it was to be held responsible for raising youth like so many I saw in Nekhen and Tjeni today. Far too many were arrogant, thinking they know more than their elders, even bordering on disrespect. Yet, what could we expect? So many of their parents today were absorbed in their pottery and basketry and brewery businesses to the point that they neglected the moral education of their offspring.

We continued our sail north, all the while my fears about the spies Mersyankh and Ihy were purchasing within our Court pushing me ever inward. We took the easternmost fork of the Nile, passing through the marshlands of the Delta, where I could once again observe the daily occupations of its lowly people.

The farmers of Lower Kem eked out an existence with the most primitive tools imaginable. They rarely used copper adze blades or axe heads or the newer farming implements. On those occasions when we stopped to replenish our supplies, we would be delayed by the admiration these people gave to even our simplest wares. They would call their friends or family members to admire the thin, elegant jars made by the professional potters in Nekhen, some with decorations inscribed, others topped with a black band formed by inverting the pot in the ashes of the kiln in its final stages of firing. By contrast, the Delta dwellers had only heavy, ungainly creations that broke easily and looked as if they were made by simple-minded children.

I thought again of the man I had seen along the shore and wondered if it could be that Mersyankh and Ihy would dare to have me followed. Was I was wrong to suspect the man? We sailed leisurely, and boats passed us frequently throughout the day. It was unlikely that someone would be leapfrogging us on foot just to observe our activities.

On the fourth day of our journey a disturbing event occurred. We were solidly in the land of Lower Kem, when I noticed a single, smoky fire on a hill on the east bank of the river. That appeared to me to be unusual, for potters usually clustered their fires together in places where the winds proved constant. It was at this point that the mighty river took a sharp bend toward the west. Once we passed the spot where the fire blazed, I happened to look back. The smoke that had been rising steadily from the fire had mysteriously stopped. Then, suddenly, the smoke rose again in one great puff. Yet again did this happen and I shot a glance toward the west bank directly in front of us. There I saw a blinding flash of light from a mirror. My blood ran cold.

In five days we reached the Wadj-wer port village of Ahnpet, there to provision ourselves with supplies. My young assistants, as well as the captain himself, had never before seen Wadj-wer and were immediately taken with its emerald beauty. They were captivated by the ebb and flow of water that, unlike Mother Nile, rose to cover the shore, then receded within hours, repeating itself continually during our stay. The captain spent many hours discussing this strange phenomenon with the farmers and fishermen of Ahnpet.

As we prepared to leave, the captain became more and more agitated. The local fishermen had filled him with stories of sea monsters and Wadj-wer's unpredictable storms that swallowed boats whole, never to be seen again. Rather than shaming him back to his senses, I used his fear to enable us to make greater haste without insulting his pride. That night, to his relief, I enlisted his promise to wait for us and learn as much as he could about Wadj-wer's mysteries, while we hired a local fisherman to take us along the coast.

We sailed toward the east as soon as Ra appeared in the sky and I had performed the requisite blessings. Whether through my intercession or by the plans of the gods themselves, we found favorable winds, but also high swells, that carried us to the port city of Rafiah in only a few days time. My young apprentices and a few of the soldiers became terribly water sick, turning a shade of green that the captain of our vessel swore he had never before seen. But, shortly after they felt the solid footing of earth under their feet, they regained their composure. As young men will do, Panehsy and Surero soon resumed their ceaseless banter and insults aimed at each other and anyone else they could think of. Listening to their mirth, I felt hopeful that I would find a cure for Meni.

In Rafiah's bustling harbor I arranged for a small caravan to take us inland, there to meet with a shaman who was well known for his treatment of the holy illness. His people were more prone to this peculiar disease and the desert tribes respected him as a great healer. In two days journey, we were in his village.

"Anhotek!" Kittar the Healer greeted me as if I were his brother returning from a long journey. He hugged me in the custom of his people, first laying his cheek on one side of my face, then the other. "Welcome. My house is your house, my food, your food, my daughters yours to serve you," he said, winking.

Kittar was more youthful than his reputation would have led me to believe. He was also more jovial than I had anticipated, for if there is one thing all healers have in common, it is a profound sadness concerning our limitations to effect a cure in those who come to us pox-stricken, legless, blind or mad. Yet, once I saw him treat his people, I knew that he was blessed by his gods. His tent was crowded day and night and more people walked away from his treatments better for it than worse.

For a full day after our arrival I only watched and assisted him, not wanting to offend him by suggesting treatments known to me. But, toward the end of the second day, a boy knocking on the door of manhood appeared out of the desert with his father. They had no sooner arrived than the boy fell down in the sand in front of Kittar's tent and shook so violently I feared that he would tear his limbs from his body. Kittar gently cradled the boy's head and waited until the shaking subsided. Then he brought the boy into his large tent, where a bed was always ready for anyone who was in need of his ministrations.

From his goatskin bag, Kittar removed a jar containing a dried herb such as I had never seen before. He crushed it further in his pestle and added various ingredients, before calling the boy's father to his side.

"Take this mixture, Jerrel, and administer it to the boy every day, after his morning meal. Be diligent about this, my dear friend, for the boy's illness is made all the worse by his impending manhood. If you do not give it to him faithfully every day, he may have the shakes without end one day, such that he will pass from this world."

When the father and son left later that evening, I approached Kittar without hesitation. "What is this herb that you gave the boy?" I asked. "It is a treatment for this very condition that I seek."

"So I have heard, Anhotek, for when news is bad it travels on the lightest of breezes." We were as one heart.

"There is a plant that grows at the edges of fields that are disturbed by cultivation. I have an abundance of it right now which I am happy to share with you. The fruits of this plant are but tiny red berries and are deadly when more than a few are eaten."

From a corner of his tent, Kittar brought out a small, coarse pottery jar that was sealed with beeswax. "I will tell you how to prepare the potion for the shakes," he continued. "However, you will need to find the right dose for the Prince, for I have found that I must vary the dose depending on how large the person is and whether they have an active or quiet spirit." With that, Kittar opened the jar to reveal a powder the color of the very sand beneath our feet, but nearly as fine as talc. "The contents of this jar will last you for a long time, since the Prince is yet an infant."

Kittar showed me how to prepare the ingredients that would calm the Prince and prevent the royal illness. Kittar assured me that he would always keep a supply on hand for my messengers to retrieve from him, for he was sure that he would need to seek out my counsel at some future time, such is the way with shamans. Before I left I gave him a special preparation that would keep wounds from festering, which he much appreciated.

Throughout the inland journey, I was sure we were not followed, for the path is desolate indeed and a spy would surely have been noticed. But, on the return to the crowded harbor of Rafiah, I noticed that the man with the limp was aboard a neighboring vessel. When our ship was at the mouth of the harbor I saw his smaller and faster boat take off from its mooring.

Our captain was indeed jubilant upon our return, swearing that the Wadj-wer was no place for god-fearing men. He had hired twelve rowers for the journey upriver, experienced men who were happy for the money. For the next few days, our captain smiled uncontrollably, praising Mother Nile's virtues, breathing in the muddy scent of her banks and quaffing its pure waters. Being back on the river brought me much contentment, too, and I eagerly looked forward to trying the new potion on Prince Meni.

As dusk fell on our fifth day, we approached the area of Dashur once again and as I gazed upstream I noted that a boat flying Scorpion's pennant was anchored in the middle of the river. As we approached, the captain hailed us.

"Anhotek, is it really you?" a man standing on the deck called once we were alongside. "I have waited these many days for your return and began to think that the Wadj-wer had swallowed you and your boat." I recognized Butehamon, one of Kagemni's trusted officers, a sailor who ferried men and supplies for Scorpion's army. Helping me on board, he motioned me to be silent and ordered the captain to sail to the west bank and there to await us.

No sooner had the boat cast off then Butehamon said to me: "Ask not any questions, dear Anhotek, for I would be unable to answer them anyway... except to spread rumors." He set out for the east bank and I was left to wonder what was of such import that Kagemni would send an emissary after me.

We reached shore after dark and Butehamon accompanied me up a steep hill to a small temple overlooking the river. The moon had risen and cast long shadows through the mud brick arches. "In the temple another of Kagemni's officers will tell you what has transpired in Tjeni during your absence. I will wait for you here."

Inside, the temple was no larger than ten square cubits, with a small altar and offerings of food that now lay scattered about by wild animals. The moonlight silhouetted a man with one arm, so I knew at once who it was that Kagemni had sent. That knowledge chilled my body.

"Anhotek, it is g-g-good to see you again, although I wish it were under b-better circumstances," Ineni said with great effort. I returned his embrace with little enthusiasm, so concerned was I about the message he bore.

"These are difficult times in the royal compound. Kagemni has sent me to g-give you advance word, l-l-lest you be surprised by recent events." It was hard to read Ineni's face and body language in the darkness, but his stuttering, more pronounced than usual, told me all I needed to know about his agitation.

"Ihy reported he saw your ship on their w-w-way upriver. On their second or third day in Tjeni, Prince Meni took ill with a runny nose and high fever. Hemamiya claimed his illness w-w-was brought to Tjeni by Mersyankh's swamp dwellers."

"To the point," I chastised Ineni, for my hairs stood on end with foreboding, worried about what tragedy would have caused Kagemni to resort to such subterfuge.

"The... the illness caused the Prince to have many shakes. Ihy and Mersyankh b-brought the incident directly b-b-b-before Scorpion. Mersyankh told the King that in Lower Kem they would have drowned a child with the Prince's illness. They... they persuaded him to have the w-w-wet nurse killed."

The significance of this act was unmistakable. Ihy had

usurped my role as counsel to the King. The fact that Scorpion allowed this manner of intercession was an unforeseen and dangerous turn of events.

"What about Hemamiya?" I asked.

"She fears for her life, Anhotek. She fears she w-w-will be the next to be sacrificed. Her love of the Queen, may Ra protect her ka, and her hatred of the King are w-w-well known. She secretly appealed to Kagemni to send me here. Kagemni w-w-worries himself about w-what happens in the Royal court."

"Is there more?" I inquired.

Ineni hesitated. "If... if I may express my b-beliefs to you, Anhotek... you who has healed my b-b-battle w-w-wounds, who cut off my arm to save my very life. I, too, see the King's w-weaknesses in managing the court." It was difficult for Ineni, a loyal warrior, to express such a thought.

"You know that I w-would not hesitate to give my life for Scorpion in b-b-battle," he said, raising the small stump of his arm. "I w-would follow his orders, no matter how wrong-headed they might at first appear, for I do not fear death any more than any soldier. Yet, as surely as Scorpion is a great w-warrior, he knows not about managing the affairs of state. Your presence is sorely missed, Anhotek and we w-wish you back speedily b-before all of Upper Kem becomes but a province of Dep."

And so I learned that night of the changes that had already occurred in Scorpion's court and of the enemy troops that were massing on our borders. Change was in the winds and not merely the gradual changes that shape our life's journey. Meni's tremors were like harbingers of the tremors that periodically shake the very ground itself and wreak havoc on entire nations. The spirits of the gods once again roamed the Two Lands, as they had in the ancient times, and only a fool would predict what was their fancy. I trembled in fear all that night, but it was only the beginning, only the beginning of many fearful nights, as I was soon to learn.

# SCROLL FOUR

*Questions*

It was the time of Akhet, when Mother Nile's Inundation spilled over its wide banks and spread its fertile reach over the land like a blanket, birthing the Black Lands anew for our people. Throughout the land, villagers had time to relax and visit with each other. The poor were able to catch up on those many activities that often meant the difference to them between life and death once the waters receded.

But, in Scorpion's court, as it was for the wealthy in many of Kem's cities and villages, Inundation was a time for excesses of every manner and description, a time when idleness led to exhibitions of people's worst traits. It was a time I dreaded, even more so as I got older, and I was committed to not allowing this infectious attitude taint Prince Meni. He, on the other hand, probably came to dread Inundation for entirely other reasons, for it was during these few months that I forced upon him an even more rigorous schedule of lessons from sunrise to sunset.

Now, just two weeks since the height of Inundation, the air was hot and hung heavy with vapors so that we could feel its dew all around the Royal quarters. The steamy mist arising from Mother Nile oppressed the ka so that few willingly walked about, and those who did avoided each other lest the recipient of one mistaken word or gesture might fly into a rage.

In his room, Meni lounged next to his bed with his white cat, Mafdet, on his lap. His clay lesson tablets were stacked next to him. Sweat stood as a sheen on his little body. His pleated braid of black hair hung to his side, its tip wet from perspiration. As he petted Mafdet, pieces of her hair drifted on Ra's currents and each stroke elicited a renewed purr from the fortunate creature. So heavy did the weight of the air weigh on him, Meni hardly moved when I entered.

"Sit with me, Anhotek," the little Prince enjoined me.

"Gladly, my Prince," I replied, feeling that in all of Kem at that moment no father felt more love for his child than did I for Meni. I sat on the pillow and he snuggled next to me, still stroking Mafdet. Thus we sat, both of us content, the rays of Ra's light falling on our arms and legs. Despite the already oppressive heat, I felt as if each ray saturated us with his blessings, and for those few precious moments I was able to rid my heart of thoughts of Mersyankh, Ihy and Scorpion.

"Why does Mafdet purr so? Meni asked dreamily.

"Because he is so content, Meni."

"Yes, but I mean what allows him to purr, yet not be able to talk?" The Prince's mind was so inquisitive for a boy hardly more than six years. "He can meow and hiss and even screech when I step on his tail, but he cannot form words."

"That is a good question, and one that I, too, wondered about when I was a boy." I pulled him onto my lap and he leaned his face against my chest so that I could run my fingers over the bald parts of his head, as he liked me to do.

"To my knowledge, humans are the only beings who can speak... except for the gods, of course. The gods gave lions more speed, crocodiles more strength, fish the ability to breathe in water, birds the ability to fly, but... but to humans they gave speech and cunning."

The Prince's rhythm of petting Mafdet slowed. "The gods created the animals, as you have told me before... but... how? How did they do this?"

Lessons are best taught in the proper order, starting with learning how to read the picture words. But, sometimes an adult must take advantage of a child's natural curiosity and answer questions they raise on their own, at the time that they raise them. Yet, Meni was so young, I wavered, debating whether or not I should address his question directly.

"Anhotek?" he asked, turning his head to look up at me.

"You ask a very difficult question, my dear Prince Meni, and one I am not sure I can explain in a way that you will understand."

"Please do not call me 'Prince Meni.' I am too little to be a real Prince and... and no one would listen to me anyway if I were to command them to do something."

"Oh, but you are mistaken, little one. You are indeed a Prince, son of King Scorpion and Queen Neith-hotpu, who now lives in the next world. As you grow older and wiser, you will command all who appear before you."

"Even you, Anhotek? My teacher?"

"Yes, even me."

"Good," he said, pushing poor Mafdet off his lap and turning toward me with that beguiling smile on his lips. "Then I command you to answer my question, even if I cannot understand it." With that, he put his hands on his lap and stared directly at me, looking every bit as determined as his mother once did. It took all of my training to keep from rolling on my back in laughter.

"Okay, Prince Meni, it shall be as you have commanded," I said, bowing my head. "Then I shall tell you the story of creation and how the Land of Kem and all its animals and plants and people came to be." His eyes lit up. "But, you must promise that you will listen until I am done before asking me your questions, of which I am certain there will be many." Meni nodded.

"In the beginning there was Nun, the waters of darkness and chaos. Throughout Nun there was no form to anything, no ma'at, and bad and good were mixed together so that only confusion reigned. Yet, even within Nun the essences of the gods swirled through the fog of chaos and one day they agreed to come together and form a cosmic egg."

"But, how..." Meni tried to interject.

"Quiet, please, Meni. Allow this old teacher to finish his lesson before you interrupt." Meni's face twisted in frustration, but he relented and leaned back on his elbows. Mafdet sauntered back to Meni and nestled down next to him, turning over on her back and swatting at him with her front paws.

"Now, in the middle of the waters of Nun there arose a mound of earth, the Island of Creation, and on that island rested the egg." I watched Meni follow every movement of my hands, as they mimed the primeval mound and the egg.

"Then, one day, Ammon slithered through the waters of darkness in his serpent form and fertilized the egg. From this egg came Atum-Ra, the Creator Sun God, in all his glory. As he grew, he was lonely, and so he sprinkled his seed on the mound and a divine couple came forth, Shu, the air god and Tefnut, the water goddess." The Prince's face revealed that he was bursting with questions. This was good, for the boy must know the story of Creation and it would probably take many tellings, at many ages, for him to understand it at its deepest levels.

"Now, Shu and Tefnut were inquisitive... like you Meni... and they went out to explore the darkness of Nun, to try to make sense of the chaos, but it was dark... so dark not even the smallest speck of light lit their way. They soon became lost.

"Atum-Ra was very upset when they did not return, so he removed his Divine Eye from his forehead to send it out searching for them. He... ummm... can you imagine what the Divine Eye of Atum-Ra is, Meni?"

He thought but a second. "Yes, it is Ra's sun disc, is it

not?"

"Yes, yes, you are correct, little one! Even today it lights our sky. But, during the time of Nun, Atum-Ra used his Divine Eye to search for his two children. It lit up the darkness and found them and returned them to Atum-Ra. When he saw them he cried with joy, and his tears fell upon the Island of Creation and each one formed a human." My fingers imitated the rainfall and Meni's eyes were wide as I raised my hands to mime how the humans were formed.

"It was magic, was it not, Anhotek?"

"Indeed it was magic, dear Prince. A magic that continues even to this day, for the forces of Nun battle the forces of Atum-Ra every day. Only through our prayers, and through the magic that has been given to us, are we able to keep the darkness and confusion away from us. Each day that Ra rises is celebrated by the Horus priests. This is what we call ma'at, little one... when through our actions we are able to maintain balance in the world, to keep the forces of chaos from overwhelming us."

"What are the forces of chaos?" he asked.

"Oh, there are many, Meni. If not for ma'at, lions would be hunting us rather than the reverse, crocodiles would eat anyone approaching Mother Nile, hippopotamuses would trample even more of our men and women who draw water from the river. If not for our prayers, Inundation would continue without end and the waters would never recede to allow us to plant. Locusts would devour all our crops and plagues would ravage our people and... and Ra might not arise one morning to chase away the darkness."

I stopped, not wishing to burden Meni with fears and bad dreams. But he was not to be so easily placated.

"Now I understand how people were created. But... but what about the animals? How did the gods create them?"

As I was about to tell Meni about the creation of the animals, I heard someone in the courtyard clearing his throat and looked up to see Khonsu, one of Kagemni's valets, standing near the entranceway, motioning to me. I nodded my head and he quickly disappeared into the shadows.

Turning back toward Meni, I said: "Meni, I think we have done enough for today, I would..."

"It looks important," Meni interrupted. "You should go."

The Prince's ability to perceive the essence of a situation, even at his tender age, was uncanny. "In any event, you look tired anyway. The day will be a hot one and you should rest. Did Hemamiya give you your medication this morning?" From the dark rings under his eyes and the manner in which the muscles in his face sagged, I already knew the answer.

"Yes, Anhotek," he replied and shoved Mafdet off his lap. He yawned. I was struck by the fluid manner with which he could move from energy to lethargy in just a few short moments and, at times like these, worried about the effects that the herbal remedy for his shakes might be having on him. For, so it is with medicines, that oftentimes one amount of it will heal and a slightly larger amount will harm or even kill.

"What is it?" I asked of Khonsu as soon as I saw him emerge from the shadows of the pillar.

"Kagemni has sent me to tell you that there is trouble brewing with Ihy. He is alone with Scorpion right now. From the tone of their voices, Kagemni has cause for concern. He begs you to join him in his quarters."

The Prince was already asleep, so I left to join Kagemni. Years ago the two of us had agreed that no good was to come from Scorpion's marriage to Mersyankh. With Ihy's addition to the court, we were proved right within weeks. From that time on, not a day passed that I did not thank the gods for Kagemni's friendship and trust. For, since the birth of Neter-Maat, Scorpion's son by Mersyankh, the Royal court had been torn asunder by the arrogant ambitions of the swamp-dwellers.

"Good to see you, Anhotek," Kagemni whispered as we embraced.

"As well for me," I replied, smiling at the man who, but for the fortunes of birth, should have been leader of Upper Kem.

"Did I interrupt something important?" Kagemni asked, as he poured us both cups of water.

"I was telling Meni the story of Creation," I said, sitting down in one of Kagemni's reed chairs, one of the few pieces of furniture in his sparsely decorated room.

"Creation?" Kagemni asked in amazement. "And you were able to get through it without being interrupted by a thousand damned questions?" We both laughed.

"I did not say that," I responded before sipping from my cup. "Have you ever met such an inquisitive youth?"

"Never... truly never," he answered. "The other day I did as you asked and began teaching him battle strategies. I had with me clay soldiers, some with spears, others with bow and arrow, others with maces... a box of them. I placed the troops to illustrate a basic battle maneuver, not minding that I had put the archers in front of the soldiers with maces and swords. I just meant to show a point about troop movements. He scolded me for not having the damned archers provide cover for the frontline soldiers!

"You laugh, Anhotek, but the boy has a gift of genius. He juggles so many damned thoughts in his head at so young an age, it is sometimes... unsettling." Kagemni slumped into a chair opposite mine.

"I have no doubt that his illness contributes to his special abilities."

"Nor I," Kagemni agreed. "But others do not agree with us, Anhotek, and of that we must talk."

So we were able to spend an altogether pleasant hour together, despite the subject matters under discussion, catching up on court intrigue, solidifying our resolve to maintain a balance in the court between Meni's interests and the younger Prince, Neter-Maat. For if one thing was clear, even at his young age of barely two years, Neter-Maat was hardly the equal of Meni in spirit or cunning. In size however, he was already as big as Meni, having received the essences of Scorpion's large stature and that of his mother's family, for the women of the marshlands are larger and heavier than are the women of Upper Kem.

With our agreement that it would be best for Kagemni

to distract Ihy from bending Scorpion's ear, I wandered back to the Prince's quarters, all the time hoping that the Prince would still be asleep, so I could prepare his medicines for the next few days.

As I approached the Prince's chambers, I heard a commotion within. "Find Anhotek and ask him to come here," Hemamiya said to one of the servants.

"I am here already," I said.

"Little Meni here..." Hemamiya started to say.

"She will not listen to me, she..." Meni yelled over her voice.

I stopped where I was and rapped my staff angrily on the floor so that both of them ceased their chatter. "What is going on here? Starting with you, Hemamiya," I added, pointing my staff in her direction.

"You always take her side!" the Prince whined, most unpleasantly.

"And, you, my dear young Prince, must learn patience... a very noble trait, that you will need to perfect if you will ever be King." With that, the Prince scowled at me, but silenced himself. However, he was obviously distraught about something beyond his disagreement with Hemamiya.

"He had a bad dream, that is all," Hemamiya said with an air of finality. "He just will not let it go."

"That is what she says!" the Prince yelled. "But how would she know if she was not inside my heart?"

Whatever it was that upset the Prince, he would not easily be distracted. Later I would speak with Hemamiya about how she might better handle the Prince when he stubbornly held fast to his position. "And this dream..." I began.

"It was not a dream," he uttered so convincingly, I felt the flesh of goose raise along my arms and neck. "It was as real as if it were happening before my eyes. I do know the difference between a dream and what I just saw," he said, crossing his arms on his chest, for all the gods looking like Sisi, my mentor in Ta-Sety, when he pronounced an important decision in a dispute that was put before him by his villagers.

"Hemamiya, take your women and leave. The Prince and I will discuss his dream... or whatever it is he saw."

"It was just a dream!" Hemamiya muttered under her breath as she made ready to leave. "And, he is spoiled beyond measure!" she added before departing.

I lowered myself next to Meni, but in his stubbornness he wiggled a half-cubit away. "Tell me of this... this... of what you saw," I stumbled.

Meni hesitated. "I... I was asleep, but it was very clear. I was standing right there," he said pointing toward a small garden area not three cubits from where I sat, "watching myself sleep. Then, I saw Neter-Maat creep in. He took a knife from his tunic and crept ever closer. I could feel his breath hot upon my neck. Then he raised the knife and plunged it into my back again and again!"

Meni looked at me with such a deep and profound sadness, I felt as if someone had knocked the breath from my chest, for no child's face should be able to reflect such inner sorrow. It was not the first time I had been at a loss of words with Meni, nor was it to be the last, of that I was certain. But, I could not deny him his vision.

"Dear, dear Meni," I began, holding my hands outstretched to him and leaning toward him. He sat on my lap, both of us looking out toward the gardens, their orderliness and beauty the very embodiment of ma'at.

"What you have had is indeed not a dream, but a vision." He relaxed, and with that gesture my heart sunk in my chest, for I knew that a deep secret of his soul had been revealed. "Nor was it your first vision, was it?"

"No, it was not," he whispered, shaking his head from side to side. "Sometimes my mother visits me... or... but this vision of Neter-Maat... it was different."

"I know. I know," were the only words I could think to utter, although they were by no means sufficient to calm his aching heart. We sat this way for a time, listening to the sounds of Mother Nile percolating through the soil, the birds singing, and the tree leaves rustling in the gentle breeze.

"There are some things you must understand about

visions," I started to explain to him, holding him close to my chest. "They are gifts from the gods, so…"

"They are not!" Meni rejoined angrily. "Or else you are lying to me!"

"Why do you say such a thing, Meni? Look at me." I turned him to face me. "You are young, but know this. For as long as you shall live I shall never knowingly lie to you. You may not like what I say and you may disagree with me, but I will always… always tell you the truth as far as I know it. Do you understand?"

He looked away then, sadness encircling him like a tent. "If that be so, Anhotek… if it is true that my visions and… and my shaking are gifts, then why do they hurt so?"

"Oh, Meni, you ask such difficult questions. Your… your shakes are indeed a gift, although you are little now and do not recognize them as such. But, one thing you must understand is that not all gifts are easy to bear. The most cherished gifts of all are both blessings and curses." He lifted his eyebrows.

"Do you doubt that Hemamiya loves you, little Prince?" I suddenly asked.

"She is cruel to me sometimes," he replied quizzically. "But, I know she loves me."

"Look at it this way. Even though you know she loves you, she sometimes angers you. So, her love is both a blessing and a burden at times, right?"

"Yes," he responded. "And so it is with my shakes, you will say. But… so far I have not seen the blessings of them."

"You will, Meni. Trust me that you will. But, now let me tell you something about visions. Did you know that people from all over the land come to me to interpret their visions?" He shook his head. "Well, they do and for good reasons, Meni. I know how to interpret them, but I also have visions of my own."

With that, the Prince spun off my lap to face me. "You do? Really, Anhotek, you do?" He was beside himself with joy, as if I had lifted a heavy burden he was carrying.

"Yes, my Prince, ever since I was your age, or perhaps

before, although I cannot remember exactly. But, here is a secret about visions. They represent truth in some way, but they do not always come true. There is a difference and I will teach you to distinguish between a vision that predicts the future and one that lights the way toward two paths, allowing you to prepare and choose the best one."

"But... but the vision of Neter-Maat was so real," Meni protested. "I could smell his perfume. I could feel pain as the knife blade cut my skin. How could this be true, yet not true?"

"I did not say true and not true, Meni. I said visions are truth, but do not always come true. The truth in your vision about Neter-Maat is that the poor child is being trained by evil forces to compete with you for the throne of Upper Kem. Since Neter-Maat is younger and not nearly as cunning as you are, he may be persuaded to actions that may bring him disgrace. That is the truth of your vision. You have been warned by the gods. By making it seem so real, they have warned us. They have given us ample time to prepare."

He sat thoughtfully, absorbing my words. "Now, you may be wondering how I know that Neter-Maat's knife could never cause you harm. And, I will tell you, for your vision is an omen. I, too, had a vision concerning you. It was when you were still living in your mother's womb. I saw you grown into manhood, King of Upper Kem. Then, when you were born, the sky was covered with tiny clouds and Ra, in his haste to fly his golden disk to the west, illuminated them so that each one flickered as if they were radiating his golden light. The sky looked like the outstretched wings of the falcon-god, Horus. This is a powerful omen, Meni, to be so cherished by Horus. Thus, you will live long, protected by the messages contained in your visions. You are Meni, the enduring one. You will always be secure under the dappled wings of Horus."

"And the shaking?" he asked me feebly.

"The shaking is a holy condition, Meni... very holy. When you shake, the ka of the gods themselves enter your body. When you are ready, you will begin to hear what the gods are saying when they are inside you. You will begin to see the world through their eyes. Then you will know, as surely as we sit here today, why they gave you this gift."

He looked up at me then and I swear to Horus that I saw reflected back the soul of a man, not a boy, for that is how it has always been with Meni. Outwardly there is the child, inwardly the ka of the man peeks out, and I pity those in his life who are not able to comprehend the full depth of the man inside.

By the next day, the northern winds picked up and blew away some of the oppressive heat, so that the mood of the entire court was thus lifted. Being the middle of the ten day cycle, the morning was to be spent with Meni and Neter-Maat playing together, as Scorpion had instructed since Neter-Maat's birth. Yet, I always wondered whether it was Scorpion's desire for the two Princes to know each other that had motivated his proclamation or some other, secret desire by Mersyankh and Ihy to have access to Meni, to keep him under their thumbs. I suspected the latter. That is why I had arranged for their play time to be supervised by me or Hemamiya, and why Mersyankh naturally insisted that she or Ihy be present, too.

On this particular day, I was curious how Meni would handle Neter-Maat, since the dream would still be vivid in his mind. Meni nervously ate his morning meal, acting uncharacteristically silly and becoming distracted by everything around him. When Neter-Maat was delivered to Meni's room, Meni occupied himself in the corner studying picture words on his clay tablets, glancing up furtively now and then to observe what his half-brother was doing. As usual, I sat on the side of the room, reading and correcting the medical scrolls I had written the previous week, before handing them to my scribes for them to make the final copies I would use when I trained other priests.

Mersyankh had sent Neter-Maat with his handmaiden, which she often did, for in maternal instincts she seemed sorely lacking although, to her credit, she was highly protective of her son. Neter-Maat sat on the floor playing with his clay soldiers, picking them up and throwing them down in no particular order. Even after thirty minutes, Meni had not yet approached his sibling. Neter-Maat, in his gentle and eager manner, began to call out Meni's name. Mersyankh entered the nursery area and stood on the opposite side of the room from me, looking coolly in my direction until I nodded and smiled to acknowledge her presence, at which point she sat down with all her pretentious bearing.

Mersyankh had lost little of her striking beauty since she had birthed Neter-Maat. Her nose and her hips had widened a bit, but her use of clothes and cosmetics was masterful. Her hair hung in tight braids with orange carnelian beads and gold threads woven throughout, accenting the sheen of her dark black hair. But her eyes were as cold and penetrating as ever. She quickly assessed the situation in the room. Neter-Maat stood and toddled over to her and she whispered to him, turned him around and pushed him in Meni's direction, for I do believe that she desired for them to get along with one another. The boy's face lit with glee and he threw himself headlong across the room, his chubby legs propelling him forward, his hands in the air, barely avoiding tripping on his toy soldiers.

When he reached Meni, he could no longer maintain his balance and he fell on his rump next to Meni's desk, spilling one of the clay tablets from the desk onto the ground, where it shattered into pieces.

"Oh, no, look at what you have done!" Meni said in a tone that was admonishing, but not overly so.

"It was an accident!" Mersyankh immediately yelled from across the room, defending her son and standing as if ready to admonish Meni. The Prince looked up at her with disdain.

"You impertinent thing!" she continued. "How dare you look at me in that manner!" But Meni simply continued to stare at her, so fixated on her face I thought for a moment he was about to have the shakes.

At that moment Scorpion entered the chambers, dressed in a dirty linen tunic that hung from his neck to his knees.

From the way he walked, I could see that he had already been drinking barley beer heavily, for his gait was unsteady. Meni wisely broke his gaze from Mersyankh and bent over to pick up the broken tablet shards.

There can be no doubt that what happened next is one of those events the gods orchestrated, as a musician writes music for the lyre and flute, knowing beforehand how they will ultimately flow together to shape a man's soul.

As Meni bent over to pick up the pieces of broken tablet, Neter-Maat, who was already holding one of its sharp, pointed shards, threw his hands up in joy at seeing his father entering the room, a smile covering his face from ear to ear. It was as if time stood still in that room at that moment. I watched as Neter-Maat's hand reached up and up and Meni's head bent lower and lower, as if both boys' actions were slowed, yet propelled forward by irresistible magic. Then, the shard punctured Meni's eye socket and the pieces so carefully arranged by the gods began to tumble into place.

Meni screamed in pain and threw his hands to his eye, blood spurting out in rivulets. With his good eye, he saw the blood dripping from his hands, which caused him to panic and scream even louder. I immediately ran to his side, as Mersyankh grabbed up Neter-Maat, who sat in blissful ignorance wondering what had caused all the commotion.

I tried to calm Meni enough to examine him, but he was beside himself with pain and fright, so much so that I, myself, was surprised at first at his hysteria. Then I realized that the wound must have represented to his young mind a coming to pass of his vision about Neter-Maat.

"You lied to me!" Meni screamed at me. "You lied!" And with that he cried so hard I thought my heart would break. But, as a healer I hardened my heart so that I could treat his wound, praying as I did so that I could save his sight.

I pried his hands away from his face and saw that the pointed shard had punctured the inner eyelid and had probably severed a small blood vessel, but had miraculously missed his eyeball. By now Hemamiya was at my side and scooped up the Prince and sat him on her lap, holding his hands as she hugged him, so that I was free to treat the wound. Panehsy brought my medicine bag and I immediately washed the puncture wound with juniper water and quickly applied dried flax fibers to make it clot more quickly. Meni continued to sob, more so from the shock of his vision becoming real than from the actual pain of the wound itself.

As I prepared a linen bandage to cover Meni's eye, Scorpion stumbled toward us. "Let me see your eye," he commanded, roughly grabbing the boy's chin as if he were a slave of war being examined. Mersyankh held tight to Neter-Maat, but he struggled to be free of her.

Instead of cooperating, Meni wrested loose from Scorpion's grip and tried to run, but Scorpion quickly grabbed Meni's arm and held him fast. At this, Meni began to cry anew and without thinking, Scorpion slapped the child with the back of his hand.

"Stop it! You are acting like a little girl!" Scorpion yelled, looking down at the boy, his face bright red from a combination of the heat, alcohol and anger. Several of Scorpion's soldiers ran into the room.

Rather than tense and scream harder, Meni exhaled, then breathed in quietly, without a spasm, without even a trace of his just having cried. He stood tall and glared at Scorpion with his good eye, enraging his father. Scorpion grasped the Prince's arm tightly, locked in a contest of wills that he was destined to lose.

"What? What are you staring at, you brazen child!" Scorpion shouted, pulling the boy onto his toes so that he might be closer to his face. His muscular biceps swelled from the effort. Yet, the child still only came up to his waist. The mismatch made Scorpion small by comparison; such is the result when power is misused.

Scorpion slowly clenched his right fist. I acted immediately, afraid that he might strike his child again in his drunken rage. With his strength, the unthinkable might occur. My action might as easily have resulted in my execution as defuse the situation.

In a second, I was at Scorpion's side. "You know, dear Scorpion," I said, controlling my voice to calm him as I had done so many times over the years. At the same time, I placed my hand on his neck and began to press into the soft tissue. As I spoke, I increased the pressure of my fingertips until his brow furrowed from following my moving lips, uncomprehending. I knew that his effort would be in vain. He let loose his grip on Meni and passed out.

"Quick... come quick," I yelled to his soldiers. "Scorpion has passed out from too much drink." I winked at the most senior officer present and took him aside. "Look, make no mention of the King's behavior to anyone. Not even to him when he awakens. Pretend that no one else was here to witness these events, except for me and Mersyankh and the two boys. You simply came when I called." The officer was happy to have someone tell him what to do. He summoned a few other soldiers to bring a litter to carry Scorpion, who was already taking the labored, snorting breaths of drunken sleep.

Mersyankh stood staring angrily at something behind me. Neter-Maat began to cry and reached out his hands toward his father. She picked her child up without taking her eyes off the object of her attention and stormed out. Then, I turned slowly and looked behind me. There stood Meni, the bandage over his eye, his child braid hanging from the side of his head, his fists clenched tightly. With his good eye he peered down at the crumpled body of his father and the hateful expression on his face sent shivers straight through my soul.

# SCROLL FIVE

## *A Severe Remedy*

"Okay, then, here it is," Kagemni said earnestly, as he leaned over and arranged a set of clay soldiers on the mud-brick floor. Piles of sand had been strategically placed to simulate sand dunes. "The swordsmen are here and... and the archers are here," he said, stretching to place them on a high dune. "And here are the spearmen. Now, what would you do?"

Meni scanned the groupings carefully. He breathed in slowly, as I had taught him to do during those times when he was tested, then he sat up straight to his full ten year-old height. His wiry build made his chest appear concave and his long braid down the side of his otherwise shaved head gave him a yet more boyish appearance.

"The position you placed them cannot be defended," the Prince stated dismissively, pointing to the toy soldiers. "Too many would perish."

"How would you know that?" Kagemni asked derisively. "You are young and impertinent! And," he added for emphasis, "a child that has no... that is too damned smart for his age. A terrible combination of traits!"

Kagemni looked directly at me. "He is hopeless, Anhotek. He is not trainable. I will have to give up on ever making him into a warrior."

I smiled at them both, for this had become their way of relating to each other, to mask their love behind a warrior's bravado. "But, he may have a point, General," I suggested. "Perhaps you should listen to his reasoning."

"You are no help at all!" Kagemni scoffed, waving me away with his muscled forearm. "He learns nothing but evil behaviors from you. He even talks like a damned Horus priest!" Feigning frustration, he turned back to the Prince.

"Explain to me… that is if it pleases you, dear Prince Meni, why this battle strategy is so dangerous for my men."

"Our men," Meni corrected, bringing a smile to my face. Kagemni hung his head down, to hide a similar reaction, I suspected. "But first I must ask you a few questions."

"More damned questions!" Kagemni sighed.

"In this situation, how many troops do each of these toy soldiers represent?"

"What is the difference?" Kagemni answered coyly.

"What is the difference? How is it that Upper Kem wins so many battles against its enemies if you, the General in charge of the troops, do not think it matters how many troops he commands? This I cannot understand." Meni's eyes were opened in wonderment.

"Hmmmm," Kagemni responded. "I suppose each figure represents one hundred men."

"Our own trained warriors or mercenaries?"

"Will you pester me forever with your unending questions, little Prince, or will you show me how you will fight this damned battle and save our land?"

"You yourself have told me that mortals rush in where the gods themselves fear to enter. If I were leading these men, I would want to know everything I could about them."

"Ahhhh!" Kagemni pretended to pull his hair in frustration. "Alright then! They are trained troops, although our Ta-Sety mercenaries are fine warriors, in some ways better than our own."

"Alright, then, here is my plan," Meni continued. Despite Kagemni's barb about speaking like a Horus priest, I was proud of how his verbal skills shined of late.

"First, you taught me that archers are used to best advantage when they can shoot their arrows from afar, without worry of being picked off by opposing spearmen or archers. Therefore, I would place the archers here," he said moving the soldiers to the top of a flat rock that Kagemni had set up beforehand.

"In this way, they not only have freedom of target selection, they also are protected by the rocks."

"Yes, but..." Kagemni started to counter.

"I would also place the spearmen on both flanks," Meni added, bending to relocate the spearmen and swordsmen. "Their spears might break up the ranks of the charging enemy. However, if our enemy was cunning, he would charge the central column of our swordsmen and break our own ranks. You have told me many times that breaking through ranks gives a big morale advantage to the side that accomplishes this.

"I would instruct my swordsmen to intentionally open ranks upon the enemy's charge," he said, rearranging the toy soldiers, "revealing two columns of spearmen here, behind them, backed by another group of swordsmen. That would enable us to surround and overpower the enemy." Now it was Meni's turn to sit back on his heels.

Kagemni sat, unmoving, reviewing the Prince's strategy. "By the gods, you are correct, Meni!" he said slowly, his voice so low I could barely make out his words. "Your strategy is damned cunning. It shows boldness and concern for your troops. I bow to your efforts," he said, bowing low toward the sandy floor.

"Can I play now?" Meni asked expectantly, looking at me.

"Yes, Haankhef is here already. Play together until after the midday meal." The Prince bounded from the room.

Kagemni turned to me, his face blanched. "By all the gods that wander the earth, even I cannot juggle as many damned possibilities as he does. He will be..."

"A formidable opponent?" Kagemni nodded. "He already is, Kagemni, and he is merely a child."

"He considers the morale of the soldiers and the momentum of battle, the very things that make the difference between victory or defeat. He is destined to be a strong leader."

"I would agree, but you better than anyone knows there is a big difference between manipulating toy soldiers and fighting a real battle. Which brings me to a question I have been meaning to raise with you. Although he is thin, I have been thinking of beginning Meni's martial arts training. Not with weapons, for he is far too small, but with the fighting movements I have learned from other shamans. Do you think this wise?"

Kagemni thought for a moment. "He is nearing the end of boyhood. It might encourage his skinny body to sprout toward manhood. I will make small weapons for him from wood. That is how I begin training the new recruits, although those dung-throwers rebel against it. They think they are born warriors and should be armed immediately." Kagemni smiled his contagious grin.

"So be it, then," I said. "However, I think it best to keep this between you and me, Kagemni. I see no point stirring the pot between the two Princes."

"I agree, but Neter-Maat has just started to receive training. He is already huge and as strong as a baby bull. Scorpion commanded the lessons and so I was obliged to arrange them."

"I am aware of them, of course." My informants now regularly apprised me of any developments involving Neter-Maat, Mersyankh or Ihy. I rolled my scrolls into their jars and stood. "Now I must tend to some of the nobles' children, who are falling ill with the typical fevers of summer." I clapped my hands to summon Panehsy. "How I hate this season, when every plague that bedevils us makes its appearance."

"Me, too," Kagemni agreed. "The plagues are attracted to my barracks like infernal flies to dung."

Kagemni left and I walked slowly through the Royal compound, accompanied by Panehsy, who carried my bag of herbals and healing tools. Immediately outside the palace were the Royal workshops, where artisans in metal, wood and cloth manufactured their various goods for Scorpion's extended family and for the families of Tjeni's wealthy residents. The workshops were a cacophony of clanging, hammering sounds, interspersed with the shouts of master craftsman and of laborers and apprentices calling to one another. Smoke from their fires hung in the air thick and pungent.

The quietest of the workshops was devoted to linen cloth making, for the past ten years under the direction of Baktre, a woman slightly older than me. Most of the weavers were women and while they chatted incessantly, they did not shout to each other like the workers in the other workshops. Instead, they settled into a comfortable rhythm, sending their shuttles flying across their looms in a click-clack cadence, with the regularity of a water clock.

Behind the weavers, on the far end of the shop, three huge copper kettles simmered. The master dyer mixed crushed malachite stone into one of the kettles, while another women added a bolt of linen cloth. As the dyer stirred the cloth, I could see swatches of green bubbling to the surface and peeking over the rim.

Outside the walls of the shop, in the heat of Ra's disk, other women sat bare-chested, beating flax plant stems with a wood mallet to separate their fibers. As many as a dozen women took the fibers, a few at a time and spun them on their drop spindles into a long, continuous thread. Every so many feet, they wound the thread onto a wooden stake. As the stakes filled with linen thread, a young girl, her breasts showing no signs of budding, ran the filled stakes to the weavers. Everyone in Upper Kem knew his and her place in the order of the land. Ma'at was strong today.

Just beyond the workshop, Panehsy and I came to a neighborhood where various of Scorpion's many relatives and other wealthy Upper Kem landowners and merchants lived. Accommodations close to the King's compound were highly desirable, the better to curry favor with the King and, I must say with all modesty, with me. However, my influence had lessened somewhat in recent years due to the scheming of Mersyankh and Ihy. But, despite Kagemni's repeated warnings to strengthen my position in the court, I felt no urgent need to do so. The Horus priests of Upper Kem pledged their allegiances to me alone and would hardly risk an unlikely alliance with Ihy and the swamp dwellers. If nothing else, my insistence that the head priest of every temple be literate, while not well received initially, ultimately meant extra income for them as they served as scribes for reading and writing legal documents. Some tutored the children of the wealthy in how to read the increasingly popular picture words and the extra goods they earned in barter for their services did not hurt my position with them.

At the house of Uni, one of Scorpion's many cousins, I was greeted by their servant. He rushed to get Uni's wife, Pakhet, a fat and slovenly woman who was a frequent patient of mine. In truth, I tired of her maladies, most of which I had come to believe were due to her unhappiness. However, by administering harmless potions and herbals, I endeared myself to her. She frequently had her servants send me sweets and breads and even an occasional piece of meat from her husband's hunts.

We waited in their spacious entranceway for what seemed like a long time for Pakhet to appear. The house had been expanded to two stories, now the rage in Tjeni. When Pakhet made her entrance, in a fine white, linen robe that was still wet from her bath, she behaved oddly. Her hair was wrapped in a thick towel. "Why, Anhotek, how pleased I am to see you!" she said blushing. "Why... to what do I owe this visit?"

Panehsy looked at me and shrugged his shoulder. "Dear Pakhet, are you feeling well?" I asked.

She stood, staring at me as if I were asking her to read a scroll of incantations. "Why, yes... yes, I am fine. I thank you for asking. But..."

Thus we stood, neither of us comprehending. "Did you not call for my services?" I finally asked.

"I... yes... I did, but... but that was days ago," she stammered. "I had Uni send word to you when he met with Scorpion about the wheat crop, maybe... perhaps three days ago. Khahor, our youngest, was ill with the summer fevers and our usual ministrations were to no avail. So I had Uni summon you."

Something was yet not spoken. "And, so here I am!" I replied, trying to be as cheerful as possible, for it seemed to me now that Pakhet was either showing the effects of aging or was ill herself or, unlikely as it seemed, had a lover in the other room. "I was only informed today of your need."

"Anhotek," she began, taking a deep breath to collect herself. "That day... the very day that Uni made his request, Scorpion sent Ihy over to minister to Khahor. He... he said some prayers and made a sacrifice and then I... I think it was the next morning, the fever broke."

Had Pakhet hit me over the head with a throwing stick it would not have surprised me any more, nor hurt any more. "I... I'm sorry..." I stammered, searching for words.

"It is no harm done," Pakhet graciously replied. "He... this Ihy said that you were probably busy and that therefore Scorpion had requested that he minister to Khahor. He praised you highly, Anhotek, praying that his ministrations would be even half as effective as yours. His prayers were obviously powerful."

I bowed and left as quickly as I could, taking a different route back to my quarters, for I did not wish to face Scorpion by happenstance, I was so enraged. I also needed time to analyze events and plan how I would deal with this new reality.

But, I had no sooner arrived in my quarters when I was summoned to Scorpion's chamber by a servant I did not recognize. I changed my clothes, groomed myself, and walked with the servant to Scorpion's side of the compound. As we approached, I heard several voices talking heatedly, but as I entered the room they desisted and Mersyankh scurried out of view.

"Greetings, Anhotek!" Scorpion called out, acting cheerfully, although I could see from his body that it took

85

considerable effort. He was clothed in a loincloth and I could not help but notice that his torso showed signs of disuse.

"Blessings upon you and all of Upper Kem," I responded, intentionally leaving out Ihy. I bowed deeply and held out my hands to the level of my knees.

"Arise, Anhotek. No need for formalities." Scorpion's tone was measured. Ihy stood stiffly on the side of the room, dressed in his customary lion skin, his eyes darting continually between me and Scorpion. I suspected that Mersyankh listened from behind one of the columns that adjoined her sleeping chambers.

"To what do I owe the honor of your summons?" I asked, not wanting to dally with Ihy present. From the corner of my eye, I caught Scorpion casting his gaze toward Ihy, who nodded and tipped his staff slightly in my direction, as if to prompt the King to proceed.

"I... I was wondering if you had heard of the illness that is even now spreading through my Royal court here in Tjeni," Scorpion started.

"It is Shomu, Scorpion. The gods always send illness and plague to us in summer to test us. Of course I have heard of the latest wave of plague."

"Well... ummm... well that is the reason for my summons, Anhotek," Scorpion said, now looking at the floor. "It appears as if this latest wave, as you call it, is far worse than usual, for it seems... for it appears to be especially hard on our children. Ihy has visited some of the ill children and he confirms that to be the case. Is that not so, Ihy?"

Ihy pulled himself to his full height and leaned on his staff for authority. "Yes, it is so, King Scorpion, for I have seen it with my own eyes."

I looked from Ihy to Scorpion to see where all this talk was leading. Instead, Scorpion stared back at me.

"Excuse me, Scorpion," I finally offered, "but my understanding is that you have sent Ihy to treat the children of the court who have been stricken. And, by all counts, he has done a good job although, I must say that their illness is of the variety that they would have recovered by any means."

I supposed that the reason for my being summoned was to enlist my aid in the task of ministering to the children, as such waves of plague had a tendency to overwhelm the healers of a community when they peaked.

"Well, Ihy says the illness is not the typical plague of summer. He... Ihy believes that this plague is far worse and that were it not for his magic, many children of the court would have died. As is, Nehasy's son died last week."

"Hmmm..." I moaned, trying to keep my disrespect from showing. Nehasy's son had died because his stupid father insisted on taking the ill boy fishing that day and he drowned when he fell feverishly into the water. Was Ihy so desperate that he would set the stage for my help by making the usual plagues of summer appear more terrible than they really were?

"And the point of all this talk of disease is what?" I asked, mystified.

"The... the point is... what I am trying to say, Anhotek, is that Ihy... that the conclusion we have come to is that the children have been made more susceptible to the plague by their exposure to...by..." Even Scorpion could not finish the sentence he had started and with a sickening feeling in my stomach I finally understood the reason for my summons.

"Before you go on," I said, interrupting the direction of the meeting, "let me say that I find it odd that Ihy would judge the severity of plagues in Upper Kem when he has had no experience with them. The plagues of the marsh dwellers are different, for they live under more... more difficult circumstances," I said pointedly.

"That may be true, Anhotek," Ihy shouted at me, "but these children are experiencing high fevers and are... they are having shakes. I have seen them with my own eyes."

I became enraged then and pointed my staff at him. "That is because you choose to see them only with your eyes, Ihy. You choose only magic remedies, rather than use our superior healing arts to hold down their fevers to prevent the shakes in the first place. You are a magician, not a healer and definitely not a Horus priest!" I turned then to Scorpion. "Ihy knows full well that high fevers often lead to temporary shakes in children, Scorpion. This is a fact known to healers for as long as our memories go back."

"Enough, both of you!" Scorpion commanded and stood up. He walked past me to the entranceway and then turned back again. "There is more to this, Anhotek, but you will not listen to Ihy and so I will be the one to tell you." His gaze burned through me like a brand.

"It has come to my attention that every child in the nursery has come down ill... all that is except for Meni. He appears healthy, except for his shakes. Why do you suppose that is?"

Bitter bile rose to my throat. So that was it! Ihy and Mersyankh feared that their own Neter-Maat was imperiled, that somehow Meni's spirit would invade the second-in-line to the throne. Only such a threat could spur Scorpion to such ignoble action. But to engage Scorpion's anger now would be fruitless. He fed on anger and on challenges to his authority. Instead, I lowered my voice to a near whisper.

"I suppose he is protected because of the herbs and the care I give him," I said simply. "Yet, I seek not to persuade you, King Scorpion. You now have the counsel that you desire and that you deserve," I said looking from Scorpion to Ihy. "I shall not come between you and your counsel, for many is the time I have advised you thus when you relied on my guidance. A leader must trust that his advisor always seeks to fulfill his best interests... and the best interests of Upper Kem," I said, hoping against hope that Scorpion would understand my veiled message. But, of course, he did not.

"For that, I thank you," he replied, sitting back down. "I had hoped you would be reasonable."

"May I be so bold as to make a suggestion," I went on, "to... to attempt to resolve this unfortunate situation?"

Scorpion looked relieved, although Ihy stiffened. "Yes. Yes, go ahead, Anhotek."

"I had been thinking anyway that Meni needs to begin

his travels. He matures in wisdom beyond what the immediate environment can provide for his learning. I seek your permission to take the Prince away for extended periods of time over the next few years." With those words Ihy let out an audible breath, so loud he embarrassed himself and in so doing revealed that my strategy might work. "Of course, I shall give you an itinerary of where we intend to go in each case, should you need to summon the Prince back to the Royal Court... for whatever reason," I added.

Scorpion looked at me, not realizing that I confirmed in the slight nod of Ihy's head that I had upstaged the plans that they, along with Mersyankh, had stealthily crafted. I was sure that behind the brick column to the King's right, Mersyankh burned with rage.

"I... that is a severe remedy you suggest, Anhotek," he said unsteadily, stealing a glance at Ihy for a hint of what he must say next. At that moment I pitied Scorpion more than ever before and I had the urge to reach out and hold his hand as I had when he was a boy, and reassure him. "I must think on it for a while... for a day or two. I... I will let you know my decision." But I could see that the decision had already been made. Short of ridding the palace of Meni permanently, Ihy and Mersyankh would settle for having him, and me, absent from the Court for long periods. They could believe, at least in the short term, that they would have sole influence over the King and thus firmly position themselves in the line to succession.

I took my leave and, with troubling thoughts racing through my heart, proceeded straight to the Prince's chambers, where I instructed Hemamiya and my assistants to begin to prepare for a long journey, although at that moment I knew not where we would go. I sat down and wrote several secret messages to my shaman peers in Ta-Sety and sent them by my personal messenger to the head Priest at the Temple of Horus in Nekhen for delivery upriver by his most trusted priests. As for my messages to my mentor in the Eastern desert and to my contacts in Setjet, I summoned the leader of a nomadic tribe that I knew well. I paid him handsomely in gold to leave immediately under the guise of a trading mission to those lands.

The next day I received word from Scorpion that he thought my suggestion a good one and that he would provide whatever support I might need in my journeys with the Prince. The court was abuzz with rumors and it was all I could do to keep myself from being constantly drawn into whispered conversations under shaded porticos or behind mud-brick columns.

By the end of the ten-day cycle, no more than six days since I had met with Scorpion and Ihy, we were ready to leave. I decided to take Meni on his first trip upriver past Nekhen, to Abu island, which was the southernmost outpost of Upper Kem. The trip itself would be fraught with peril, but not nearly as perilous as was leaving the Royal court to the scheming of Mersyankh and Ihy. So I arranged a series of meetings with the priests of every temple along our route to mortar their loyalty. Yet despite the ambitious agenda I had set out for us, once we were in the boats, I felt as if a burden had been lifted from my shoulders. It was now in the hands of the gods themselves to determine what was to become of the Prince and of Towi, The Two Lands of Kem.

# SCROLL SIX

## *The Vision*

Sailing with Meni on Mother Nile, as I was at this moment, I had to admit that the past two years of near exile had not been as bad as I had imagined they would be. Not that Mersyankh and Ihy made things easy. To their credit, they were persistent. Whenever they heard a rumor of a disaffected priest or a wealthy merchant who complained too loudly about the taxes the priests collected for Scorpion's treasury, they sent their advisors to curry his favor and thus endeavor to persuade him into an alliance. Fortunately, my network of spies relayed such attempts to me and I dealt with them quickly. Many of Ihy's and Mersyankh's attempts had thus been thwarted, but I was not so naïve as to assume that their unholy alliance had not won over more than a few of Upper Kem's rich and powerful.

In the past two years our entourage had journeyed throughout Upper Kem, so that Meni was able to see for himself how his people lived and worked, played and died. We traveled throughout the annual cycle, coming home only for brief periods during the start of Akhet, when the raging Nile made travel upon it too hazardous, or during Heriu-renpet, the five days before the New Year, when the gods roamed the earth and I feared bad luck might befall us.

Soon after we left the Royal compound, the plague in Tjeni subsided, as I knew it must. Ihy, however, took great pains to point out to Scorpion the fact that fewer children were ill after we left, as if to validate his mistaken beliefs that Meni was to blame. Yet, once we were gone a few months, the illnesses returned, only this time with a vengeance. Many of the children of the wealthy became gravely ill and several of them died, that year and the one following. Even now, the second summer since we left, Ihy's magical spells and incantations did little good, but Scorpion was too proud to call for my help, despite the pleas of many within the court. My spies had informed me of these heartfelt pleadings, but Scorpion was now fully under the sway of alcohol and the two swamp dwellers.

At this very moment I hardly cared, for we sailed lazily back and forth across the mighty river, three days journey south of Abu island, where the rapids form the first cataract on the Nile. The huge boulders in the middle of the river at Abu island looked just like the rounded backs of elephants crossing from one side to the other, hence its name. On Abu island itself, which stood high above the river, its industrious people had dug a series of shallow canals, into which they poured buckets of water portaged from Mother Nile. Much of the island was lush with emmer wheat, barley and flax. Across the river from Abu island were immense white sand dunes that sloped down to the river's edge.

Abu was the most prominent strategic site at the boundary that separated Kem from Ta-Sety. We had rested and provisioned ourselves in the main village while Meni, already on his third visit to the island, reacquainted himself with the fishermen that plied the waters of Mother Nile for the giant catfish. He accepted their gracious hospitality and exchanged gifts with them, a practice I encouraged, for I foresaw the day when he would need all the allies he could muster.

And so we sailed, idyllically, upriver, each day passing a

multitude of boats loaded with grains or livestock or fruits of every manner. We were now well into the territory of Ta-Sety and with each passing day I felt the excitement of the journey grow. In truth, I was eager to acquaint Meni with our Ta-Sety neighbors and their customs. With each day that passed, the complexion of the people inhabiting the river grew darker and darker.

One day, Meni approached me after we had finished the afternoon meal. He had been in a somber mood for several days and I had begun to consider reducing the dosage of the medicinal herbs from Setjet that he still took. Children in puberty are the most difficult to treat, since their moods are so changeable, and I am often confused about whether it is my skill, the medicines or their behaviors that most affect the treatment.

"Anhotek, I have been wondering," he started. "As far as these Ta-Setys go, I have always heard our people brag of our superiority, yet... yet as we sail by their shores, aside from the color of their skin or perhaps their greater height, I can tell no difference between our two people. They seem to farm in a similar way. Their villages, their way of life look much the same."

"That's true. Always consider the sources of your information, Meni. Those who compare the Ta-Setys unfavorably to the people of our land speak out of ignorance." The green banks of the Nile were spread before us, lush with reeds and rushes and filled with birds and animals of every description.

"When I lived among them, the Ta-Setys told stories of their long history much as we speak of ours. They have lived in villages for as long as have we... perhaps longer. Like us, they have Kings and Queens and they trade among themselves and with us, as well as with the lands to their south. They are great hunters, for their land south of here is even more lush, with grasslands and with forests that defy description. They have lions even more numerous than have ever lived in Kem, even when our gods roamed the earth. In places they have elephants so numerous, they are like trees in a forest. That is where all the ivory used in the royal workshops comes from."

"And our ebony comes from their forests," Meni added.

"Yes. And their grasslands produce ostriches, which we use for eggs and feathers."

"So they are primarily our trading partners?" Meni asked.

"Yes... and no. We do trade our grains for their goods, but we also gain more. You, my dear Meni, would never have been born if not for what I learned from their healers. Their magic and their medicines are very strong, every bit as powerful as ours.

"I have much respect for their land and people. But, I would not be serving you well if I did not also caution you about these people. They may someday represent a threat to Upper Kem." Meni turned toward me, sensing my change in tone.

"But, they seem peaceful," Meni countered. "I have not seen any soldiers."

"True. And we may proceed on our entire journey through Ta-Sety and not encounter a single soldier, or at least not one that you could easily identify. That is because the Ta-Setys train even as young boys in the art of fighting. They don't have an army such as your father commands. Instead, they sometimes raid another village or defend their own against attack. But, in these actions they are fierce warriors, indeed, for I have seen with my own eyes how brutal they can be with each other. You already know that Kagemni hires many as mercenaries. So, you would be well advised to remember that given the right circumstances, if they feel mistreated or threatened by Upper Kem, they could very well rise up in arms and threaten our southern border."

Meni looked away from me and surveyed the scene before us, trying to fit my observations into his own. "I will heed your advice," Meni finally said. "When we travel through their land, I will look for signs of aggressiveness on their part."

Our ship swayed as waves from a fishing vessel lapped

against its side. "There is yet another, even greater threat the Ta-Setys pose, one you would be wise to consider during your idle times." Again Meni looked at me.

"They control all the trade routes to the south. Without the luxury goods we get from them, without the ebony and ivory and gold, we would live like the swamp dwellers of Lower Kem. The luxury goods from Ta-Sety support our craftsmen, who produce the products so admired by the rest of Kem and the eastern lands. If they were to deny us access to those goods, the wealthy would be dissatisfied and that would not be good for a ruler."

Just then, Butehamon called out to a tall, thin black man standing on the bank, dressed in a coarse loincloth. He asked him to catch our line and within minutes all three boats were secured and we stepped ashore to stretch and relieve ourselves. When we were done, I spoke to the man, who was a fisherman.

"He says the catfish are biting well today," I translated to Butehamon, who responded with great enthusiasm. He quickly made the smallest of our boats ready to drop some fishing lines before night fell. Meni accompanied Butehamon and three other soldiers as they rowed slowly and dropped their anchoring stone only a hundred or so cubits from our camping ground.

While the rest of us set up the tents for the night, we could hear the men enjoying their fishing outing. Every few minutes we watched them pull up a perch or small catfish, to much excitement or derision, depending on the size of the fish. But we all dropped what we were doing when a series of loud yells burst from the boat all at once.

"By Hapy, he must be a monster!" one of the sailors shouted as he peered overboard. We could see the boat being dragged to the middle of the channel, anchor rock and all.

"Quick!" Butehamon shouted, "pull that anchor before the rope rips a hole in the boat!" One of the sailors rushed to heave on the anchor line. As soon as he lifted the huge stone from the bottom, the boat took off as if pushed by the wind.

On the bow we could see one of the sailors battling the fishing line, trying to pull in the fish. "Meni!" we could hear Butehamon shout from the stern, "grab that fishing line and help land the beast! Feel what it is like to take one of Mother Nile's monsters!"

My heart sank as I watched Meni jump over ropes to get to the bow. The soldier grabbed Meni, positioned him in front of his chest and wedged him between his massive legs. Then he handed the rope to Meni. Together they pulled, then let the line go for a few seconds, then pulled again, hoping to tire and thus land the fish. Each time they pulled, the bow of the boat bobbed low to the water, giving an indication of the size of the beast they had hooked.

It took more than an hour for the men to exhaust the fish, and even when they brought it alongside the boat, it was too heavy for them to lift. Instead, Butehamon himself took one of the oars and beat the fish senseless. Then they tied it to the side of the boat and rowed to shore.

When I finally saw the fish, I gasped. It was a monstrous catfish, easily longer than any of us, more than two cubits in length. Its snake-like whiskers hung down nearly a half-cubit and its girth was larger even than Butehamon's barrel chest. The copper hook that it had swallowed was bent nearly straight from his valiant efforts to escape.

Meni was prouder than I had ever seen him and throughout an entire night of retelling how they had landed the catfish he never complained about the rope burns that blistered his hands and left them bloodied.

Butehamon's men filleted the beast and we gave a large piece of it to the local fisherman who had befriended us. We then made sacrifice to Hapy, the god of the Nile and still the remainder of the monster's flesh was plentiful enough to feed three boatloads of hungry men. It was a rare experience that connected Meni directly to Mother Nile and her bounteous gifts. I felt sure he would never forget it, nor the rich lessons it provided.

In the morning we woke to a chorus of birds in the shallows. After the morning meal of leftover fish, bread and cheese, we began our journey inland, leaving our boats under the protection of four of Butehamon's soldiers. For three days we walked along a well-worn trail that meandered inland toward a hilly and forested region. Once we reached the base of the foothills, we were greeted by a group of tall, black tribesmen, as I suspected we would be, for the hills commanded an unobstructed view of the plain we had just crossed. Much to Meni's delight, behind the men were several elephants, waiting to transport us and our goods further into the forest. The men tapped the forelegs of the giant beasts and they kneeled before us. With little prompting, Meni scrambled up the side of one of the beasts enthusiastically and sat upon it, gazing around in wonderment as it stood and began to lumber forward.

Thus we traveled for the remainder of that day until, as the disk of Ra began to sink and the forest grew dark in shadows, we came upon the village that I had not seen in more than twenty years. I eagerly scanned the faces of the people who came out of their huts to greet us, but could not find the face that I sought. I anticipated bad news, for when I had last seen him Sisi, the shaman with whom I had apprenticed after my ordination as a Horus priest, was already old.

As I began to descend from the elephant's back, the crowd split and a man nearly my age walked through the crowd toward me. To my amazement, it was Sisi, and he appeared as if he had not aged at all. His body was lean and muscular and he easily stood a full head taller than me. His hair hung in four twisted locks from his head to below his shoulder, characteristic of Ta-Sety men, and on his arm he wore a series of gold armlets. He wore a large leopard skin draped over his shoulder and a leopard skin tunic.

"Anhotek!" he called out in a deep voice, bowing low to the ground in their sign of respect. I held tight to my staff, still shocked by his appearance. "It has been far too long since we have seen you. My father waits for you to bless his home with your presence, dear brother." Only then did I recognize Atuti, Sisi's oldest son, who now wore all the attributes of power.

"Atuti, for a moment I thought I gazed upon your father in his youth. You… you have grown to a fine man. I…" But before I could finish my words, he grabbed both my arms in his and squeezed them tightly, as is their custom. The villagers murmured their approval and I could see that several of the older ones recognized me, and I them.

We were led immediately to the same mud and straw hut within which I had spent three years of my life, learning the customs, as well as the healing potions and practices, of these Ta-Setys.

"Father," Atuti called out, "I have brought home a gift from the gods. Will you accept their blessing?" This was their custom for announcing the return of a hunter or announcing visitors. Sisi once explained that the custom celebrated the fact that visitors nourished the soul of the tribe, just as food nourished the body.

Sisi sat upon a large wooden chair, upon which were cushions for his comfort. Yet, instead of the large man that filled the chair during my apprenticeship, here sat a thin and shriveled old man, covered in a long tunic of a coarsely woven plant. A small fire burned in the middle of the hut.

"Oh! Oh, the gods are good!" Sisi exclaimed as he tried to rise from his seat to greet me. "Look what they have brought to me as a comfort in my old age!" I hurried to grab Sisi so that he would not expend the effort required just to stand. I bent low, even touching my knees to the floor, as tears filled my eyes from the joy, and the sadness, too, of seeing my mentor.

"No, no, you must not bend down before me, dear Anhotek, for a son never bows to his father once he is grown to manhood. Rise, my son, for tonight and tomorrow are times of celebration." Holding onto my shoulder, he raised himself to standing and we embraced for a long time. The effort had exhausted him and I eased him back into his chair.

"And, who is this fine young man you have brought with you?" Sisi asked as soon as he regained his breath.

I moved closer to Meni and bent low to the ground,

both my hands stretched out before him. "This, dear Sisi, is my master, Prince Meni, firstborn son of King Scorpion and the future King of Upper Kem, greatest of the Two Lands." A murmur from Atuti and his friends went up in the room and spread to those gathered outside. Meni, not knowing what to do, stretched himself to his full height and tried to look casually around the room.

"Meni. Prince Meni," Sisi said as if practicing the name. "You will always be welcome here, for anyone who Anhotek loves, is beloved in this village. Forever shall this be your refuge when you visit Ta-Sety. Now, come here, my child, that I may gaze upon your face."

Meni glanced toward me, not in fear, but with a questioning look. I motioned him to go closer and he walked proudly toward Sisi. Atuti sidled over next to me, his shoulder touching mine. When Meni was in front of Sisi, his body revealed he was unsure of the protocol. Should he bow or accept the tribute of Sisi? He closed his eyes for just the merest of seconds and then his heart filled with its own answer. He bent low to the ground, spreading his hands wide in front of him, below knee level. Atuti turned toward me and beamed his approval.

Sisi reached out and pulled the boy up and studied him from his feet to his head. He ran his fingers lightly over Meni's face, then closed his eyes and placed his hands on Meni's bowed head for several minutes, all the while blinking behind his eyelids, his chest rising first with shallow, then deep breaths.

For his part, Meni stood silently. He tensed at first, then relaxed until, by the end of their time together, I could see them breathing in identical rhythms. As Sisi removed his hands from Meni's head and held his cheeks in his hands for a moment, I could see their eyes locked. Then, it was over and Meni walked back to my side. It was difficult to gauge his reaction. He appeared saddened.

Sisi clapped his hands weakly and a tall, muscular young man, with radiant, jet-black skin and many twisted locks of hair, emerged unexpectedly from the shadows. He wore a simple loincloth and a leather herbal pouch around his waist. Sisi whispered something to the man and he approached us.

"Sisi wishes me to show you to your hut, Anhotek." He surprised me by speaking fluently in our language. "My name is Meruka. Sisi has spoken of you often and I am most honored to meet you," he said, bowing. "I am Sisi's apprentice and also his youngest son."

"And his mother was the prettiest of all Sisi's wives," Atuti said, smiling at his half-brother. "She still is."

Over the two, ten-day cycles of our visit, Meruka accompanied me on several plant-gathering expeditions so that I could restock my dwindling supply of herbs from the forests and mountains of Ta-Sety. He amazed me with his intimate knowledge of herbs, for he was no more than twenty years old. He had been in training with Sisi since he was a child. The young man possessed a keen intelligence and a deep curiosity and I had not had such an enjoyable time with another healer for many years. Sisi had delegated much of his healing practice to Meruka, although I did not have occasion to watch him heal anything but minor conditions.

On the days when I stayed in the village to dry and prepare the medicinal plants, or to take a day's rest, Meni and Meruka talked in animated tones or left early in the morning for long expeditions, often arriving back in the village with fish and game they had killed. Meni also persuaded Meruka to teach him some of their fighting techniques, and I noted that Meni practiced relentlessly in our small hut whenever I was outside. Over the course of our visit, the two had grown close, much to the delight of Sisi and Atuti.

Toward the end of our visit, Butehamon and his men become restless, although Meni and I would have gladly stayed another two or three cycles. Sisi noticed this, too. One night, after the evening meal, he called me and Meni into his hut. Meruka sat on one side of him, while Atuti sat on the other.

"Sit, my sons, for I fear that the time is drawing near for us to part once again, and our next meeting will doubtless not be in this world." He held up his hand to stay my weak protest.

"I have been thinking about many things," he said, looking at each of us in turn. He sat silently for a long moment, collecting his thoughts. "There are changes... in the sky, in the water, on the land... such as we have not seen as far back as the memory of our tribe goes.

"The air is drier now... the seasons hotter than ever before. Our water dries up and the sands claim more of our land with every passing year. Tribes are leaving their ancestral lands and roaming the earth seeking pasture and land for farming and hunting. This brings our tribes in close contact with each other, which has not always been good.

"Now, we learn that your father has defeated all the villages of Upper Kem," he said looking at Meni. "I ask myself how long it will be before he attempts to do the same even in Ta-Sety?"

"Sisi, I assure you..." I began to say.

"I have had a vision, Anhotek, although... although I am uncertain whether the vision is near or far off. I see in the future that Kem will threaten the people of Ta-Sety." I was beginning to feel anxious about where Sisi's speech might yet lead.

"So, I have made a decision," he said with finality, "a decision that I pray will bind our people together in peace forever. It is a decision about our two families, Anhotek, for I have seen that Meni has... I have seen a glimpse of his visions. He suffers now, yet he is destined for greatness. He will need ministering as he grows, and while you have grown to be a great healer, there will be times when you, too, will require able assistance.

"I have decided that Meruka will accompany his brother, Anhotek, to Kem." Sisi had obviously not discussed his decision with Atuti or Meruka. They demonstrated admirable restraint. They neither looked at their father, nor at me, nor at each other. Meni's reaction, however, was less subtle. He glanced at Meruka, with delight.

"Will you accept counsel on your decision, father?" Atuti asked. "Or is your decision final?"

Sisi looked up at his eldest son with a pained expression. "On most decisions a wise leader seeks the counsel of his people," Sisi offered. "On others, he consults the gods and acts alone. In this, I act alone, for the signs from the gods are unmistakable to me."

Atuti closed his eyes for a moment. "Then I accept your decision, father, although it also raises other... complicated issues," Atuti said. "You are the greatest of all healers. But without Meruka, who you have trained since he was barely old enough to walk, we are without a healer and shaman to care for our tribe. Our prestige among our neighboring tribes will diminish. They will take this as a bad omen and may attack."

"Yes... yes this does raise difficult issues for us," Sisi agreed. "However, I will also tell you this, Atuti, my eldest. You are the chief. Yet you have lived in the shadow I have cast. Great challenges make great leaders. How you meet these challenges will determine how our people whisper your name in the fire circle for many generations."

I admired the respect and orderliness that infused Sisi's household, for it is always thus with great leaders, that they need not wield their power with a mace to move others toward a better future. Instead, through the respect they have earned, the people willingly follow. I hoped that the lesson was not lost on Meni, who sat silently, intensely observing the discussion.

"As for you, young Meni, future King of Kem," Sisi said, "my decision is only a half decision unless you allow Anhotek to accept Meruka. Although I give my youngest to Anhotek as an assistant, it is more done to serve you." Sisi and Meni locked eyes and deep understanding flowed between those two in that moment.

"I accept, wise grandfather," Meni said quietly, showing how adept he was. "I am honored to have Meruka assist Anhotek."

Sisi smiled. "There is but one thing I must ask of you," he added. "After I leave for the next world, Atuti will rule alone. I pray that the gods give him long life and many sons and daughters. But, if his fate is to join me before his sons are old enough to rule, and Meruka is still alive, I ask that you release Meruka so that he may come home to lead our tribe."

"I give you my word," Meni answered solemnly.

"Then step forward, Anhotek, Meruka," Sisi said, his voice now weakening from emotion. He drew his flint knife from his medicine pouch. "Give me your right hands." As we extended our hands, Sisi cut into the fleshy part of our palms at the base of our thumbs until he drew blood, then held our hands separately in his.

"Though you come from different lands, though your outer skin is a different color, know that your blood is the same. You are both my sons. Although you are my adopted son, Anhotek, we long ago mixed our blood in a ceremony before our gods. So, my blood runs through both of you. Now, I mix your blood together," he said placing Meruka's smooth, black hand upon my pale and wrinkled one, and squeezing them together. "Forever are we family." I looked deeply into Meruka's dark eyes and knew that Sisi had spoken the truth, for I could feel the magical bond that Sisi had created.

Throughout that night, the village both celebrated and mourned Meruka's leaving, with dances and stories around a huge bonfire. Meni tried to stay awake, but the emotions of the past few days were too much for him and he fell asleep after the feast, sitting between Sisi and Atuti. As the night wore on, the village was spellbound by the stories that Sisi and I told of the days when the gods walked the earth. But Sisi also made the villagers laugh until their sides hurt with stories of my tasting the wrong herbs when I apprenticed with him, so that I had to live in the jungle for a week only a few steps from the latrine pit.

In two days more, we were gone, retracing our steps back across the dense savannah toward Mother Nile. As Meruka's village faded into the distance, he grew silent and uneasy, so that he seemed as if pins were stuck into his skin. The slightest sound from the grasses that surrounded us spooked him and he sprung into action with his dagger at the ready. Meni noticed it, too, and he spent more and more time next to me.

With another half-day's walk ahead of us, Ra's disk began to set, so we camped at twilight atop a slight rise that gave us a view of Mother Nile and the ribbon of green that accompanied her through her journey. As Butehamon and his men set up tents, Meruka crouched down at the edge of camp, leaning on his spear and lost in thought. Meni was tired from the long walk and crouched against a tree while the tent was being readied.

No sooner had I sat down next to Meruka when a shout arose from one of Butehamon's men, then another. I turned toward the encampment, but the tall grasses prevented me from seeing what caused the commotion. But Butehamon's booming voice soon roused me. "Anhotek! Come quickly! Meni is shaking!"

In an instant I rushed to Meni's side, with Meruka right behind me. "These are the shakes of which I have spoken to you," I said without even glancing at him. My hand cushioned Meni's head from hitting against the trunk of the tree. Meni's right hand, however, lashed out furiously and his knuckles repeatedly hit one of the large roots. Meruka jumped over Meni's body and grabbed his right hand tightly.

"No, do not restrain him!" I cautioned Meruka and he immediately let go Meni's hand. "You can cushion the hand, but do not prevent it from shaking. People with shakes can break their limbs from others trying to restrain them." Meruka was a quick study and he gently placed his own hands between Meni's arm and the root. "And quickly give me your medicine pouch," I added. Once he had removed it, I forced the edge of it between Meni's teeth.

"We dare not move a person who is shaking," I instructed Meruka. "Once he is done, we will move him to the tent and medicate him." By then, Butehamon had removed everyone else from the scene, lest they witness any more of the Prince's illness than necessary. In a moment the shakes ended. Meni had bitten his tongue and blood ran from his mouth.

We carried Meni to his tent and laid him on a

makeshift bed of dried grasses, covered by a cloth. "What will you do for him now?" Meruka asked, his hand shaking.

"He usually sleeps for several hours, perhaps a whole day, after a shake as severe as this. Since we are traveling, I will give him an extra dose of the medicine I got from the healer in Setjet." As I turned to retrieve my medicine kit, Meruka roughly grabbed my arm and spun me back around.

Meni was about to have another bout of the shakes. The whites of Meruka's eyes shone brightly in the dim tent. But, his fear, a fear based on ignorance of the holy illness, was no match for my fear at that moment. I could not administer the medicine that Meni so desperately needed for fear of him choking.

"This has never happened before, Meruka... two episodes of shakes in a row." As I said those words, the Prince began shaking again. Yet, this incident was different from the one we had both just witnessed, different, in fact, from any others Meni had experienced. Rather than the violent shaking, his body became rigid. His arms were pressed close to his torso, so that his whole body shook in unison, but mildly. His face was not contorted, as during a full-blown shaking episode. Now only his brow was furrowed. In this state he continued for several minutes, although it felt more like an eternity to me.

Finally, it was over. A few sporadic shakes more and the Prince rested, his body limp, his loincloth and bed covering soaked in his own urine. As Meruka brought his hands toward the Prince to untie his loincloth, I recoiled at the contrast between his glossy, healthy black skin and Meni's frail, white skin. I rushed to mix Meni's medicine, while Meruka lifted the Prince to sit him up.

As I approached Meni with the medicine cup, the oddest thing happened. He opened his eyes, underlined by purplish-black circles of fatigue, and stared at me with a look that was indescribable. No one, other than another shaman who was in the throes of a vision quest, had ever glanced at me with such deep, knowing in his eyes and such utter resignation. As I brought the cup to his mouth, he reached up weakly and grabbed my hand and shook his head ever so slightly. Had I persisted, he could not have resisted my efforts to medicate him. But, I swear in the name of Horus that at that moment I knew Meni was not alone. He was in the midst of his own vision quest and I, despite my good intentions, had interrupted him.

I instructed Meruka to lay him back down, and he had hardly done so, when Meni began another series of shakes, still longer than the second, but even milder. Meruka looked at me questioningly, but I shook my head and neither of us uttered a word. I, myself, shook in awe in the presence of the gods' visit, channeled through the Prince.

So it was that Meni had his final shakes that evening, for the disk of Ra had now settled in the west and darkness, along with a deep sense of gloom, had descended with it over the camp. I dared not leave Meni's side and Meruka brought the makings of a fire to take the desert chill from the tent. Once the fire established itself, I arranged my shaman tools and bade one of Butehamon's men to run to Mother Nile to fetch some water, which I blessed. With Meruka's help, I prayed to the gods, such as I had never prayed before. I prayed for Meni and for Upper Kem, but also for the goodness of Ta-Sety that Sisi and Atuti and Meruka embodied.

That evening, as I dozed while sitting by Meni's bed, I was awakened suddenly by a chilling presence. Yet when I blinked open my eyes, nothing had stirred. The fire had dwindled and the evening chill was back in the air, so I tossed on more brush and a few twigs to rekindle its warmth. I turned to check on Meni, who sat still and silent, staring at me, the dancing flames reflected in his brown eyes. I felt gooseflesh rise along my arms and spine. But, he was in no distress that I could see. Quite to the contrary, he seemed calmed.

"It was as you said, Anhotek," he whispered. "The visions, they... they came... they..."

"Shhhh. You need not talk now, my Prince. You must rest," I insisted.

"No, it is you who must be quiet now, Anhotek. Horus himself has given me a vision... many visions. I must reveal them to you, for my fath… King Scorpion does not favor me. A big part will fall on you to see that the visions come to pass. Thus it was revealed to me."

What could I say? Here was a boy, staring at me with eyes that penetrated to my ka, eyes that revealed a power behind them far in advance of his years. That he experienced a vision there was no doubt in my mind. I was spellbound by the holiness that he radiated in the feeble light of the fire.

"There are not two kingdoms of Kem, Anhotek," he continued, looking into the fire, "except in the minds of men. Mother Nile cannot serve two masters once it flows into Kem. The gods will that there be only one Kem and I its only ruler. This I saw.

"The Kem that the gods revealed to me is a land of such majesty it took away my breath. I saw temples of white stone, monuments so large they dwarfed the size of men and reached to the clouds. I saw irrigation canals crisscrossing the land to spread the gifts of Mother Nile far from her banks and there was grain… grain and foodstuffs in abundance.

"I saw all this and more, Anhotek. Much more," he said almost pleadingly. "Yet, even now I cannot bring forth all the images that were shown to me. There were priests, many, many priests and they all possessed great knowledge of the gods and medicine and magic and… and they read from the divine words, the picture words that you have taught me, but… I cannot explain it… there were many divine words that I have never before seen. Oh, it was so grand, Anhotek, so grand our Kem!" His eyes shone bright.

I could hardly contain my enthusiasm, for Meni's vision had rekindled my own visions, ones that were given to me by the gods after I had returned from my many wanderings and had settled back in Tjeni.

"I, too, have seen what you describe, Meni," I said excitedly, rising onto my knees. "Not in such detail, but similar… similar enough. I have dreamed of a Kem of such grandeur it makes me giddy. I have always believed it possible to achieve if the right leader were to ascend to the throne." I stopped, for I feared putting too much pressure on Meni. Vision without power, without a plan to achieve it, has been the ruin of many a man and his followers.

"Meni," I went on, reaching out and holding his right hand in both of mine. "The teachings of the Horus priests tell us that a person can only fully understand by dreaming. This is a grand gift you have been given, but also an awesome responsibility, for you are still young. You have much to learn in order to lead men, to create the Kem of your vision. I give you my oath and swear to you my allegiance, that we might turn your vision into reality. This I promise you, that we will write down your vision and devise plans to achieve it and… and not rest until…"

"The vision will not be achieved in my… in our lifetimes, Anhotek," he said with authority. "As I flew over our very Kem on the back of Horus, Mother Nile rose and fell with every beat of his wings. However, we must start upon the path that Horus revealed. If we do not, I saw a glimpse of the chaos that will overtake our land. It… it was terrible!"

"I will walk that path at your side." I could see his strength was ebbing. "However, right now you must sleep, for you cannot help the gods achieve this vision from the next world."

As soon as his head felt the soft grasses, he fell into a deep sleep and I sat by the fire for an hour or more watching him toss and turn and grimace and moan, as if he sought a way to shoulder the immense burden that his vision now thrust upon him. That night will forever be etched into my memory, for even as I prayed for Ra's appearance in the morning sky, I understood that it was the last time that I would gaze upon the sweet face of Meni, the boy Prince. Like all great visions, it would take the shoulders of a grown man, even with all the gods behind him, to lead a people to greatness.

# SCROLL SEVEN

## *Ra's Glory*

If there is anything more frustrating in the world than raising a boy through the transition into full manhood, the gods have mercifully not yet thrust it upon me. I now look back with embarrassment upon the many times a parent came seeking my counsel in raising their son or daughter through these years and I, haughty and smug, dispensed advice as if it were but a simple task, involving only a minor correction here or a scolding there.

How wrong I was! Dealing with Meni is hardly easy any more. I often spend the early part of what should be my sleep replaying the latest argument I had with him. I wonder whether this young man is indeed the same gentle child I once knew, or whether the evil mut spirits have secretly exchanged his ka for one their own. There are times when he stares at me with a look of utter disdain, as if my body stank like a rotting corpse and he were suffering my presence only at the peril of his own life.

Yet even when he is at his insufferable worst, when I feel as if I would be doing Kem a favor by drowning him in an irrigation ditch, in the very next instant his original ka returns to his body and he becomes a considerate, thoughtful young man, redolent of the boy I once knew. One moment he thinks my counsel worth less than the toothless beggar's in the street, the next moment he falls all over me with gratitude for helping him make a simple decision.

It was Proyet, the season of Planting, when due to the intercession of the gods Mother Nile retreats to its banks, leaving its rich, musty smell and the heady promise of renewal upon the land. From the river to the desert's edge, a thick carpet of black, with a downy covering of green could be seen. Farmers spread over their fields like ants, tending the emmer wheat, oats and barley seedlings that pierced the fertile soil on both sides of the river. We were in Tjeni for the Festival of Planting, when King Scorpion would bestow his blessings upon the farmers and their crops. These ceremonies had come to bring out the worst in Meni, for he both loved what they represented to his people, but also dreaded the time he would have to spend with his father and half-brother.

"Have you seen the Prince?" I asked Hemamiya, as she tidied his room. The way the mid-day light shone straight down on her long hemp robe made Hemamiya look squatter than usual, but the truth was that as we aged we had both gained weight around our mid-sections.

"This morning… when he awoke and packed his bag. He left before Ra appeared in the sky," she answered me, not breaking stride in her chores. There was an edge in her voice.

"To…?"

She stopped her work, stood straight up and placed her hands on her hips. "How am I to know?" she snapped. "I long ago gave up pretending that I have any control over him, as you still do. He does as he pleases. I sometimes wonder if what he needs most from us he does not receive."

"And what is that?"

"A switch! A stick… whatever it takes," she said in exasperation. "He is so insolent at times. He insults me as if

I were nothing to him but a slave."

"Hemamiya, look how we argue over him, like a husband and wife. He is just a young man and you... you have raised only girls. Boys are a different animal altogether."

"Yes, animal is the word for him. I fear he will... never mind," she added and turned back to her work.

"What, Hemamiya? You fear he will...what?"

She stopped again, but this time did not turn toward me. "I sometimes fear he will become like his father."

Her shoulders hung heavy with her admission. "I understand your fear, Hem..."

"Do you?" she shot back, turning to face me. "Do you really understand how much I despise him, Anhotek? Do you?" Her face was crimson with fury.

"I think I do, dear woman, for you have detailed your grievances to me for these many years. What are we to do about it? We are but servants of the King, Hemamiya. I have tried everything to change him for the..."

"I know that!" she shouted back at me. "But your influence is no match compared to that... that sorceress," she said, pointing toward Mersyankh's chambers, "and that evil magician. I believe the King has worsened, although I swear by the gods that I could not have imagined that were possible. He is constantly drunk and Mersyankh twists him to her purpose like a vine on a tree." She sunk down onto Meni's bed and absent-mindedly smoothed the sheets with her hand.

I waited for a moment before continuing. "Hemamiya, did the Prince say where he was going?"

"No. He confides nothing to me anymore."

"He loves you, Hemamiya. Surely you know that." My words seemed to calm her and she breathed in deeply and sighed. "In any event, I must find him, for we have to prepare for the Blessings of the Crops. If he returns soon, please advise him that I seek him out."

The Prince had probably taken his boat to the east bank of Mother Nile to wander in the desert again, a practice for which he had been reprimanded many times. By rising early he managed to escape his body guards and had long ago figured out how to sneak down to the water unobserved. The desert seemed to offer him solace, for he invariably arrived back by day's end with a more cheerful demeanor.

I returned to my quarters and began to write in my medical papyrus. With the Prince gone, my rooms were unusually quiet and I enjoyed hours of satisfying work. With Ra low in the sky, I began to feel unnerved that Hemamiya had not sent for me.

I sent Meruka to search for the Prince within the Royal court, but he returned in an hour empty-handed. By now Ra's chariot was quickly receding to the western lands and I felt a sense a foreboding in my heart. Never before had Meni been gone past dark.

I sent Meruka to fetch Butehamon and Kagemni. Within minutes, Kagemni arrived dressed in his full military regalia, for he was in the midst of rehearsing with his men for the Festival.

"How long has he been gone?" Kagemni inquired as soon as he and Butehamon entered my quarters.

"Since before Ra rose this morning," I answered, feeling my stomach twisted in a knot.

"To where?"

"To the east bank, I believe. He is probably walking in the desert, as he sometimes does when he needs to be alone and think."

"Hmmm," Kagemni muttered. "This afternoon, one of my officers arrived from the east bank. He said there were damned heavy windstorms in the desert, just beyond the mountains." My heart skipped a beat, for Meni loved those mountains and often walked among its peaks and valleys. He once begrudgingly confided in me that the mountains gave him the best opportunity to use the meditations I had long ago taught him.

"Kagemni," I said, "he is probably in those very mountains. We must do something."

"Butehamon," Kagemni ordered, "assemble a battalion of men and have them meet us at the docks. Have your boats ready to ferry us in an hour."

"It will be almost dark by then," I said.

"If we hurry we can reach the east bank and still march for an hour. That will bring us closer to finding him in the morning. We might even bump into him tonight, scrambling to return home."

By the time our boats reached the east bank, Ra's disk had sunk nearly behind us into the horizon, bathing the mountains we faced in a warm, reddish hue. A hurried search by Kagemni's men turned up Meni's boat moored in a stand of papyrus plants. Kagemni instructed his men to split into three groups in order to cover a wider area and then to march in double-time toward the mountains where I knew Meni liked to roam. I stayed with Kagemni's group, and Meruka with Butehamon's, and we all arrived at our encampment shortly after nightfall, still short of the mountains themselves. The temperature had already dropped while we set up a simple camp in the dark. Kagemni posted sentries to be on the alert for the Prince walking back toward Mother Nile.

I had trouble falling asleep that night, but finally succumbed to a blissful dream. Just before Ra rose in the sky, Kagemni woke me. "Where should we focus our search?" he asked, as I rolled out of my blanket with difficulty, for my bones no longer adjusted easily to sleeping on the pebbly sands of the eastern desert.

"He likes to wander through the gorge that cuts through the mountains," I said, recalling the many times we had walked there together. "But in the past year I have not accompanied him. He wanders alone and I know not where. I suggest we start through the gorge and then spread out afterwards."

Kagemni thought for a moment. "No, we might miss him. We will split into three groups. One will go through the gorge, but the other two will circle wide and meet us on the other side."

After a quick morning meal of flat bread, honey and water, we left. I accompanied Kagemni's group, which was to take the route through the gorge. We marched thus for an hour, the gorge looming larger and larger ahead of us, for all the world looking like an immense gateway to the next world, ill-omened and forbidding. We were still a solid hour's hike from the base of the gorge when the skies suddenly darkened and we could see the advance wave of a huge sandstorm blowing in from the east and hovering over the mountains. The storm was frightening to behold, for it stretched the entire width of the mountains and dwarfed even the highest peak, ominously darkening the skies. There was not a man who did not tremble in fear.

"Quick!" Kagemni shouted to his men. "Dig a trench and lay your blanket over you! No man is to be alone. Pair up!" They immediately followed his orders and we jumped into the trench just as the first grains of sand began to blast our skin. For the next hour we were stung by a sandstorm that waxed and waned, sucking the very air from our lungs and covering every inch of us with fine grains of sand and dust. Every man coughed and choked from the furious assault, yet such it is when faced with the awesome chaos of such storms that not a man spoke a word to his trench mate during the entire ordeal.

As soon as it passed, Kagemni clawed at the sand and dug us out of the pit, which now lay covered a cubit deep. He ran along the trench line and helped dig out every pair. It was easy to see why his men loved him so and pledged him their loyalty to death. I ordered the men to drink as much water as they could prudently spare to offset the desiccation produced by the hot desert winds. In another hour we were ready to resume our march through the mountains.

"That sandstorm was fierce," Kagemni said to me as we walked. His voice betrayed his worry over the Prince.

"He will be fine," I said, trying to convince both of us with my words. "He knows where the pools of water are within the caves of these mountains." But I feared greatly that Meni would not know how to defend himself against such a force of chaos.

As we marched, Kagemni kept looking to his left and right, trying to determine whether his other troops had fared as well as had we. By the time we reached the gorge and had traveled halfway through its corridor, we saw one of the other groups waiting for us. It was Butehamon and Meruka, with his twisted locks of hair covered with fine sand dust.

"We saw nothing of the Prince," Butehamon said as soon as we were within earshot.

"Have you seen anything of Asheru and his men?" Kagemni asked.

"Nothing. We marched double time to the mountain and managed to gain refuge in the rock caves before that monstrous storm hit us. Before Ra rose, we spread out to search for Prince Meni. Asheru must be doing the same on the other side."

"Let us pray you are correct," Kagemni replied. "Still, have two men climb that ridge," he said pointing to our left flank, "to be sure Asheru's men are unharmed."

With that, two soldiers ran at a steady pace to climb the ridge. But, before they reached the peak, one of the men in Asheru's contingent appeared at the peak and hailed them. We watched as the three soldiers conferred and then split apart, each retreating the way they had come.

"Kagemni!" one of the men said breathlessly when he returned. "One of Asheru's men was bitten by a viper when they dug out from the sandstorm. He is in great pain. Asheru asks for Anhotek to come at once."

Of all the forces of evil in the desert, the troops feared the viper the most and with good reason. It hid stealthily among the rocks and sand, camouflaging its light brown, scaly body, tightly coiled below the surface so that it could strike with ferocity when threatened. And its poison infected the body with equal ferocity, attacking its victim's vital organs with painful venom. To die from the bite of a viper was an agonizing, painful death.

Meruka came with me and we made haste to follow our guides. But I had to rest several times, for the trek took us up and down rugged hills. We arrived at a scene of confusion. Many soldiers swarmed around the bite victim, while others sat around complaining of the desert and its demons, wishing aloud that they could march back to Tjeni.

"Anhotek!" Asheru called to us as we descended. "Thanks be to Horus that you have arrived while Harnakhte is yet alive. My... my men are taking the storm and the serpent as bad omens." Asheru's eyes were wide with indecision and even fear.

"Storms and serpents roam the desert at will," I whispered into his ear. "If you do not take control, chaos will surely govern your men, and not you!" Asheru moved his head slowly away from me.

"Yes. Yes, you are right, Anhotek. I... I was distressed about the Prince and..."

"There is no need to explain yourself," I said, eager to get to the stricken soldier. I made a mental note to tell Kagemni about Asheru's lapse of command. "Did you see the serpent that bit Harnakhte?"

"I killed it with my own sword. It was a sand viper," he replied, eager to be of some use.

When I saw the bitten soldier, I knew at once that he would soon journey to the next world. Despite his large size, Harnakhte writhed in pain. Periodically, he tried to stand up, but three of his soldier brethren held him down. His left forearm, where he was bitten, had swelled to the size of his thigh and the site of the bite itself was a deep purple, for the bite of a sand viper will cause the blood to leave the vessels and pool near the wound. His tunic was soaked with his vomit.

I squatted next to him in the sand and immediately felt the heat of his body. Though he tried to pull his wrist away from me, I could feel a shallow, racing pulse.

"Harnakhte, can you understand me?" I asked, looking into his eyes. He was frantic with the knowledge of his own impending death. He nodded.

"Is the pain very bad?" Again he nodded.

"Do you taste metal in your mouth?" He nodded once more, never taking his eyes off me. He rubbed his swollen lips against each other, indicating that he was experiencing the tingling sensation that accompanied a viper bite. "I will try to help you, Harnakhte, but you must also help yourself. Listen. Listen to me," I repeated, holding his head in my hands. "You must try to relax, so that the poison doesn't spread so rapidly."

"Meruka," I called as I arose, but he was already at my side. 'We must work speedily. Give me your assessment." By now Meruka was used to analyzing patients by the symptoms they presented, as was our practice in Kem.

"In my opinion, he is beyond saving," he whispered.

"I agree with you, Meruka. Assuming he will die in any case, what might we do?"

All that day we worked on the afflicted soldier while Asheru regained control of his troops. He sent a messenger and escort back to Kagemni. While Meruka ground fennel seeds and fleabane for application to the wound, I incised the man's arm and cut out the part of the arm that the serpent's poison had destroyed. Gruesome work it was and each of the soldiers that stayed behind made sure he was occupied with another chore while Meruka and I worked. Once I sewed the incision, I packed it with natron salts to keep it from festering and wrapped linen bandages around it.

We forced copious amounts of water into Harnakhte to dilute the poison, as well as a mixture of onion, honey and the blood of the viper that had bitten him. He swallowed them feebly, although he had not eaten anything since the evening before.

Once we had completed the first treatment, I paused to offer a prayer to the gods. Meruka and I knelt over Harnakhte.

"Horus, god of Nekhen, protector of the Kings of Upper Kem, I kneel before you in your service," I began, while my hands passed over Harnakhte's body. "You granted me my healing gifts. I have served with healers and shamans from Setjet to Ta-Sety. Meruka's father, the greatest healer of the Ta-Sety people, taught me his magic. Let me honor your name by healing Harnakhte, who himself serves King Scorpon of your divine lineage. By your will, make the poison flow out of Hernakhte. Make it come forth and spill out on the ground. Exorcise the poison, Horus!"

The soldiers stood watching in rapt attention, for it is common knowledge that the treatments from healers who have been trained as priests are aided by the intercession of the gods. My skills had to have been god-given, for who better than I knew of my own doubts and failings? Meruka then offered prayers to his gods, for they are powerful, indeed.

That night, the other two contingents of soldiers joined us, having been frustrated in their attempts to find the Prince. Kagemni ordered a fire to be lit, as much to ward off evil forces as to serve as a beacon for Prince Meni. By now Harnakhte was quieted and the swelling in his arm reduced. Meruka tended to him without cessation, changing his dressings frequently and murmuring his own incantations against evil demons.

"Will he live?" Kagemni whispered to me once his men had settled around the fire.

"No one but the gods can say for certain," I replied. "But, he seems to have strengthened over the course of the day. I believe Horus has looked kindly upon him."

"He is one of my best damned warriors," Kagemni told me. "We can ill afford to lose such men."

"He may yet be lost to your service," I whispered back. "His arm has putrefied. I fear we will need to amputate below the elbow when we return to Tjeni."

Kagemni stood still for a moment, staring at the fire. "If that is the will of the gods, so be it," he continued. "He is alive only because of your skills, Anhotek. Yet, even missing a hand, I would welcome him as an instructor." Leaders like Kagemni know that to discard such a man as Harnakhte, after a life of valorous service, would be a dreadful lesson for younger troops.

"One more thing, Anhotek. The men fear that the cursed serpent bite and dust storms are ill omens. I beg you to conduct a ceremony that drives the evil forces away and helps us find the Prince. I am fearful that we have seen no trace of him today... not even a damned footprint in the sand. We..."

"Meruka and I will prepare at once." With that, I left

Kagemni and knelt next to Meruka at Harnakhte's side. The soldier looked up and smiled at me and I took his good hand in mine and squeezed it.

"He is much improved," Meruka said to me. "I have learned a great deal today, Anhotek."

"You have also contributed much, Meruka. Come... now we must conduct a ceremony to drive away the evil mut that still lurk in the desert all around us," I said, standing with difficulty.

"Bring me all the garlic cloves you can find, even if you must take them from the men's rations. Bring your rattles, for they contain powerful magic against the mut. Wear, too, your bangles, for tonight I believe you shall dance the spirit dance of your people."

We gathered all the materials we would need to conduct the ceremony. The men sat around the fire in loose clusters, except for two that remained by Harnakhte's side. However, every man was riveted on Meruka, for he wore only a piece of coarse linen wrapped around his manhood and had rubbed his body with oil so that it shone bright and black, his tensed muscles accented by the firelight. On his arms and legs he wore gold bangles and a necklace of immense lion claws.

From my bag I removed my four magic wands, made of hippopotamus ivory and carved with powerful representations of the gods triumphing over evil. Meruka and I laid down the wands to delineate four corners. We raised our hands toward each other, to create a magical protective tent over the men emanating from the wands.

We then placed cloves of garlic in straight lines between the wands, for the smell of garlic wards off all manner of insects and scorpions and serpents. Then Meruka and I walked inside the protective space and toward the fire. We raked the fire outward, rearranging it into a ring, with us in the center and the men a respectful distance outside, but still within the protection of my wands and the garlic cloves.

"Horus! Thoth!" I shouted, so loudly and for so long it startled several of the men. The echo from my voice reverberated back over us from the mountain's wall. It created a mood that I knew the gods themselves preferred in order to work their magic. "Make your presences known to us, humble servants of Ra. By the magic powers you have placed in my keeping, I beseech you to protect these men against the evil spirits that are even now wandering the desert." Several pairs of frightened eyes peered intently into the darkness that surrounded us.

"Horus! Thoth! Protect us against the mut, the dangerous dead that roam these deserts as serpents. Change those serpents that seek retribution against the living. Transform the mut who join together to form dust storms that threaten to kill us without proper burial. Force these restless spirits to resume their journey to the next world so that they may transfigure into an akh. This we ask in your names."

As I began to repeat the prayer seven times in a sing-song, chanting cadence, Meruka started to sway. Soon his upper body shook and he stamped his feet to the rhythm of my voice, somehow making the bangles on his ankles and arms ring in perfect unison. By time I was halfway through the fourth rendition of the chants, he had already entered his trance state. His eyes were rolled up in his head and a sheen of sweat dripped from his body. He danced over the ring of fire and back again, his twisted hair locks bouncing off his forehead and neck. The men backed away from him out of fear and respect. Then he did a remarkable thing.

With his eyes closed, he reached into his goatskin bag that lay in the center of the fire circle and withdrew a large, squirming viper. The men gasped in unison, even Kagemni. Meruka paid no heed to the men, for he already traveled into the spirit world. He held the sand-colored serpent by its neck and it slowly coiled its thick body around his arm, its terrible tongue slithering in and out of its triangular head.

Meruka continued his dancing as I chanted. He brought the serpent near to his face, their eyes not more than a hair's breadth away from each other, so that its forked tongue actually touched Meruka's face. He swayed and twirled with it, slowly removing the serpent's coils from his arm. The serpent's body drooped straight down, held only by Meruka's grip on its neck. Though he held the monster as high as he could reach, the tip of its tail still touched the ground.

With his free hand, Meruka stroked the serpent slowly on its front side, from head to tail, all the while swaying back and forth, back and forth, until the serpent appeared to sway by itself. Then Meruka gently grabbed it close to the tail and the serpent stood straight as a stick in his hands while they swayed back and forth! Never had any of us in Kem seen such a magical sight.

As I finished my last chant, Meruka took the serpent closer to the fire and with a smooth motion, he threw it in. It took the serpent a few seconds to break from the spell that Meruka had cast upon it, but by then it was too late. As if recognizing its awful predicament, it coiled and reared up, as if to launch itself from the fire at Meruka. It made a horrible hissing sound that drew gooseflesh on everyone who witnessed the spectacle, myself included. But, instead of flying out of the fire, it collapsed dead, the lower part of its body still searing in the flames and its upper body sprawled on its side in the sand. Meruka reached down, picked up the serpent, and in one quick motion, bit off its head. The serpent's blood spurted down his chin and upper chest and mixed with the sweat on his black body.

The men stood or sat silently at first, wide-eyed, stunned, as if they had all suffered through a great shock. Yet their spirits felt the power of what their eyes had just witnessed. Then, one of the men, who had picked up his spear as a precaution when Meruka pulled out the serpent from his bag, began to hit it upon the ground. One by one the other men joined him, until they pounded the butts of their spears into the ground in unison chanting: "Anhotek! Meruka! Anhotek! Meruka!"

Not until I held up my staff did they quiet down. "Behold, you have seen the power of Horus flowing through Meruka's body," I called out. "Know, then, that Horus the falcon god of Nekhen, protector of King Scorpion, favors each and every one of you in your mission to find the Prince. You shall no longer be bothered by scorpions or serpents or even dust storms. Sleep now, in peace, but stray not beyond the borders set by my magic wands, for I cannot guarantee that the magic is strong enough beyond them. The gods surely stand watch over you tonight."

Although the soldiers told us they felt the blanket of protection we had woven over them, most did not rest easy that night. Some stayed awake in pairs or small groups, whispering among themselves, recounting what they had witnessed. As I overheard snippets of stories here and there, Meruka's serpent had grown by at least a cubit by time the moon had set low in the desert plains behind us and the serpent had not merely hissed before dying, but had shrieked a foul breath that had nearly pierced their eardrums. So it was on that night that our magical abilities grew. Far was it from me to dissuade them from such tales. In my own eyes, Meruka had elevated himself. From that time forward he and I would serve Kem as equals.

Before dawn, Kagemni woke us to the smell of a fire, tea and roasted bread with honey. Hernakhte was sitting up in a carrying chair the men had rigged from their spears and leather tunics. Although his arm was beginning to show signs of putrefaction, he appeared in good spirits.

"Today is the day we shall find Prince Meni." Kagemni announced to his troops. "Ra's disk will soon rise over the mountains. We must be on the move with it. We will march out as one unit through the pass and then split again into three. Whichever group finds the Prince will sound its ram's horn… loudly… three times. And extra rations of beer for that lucky group!"

As Kagemni's thirty troops moved in pairs toward the far end of the dry river bed that ran through the mountains, we could see a sliver of Ra's orb just break the horizon. Kagemni led his troops and Meruka and I carried the rear, along with Hernakhte and his four carriers. As we broke through the holy mountain pass, directly in front of us Ra's disk rose in its full splendor along a huge sand dune in front of us. It's orb shone a deep orange as it rose, almost red, as often happens after days of dust storms.

Every man stood there watching, transfixed by Ra's glory. Then a small round object appeared in view along the dune line, bobbing up and down and increasing in size, until it grew a neck, then a chest and arms, then legs. No one spoke a word, nor made a sound, save for the creaking of leather breastplates, for we all sensed at once who it was that walked toward us. Silhouetted in black by the shimmering disc of Ra himself, the Prince strode confidently toward us.

Although it was later told, even sworn to, that Ra had delivered the Prince to us on a cloud, even I could not have sworn otherwise at that very moment. He seemed to materialize from the shimmering vapors of Ra's very rays.

As Ra rose in the sky still further, the Prince stopped atop the dune and for a long moment it appeared to us as if he were wearing the sun-god's crown atop his head. I knew then that Meni had found us, and not the other way around. He appeared healthy, even radiant. He looked down upon us as a god must look upon his worshippers, for at that very instant every soldier, even Kagemni, knelt in silent praise to their future King.

# SCROLL EIGHT

## *Mother Nile*

"And this... what you are telling me... it is really so? Like... like animals do it?" Meni asked, sitting in front of me in our boat.

What could I do but smile at the future King asking me such a question? The boy had matured into the man. His large brown eyes had intensified and his jet black hair now filled his head, replacing the shaved head and single braid of his childhood. Each feature complemented his well proportioned, muscular, sixteen year-old physique. It was only natural that his attention was now focused on sexual matters.

"Well, yes... in some ways, but not in all ways," I responded, tilting his head to the side so I could trim his hair. "The basic elements are the same. The man's organ becomes erect and he places it inside the woman's private place. In this the gods designed the perfect system."

"How does this happen?" he persisted. I had hoped for this discussion for several years now, but accepted the delay as caused by his medicines, which sedated him and surely suppressed his sexual desires, and also by the protected life that was forced upon him. But now, no medicine known to any healer could halt his raging desire and I could not help but notice his bodily reactions lately when he observed a pretty girl. "How does the girl... you know... signal when she is ready to accept the man?"

"That is one of the ways that people differ from cows," I answered. "Cats know when the female is receptive by the scent that she gives off. But with humans, it is more of a game. If a man likes a woman, then he courts her."

"What..."

"The man will begin talking with her or she with him. If they are attracted to one another, they will talk more, take walks together, spend time with each other's family. If the attraction persists, they begin holding hands and kissing."

"Hmmm," Meni sighed. "This is perplexing. With every word you say I have ten questions." He bent his head forward to allow my knife to do its work.

"We have time, Meni, but if you do not hold still I shall cut off the tip of your ear!" For a moment I feared that his frustration at not understanding the mysteries of the sexes might plunge him into a foul mood. But, his desire to understand his sexual yearnings compelled him to continue.

"I see women walking along the banks of Mother Nile or... or I see them in the towns we visit and I think... I find myself wondering what it would be like to place my manhood into them. It instantly becomes stiff, before I even know it, as... as if it has a mind of its own. I do not know how other men keep it under control."

"Meni, what you describe is normal. Young men have very active organs. Most boys spill their own seed when it becomes too agitated," I said as evenly as I could, not wanting to embarrass him. He blushed and turned aside, pretending to look at a passing boat. "That, too, is normal. As you get older, you will be able to control your manhood ever better. Now, hold still." I made my final cuts with my knife.

"But, what does it feel like?" he asked in utter desperation.

"Do you mean the act of placing your manhood into a

woman?" He nodded. Just a few days ago, one of the other boat captains told me that he had overheard Meni and Haankhef periodically making lewd remarks about women they saw and giggling, as they pretended to play Senet or Dogs and Jackals on their ivory playing boards. According to the captain, they apparently spent considerable time filling each other with false knowledge about sexual matters.

"I do not know how to answer that," I replied carefully, sweeping the hair from his head with my brush. "It... it is like no other feeling on earth. The gods have created a man's and woman's body to..."

"Is it rough inside or soft?" he interrupted.

I smiled. "What do you imagine it to be?"

He got up from his seat and leaned back against a sack of grain and shut his eyes. "When I think of it, I imagine it to be soft... very soft."

"It is," I assured him, sweeping up his hair and carefully placing it in a cloth bag.

"And how would you know, Anhotek? You are a priest. I have never even seen you with a woman."

Again I smiled at Meni's roguish nature. "Meni, most Horus priests marry. I have known many women in my youth. Even now, periodically, when I visit places where I know a woman well, I indulge from time to time. But, I have a sworn duty. Yet, I am... on the whole I am satisfied with my life."

Meni looked away then, for my intimate remark seemed too close for him when he was in such a vulnerable mood. "Besides," I continued, "being with a woman is not only about sex. This I know, for I have been dispensing advice to men and women about their mates for more years than you are old. They have confided in me their most secret desires, the deepest wishes they have regarding their partners.

"You see, Meni, sex is best when two people love one another. Once a woman loves her man, sex teaches itself to the couple. A woman will surrender herself, will do whatever it takes to please her husband... and in so doing please herself, too. For it is not only the man who spills seed. A woman, too, when she is in the throes of her own pleasure with her man, also has a spilling of seed."

Meni's eyes lit up. "Really? Is this true, Anhotek? How does this happen, for... for she does not have anything hanging between her legs to become stiff at the slightest provocation."

"Oh, but you are wrong, Meni! Women do have such an organ, but it is very tiny... hidden... as if it is a delightful treasure to be uncovered by a caring lover. It is at the entrance to her private area and I shall teach you about it soon, now that you are ready. When she is in the deepest passion with the man she loves, a woman reaches a high fever, just like a man. But, instead of shooting her seed out, she releases it inside her, wetting her pleasure passage and increasing the delight to both her and her man."

Meni was becoming uncomfortable with this new knowledge that at once sexually excited him and also constrained him through his inability to act upon it. I thought it best then to abandon the conversation for now. But it was a good start and we had been comfortable enough together discussing it that he would approach me with other questions.

"On this journey, Meni, I will help enrich your knowledge about sexual matters. We will continue this conversation, but now, with your permission, I must spend time with Butehamon. You have much to think about already." I gathered my things and turned to leave.

"Oh, and be sure to spend some time today with your martial arts training. I have not seen you practicing in many days." He nodded his agreement, but he seemed still preoccupied with sexual matters.

The wind blew us steadily away from Tjeni and toward Lower Kem. Although our stay at Scorpion's court to restock our ships had been brief, it was also full of the stresses that had become commonplace in the Royal court. In particular, Mersyankh and Ihy now blatantly manipulated Scorpion. He was continuously drunk now, slovenly, his eyes pitifully bloodshot. Yet, who could he blame but himself for his misfortunes?

Scorpion's sad condition helped shape our present itinerary. It was critical that I visit the temples along the route to Lower Kem to reacquaint myself with the priests and to keep the alliances intact with the wealthy houses of Upper Kem, for I feared what was surely to come when Scorpion had drunk himself to his death.

In a few minutes I was in Butehamon's boat. We dispatched all but his most trusted deckhand to the other two boats so that we might talk in private. For the length of our stay in Tjeni, Butehamon had spent most of his time with Kagemni, who was forbidden by Scorpion to even lay eyes on me.

"At last," Butehamon started. "We have much to talk about. I feared you would have no words left after talking so long with the Prince."

"Ah, he is of that age, dear Butehamon," I replied, smiling broadly at him, "when the thoughts of sex crowd out any other rational thoughts in a young man's heart."

"And about time," Butehamon teased, poking me with his sturdy elbow. "I have heard of his preoccupation with this topic lately. Better for you to explain such mysteries to him, rather than my deck hands." The breeze suddenly stiffened and the ropes pulled on the boom, snapping the sails.

"Here is our Prince's hair," I said, holding out the wrapped bundle to him. "Be..."

"Yes, yes, be sure to dispose of it with utmost care. I know. I will burn it this evening."

"We can never be too cautious," I whispered to Butehamon. "The evil eye sees far," I added and spat overboard. He took the cloth and stuffed it in his belt.

"So, what have you heard from Kagemni?" I asked.

"There is much amiss in the Court," Butehamon replied, as if he were eager to relate to me every juicy bit of gossip. "Did you see Neter-Maat?"

"No, I was not able to invent a pretense for doing so. Is it true what they say about him?"

"He is huge, a... a giant. It is as if the gods took the strongest parts of Scorpion and of Mersyankh's people and combined them into Neter-Maat's body. He is but twelve years old and has the body of a man twice his age." I tried to reconcile that image with the baby that toddled after Meni in his nursery.

"Ihy has persuaded Scorpion to increase Neter-Maat's military training. Ihy and Kagemni have been instructing him in the art of battle, although… I…"

"Go ahead… out with it!"

"He is… stupid, to put it bluntly. Kagemni is at his wit's end trying to explain battle concepts to him. However, Ihy trains him in the warrior arts and his power is extraordinary. He is slow, but even at his age he could bash a man's skull with one swipe of his mace." That thought did not sit well with me. Meni was well-balanced, but his body was far smaller.

We sailed in silence for a few minutes. "And what about Mersyankh?" I asked.

"That is troubling, Anhotek. Neter-Maat is completely at her mercy. The boy has no will of his own. When in her presence, he hangs his head in shame or fear… I know not which. She taunts him mercilessly. 'Stand up straight!' she screams at him. 'What kind of King shall you make when you look so slovenly!' she scolded him once in my presence."

Butehamon was exceedingly perturbed and the sound of his voice might make his words be overheard. Yet I did not want to subdue his emotion, for it is often true that I receive my best information when the passions of the teller are revealed.

"And Kagemni?" I asked. "What of him?"

Butehamon looked at me as if I were speaking in a foreign tongue. "What do you mean? He… we both feel exactly the same. He makes every excuse to be away on military business, but he cannot avoid his responsibilities to Neter-Maat altogether."

I knew that Ihy would quickly tread a path to Scorpion if Kagemni ignored Neter-Maat, since the only prospect Neter-Maat might have to assume the kingship would be to gain legitimacy with the military.

"Kagemni says that those two evil spirits are presently engaged in great intrigue within the Court. Ihy has brought to Tjeni some of his own priests from Lower Egypt. Chekhnew!" Butehamon spit over the side of the boat. "May they be cursed through eternity... the whole lot of them!"

"Be careful, Butehamon," I cautioned, "for some day we may rule over all of Kem, both Upper and Lower. The people of Lower Kem live and die and raise their families along Mother Nile, as do we. To refer to them as foreigners may not serve us well in the future."

"No disrespect intended, Anhotek, but your ideas are too noble for a low-class soldier such as myself. I see the chekhnew as trouble and the sooner we march in and force them to bow down before the King, the better, I say!"

I let his words settle between us before speaking again. "Butehamon, loyal soldier of Upper Kem, I do not dispute your beliefs. Understand that I, too, feel that the people of Lower Kem are... how shall I say this?... not equal to the people of Upper Kem. I, myself, have referred to them as swamp-dwellers. All I am saying is that we must weigh our position carefully. Would you conquer them at this moment, with Mersyankh and Ihy controlling Scorpion as they do? We would all be their servants if we did. Bide your time, Butehamon. We will act when the time is right, but now is not that time."

Butehamon stood with his hands on his hips, peering far ahead downriver, drawing solace and strength from Mother Nile. He breathed in the river air. "I am but a soldier, Anhotek. I serve by taking orders. I do not pretend to understand the plotting that goes on in the Court. Until now I would have followed only Scorpion. But, Scorpion no longer..."

"Say no more," I comforted him. "Your heart speaks better than can your words." We sat quietly for a few moments before Butehamon moved toward the stern to take back the tiller.

With the approach of evening, we anchored in a remote area and Butehamon's men scouted a site for us to make camp. After several days on board, we were eager to feel solid ground beneath our feet. As the men put up tents, I wanted to focus my mind, and so trampled down a circular area of papyrus sedges within which I could practice the meditative movements that I had learned when I lived in Setjet studying their herbs and religious practices. Soon I felt the rhythm of the movements circulate the life force inside me and I felt energized, my mind clear. Just then, Meni passed by and watched me finish my routine.

"That is interesting," he commented. "I note some fighting moves in what you did, although you did them slowly and more precisely... like practice movements for children."

"Do not to fool yourself by its apparent simplicity, Meni. It is a very advanced form of fighting, one for which you are not yet ready."

"Not yet ready?" Meni mocked me good naturedly. "You, yourself, have been training me in far more active forms of hand combat."

"Ah, yes... more active," I mused. "More violent... the most primitive form of fighting. This ancient art is taught in faraway lands, over the mountains of Setjet and Babylon and farther still to the eastern lands. It is a high form of combat, but one that is designed to deflect violence, to turn the aggressor into his own instrument of destruction."

Meni looked at me, uncomprehending. "How is this so, Anhotek? You speak again in riddles. If you were not so old, I would show you that no such simple maneuvers are capable of defending against an aggressive enemy. Your words are... they are just words!" The muscles of his boy-man chest puffed out as he flexed them.

I laughed then, which infuriated Meni. "Come then, my little Prince," I said to bait him further. "You who have no time to practice his fighting, who is too busy loafing on deck while others do your work for you. Come, child, and show this old man how you can hurt me." With that I squatted ever so slightly, dipping my lower body to assume a more stable base. I raised my hands and bade him to enter the circle.

Poor Meni did not know what to make of the situation. "This is folly, Anhotek! Your body is no match for a younger, more powerful man."

"And, pray tell me who is that man?" I asked, looking behind him, while smiling. "Certainly not you!"

Meni was conflicted now. Never before had he raised a hand with malevolent intent against me. His brow was screwed up, his muscles taut. He stepped warily into the circle. "Alright... alright, then, I will do this, but... but only to teach you a lesson, Anhotek, for I swear that I do not want to hurt you. I will go easy."

"That is wise, child. For the easier you go with me, the easier will be your falls." He could take my baiting no longer and rushed at me, hands outstretched to push me out of the circle. I half-turned my body at the last moment, put out my foot, grabbed his arm and tossed him forward. He tripped and sprawled on his face and stomach, skidding along the moist reeds. I laughed heartily. Butehamon and two of his men had walked over to see what the commotion was all about. With the Prince still bent over on the ground, I waved them off, lest the Prince be embarrassed, for the lesson seemed destined to be a painful, if valuable one.

"That was unfair!" Meni complained to me as he stood up and brushed off his kilt. Raised welts appeared on his abdomen from where the sharp edges of the reeds had scraped away his skin. Seeds from their flowering heads dusted his hair. "You tripped me!"

"Unfair? Did you say 'unfair,' Meni? Will your headless torso complain so when it is parted by an enemy's unfamiliar sword play? There is a lesson to be learned here, but you are still too impertinent to have learned it. Your ba blinds you! Here is a stick," I said, throwing my staff to him. "Make believe it is a mace and attempt to bash my skull with it. You need not worry. I'll try not to hurt you!" Again, I wiggled my finger to taunt him.

Meni was irate. His body quivered as he grasped the stick, his knuckles white. He rushed at me, yelling a war cry, and brought the stick over his head. He feinted one way, spun around as I had taught him to do, and with one smooth motion, brought the stick down toward my head. But, I had already seen his intention and instead of backing away, I crowded him, crouching still further. As his blow crashed down behind me, I dropped to the ground and somersaulted backward, flinging him on his back. I rolled sideways, picked up my staff that he had dropped and struck to within a finger's width of his throat.

He looked at me wide-eyed, with a mixture of fear and new-found admiration. "How... how did you do that?" he asked in disbelief, breathing hard. "For a moment I felt the fear that must accompany a man about to die on the battlefield. Yet... yet it was over in a second. It... it was not what I expected."

"Indeed," I said, standing back and reaching out my hand to him. He pulled himself up and bowed, his hands stretched low.

"Stop! Never do that!" I said sternly, looking around to see if anyone was watching. "The future King bows to no mortal!"

"But, I am not yet the King, Anhotek, and you are my teacher... now, and always. And... and I feel quite foolish. I have given you so much grief lately. It is as if sometimes... a foul mood descends over me and I am angry with everyone who crosses my path... even you." He looked utterly dejected.

My heart reached out to him then. "Meni, my son, do not apologize. What you feel now all young men your age feel. The powerful essences that flow through your body to transform you into manhood also affect your heart and moods. This, too, will pass. But, today, right now, the way you have conducted yourself in defeat is a great credit to the man you have become. I feared you would be angry and belligerent, but instead you are contrite. That bodes well for you. That shows strength of ba."

He seemed relieved then, as if the weight of guilt had been removed from his shoulders. He looked up at me impishly. "But, Anhotek, will you teach me those moves? Will you instruct me in the ways of these battlefield arts?"

"When you are ready," I answered. "But honestly, you

are far from ready right now, Meni. However, if you practice diligently and master what I have already taught you then, yes, I will instruct you in these arts such that you will be nearly invincible on the battlefield." He seemed pleased and we ended the meeting, which the gods had obviously arranged, in good spirits and together we walked slowly back to the boat.

We had left Tjeni at the beginning of the season of Shomu, when all of Kem is busily harvesting, transporting, storing or selling the year's crops. Mother Nile had not flooded as high as usual and the crops threatened to be less than in an average year, which created apprehension up and down the mighty river. Grain prices rose and the poor complained bitterly. There were few granaries, so neither King Scorpion nor King W'ash could distribute much to their people from their stores, for there was little left from last year's bounty. This was bound to encourage cross-border raids and exacerbate an already tense situation between Upper and Lower Kem.

Our entourage stopped at each temple along the river and I used the occasions to both mortar my position with the priests and also to introduce Meni to them. His natural curiosity and grace went far with them and under my tutelage he achieved a remarkable balance between a regal bearing and an approachable manner.

Our frequent excursions upon Mother Nile achieved another purpose. Meni gained a true appreciation for how closely the fate of his people was bound to the mighty river. Ever since the evening he caught the huge catfish, he loved to fish and hunt the abundant life the river gods gave to us. At first I was cautious about his new-found passion, for I have seen far too many men gain a thirst for the killing itself, hunting for the sheer sport of it, slaughtering large numbers of waterfowl or catching many more fish than they could ever eat or hope to sell.

We talked frequently about how much hunting the river could sustain and early on I taught Meni the various prayers and offerings he should make to appease the gods before and after the hunt. One day he returned to the boat after a frustrating day of hunting for waterfowl.

"It is no use," he sighed in frustration, tossing his heavy throw-sticks on the deck and slumping against a sack of barley grain. "I shall never be the hunter that Butehamon is."

"But, Meni, Butehamon has plied the waters of Mother Nile his entire life."

"Yes, but I toss the throwing-sticks more accurately than he does. Not as powerfully, but more accurately for sure."

"And what did you hunt today?" I asked.

"The river rail," he said. "The bird with brown and white stripes that stands straight in the rushes. It was frustrating. I could not get in a shot until I was closer, but by then they would explode from the rushes so suddenly, it was impossible for me to aim. Aaaah!," he grimaced, holding his hands to his face in his typical gesture of frustration.

"What if I were to say that tomorrow I will show you how to properly hunt these birds?" I asked.

"Anyone can hunt rails," he replied, sarcastically.

"Ah, yes. Meaning that if you cannot land one, no one else can, correct?" He looked away from me then, a sheepish grin on his face. "Well, if you will point out where exactly it was that you saw them, I assure you that you will have some by lunch tomorrow."

So it was that I awakened Meni before Ra rose in the sky and we slid into the chilly water up to our waists. We smeared our faces and hair with mud and I insisted that we rinse our mouths well with muddy water. I then tied rushes to the reed headbands I had hastily woven for us the night before.

Thus camouflaged, we stealthily waded toward the spot that sheltered the rails, only our eyes and the reeds of our headbands peeking above the water line. Finally I stopped and we sat motionless, although shivering slightly, as ever so slowly Ra began to illuminate the heavens above us. Meni's eyes darted about him and I watched his reaction as he saw our predicament. We were literally surrounded by rails, some not more than a cubit from where we crouched.

Under the water, I gently grabbed Meni's hand and squeezed it repeatedly, until he understood my meaning and we both squeezed the hand of our throwing arms. Then I placed one of my throwing sticks in my right hand and held the other ready in the left. I watched Meni do the same. If we waited even another minute, Ra's light would shift to the favor of the birds.

I burst from the water, my stick high above my head and flung it at a bird that sat calmly three or four cubits away. As the stick sailed through the air at the startled bird, I transferred the second stick to my throwing hand and heaved at a bird that was closer, but already rising. The air and water around us erupted into a raucous maelstrom, as thousands of rails, geese and ducks took to flight, squawking and honking in alarm. By then, both of my birds lay on the water, one instantly dead and the other fluttering with a broken wing.

Meni's first stick missed its mark, probably more due to the suddenness of my attack. But the second hit a rail squarely in the head as it rose low over the water about five cubits ahead of him.

"Yahaaah!" Meni shrieked at the commotion that surrounded him. "Did you see that, Anhotek? Did you see him fall?" His chest stuck out as he waded to retrieve his bird. I, too, had reached my birds and promptly twisted the neck of the injured animal to end its pain and send it quickly on its journey west. With Meni itching to show off his catch, I grabbed his arm. Together, we offered a prayer of thanks to Hapy for the bounty he had placed before us.

That evening, as we feasted on our bounty of rail, goose, fish and vegetables, Meni sat next to me.

"Anhotek, I learned much from the hunt today. Until now, I have looked upon the hunt as... as a game. Human skill and cunning against animal instinct. Yet... yet today, as we waded into the reeds and waited, I realized that I was thinking like a bird, that I was feeling the water and smelling Mother Nile's mud. My senses were on high alert. This was a true revelation." Never was I prouder of Meni, for he had learned an important lesson that would serve him well, whatever the hunt.

True to his intention, Meni also practiced his fighting moves every day, whether on the boat or on land. When we did find a suitable camping spot, he would engage in simulated combat with one of his friends who would periodically accompany us. By the end of the first month, there were none who could defeat or defend against him in hand combat. Although he was neither large nor very strong, he was bold, graceful and, above all, cunning. He had a discerning eye and could quickly gauge an enemy's weaknesses and exploit them.

By the start of the second month of Shomu I began his defensive training in earnest and, as I suspected, it was difficult indeed, for youth are impetuous and believe themselves omnipotent. Boldness sometimes has genius to it but, more frequently, foolishness.

"If you are rigid and tense, you will not be able to defend properly," I would tell Meni.

"How can I not be tense when you rush at me with your staff, ready to strike me over the head if I do not defend myself?" he would ask in exasperation.

I found that he was most receptive to this more contemplative martial art after we had meditated together, when I would sometimes guide him through visualizations until he could see and feel what I described. Then, he would allow himself to be supple, calmly observing my moves and joining in their motion in ways that magnified them and allowed him to thrust me about where he desired. As he became more successful, it motivated him to practice yet more, until none of his friends were willing to engage him in combat any longer. Soon, he was playing at combat with Butehamon's sailors and regularly defeating them. But, instead of swelling his head, I found that his increasing mastery made him ever softer and more introspective, as if he understood the power of his new skills and, upon reflection, they sobered him greatly.

Yet, little did I suspect that soon the Prince would have occasion to put his new skills to the test and that the outcome of that bloody conflict would help shape the future of all Kem.

# SCROLL NINE

## *Light of God*

In two weeks more, we had sailed downriver as far as the border of Lower Kem. I dared not go any further for it had slowly dawned upon most of the people that the harvest was far poorer than even the most pessimistic had predicted. The priests near the border areas complained that they heard grumbling among the swamp dwellers that the people of Upper Kem had far greater abundance in their harvest. They grumbled about grain sold to them at highly inflated prices.

We stopped at Turakh, a village on the east bank just south of the delta where a small Horus temple stood. The head Priest was a fellow initiate with me in Nekhen, whose position I had secured many years before.

With three of Butehamon's men leading the way, and with Meni accompanying me, we walked past the meager barley crops and up a steep, rocky hill toward the mud-brick temple. From the top we could see the commanding view that the priests enjoyed, able to watch the farmers that toiled the fields below, as well as observe the traffic along the river.

Once inside, we were warmly welcomed by my friend, Denger, who looked like he was ready to depart this world. He was as thin as a Nile reed and had a terrible pallor to him that whispered of death. As we embraced I detected a faint odor of the illness that grows within the body and quickly consumes it. I felt saddened, but also began scanning a mental list in my mind of potential replacements.

After I introduced Meni, Denger's eyes lit up and he dispatched an initiate to fetch some thin barley beer to quench our thirst. Denger informed us that King W'ash was not in solid control of Lower Kem. A number of smaller provinces were resisting his taxation and the King's forces were spread thin trying to keep them in line. Meni probed Denger with a well placed question here or a raised eyebrow there that elicited valuable information.

As we were about to bid him farewell, Denger said in passing. "Do you remember that man from Setjet we once knew, Anhotek? His name was Me'ka'el, a nomadic trader. He and his daughter visited me recently. In fact, he is in Kherdasakh right now, negotiating grain purchases."

I was delighted, for I had spent many an hour with Me'ka'el from the time I was a youth, when he traded with my father. It was from him that I first learned of the strange beliefs and customs of some of the tribes from Setjet.

"Who is like god?" I muttered.

"What are you saying?" Denger asked.

"Me'ka'el once told me that is the translation of his name from their language. 'Who is like god?'"

"What a strange name," Denger mused. "His name is a question!"

"His people seem to question everything, so I suppose their names are not strange to them." I thought of how many years had passed since I had seen the trader. "Oh, but he must be ancient now!"

"Ancient? Yes, but he is destined by the gods to walk the land longer than shall I," Denger said. He understood this would be our last meeting. We embraced for a long moment before we departed.

As we walked back to the boats, I made an impulsive

decision. "Meni, I should like you to meet Me'ka'el, the man that Denger just spoke about. He is only a few hours sail downriver and it would be instructive for you to know about the customs of the people of Setjet. They are important trading partners."

Meni thought for a moment. "But that will put us in King W'ash's territory. Do you think it safe?"

"Perhaps I should not have decided so impulsively, but I desire for you to know a people who are far different from us, with strange customs. I think that it would be wise."

We watched the farmers and their sons rhythmically cutting barley stalks, while the women and girls gathered them and stacked them to dry. "I agree. We should take advantage of this opportunity," Meni finally said. "But I think we should only take one boat, so as not to draw too much attention to ourselves," a point to which I readily agreed.

Once arrangements had been made as to the contingent of sailors and servants who would stay behind, Butehamon and five of his best men set sail, complaining all the while amongst themselves about our foolish decision. The Prince stood by my side at the bow as we made sail.

"Why is it that you dislike the Lower Kemians so, Anhotek?" Meni asked. I was unsure of my answer, for like other educated people I did not like to have my prejudices exposed. "They are, after all, Kemians."

"That is both true and untrue, Meni. You are right, I should not be so prejudiced against them. But… but it is far more complicated than that."

"As you have said to me before, we have time."

"Hmmmn. Alright. You have seen how different the people of Lower Kem are, how much more primitive they are than our society. Their ancestors came to Lower Kem from Ta-Tjehenu, far across the Western Desert. They are mostly poor farmers with implements that are far behind ours. Their pottery is thick and crude and… quite frankly, ugly. They use foul-smelling castor oil in their incense.

"In contrast, our society has developed so highly because everyone knows his and her place. We have an elite class of merchants, we have a priestly class, administrators, rulers. Our people have more time in their lives to develop new innovations, to perfect our pottery and implements. Our priests devote more time to defeating chaos and restoring ma'at.

"And another thing. Our art and music, our medicine and even religious customs, are more highly developed. We have people able to devote themselves to pursuing such high ideals because the ruling class supports them. Since Scorpion defeated Nubt, our writing advances day by day, while the Lower Kemians hardly have writing at all. "

Meni turned back to look at the shore. "I have seen what you describe with my own eyes. Perhaps the sadness of your observations has caused me to shield my eyes from their truthfulness.

"So, how will we elevate the Lower Kemians to our higher state as quickly as possible once we conquer and unite with them? Think on that, dear teacher, for as they develop, so will all of Kem prosper."

Just then Butehamon came forward to review security arrangements. In a few hours we reached Kherdasakh. A runner went ahead into the village to let Me'ka'el know of our arrival. In an hour, he returned with a message beseeching us to come at once, to participate in their evening meal.

In high spirits, Meni, Meruka and I, along with Butehamon and two of his men, hiked up the narrow path along the bank to the small village. On a hill to the north of the town, Me'ka'el and his family had set up several tents. With Ra's light fading in the west, we announced our arrival.

From within the largest tent, an elderly man, small of stature and with a gray beard, emerged. He took a long look at our group and in a second his wrinkled face broke into a broad smile and he shuffled eagerly toward us. I ran to meet him and we embraced for several moments, first locking arms, then hugging, since we had not seen each other for many, many years.

"You look well, my friend," I said, looking into his eyes.

"And I thought that the priests of Horus do not lie!" he replied, laughing. His front teeth were entirely gone now, and his nose curved nearly down to his mouth.

I then turned him gently to face Prince Meni and, holding onto my arm for support, he bowed low.

"Please," Meni graciously said, "do not trouble yourself, for it is my honor to meet a man that Anhotek so highly esteems."

Me-ka'el stared at Meni and then looked from him to me and nodded approvingly. "You have done well, Anhotek," he whispered into my ear, "very well, indeed.

"Come... come all of you into my tent. Honor us with your presence," he said, waving us to follow him. He held onto my arm as a woman swept the tent entrance flap aside and we entered.

Spread before us was a mighty feast, the likes of which we had not seen since we had left the Royal compound in Tjeni. Freshly baked breads lay on a blanket, surrounded by figs, dates and spiced bean mixes. The smells alone were enchanting.

"You have arrived at a special time," Me-ka-el said to us. "Come sit down as I say the blessings. The harvest was meager this year, but we are fortunate to have enough to eat to share with our friends."

Once we were all seated on the colorful wool blankets, Me-ka-el raised his hands and we fell silent. He began chanting a prayer in their language, his raspy voice not able to hold any two consecutive notes in tune. It had been so long since I had heard the peculiar words and cadence of his language, yet I recognized some of its sounds and even a few of the words that Me'ka'el had taught me so long ago.

Once he was done, he switched to Kemian, so that all might feel welcome. "Blessed King of the heavens, we thank you for the blessings of grains that grow from the soil and wine that grows from the vine."

"I also thank you for my wife, who you have blessed me with in my old age. Together, we thank you for the blessing of our daughter. And, we also thank you, dear God, for bringing Anhotek and Prince Meni and his loyal soldiers to share in our meal." He bowed his head and we sat silently for a moment, the enticing odors of the foods making Butehamon's stomach growl loudly enough for all to hear.

"And now we eat, or else be forced to listen to a chorus of hungry stomachs!" he exclaimed, and with that he broke the bread and passed it around for all to partake.

Once we began eating, Me'ka'el introduced me to his new wife, Sara, who I estimated to be about my age. Her skin was deeply tanned, but wrinkled. She must have been quite beautiful in her youth, but now her teeth were worn badly, as happens to nomads who have to contend with sand dust in everything they eat.

Meni followed every word of our conversation. "This god you referred to, is he your patron god?" Meni asked.

Me'ka'el laughed. "No… no!" he said. "Our tribe believes in only one God, not many." Meni raised his eyebrows.

"On the surface it seems like our beliefs are different," I explained. "But when you examine them, they are similar. If a man from Me'ka'el's tribe sees a sledge, he says, 'There is a sledge.' But when a Kemian priest sees a sledge, he says, "Look at all the parts that make a sledge. The hardwood rails, the sideboards, the wood dowels, the caning to bind it all together.' They each refer to the same object. We may have more gods than Me'ka'el's tribe, but they form the same whole." Both Meruka and Meni nodded.

"Now, Me'ka'el," I said, "how goes the trade between Kem and your lands?"

"We are constantly harassed," he replied passionately, as if he had waited for me to ask him this very question. "From the time we leave the banks of the Nile until we arrive in the eastern kingdoms we are forced to pay fees… to cross a strip of land no more than a few hour's walk and then again a few hours later, until we are well into the desert crossing. But, the robbers in Lower Kem are the worst, may their names be stricken from the Book of Life. I must pay for guards to accompany me to keep the robbers away. It… it has only worsened in recent years. I am getting too old to deal with this and I have the safety of my family to consider. I am thinking of ending my trading trips to Kem."

I looked at the Prince. "I have heard this from other traders, too. The trade routes to the east must be protected or we will lose access to timber, lapis lazuli and other jewels, let alone medicines."

We discussed several possible solutions, drawing on Me'ka'el's knowledge of the eastern desert. By the end of the conversation, I promised Me'ka'el that I would raise the issue with Scorpion, but Meni interrupted. "The King is currently busy dealing with rebellions along the border with Lower Kem. However, my friend," he said turning to Me'ka'el, "I give you my promise that I will personally deal with the matter." While Me'ka'el's expression revealed that he was pleased, Butehamon's indicated surprise. To his credit, he said nothing about it that night.

We were nearing the end of the lengthy feast, when Me'ka'el's wife came to kneel at his side. He whispered in her ear and she left the tent for a few minutes. When she returned, a young woman followed along behind her.

"Prince Meni, Anhotek, Meruka, Butehamon and… and the rest of you," Me'ka'el said waving his hand in good nature to encompass our entourage. "I should like to introduce to you my daughter, El-Or." With that introduction, the women sat on either side of Me'ka'el. The effect of his daughter's presence was palpable. Each of us was struck dumb and not a word was uttered for a long few seconds. I noted that Butehamon and his men cast down their eyes, lest they appear lascivious in front of our gracious host.

"What a lovely name… and for such a lovely presence," I said to aid my companions in bringing their tongues back into their heads. "Pray tell us what the name means."

"It means 'light of God,'" Me-ka'el said proudly. "And she is truly a blessing in my old age."

El-Or averted our looks by glancing down in modesty. To observe that she was beguilingly beautiful would have been an insult to her. Her skin was copper-colored, as was characteristic of the people of Setjet. Her features were delicate and her body petite. She wore just a trace of kohl, just enough to accent her large, brown eyes, which reflected the dazzling beauty of the simple gold necklace around her neck. Her black hair shimmered in the light and hung loosely down her back.

Meni simply stared at El-Or and I do not believe he was aware that his lower jaw had dropped, exposing his teeth and tongue in an embarrassing manner. I dared not peek at his private area, for fear of what I might see stirring, so blatantly was he struck by her beauty.

"El-Or, allow me to introduce to you Prince Meni, son of King Scorpion, ruler of Upper Kem," I said, gesturing from one to another. Only then did Meni return from his dream world.

"I... I am sorry... I... I have been rude," he started, stumbling over his words. He did not seem to know whether to look at her directly or to cast his gaze to the sand, so he alternated back and forth, making himself appear even more buffoonish. I had never before seen poor Meni so befuddled.

"No, you were not rude," she offered sweetly, saving him further embarrassment. The two locked eyes in an unmistakable manner. "Would you like... would all of you like some tea? Father traded for it with people from the far eastern lands."

Butehamon declined, making up an excuse about the duties he and his men had to the Prince. They left the tent, although I had never before known Butehamon to refuse any manner of food and I had no idea to what duties he referred. I was beginning to enjoy the spectacle unfolding before us. Meruka, who sat opposite me, sent me a smile of recognition.

"I must prepare medicines for tomorrow," Meruka offered. "With your permission, Prince, I shall return to the ship," he said, bowing low. Thus I was left alone with the Prince and Me'ka'el's family.

"Me'ka'el, do you have any medicinal herbs in your caravan, ones I can trade for?" I asked of him and before long we, too, exited the tent, leaving Sara behind with the two youth.

For the next few hours, well past the mid-point of the night, Meni and El-Or talked. Me'ka'el and I could hear them laughing and, at one point, even arguing, before their voices turned to laughter once again. I had never before heard the Prince's conversation so animated.

"Well, it is either you or I that must break the two of them apart," I finally said to Me'ka'el, for he was no longer able to keep himself awake. "I do not think it is my imagination that sees a future for these two, even if as good friends."

"I wish that it be so, dear Anhotek. But I cannot stay awake any longer. My very bones ache. I will fetch my daughter, but you will owe me on our next trade, for I will surely bear her barbs for separating them." We both laughed.

Despite their protests, we managed to wrest the two away from each other. Even at the edge of the camp, far from the fire pit, their faces glowed with delight at their fortuitous meeting and the sweet sadness at their parting. The Prince promised to send a messenger to her soon and Me'ka'el agreed to bring his family to Kem at the next harvest by the desert route that ended in Tjeni.

In the eastern sky, over the flat marshlands unobscured by sand dunes, I could see the faint light of Ra's disk as it prepared to emerge in another hour. One of Butehamon's men woke him and he quickly dressed in his uniform, placing his captain's rank and Scorpion's insignia on his armband. Together we walked toward the ship, although the Prince's step seemed lighter than usual. While the rest of us talked, Meni was lost in reminiscing.

"She is beautiful, is she not?" he finally asked, interrupting a conversation I was engaged in with Butehamon. "She is bright as Ra, and… and…"

"This is serious," I warned the Prince, "for you were bewitched by a sorceress and I do not possess an antidote for such treachery." Meni looked to see if I was truly serious and saw my broad smile.

When we were but a few hundred cubits down the

embankment from Me'ka'el's camp, in the dim light of dawn, we noticed a commotion below us in the direction of our boat. We stopped to take our bearings and Butehamon turned this way and that, no doubt searching for escape routes. The path was narrow and steep and if there were any danger our only option was to retreat to higher ground and a more defensible position. But, before we could act, a contingent of King W'ash's soldiers suddenly arose from behind us, while another group ran up from below. We were surrounded by twelve armed soldiers.

"By whose orders do you confront us?" I shouted at the captain, who wore a distinctive silver armband and a decorated leather tunic. His sword was drawn, but he held it at his side.

"I am an officer in King W'ash's army," he replied authoritatively. "We received a report that you had arrived here, Anhotek."

I immediately suspected Ihy's treachery, for how was a lowly soldier to know who I was? My mind raced through several questions. Did they know that the Prince stood next to me? How did King W'ash know so quickly of our presence?

"How do you know who I am?" I asked softly, trying to keep the confrontation from deteriorating.

"We know who you are, Anhotek, advisor to King Scorpion, may his name be banished from both worlds for all eternity!" the captain said, spitting on the ground. "He has sent you and the Prince to steal our meager harvest from under us. You have come to make deals with the Setjet traders. It… it is not enough to attempt to kill us with your troops, but now you would starve our women and children, too! Kill them!" he suddenly shouted at his men, holding his sword high in the air.

Upon his order, the entire contingent of soldiers charged us, thrusting their spears, their swords whooshing through the air as they slashed at us. We had no time to prepare. The fact that our own soldiers from the boat did not immediately come to our aid could mean only that the enemy had already surprised them. The horrible thought that Meruka might lie dead or wounded, and perhaps soon the Prince, spurred me to action.

Butehamon had wounded one swordsman, barely out of boyhood, in the initial charge and was now engaged with another enemy soldier off to my left, at a higher elevation. The path was narrow here and the first enemy to come toward me I easily disposed of with a thrust of my staff. He tumbled down the embankment into the reedy water. The Prince was to my right and he had not a single weapon at his disposal, not even his dagger.

An older soldier reached Meni in the next instant and slashed his sword fiercely at his head, all the while making a blood-curdling battle cry. Meni ducked the blow and using my training and the man's own momentum, tossed him into the embankment opposite them. As he tumbled, the soldier dropped his sword. In one smooth motion, Meni picked up the man's sword and ran it through his side. Although I was also besieged, I witnessed Meni's blow puncture the man's lungs. As the enemy looked at his own side, blood gushed out and foam bubbled from the gaping wound. He looked from his wound to Meni's eyes in disbelief, then collapsed on the ground. The Prince stood staring at the lifeless body.

"Meni, be quick!" I shouted, as another soldier jumped at him from above. As the man lunged toward him with his sword, Meni fell to the ground and used the man's charge to fling him over the embankment. The water now churned with the blood of the first soldier. Two crocodiles fought over the poor man's limbs.

For now the Prince faced no opponents, but two enemy soldiers faced me on either side. They advanced hesitatingly toward me. I spun to the left and hit the first soldier squarely in the face with the delivery end of my staff, knocking him off his feet. Blood spurted from his nose and mouth.

As the other soldier advanced toward me, the sound of a swift, slashing sword blade came from behind him. He began to turn toward it, but in the next instant his head exploded from his body and his torso crumpled to the ground in a heap next to me, blood spurting copiously from his neck. For the most fleeting of moments, the Prince stood above him, his sword dripping blood. But the momentum from his sword threw him off balance and he slipped, sliding and rolling, head over heels, down the embankment and into the water. My heart stopped, despite my being besieged by other enemy soldiers.

Just the merest second before the Prince hit the water, the head of the soldier he had decapitated tumbled in first. The crocodile that had lost the hideous tug-of-war to his rival raced for the head and, unhinging his monstrous jaws, sucked it in with a gulp. Meni landed with a great splash between the two crocodiles, both of which were occupied by their morsels of fresh human flesh. Thus, through the intervention of the gods, they hesitated a few seconds before striking off toward Meni.

Meni surfaced already swimming for his life toward shore. As he gained purchase on the muddy river bottom with his legs, the slithering bodies of Apep's hideous monsters raced toward the Prince. The mud caught Meni's legs and he struggled mightily to free himself, only to fall again and again.

The silence from behind me made me glance back. Three enemy soldiers looked down the path past me, their eyes wide. I glanced back down the embankment and saw Meruka, blood dripping from his mouth, running along the river bank, brandishing a mace in his right hand and a dagger in his left. His muscular body was drenched in sweat and blood, creating a fearsome sight in Ra's emerging light.

The smaller of the two crocodiles was almost upon Meni when he slipped again. I watched in horror as the beast turned on its side and opened its toothy jaws. It had already begun to snap them shut on Meni's legs when Meruka's mace caught it full on the underside of its jaw. In the next instant, Meruka extended his hand, grabbed Meni's arm and pulled him from the water. He dragged him further up the embankment, but the larger of the crocodiles was not to be denied his prize. As Meni and Meruka sat on their bottoms, heaving with exhaustion, the crocodile exploded from the water, its scaly tail propelling it forward.

At the last moment, Meruka used every measure of his strength to push Meni aside. As the crocodile snapped its horrible jaws together in the space between them, Meruka plunged his dagger down between the creature's eyes. It roared up, hissing in pain and crashed down to disappear into the watery abyss.

I turned to see two enemy soldiers who lay wounded near Butehamon. One of his own men had been slashed on the upper arm and was bleeding profusely. What was left of the enemy contingent immediately fled. Butehamon himself had watched the last exploit of the Prince in amazement.

From below us, the Prince's scream reached our ears. "El-Or!" Meni shouted, pointing toward the hilltop above us. There, watching the entire engagement, were Sara and El-Or, holding tight to each other.

The Prince ran up from the bank. "Butehamon," he shouted. "Take your men and round up Me'ka'el's entire caravan. Have them packed in an hour." Next the Prince looked at me.

"Are you alright, Anhotek?" he asked, as I sat, squatting on the ground from exhaustion. I nodded, afraid that my voice would crack from the emotions of the moment.

"Good. Then tend to Butehamon's man. Meet me at the boat in an hour. But first commandeer another boat or two, for we shall soon have company."

# SCROLL TEN

## *Crossing The Line*

For three days now, Meni had stayed apart from us, eating separately, doing his writing exercises and faithfully practicing his martial arts. Whenever someone approached him, he fell stonily silent, answering only those questions he must, and no more.

It had also been three days since Meni had bidden farewell to El-Or. After escaping Kherdasakh, we sailed upriver and dropped them off on the east bank, near a well-worn trade route to Canaan. There I recruited a dozen soldiers stationed near Denger's temple and the Prince pressed them into service guarding the caravan until they were safely delivered home. At that point, Meni gave the soldiers instructions to return to Tjeni to report directly to him, and only to him, and receive a well-earned reward. If anything happened to El-Or, he cautioned them privately, they would pay with their lives.

Meni's second parting from El-Or was even more bittersweet than the original, since he now placed upon himself the added burden of her security. The two young people were bitten by love, as if suddenly their destinies were incomplete without each other. For her part, El-Or displayed an uncanny sense of presence for her young age, an ability to focus her attention on Meni, yet be aware of when her parents or guests might need her. When they parted, El-Or promised to send a message back with the soldiers as soon as they arrived home.

Once she left him, Meni became sullen. No medicine in my pharmacopoeia could patch his broken sixteen year-old heart and no advice I could give would serve him as well as the passage of time. Thus, I left him alone to mend and to sort out his feelings.

Part of his distress surely involved his first experience in battle, although his performance was admirable. Butehamon's soldiers, one of them still healing from his own infected wound, talked incessantly of the Prince's valor and cunning. They had never seen the type of hand-to-hand combat maneuvers the Prince had used. They pestered me thoroughly in the days that followed to teach the combat to them.

To emerge victorious in battle is not what those who have not experienced it imagine it to be. It is a shallow victory at best, to kill another man, to rob him of his life, knowing that he, like you, has brothers and sisters, a mother and father, perhaps even his own children who will never again see him in this world. The Prince probably replayed his actions many times and his heart pained with each replaying. His muscles were tensed and his face contorted when he sat alone on the bow of the boat, staring ahead and seeing nothing but that which passed before his eyes from within.

In fact, much did pass before our eyes in the few days it took to return to Tjeni, for it was in the midst of harvest season, meager though it was. On one stop, we anchored near a group of men and women making paper from the papyrus reeds they gathered from the banks of Mother Nile. It was the first time in days that Meni watched something with interest. Half the village seemed to engage itself in this task. The policy I had established of hiring villagers to make papyrus scrolls for the temples of Horus yielded much good will during hard times like this, when the food crops returned little for the hard efforts of the farmers.

The men, dressed only in mud-covered kilts, stooped to cut the tall, triangular reeds as close to the roots as possible. Their sons then grabbed the reeds by small handfuls and ferried them to the banks where they stacked them carefully. Young girls then brought the reeds, a few at a time, to their mothers, who deftly stripped off the outer green layer, leaving only the pithy white core. Everyone who set upon this task had cuts covering their hands and forearms from the papyrus' sharp edges.

Another cluster of women sliced off long, thin slivers and arranged them on a large, flat rock, then lightly pounded them and placed them into a large wooden vat of water to soak.

"How long does the soaking take?" Meni asked.

"Usually two or three days," I answered. "The soaking swells the fibers and releases a glue that allows the papyrus strips to adhere together. Look... over there!"

Perhaps five cubits from the women who pounded the strips, another row of women sat and methodically removed strips that had aged the right amount of time from a similar vat. They arranged the strips in barely overlapping vertical rows on top of a long frame of wood. On top of the frame was a thick sheet of linen, upon which the papyrus strips were laid.

"Look how quickly they lay them out!" Meni exclaimed. As soon as the vertical rows reached the end of the board, the women began laying strips horizontally. Once the strips ran top to bottom, they placed another linen sheet on top and then an identical sized board atop that.

Two men lifted the frames and carried them to a large, flat rock. They struggled to place a huge rock on top of the boards to squeeze the juices out of the papyrus strips.

"They will rotate the frame and place more rocks on it over the next few days," I explained to Meni. "That way the papyrus dries properly and the strips glue themselves together." I was satisfied that Meni had finally seen how the holy paper was made from Mother Nile's gifts.

The very next day, as Ra set in the western sky, we arrived in Tjeni. By then, although I could see Meni was still feeling dejected due to El-Or's absence, he tried to mask it from his enemies within the Royal court. We arrived with little fanfare, although the head priests of the temples in Tjeni awaited me with the latest news and tidbits of gossip. Very much at the forefront of my mind was the attack upon us at Kherdasakh.

Even though Ihy was now Scorpion's chief counsel, he held very little influence amongst the various priest cults and none whatsoever among the Horus priests. Accordingly, over the next few days, I entertained my many head priests and even had occasion to visit a few patients who quietly insisted that they be treated only by my hands.

Still, Ihy and Mersyankh exerted great influence within the Royal court itself, more through fear than through persuasion to the correctness of their beliefs. I heard numerous tales of beatings and mysterious deaths that accrued to those who opposed them. Scorpion hardly knew any more whether it be day or night, so possessed was he with the evil power of cheap barley beer. Kagemni, too, secretly reported to me that first evening. Scorpion had committed egregious errors on the battlefield, resulting in the loss of hundreds of men and the army was forced to retreat from our northern borders. The marsh dwellers were gathering strength once again and hiring mercenaries from Ta-Tjehenu to aid their cause. This, Kagemni warned me, put Scorpion into the foulest mood he had ever seen.

Thus it was that the next day was a rarity for me, for I did not greet Ra's disk with a sense of reverence and excitement. Rather, I turned over on my mattress, still tired, and buried my head beneath my blanket. As I was about to doze off again, I heard a discussion that was unmistakably rising in pitch and which reluctantly forced me from my bed.

"Come on," Neter-Maat insisted, "tell me. I am your brother."

"Half-brother," Meni responded, not looking up from

the scroll he was studying.

"But, is it true?" he persisted, his hulking figure towering over the Prince. "You now have a lover?" Meni did not say a word. However, he no longer pretended to look at the scroll.

"And a Setjet whore, no less!" Neter-Maat said, forcing a laugh. He bent down to stare into Meni's face. "Why bother? You might as well make love to a donkey!"

With that comment, Meni pushed his chair back forcefully and stood up to face Neter-Maat, although he barely reached his half-brother's chin. "Why say such things?" Meni protested, taking a breath to regain his self-control. "You sound stupid. You're only twelve. Do you know even one person from Setjet?"

Neter-Maat hesitated. "Does it make a difference, brother? Everyone says that's true."

"By 'everyone' I assume you mean your mother," Meni responded sarcastically, and turned to sit down.

"Do not insult the Queen!" Neter-Maat yelled. He pushed Meni, who almost tripped over his chair.

"Neter-Maat, stop this! It is nonsense for us to argue over such a trivial matter," Meni responded. "It is not worth us fighting over…"

Before Meni could finish his sentence, Neter-Maat grabbed the Prince's tunic and literally picked him up off the ground. "You weak, shaking piece of crocodile dung! I could crush your head like a fly."

"Put me down, Neter-Maat," Meni said as calmly as he could, "or I shall not be responsible for my actions."

Neter-Maat laughed heartily into Meni's face. "Sure, Meni, my master." With that, he threw Meni nearly halfway across the room, against a pillar. It was then that I noticed Mersyankh's hair jutting from behind the pillar. There was no doubt this debacle was her creation, and perhaps Ihy's, too. Then I saw him standing in the shadows in the room behind Mersyankh. It has long been said that fools scheme and gods laugh.

Neter-Maat continued to bait the Prince. "As for your kills in battle, Meni, I have heard the truth that you ran through a mere child who cowered before Butehamon, pleading for mercy."

Meni stood up slowly and for a moment I thought of stepping in and preventing the fight the gods had ordained them to have. But, I thought better of it, for if it were not this instant, it would be another, so little did Mersyankh and Ihy understand from where true power emanated.

"Neter-Maat, do not play the fool to Ihy and your mother. The path you embark upon is fraught with danger. By laying your hands upon the future King in anger, you condemn yourself and... and them. Back off now, while there is still time."

"No one, not even you, calls me a fool!" Neter-Maat shouted, and before Meni could even react, Neter-Maat swung viciously at him. With a dull thud and a sickening cracking sound his fist connected with Meni's face. Blood immediately spurted from Meni's nose as he fell to the floor. I was stunned by the speed and force of Neter-Maat's blow, but I was also troubled by Meni's inability to deflect it.

Once again, Meni stood slowly, this time holding his nose with the cloth of his tunic. "Get control of yourself, Neter-Maat. Walk away now and I shall forget about this incident!" As he spoke, Meni circled cautiously to follow Neter-Maat, his free hand out to his side for balance. He, too, now knew where this conflict would end and he was positioning himself to best advantage.

"The only control I shall get is over you!" Neter-Maat responded, and lumbered forward. As he did so, I could hardly believe the changes that had come over the youth who was so happy and mild-mannered as a toddler. Meni stayed rooted in his spot, relaxed and limber, yet still holding his nose. Neter-Maat lunged at him, his face screwed up in anger, both hands outstretched. At the last moment, Meni stepped aside, holding out his foot and pulling Neter-Maat's arm down to the ground. Neter-Maat's large bulk sent him propelling forward and his head hit the leg of the table. Jars and scrolls went flying and the table shattered. Two guards rushed in, but Mersyankh held up her hand to them and they stopped immediately.

For a moment, Neter-Maat lay there, not comprehending what had happened. Then he arose in fury and grabbed one of the broken table legs. He tore it loose from the reeds that bound it to the table top and, his eyes narrowed, advanced once again.

"Do not do this, Neter-Maat!" Again, Meni circled purposefully to open the distance between them and to keep his opponent off guard. Ihy joined Mersyankh's side, the confrontation no doubt already surpassing what they had intended. They whispered to each other frantically. Ihy then noticed me and shot me a glance, expecting me to intervene. Instead, I simply nodded at them.

Neter-Maat was possessed, his fragile mental abilities now dwarfed by his anger and humiliation. As Meni backed away and to his right, he bumped into a chair and made the mistake of looking down for an instant, just long enough for Neter-Maat to swing the table leg. Meni saw it too late and deflected it only slightly, while also spinning away.

"Aaaahh!" Meni moaned, as the blow landed hard on his left side, near the bottom of his rib cage. He put his hand up to his side and staggered away, probably with a cracked rib. Blood flowed freely from his nose and stained the front of his tunic a deep crimson.

"You know, Neter-Maat," Meni now said in a baiting tone, "for a big hippo like you are, your blow was not as hard as I expected. I wonder... is that because you are weaker than you look, or because you are too stupid to accept proper training?" As he spoke, Meni assumed the combat position, balanced evenly on his feet, his arms somewhat opened, his left foot slightly forward. I admired his strategy.

Often people who are less smart than others hate to be reminded of that fact. Rather than accept their weakness and seek ways to strengthen it, they go to great pains to avoid situations that make them feel stupid and inadequate. They are also easily enraged when their shortcoming is thus pointed out to them. So it was with Neter-Maat. He charged Meni, the table leg held high above his head.

As he had done with the soldier along the banks of Mother Nile in Kherdasakh, Meni crowded Neter-Maat's charge at the last possible moment, ducking underneath the blow and grabbing his opponent's tunic just below the sternum. Meni groaned from the pain in his ribs, but he rolled backward, thrust his legs under Neter-Maat and flung him far away from his body, while at the same time punching his fist under Neter-Maat's sternum. Meni deftly grabbed the table leg from Neter-Maat's hand. He continued his backward roll and stood above Neter-Maat's head. The wind was entirely knocked out of Neter-Maat's chest and he lay there trying to suck in air.

"By the gods I have the right to bash in your skull, my brother!" At that instant Ihy and Mersyankh came running in. Neter-Maat tried weakly to rise, but Meni brought the table leg down and held it against his throat.

"And you two, stop right there!" Meni commanded, pointing directly at them. He stood tall over Neter-Maat, the blood still dripping from his nose. "It has been a long time since you have given me a gift, my dear step-mother... not since you first arrived in Tjeni... when Scorpion was sober enough to notice your act of generosity."

Meni took a step back from Neter-Maat and threw the table leg atop his heaving bulk. "Now I repay your generosity, my dear Queen," Meni said, bowing only slightly at the waist. "You may have your son back... but take him quickly, before I change my mind!"

Mersyankh was shocked beyond speech. She stood, her jaw quivering, her eyes narrowed to two slivers of hatred. Ihy, to his credit, simply stared at the brick floor, as Neter-Maat turned over, got up and lumbered toward them, gasping for breath. Mersyankh glared at her son with utter scorn. He hung his head low and limped out after them, not turning to look back at his half-brother.

"You'd better let me look at those injuries," I said as I entered the room.

"Did you enjoy the spectacle or should we reenact it more toward your liking?" Meni said to me disdainfully. He bent to sit down, but the pain in his ribs made him think better of it.

I stood there, both hands on my staff. "Meni, what happened was destined to play itself out. Better to happen now with table legs than later with daggers, as your youthful vision dream warned you." He thought about my words. "Now may I look at your injuries… before you bleed to death?"

By mid-day Meni rested, although uneasily. His nose was broken and Meruka and I did what we could to mend it, although the break would permanently alter the contours of his face. For now, both his eyes were swollen and black and blue. His ribs gave him the most difficulty, for he could neither sit nor lay down without pain. We wrapped his chest tightly with linen bandages to make breathing easier, yet we dared not give him more pain-killing medicines. We feared that its effects, combined with the medicines he already took for his shakes, might sicken him even more. Time would be the best healer of all.

Throughout the next two days, Hemamiya tended to Meni, complaining all the while to anyone who would listen about his foolish actions. Still, she patiently applied towels soaked in the cooling water of Mother Nile to speed his recovery. To his credit, Meni said not an unkindly word to Hemamiya, but allowed her the unadulterated joy of ministering to him.

On the third day following their altercation, we received a summons in early morning to Scorpion's private chambers. I had been expecting it ever since, for if there was one thing consistent about Mersyankh it was her relentlessness.

Meni and I arrived and found Kagemni, Mersyankh, Ihy and Neter-Maat already present and standing stiffly. Meni and I had prepared as best as possible. To say that the Prince looked bad would be untruthful. His face looked horrible, still swollen and discolored. Although I knew that his cracked rib caused each step he took to be painful, I also knew he would not let on so before his father.

We had no sooner entered when Scorpion sat up straight and addressed us. "It has come to my attention that my two sons have recently come to physical blows against each other. This incident disgraces my Court. It is against ma'at. I will not tolerate this under my protection," Scorpion said, leaning back in his throne chair, which was elevated on a stone platform.

"Neter-Maat, Meni, come here before me." Meni stepped forward and as he moved toward the King, Neter-Maat sneered at him. "What have you to say?" Scorpion asked, looking at each one. Neter-Maat stood with his head bowed, looking at the floor. Meni stood erect, staring directly into his father's eyes.

"Well?" Scorpion asked, looking back at Meni.

"I hadn't realized this was to be a Court of Judgment," he said and even I could feel his voice thick with impertinence. I had distinctly warned him against this attitude and I believe had it been any other leader, even King W'ash, Meni would have been contrite and accommodating. But, the strain between father and son was too great for either of them to surmount. Kagemni and I traded looks of pain.

To his credit, Scorpion ignored Meni's challenge to his authority and turned first to Mersyankh and Ihy, then to me. "It has been reported to me that Mersyankh and Ihy saw the fight and that Meni baited Neter-Maat into it," Scorpion said. I wondered how he could keep a straight face when he uttered those words, since Neter-Maat stood a head taller than Meni and was easily twice his weight.

"Well, if nothing else, I think the Prince is smart enough to recognize the folly of such an action," I suggested, walking forward to Meni's side. Ihy then joined Neter-Maat. "And the bruises on his face would seem to underscore that point. However, in all honesty, I was in an adjoining room," I said truthfully, "and did not have the advantage of having been in the same room as the Prince and Neter-Maat, as were those two," I said, tipping my staff toward Mersyankh and Ihy.

"You do mean the two Princes, do you not?" Mersyankh asked sarcastically, while looking at Scorpion for support.

"If I may continue," I said, turning toward Ihy and ignoring her comment, "nothing of what I heard indicated to me that Meni was in need of any assistance. But what is curious to me is why, if both Mersyankh and Ihy were in the room, neither of them used their wit or authority to defuse the argument or separate the two... the two young men." I was confident that neither Mersyankh nor Ihy would acknowledge they saw me watching the scene, for to do so would have revealed even more clearly their conspiratorial natures.

"Surely, you do not defend Meni's actions against a brother who is four years younger!" Scorpion asked of me.

"No, he does not defend my actions at all, fa... King Scorpion," Meni interjected, holding up his arm in front of me. "I am capable of defending myself."

"That is quite obvious, judging by the bump on Neter-Maat's head. But are you not ashamed of picking your fights with children?" Scorpion asked, gripping the arms of his chair, the veins of his neck becoming more pronounced.

"Why should I be? I learned it well from you, did I not?" Meni retorted, swallowing hard, for he must have recognized that he had just crossed the line. The instant he vomited those bilious words from his mouth the room became deathly silent. Mersyankh gasped and Kagemni's entire posture changed. He was taut, like a cat waiting to jump on its prey.

It took a few seconds for Scorpion's alcohol-clouded mind to comprehend the full meaning of Meni's remark. When he did, he bolted from the throne chair and flew into Meni's face. "You impertinent imbecile!" Scorpion raged.

"Sorry, wrong son! But perhaps you are too drunk to tell," was all that Meni whispered into his father's face, but it was enough, far beyond enough. By all the gods that roam the land, Scorpion was no longer a match for the Prince, the cheap, thick beer having long ago destroyed his reasoning. But to be so insulted by one's own son is a humiliation few men could take, let alone the King of Upper Kem in his own Court.

Scorpion turned half around and stretched his closed fist

as far behind him as he could, preparing to strike his son. I could do nothing, nothing at all, but watch this horrible play staged by the gods. If Meni ever deserved to be severely disciplined, this was the very time. I feared Scorpion's might, but I also knew that if I interfered in his role as father and King, I would rightfully condemn myself to death.

Yet, far from fearing his father, Meni stood relaxed, looking directly into his father's eyes, not wavering, not even blinking, waiting for his father's stinging retribution. I watched Scorpion's fist fly forward in a mighty blow and as it was about to hit Meni's face, an even larger fist grabbed it from the side. Soon Kagemni, the only man the gods had placed in this play who could have done it, wedged himself between the King and the Prince. Meni was shoved backward a few steps by Kagemni's action.

"Scorpion! No! Do not do this! I beg you. To hit him in anger will bring ruin on your Court and... and all of Upper Kem." Kagemni's bare chest was pressed hard against Scorpion's, their faces not a hand's width apart, both of them panting with the madness of the moment.

"Please, Scorpion," Kagemni said, this time his voice softer. "It will bring disfavor from the gods." Every muscle in Scorpion's body was tensed for action. His fists were clenched at his side. "Please, my friend... please!"

Slowly, so slowly it seemed as if time itself stood still, Scorpion willed himself to retreat. He stepped back haltingly, first one step, then another, all the while staring at Meni, until Kagemni returned him to his throne chair.

"Out, both of you!" Kagemni commanded, turning angrily and pointing to Meni and me. "All of you... all of you, get out!" he bellowed. Wide-eyed, Neter-Maat turned and almost ran from the room. Mersyankh and Ihy were close behind.

I turned and reached to grab Meni's arm, but he waved me off. I watched as he cast one final look at his father, a look that to this day I have been unable to fathom. At first I imagined it to be haughtiness, an arrogance bred by the hatred caused by his father's neglect that had simmered within him for these many years. But, as he turned I realized otherwise, for from his eyes ran a stream of tears, a river of regret that obscured the last view that Meni would ever have of his father in this world.

# SCROLL ELEVEN

## *Turmoil*

"Meni... Meni, wake up!" Shouts came from throughout the Royal compound and people scurried in the corridors in disbelief.

"Meni!" I shook the Prince awake, for it is difficult enough to awaken a normal seventeen year-old, let alone one who took as many herbs to quell his shakes as did Meni. Behind his eyelids I could see his eyeballs moving rapidly, a sure sign that he was in the midst of a fretful dream. Reluctantly, he opened his eyes.

"What? What is it?" he asked, shifting to his elbows. I gave him the full measure of my assessment, even in the dim light of the pre-dawn hours. He measured up well for what I was about to tell him.

"Are you awake... fully awake?" I asked. He stared back at me, threw his legs over the bed frame and stood up. He was naked. He bent over to retrieve his loincloth from a bench at the foot of his bed and tied it around him.

"I am now," he said, after rinsing his mouth from a cup at the head of his bed. He spit out into a bowl. "What is it?"

"Your father is dead," I said, as calmly as I could.

Among the priests it is said that the loneliest day in a man's life is when he is told that his father has died, for then the weight of the generations, past, present and future, fall upon his shoulders. And, when he turns around to lean his head in grief against the shoulder of the one man upon whom he has always depended, he feels instead the desolate emptiness of death.

Meni turned his head partly away from me, staring at the candles on the far side of the room. I tried to gauge his reaction, but whether it was the shadows cast by the candles, or the fact that Meni hid his reaction in a darkness of his own creation I could not tell. His face was expressionless.

"That is not possible," he finally said softly, as shouts continued to ring out in the corridors. "For unless you are a ghost, Anhotek, my true father still lives." That is what he said, may Horus bless him forever and ever, into the far expanses of eternity. That was all he said. He then turned and walked outside to relieve himself, before returning and washing. He sat down in the cane rush chair that was his favorite.

"How did Scorpion die?" he asked of me.

"He... he died valiantly, in battle, according to Kagemni... who himself was wounded, I might add, but not seriously. The marsh dwellers had engaged a plot with the Ta-Tjehenus. They outflanked our troops when they moved in from the western desert."

"And the outcome of the battle?" Meni asked, dispassionately.

"Apparently, our troops drove them back to the marshlands. But we lost many men and Kagemni was worried that we could not sustain another battle. They... they prepared the King's body for a field burial, but when they decided to return immediately, they brought his body home with them. It... he is in his chambers as we speak."

Meni sat silently, absorbing all that I had told him. He sat erect, his hands on his knees and had I danced before him with sistras on my feet, he would not have noticed.

Thus he sat for ten minutes or more.

"What must we do now?" he finally asked, sighing.

"Even under the best of circumstances, there would be a large number of tasks we must do. However, given the situation in the Court... I mean with your half-brother, the Queen and Ihy... the list is long. We both know that the future of the Two Lands is at stake. We must act with all dispatch, Meni."

"And so, tell me."

"The first thing is to give Scorpion a proper burial, deserving of a warrior-King. Then we must go to Nekhen, to the Temple of Horus, to say prayers and to seek the blessings of the priests for your coronation after the mourning period is over."

"And during this interim period?" Meni asked, turning toward me.

"That will be very difficult, indeed. Mersyankh and Ihy will make every effort to seize control of the throne. It will take all our skills to develop alliances so that their efforts prove futile. We must establish you as King, with a strong power base. That will not be easy, Meni. Not easy at all."

Meni sat, his body still tense, his heart probably mulling over how the events of this still young day wove themselves into his visions. "I... I often wonder, Anhotek... I think about what my days in this Court might have been like had Scorpion not met Mersyankh, had they not birthed Neter-Maat, had..." He stopped in the middle of his speaking, realizing that he was talking aloud.

I picked up another chair and carried it close to the Prince. "I, too, wonder about that," I said, cradling his hand in mine as I sat. "Scorpion was a good man at his core. Like all men, his strength was also his weakness, Meni. He could not handle the diplomacy aspects of kingship. Instead of reaching out to his trusted advisors, he drank, and no man is strong enough to master that affliction. Had alcohol not clouded his mind and sapped his true strength, I believe he would have accepted your holy illness and embraced you as heir to the throne."

Meni held my hand, but did not respond. He breathed

in deeply and sighed. "In some ways I regret the way things turned out with him, but in other ways I do not. Had I been raised here, I would not have had you as both father and teacher. I would not have traveled as we have and learned of foreign people and their mysterious manners. I would not have met Meruka… or El-Or." He squeezed my hand.

"I have come to believe you are right, that the gods themselves set my life in motion. They prepared the road I have walked. You often say to me how I am a leader, Anhotek. But, indeed, up until this time I feel I have been led."

Suddenly, the sound of loud, ritual wailing reached our ears and we knew immediately that Mersyankh had been told of her husband's death, although she had been living with his ghost for more than a dozen years now. If nothing else, her shrieking motivated us to action.

"I have drawn up a list of things to which we must attend immediately," I said to Meni. "It would be wise to remember that your ascension to the throne is by no means assured. I suspect that Mersyankh and Ihy will make a strong play for Neter-Maat to be crowned King. She may even try to assume the throne herself as regent. You and I will need to remain focused on the tasks at hand. This is a propitious time, Meni. Chaos is everywhere. Until you are crowned, evil spirits roam Towi, threatening ma'at."

"I understand," Meni assured me, letting go my hand.

Until well past Ra's setting in the western sky that night, I held one meeting after another, first with Kagemni, to mortar our alliance, then with the priests of the Temples of Horus and Osiris in Tjeni and the Temple of Min in nearby Gebtiu. By nightfall, the head priests had dispatched their initiates throughout Upper Kem to relay the news of Scorpion's death and to hand the head priest of each temple an oath of allegiance to me and Meni, which they were to secretly sign.

On the third day after Kagemni returned to Tjeni with Scorpion's body, we met with Kaipunesut, the Chief Architect of the Royal family and a man I deeply respected. We had worked together on many projects assigned to us by Scorpion over the years and I trusted him implicitly. I suspected he did not feel quite as warmly toward me, for he detested diplomacy.

"Anhotek!" Kaipunesut called out cheerfully as soon as he entered the Prince's chambers, dressed in a fancy pleated tunic. He grasped both my forearms in his hands and shook them warmly. "It has been far too long."

He appeared to be well, his tall, thin frame now bent slightly from age. With his skinny neck bent forward, and his cleanly shaved head, he gave the appearance of a mace. "Prince Meni, good to see you again. By the gods, you have grown into a handsome man!" He smiled broadly, eagerly anticipating a new building project.

"Sadly, we have called you here to discuss an unfortunate project," I began.

"We will need you to design and build a simple mastaba tomb for King Scorpion," Meni said, trying to act like a grieving son.

"Ah, yes... yes," Kaipunesut responded. "I anticipated that. I have already begun to think of designs that..."

"Nothing fancy, Kaipunesut," Meni interrupted. "A simple mastaba, that is all."

"But... but I have already been asked by Queen Mersyankh to devise an elaborate tomb, rising above the ground, not a flat mastaba tomb... at the Royal necropolis in Abdju. I... I..."

"We understand your... conflict," I said, trying to reassure Kaipunesut. It did not surprise me at all that Mersyankh would commission an elaborate tomb. That process would take considerably more time, time she and Ihy would use to sow discontent and to solidify their base of power. So long as leadership remained in doubt, it would benefit their scheming. "However, Kaipunesut, let me explain something." I began to pace the room.

"There is no time to waste. Scorpion's ka journeys between worlds. Chaos is everywhere. Mother Nile did not flood high and the crop yields have not been good. The marsh-dwellers and the Ta-Tjenehus threaten our very way of life. Mut roam the land, their ghosts causing tragedies of every description." Kaipunesut was a religious man and he followed my every step, his eyes wide and his body tense.

"We must put Scorpion's body in his tomb and provide for him all he needs for the afterlife. Until he arrives there, and Prince Meni crowned, ma'at will not be restored. Do you understand?"

"I do, yes I do!" Kaipunesut answered, shaking his head vigorously. "But, I am not adept at... at manipulating people, like you, Anhotek. You are masterful in that regard. I am but an architect."

"I will take care of the Queen... and of Ihy. However, you must have the tomb ready in thirty days, Kaipunesut."

"Thirty days! That... that is impossible. It will take me that long just to..."

"Thirty days from today... no more," I insisted. "I am arranging the procession for that day. If you feel you cannot have a simple mastaba ready by that date, tell me now. I will understand, but I will have to bring in another architect who can guarantee me completion in thirty days."

The rest of the negotiation would be but minor details, for my implication was clear that Kaipunesut risked keeping his position as Chief Architect to the King. But, we also explained that there would be a revival of building projects once Meni was crowned. He seemed placated, but still nervous about the Queen's reaction. My assistants escorted Kaipunesut directly to the necropolis to remove him from Mersyankh's direct influence. Later that day I arranged with the priests at the Temple of Osiris, whose grand temple bordered the necropolis, to guard Kaipunesut from any distractions. I was to be the only one from the Royal Court with access to him.

The following day I arranged to travel to Nekhen, there to obtain the consent of the priests of the Temple of Horus for Meni's ascension. Every King of Upper Kem had a direct connection to Horus, the falcon god of Nekhen. I anticipated their cooperation for Meni to wear the crown, rather than Neter-Maat, whose bloodline was diluted by Mersyankh. To mortar that cooperation I would commission an entirely new and larger Temple of Horus, along with a complex of administrative buildings.

Meruka and I left in three days time, after a lengthy and secret meeting with Meni and Kagemni. Although the demands on Kagemni would prevent him from directly attending to Meni's protection, we arranged for Butehamon to serve again as Meni's personal guard, along with a contingent of Kagemni's finest soldiers.

We had no sooner arrived in Nekhen when the first of several messages arrived from Kaipunesut, assuring me of steady progress on Scorpion's mastaba. On the second day after our arrival, Meruka ran into an acquaintance from his youth, an older man from a neighboring Ta-Sety tribe, who was in Nekhen trading ivory for flax oil and emmer wheat. Amidst much hugging and laughing, they immediately took off together and I did not see Meruka for two days more. I did not begrudge him some long overdue time for himself.

It was on the fifth day after our arrival, after Ra had set and Meruka and I had participated in the evening prayer rituals with the Chief Priest, that I received an urgent message from Kagemni, delivered by one of his trusted servants. The papyrus scroll had been carefully sealed and, like all trusted messengers, Kagemni's servant carried a phial of special vegetable oil I had prepared, with which he could obliterate the text if he were in danger of being captured.

Meruka ordered food and drink brought to the messenger and then the two of us retreated to our quarters to read the scroll. Even in the dim candle light, we could see that it had been hastily written. It advised us not to leave Nekhen until another messenger arrived in a few days, who would relate more details to us.

The scroll included a few words about Mersyankh holding furtive meetings. Powerful families were being offered trading contracts and tomb placements next to Neter-Maat, should they support his ascension. Kagemni also indicated that some of his officers were being tempted with bribes, although so far unsuccessfully.

Kagemni's message was troubling, since before I left we had discussed in detail how Kagemni and Meni were to thwart Mersyankh's attempts until my return. I suspected that the real purpose of the message was to be sure that the route to us was not compromised and to assure us that the next messenger would provide us with more sensitive information.

That night, I felt evil spirits afoot. Meruka, too, felt uneasy. I tossed and turned in my sleep, the mut spirits haunting me in my dreams. Halfway through the night, I awoke instantly. Meruka stood over me and in the light from the silver disk of the night, I could see that he was sweating and shaking.

"What is it?" I asked, frightened.

"We must go back to Tjeni… now!" he said, looking outside in the direction of our home, the twisted locks of his hair silhouetted by Ra's night disk. "There is evil magic in the air, Anhotek. Powerful magic. The mut have been set afoot throughout the land. I fear for the Prince's safety. We… we must leave at once." He flared his nostrils and shifted his face from side to side, as if he was trying to sniff the scent of evil on the gentle currents of the night air.

So much did I respect Meruka's magic that without further questions we packed. By the time Ra's disk emerged victorious in the east, we were ready to leave Nekhen. The priests of the temple blessed us and brought provisions for the journey. The priests provided an extra boat crew so that we could rotate men throughout the trip and return to Tjeni in one day's journey. I thanked the gods that our journey was downriver.

The closer we sailed and rowed to Tjeni, the stronger was Meruka's worry. He peered into the darkness ahead of us. "In my land there are some who practice the dark magic… spells to unleash evil spirits," he said, spreading out his arms in front of him, "spells to make an enemy ill or to bring on an untimely death."

"You have seen these spells yourself?"

"Many, many times. A… a neighboring tribe once had a powerful shaman who practiced the evil arts. No one dared to oppose him, until one of my father's wives had a disagreement with the shaman's first wife over a goblet they had traded in the weekly market. He cast a spell and it traveled over the plain and came upon my village that night as a terrible, shrieking wind. Oh, it was awful! My father was away hunting and this mother died before daybreak. Next to the mother who birthed me, she was my favorite one. I was young and I shook with fear for days."

We arrived in Tjeni at dawn of the next day. At this early morning hour only a few industrious fishermen were about, untangling their nets and baiting their lines. No sooner had we hiked up to the palace, than Meni, walking alone, met us in the entranceway to our quarters.

"Anhotek! Meruka! Thanks be to Horus that you have arrived," he said, grasping each of our forearms. "Come quickly! Hemamiya is gravely ill." We hurriedly followed Meni to Hemamiya's tiny room, where Panehsy and Surero ministered to her. She lay in her bed, soaked in perspiration.

"What is wrong with her?" I asked as soon as we were by her side.

"Anhotek, forgive us! We have acted for your praise! Yet, we know not what ails her," Panehsy replied in frustration, tears pooling in his eyes. "She… she took ill two nights ago and… and no matter what we do she worsens." Tiny Surero nodded his large head in agreement.

Her condition was grave. Her breath was shallow and her color a ghastly blue. Her pulse was faint. She did not respond to light or to my pinching her in various places on her body. Working together, Meruka checked her body for signs of injury, while I probed her vital organs. The cause of her illness eluded me.

"What ails her?" Meni asked, looking frantically from me to Meruka.

"It is the dark magic," Meruka whispered. "I have seen it before. She is under a spell. She cannot respond, for her ka walks in the land between the worlds." His face was deeply etched in shadows cast by the oil lamps.

"Thank Horus you are back!" Kagemni's voice suddenly boomed from the far side of the room, startling us. "I just heard you had arrived. I was hoping you would return soon."

Meruka and I looked at each other in amazement. "You... you what?" I asked, incredulous.

Kagemni stopped two cubits in front of me and moved no further. "What in Horus' name? Are you ill, Anhotek?"

It was obvious that we were communicating like flies circling dung. Meruka grabbed my arm and motioned for me to open my bag. He removed the scroll Kagemni had sent us and handed it to him.

"Your message said that we should wait in Nekhen for a few more days," Meruka said waving the scroll before him, "until we heard from you again."

Kagemni opened his mouth, but no words came out. "Is this not your seal?" Meruka asked, pointing to the wax impression.

"Anhotek, I... I have not sent you a message since our battle with the damned Ta-Tjehenus... years ago. I... yes, it is my seal, but... but I have not sent you any message. I... I am..."

"It is Ihy's work," Meruka sighed. "Hemamiya's illness, this forgery... there is bad, bad evil. My blood curdles."

Ihy had masterfully executed the forgery, providing enough negative information about him and Mersyankh to make the message appear authentic. "If not for you, Meruka, we would still be in Nekhen awaiting word from Kagemni. Only we would never have received such word, except about his untimely death, I imagine."

"We must talk privately," Kagemni said, looking up from the forged document. By now Ra's disk was full on the horizon and we could hear the stirring of activity in the court.

"Let me give instructions to Panehsy and Surero," I said. In a few minutes Meni, Kagemni, Meruka and I left for Kagemni's quarters, which were private and secure. As we passed into his area, he posted guards with instructions to allow no one to pass.

As soon as we entered, we sat down at a table that Kagemni used to brief his officers. "There is much I must tell you, Anhotek" Kagemni began. "Since you have left the forces of chaos reign. There is fear and dissension throughout the Court."

"Mersyankh has rent her garments," Meni continued, "and she acts the role of grieving widow. Very convincing, although I find it impossible to believe that anyone who knows her deems her sorrow sincere. She and Ihy met with Neter-Maat and others within the court and began to plot the evil that now befalls us." Meni turned to Kagemni.

"Two nights ago," Kagemni went on, "Ihy gathered a group of people to his quarters. He has dug a fire pit in its center... did you know that, Anhotek?"

"Yes. It was necessary for his priestly rituals, he told me."

"Yes, but this time my spy tells me it was different. He... that bastard made up wax and clay figurines of you and Meni, Hemamiya and Meruka." The gooseflesh rose on my body, for I never imagined such a dark, evil ceremony would take place within the Royal court.

"Somehow, that son of a whore put hair on the clay figurines of Meni and... and he claimed it was Meni's actual hair."

"That's impossible!" I protested. "I always dispose of his hair and nail clippings properly. Always for... for this very reason. Is that not correct?" I asked, turning to Meruka.

"Always," he agreed.

"Nonetheless..." Kagemni continued.

"Except..." Meruka continued, "except when we travel. Sometimes you will cut his hair or nails on the boat and later throw them overboard." Meruka was right. But who would risk the wrath of the gods by gathering the personal groomings from the Prince's body? My mind spun with the maelstrom of intrigue.

"Continue, Kagemni, for the plot thickens. We must extricate ourselves from this muck to save Meni and our precious Kem. Leave out no details, Kagemni, for Meruka and I will need to counter Ihy's evil magic."

Kagemni acknowledged my words with a shake of his head. Meni's eyes were wide with fascination, but he hardly could have suspected the danger we all faced.

"Ihy laid out his wands to contain all the magic within the circle of the damned traitors," Kagemni said, spreading out his hands as if to define the circle. "Then he named each figurine and stuck pins in them. He called up the evil bau spirits." Kagemni looked up at us. "I am told that the ritual was so frightening, it sickened two of the traitors and they vomited all over themselves."

Meni leaned back in his seat, contemplating Kagemni's description. "Then Ihy conjured up Apep, the serpent god, and began to chant and sway. He kept calling out all your names, but most especially Hemamiya, referring to her as the one that Ra hates and enjoining Apep to send his evil bau to enter her body."

"But, why Hemamiya?" Meni asked.

"That would be just what Ihy would do," I suggested.

"First attack the enemy whose magic protections are weakest," Meruka added. "Then the other conspirators will see the effect of his spell and be cowered into submission. If he attacked any of the three of us directly we might detect his magic."

"Did he break the figurines in the fire?" I asked Kagemni.

"He opened the magic wands so that the spell could be cast from the fire circle. Then Mersyankh herself threw the figurines of Hemamiya into the fire to shatter them, laughing all the while. Ihy cursed Hemamiya's name seven times and... and a huge wind came and blew over the fire and out the door. Ihy was so possessed at this point, he foamed at the mouth and began to make vile utterances. He shouted things in a language no one understood. His voice seemed to come from the netherworld, shaking and high-pitched. Mersyankh herself... that dog bitch... stopped him from going further.

"He returned from the netherworld of the mut then. But, before he was done, he cast a spell to protect Neter-Maat against the Evil Eye that he felt Anhotek would surely cast on him."

I am certain that each of us was chilled to our very bones. "This explains what you felt that very same night in

Nekhen," I said turning to Meruka. Kagemni and Meni looked up at me, then at Meruka.

"You felt the ritual there?" Meni asked in amazement. "In Nekhen?"

At that moment, a loud shrieking arose from another area of the court. Soon we heard the quick footsteps of Surero's sandals on the mud-brick floor. Kagemni got up to retrieve him from the guards.

"She is dead, Anhotek! Hemamiya's ka has departed," he said in his odd voice, still breathing heavily.

Meni's face turned pale. He slumped his elbows to his knees and hung his head down. I wanted to place my hands upon him, to hold his head upon my shoulder. Although he bickered with Hemamiya since childhood, it was bickering borne of love and caring. Hemamiya was his servant, his nurse and his mother in one person. Yet, I did not touch the Prince, for to do so would have weakened him in the eyes of the men who would soon pledge their very lives to his service.

Instead, I breathed in and let out a large sigh. "We must act quickly if we are to battle these evil menaces. There is no time to waste!" I turned to Surero. "Surero, dutiful servant, go back and prepare Hemamiya's body. I want her buried tomorrow."

"Tomorrow? How is that possible?" Surero protested.

"Tomorrow!" I insisted. "By the time Ra's disk rises in the east." I dismissed Surero and turned back to the others.

"We must bury Hemamiya quickly, to reclaim her ka from Mersyankh's and Ihy's evil. But, we must also take control of matters in the court.

"Meruka, prepare a Reclaiming of the Ka ritual for Hemamiya. We will lead it tonight. Meni, bring to the ritual something of hers, a treasured gift or personal item she gave you." Meni nodded.

"Kagemni, to you falls the most difficult task of all. Ihy and Mersyankh have doubtless frightened all who attended their evil ceremony. In an hour, the entire Court will have heard of Hemamiya's death, may Horus protect her ka in her journey. Maintain tight control of your troops. Do whatever you must to assure that there are no plots, no mutinies, not even a hint of them. Chaos presses upon us from every corner.

"Worst of all, Kagemni, there is a spy in our midst, a festering sore that will kill the Prince and the rest of us with him. We must uncover him, to cut out the putrefaction, if we are ever to place the Prince on the throne and restore ma'at."

# SCROLL TWELVE

## Traitor In Our midst

The funerary procession stretched for as far as the eye could see, from Tjeni to The Place of Truth, the Royal necropolis in Abdju, where every King of Upper Kem had been buried as far back as the god-Kings that walked our ancient lands. Farmers took the day off from their planting and all manner of workers lined the route, eager to glimpse members of the Royal family, to mourn for their dead King and to see Prince Meni, their future ruler.

The procession began when Ra rose in the sky in his boat. He was now high in the sky overhead and we were still not at the temple, such was the length and slow pace of the procession. As the funeral bier passed, the people knelt to the ground in prayer, pounding their chests in grief and ripping at their clothing. There was a palpable fear in the air, for without a King, the people knew that ma'at eluded them. Business deals were delayed, marriages postponed, caravans halted, for it was not a propitious time.

For an hour we proceeded due west, above Mother Nile's floodplain, through the grasslands, to the very edge of the desert. Now we stood nearly at the entrance to the mud-brick Temple of Khenti-Amentiu, gateway to The Place of Truth, its columns rising to five times the height of a man. Like the Temple of Horus at Nekhen, it had a thatched roof that pitched straight down from front to back. Beyond the temple lay the three elephant-shaped mountains that gave the holy area its name, Abdju.

Eight soldiers carried Meni's gold and ebony chair, which was affixed to long poles that extended in front and behind. Even under Ra's baking rays, he sat straight. Periodically, he would cross his forearms on his chest and lower his eyelids to the crowds, which murmured its approval. His eyes were lined with kohl and he wore a pleated white tunic and a simple gold necklace. His regal bearing shone through even his modest dress.

On the platform in front of us sat Queen Mersyankh, wearing so much ostentatious jewelry, even Ihy was uncomfortable. Her pleated gown was pure white and her face and hair were meticulously arranged. Her gold and silver bracelets, anklets and necklaces glittered in the sun, while her lapis lazuli and turquoise beads and ornaments flashed their intense colors to the onlookers every time she moved. She wore earrings of the finest translucent carnelians. Fan bearers waved their large ostrich feathers to cool her. The perfume she wore was so pungent, whenever the breezes blew in our direction it caused me to gasp for air, for the women of Lower Kem still used ox fat for the base of their perfumes.

The priests from the Temple of Khenti-Amentiu refused to accede to Mersyankh's demand that Neter-Maat ride immediately behind her platform, explaining that our precedent was always the spouse followed by the first-born son. Even so, when it came time to leave that morning, she tried again to place Neter-Maat's platform right behind hers. However, the priests stood firm and she relented. He now rode behind us, infuriated by whatever attention the crowds paid to Meni.

Scorpion's burial ritual was simple, as befitted the warrior-King he was. The priests carried his coffin through the temple to the inner sanctum, where Meni and I,

Mersyankh, Ihy and Neter-Maat were the only ones allowed to enter. There, amidst a great expanse of space, the statue of Khenti-Amentiu, god of the underworld stood, his jackal head frightening to behold.

The priests accepted offerings of food from Mersyankh, Meni and Neter-Maat and placed them at the foot of the statue, which towered above us. The legend told that only those pure of heart could gaze upon Khenti-Amentiu's face without trembling. Neither Mersyankh nor Ihy dared look up. Neter-Maat, may Hathor protect his innocence, gazed curiously upon the god as if it were one of his game pieces.

All others in the procession took a path around the back of the temple and we met them in the Place of Truth, where the mastaba tomb that Kaipunesut built awaited Scorpion's arrival. The cemetery lay in the valley, in a straight line between the temple and the steep pass that the gods had etched between two of the mountains. This was the holy gateway between this world and the next that the King's body would travel when it journeyed to meet his ka and ba in the afterlife.

The burial room of the mastaba had been prepared with all manner of food and drink. The adjoining room contained all the comforts of the Royal court, so that his body would be well nourished and comfortable in the afterlife.

When Scorpion's coffin was placed on the stone slab in the center of the burial chamber, Mersyankh screamed and attempted to rend her clothes. Yet, when she was done with her performance, her eye makeup was as fresh as when it was first applied and her garments showed not a single actual tear.

Meni read a prayer for his father's journey that he had not shared with me beforehand. I was apprehensive, for I hoped he would not dwell on the rumors about his father's death. Kagemni had confided in me the truth about his closest friend's death. Surrounded by enemy troops, Scorpion plunged his own sword into his heart. I, myself, believed Scorpion's death hid a still darker secret, that he recognized that his fearsome sword could no longer solve the many problems of his own creation. So, he chose to die by its simple architecture.

Meni's prayer was a simple one, acknowledging that he had learned how to stand up to an adversary from his father's example. On the surface it sounded to those who were not intimately connected to life in the Royal court as a special tribute. In the end I was proud of Meni, for he had found the one trait that he had indeed learned from his father and made it appear to all eyes as solely a positive attribute.

Mersyankh, however, was not to let Meni have the last word. When he was done, before his prayer even settled over the assembled crowd, she turned to Ihy and instructed him to say a prayer in her name.

Ihy raised his staff and began an incantation that none of us could comprehend. It was not from the standard prayers that any of the head priests of Upper Kem knew. Ihy shuffled around Scorpion's coffin, raising and lowering his staff, changing the pitch of his intonations, and at times invoking the fearful image of Apep, the serpent god. Raising Apep's image in front of Khenti-Amentiu's priests was inappropriate and even insulting. The Chief Priest began to step forward to put a stop to Ihy's performance, but I shook my head to stay him. By then people were whispering and murmuring to each other.

Finally, Ihy became aware of their reaction and stopped his performance, put down his staff, and returned to Mersyankh's side with whatever dignity he could gather. I often wonder what possessed Ihy to engage in such a bizarre ritual. Was it something done as a matter of course as part of a Royal burial by the marsh-dwellers? Or, as Meruka believed, was it that he truly believed he would invoke the dark spirits to that place, at that time, and thus demonstrate the power of his magic, despite the light from Ra's disk shining so brightly upon us?

If Meruka was correct, I pitied Ihy greatly. The dark magic works only in the shadows, for the light of Ra is its enemy. It works only on the weak, for strength of character does not provide it with fertile fields to sow. It works only with small groups of powerless people, for true power requires light to illuminate great visions.

While Kaipunesut's masons completed the sealing of the mastaba, we returned to Tjeni. As Meni passed Mersyankh's platform to step onto his own, she called down to him from her chair in a loud voice.

"Meni, how is the one who is more beautiful than any other?" She smiled wickedly and turned to Neter-Maat and Ihy, who stood to her side. Neter-Maat laughed, as did several others in her retinue. Ihy, however, looked embarrassed.

Meni appeared shaken by her remark. As he walked by her, he stumbled on a rock and nearly fell. That, too, brought her to laughter.

"Poor Meni, how will your oafishness appeal to she who treads of the ground with a brisk step?" she remarked to even greater laughter.

Meni, now thoroughly embarrassed, quickly mounted his platform and yelled to his platform-bearers to make haste.

Throughout the ride home, I could hear ahead of us the sounds of laughter each time Mersyankh spoke. It seemed to me as if she were reading from a scroll that those around her found amusing. Meni, on the other hand, sat stonily silent, his face flushed from more than the heat of Ra's disk. By the time we reached the Royal compound, he was tense and fuming.

I whispered into Meruka's ear until he nodded with understanding. As soon as Mersyankh stepped off her platform, I began a conversation to distract her. Meruka took Meni off by the other side and spirited him to his quarters. When he was safely out of view, I made my excuses and left. Ihy did not bother to instruct the Queen that Meni had left, even though from his vantage point he looked directly at him. By the time I entered Meni's quarters, he was pacing back and forth, his voice raised in anger.

"... because those were the exact words I used, that is how!" he yelled at Meruka.

"What is going on?" I asked.

"The Prince believes that one of Mersyankh's spies must have intercepted a letter he wrote to El-Or," Meruka said to me.

"What leads you to believe that?" I asked Meni.

"Why must I always repeat myself?" he snapped in frustration. Then he sat down and sighed. "As I said to Meruka, that demon sorceress quoted from a poem that I wrote to El-Or... not just thoughts that I might have expressed to others, but the exact words I wrote. I... I feel humiliated!"

"Meni, if you are embarrassed, it is by your choice alone. Revealing your true feelings to your loved one should not be embarrassing. Our greatest poetry is written to express love. Mersyankh is jealous, for never has she had a man feel so passionately about her as to commit his feelings to poetry.

"But, this incident does reveal something far more sinister. Whoever is spying for Mersyankh and Ihy is becoming emboldened. We must deal with this immediately."

"How?" Meni asked.

"Meruka, bring Kagemni here immediately." Thus I set in motion the plan to bring to light the spy who circulated in our midst, who added to the fog of chaos that surrounded the Royal court.

The very next morning, as Meruka and I sat with Meni's in his quarters, one of his servants announced that Kagemni and Butehamon had arrived. Once we were all seated, we ate our fill of barley beer, honey bread, cheese and fruits and laughed over the latest of Butehamon's amusing stories. From my mannerisms it was clear that I was not hurrying the proceedings. That, in itself, was unusual.

"So, when do we leave?" Butehamon asked. Meni looked at me.

"Leave?" I responded. "What makes you think we are leaving?"

Butehamon seemed taken aback. "What... I mean you have asked me here, so... so, I assumed we were to sail."

"No, not this time, dear Butehamon. We... our only trip in the near future will be a short sail, actually the coronation procession, to Nekhen. No. This time we asked you here to be part of our counsel, to give us your advice."

The furrows eased on Butehamon's brow and he leaned back on his pillows. "I am honored," he replied.

"Good, then let us get right to the point. There is a rather messy situation that we have been forced to deal with lately, especially since Scorpion's death." I had everyone's undivided attention as I rose to pace. I drew out the spaces between my words, which always elicits a reaction from those whom I wish to test.

"Yes, go ahead," Butehamon said, impatiently.

"It would seem... and by the way, do we have everyone's agreement here that this council is to be confidential?" Everyone nodded their assent. "It appears that someone has betrayed the Prince's confidence recently. It would be better to prune it now, before it grows like a weed out of control."

"I agree," Kagemni added, as we had rehearsed.

"Well, then, what I am referring to here is the letter which Meni entrusted to you, Butehamon, to send by messenger to El-Or in Setjet. It seems as if it has gotten into the hands of the Queen and I was wondering how that might have happened?"

If he was involved in this scheme, Butehamon gave no indication of it. "I... I have no idea," he said, sitting up and looking at each of us. "I gave the letter immediately to the Chief Priest to send out on the first caravan. We talked for a few moments after I gave him the scroll. Others joined us. We laughed... ask him, he will surely confirm that I handed him the sealed scroll."

"Butehamon, calm down! We are not accusing you. We are... checking, that is all... to find out the true culprit." I turned away from him to pour myself more water. I dragged out my drinking as long as I could, imagining how dry Butehamon's throat might be at that moment.

"So, you gave the scroll to the Chief Priest of Tjeni, correct?"

"Yes."

"Immediately, that is as soon as the Prince handed it to you?"

"Yes, without hesitation." Butehamon's right eyelid fluttered as he answered.

"Thank you for clearing this up. I will look into the matter, discreetly, of course," I murmured, as if to myself. Butehamon leaned back on his pillows again. But I had already asked the Chief Priest the day before and he remembered Butehamon arriving late in the day.

"There is yet another matter, one that is a bit more distressing. I assume you have heard about the ceremony that Ihy conducted recently?" I asked, looking again at Butehamon.

"Yes," he responded hesitantly. "The... the entire Court has buzzed about it."

"Yes, I imagine it made quite a stir. I heard it was very powerful."

"As did I," Butehamon volunteered. Meni, Kagemni and Meruka sat still, watching my performance.

"Please help me out here, for I am in need of more information. What have they been saying about it?" Butehamon looked at Kagemni, his eyes lifted as if to ask permission.

"You may speak freely," Kagemni instructed Butehamon. "We are all servants of the Prince." I noted then that Butehamon shifted his eyes downward.

"They... they say that his magic that night was very powerful, that it was as if he was a god... that he brought down wind and fire. He... they say that Hemamiya's death was due to his spell."

"It was," Meruka replied without thinking. I glanced at him severely.

"I agree with Meruka. And if Ihy had his way, I do believe Meni would be ill, if not dead, at this very moment," I added.

"What... what do you mean?" Butehamon asked.

"What I mean is this, Butehamon. It has come to my attention that Ihy made a wax figurine of Meni that was topped by his hair and that inside the figurine were clippings from his nails. Now, that appears to me to be unusual, for as you know Hemamiya and I have always been very careful to dispose of materials from his body for fear that someone might use them to perform dark magic. You are aware of that, right?"

By now Butehamon knew where my interrogation was heading and he hung his head, seemingly resigned. He nodded his head.

"The only way I know that his hair clippings could have been retrieved was if someone did so while we traveled on Mother Nile aboard your boat. Instead of throwing them overboard, someone pretended to do so, or switched someone else's hair for the Prince's."

"And another thing, Butehamon," I added, pacing back and forth in front of him. "The morning that we were all attacked in Kherdasakh... I keep playing that scene over and over in my mind. I ask myself over and over how it was that King W'ash knew exactly where we were on such short notice? It was a last minute decision to even go to Kherdasakh. And, when you dressed that morning, why was it that you wore your rank and insignia on your arm, even when we were trying to be unobtrusive? And... and when we were attacked, why was it that the Prince was singled out by their best warriors, while you, wearing your senior rank and insignia, were attacked by the two youngest soldiers, barely men themselves? Yet, despite that fact, the story that came back to the Royal court was exactly the opposite." I stopped and looked directly into Butehamon's eyes. "That intrigues me to a high degree," I said to him. "Is it possible to explain these events? I mean, explain them in a way that assures us of your allegiance? Is this possible, Butehamon, trusted guardian of the Prince of Upper Kem?"

There I stood, staring intently at Butehamon. He stared back at me, his left cheek twitching and the muscles in his face and neck taut with malice. Finally, as if transformed, he answered, his voice controlled, even restrained.

"You have no idea who... what you are dealing with, Anhotek. None of you! Ihy possesses magic that is beyond my understanding, beyond even yours, beyond this world. He…"

"Tell me, Butehamon, what did he promise you? Immense fortunes? Great power? Help me to understand what it takes to betray the sacred trust of the future King?"

"He will be no future King!" Butehamon shouted, jumping to his feet. Instantly, Kagemni and Meruka did the same. Kagemni drew his dagger from his leather scabbard, scattering the contents of a bowl of grapes as he did so. But Butehamon was too possessed by the poisons that infected him to even take notice. Meni, to my surprise, stayed seated.

"He is weak!" Butehamon shouted, pointing at Meni. "Look at him sitting there like a girl. He is infected by the shakes. He fancies himself a poet. It is Neter-Maat who has Scorpion's warrior ka inside him. He will be the next King and nothing you can do will prevent it!"

Suddenly, Kagemni charged Butehamon, his dagger drawn high, but Meruka quickly turned and spread his powerful arms around Kagemni's chest to block his charge. "I will kill him," Kagemni shouted as Meruka restrained him.

"Stop it!" Meni said forcefully, looking amused by the entire incident. Kagemni backed off.

"I pity you, Butehamon," Meni said simply, "for this is not about me and my weaknesses, nor is it about you and your fear of Ihy. This is about a man who pledges his loyalty, then violates that sacred trust. This cannot be tolerated. I will not tolerate it."

Meni turned to me. "Anhotek, am I within my rights to remedy this situation?"

My mind raced with a flood of contradictory impulses. "On the one hand, the security of the Royal court is at issue. Yet, the forces of chaos are stronger than I have ever seen in my lifetime. To act would be prudent, to not act shrewd. I will need to think more on this."

Meni considered my counsel for a moment, then turned to Kagemni. "Invite in your guards. Have him gagged." But before Kagemni could leave, Meni spoke. "Wait! You are sure, beyond a doubt, that these guards are trustworthy?"

"Absolutely, my Prince!" he said, still shaking with fury. "Unlike Butehamon, these men have fought by my side on the battlefield. I would run this dagger through my own heart if ever they sought to betray me!"

"Then bring them in," Meni said with authority. "As for you, Butehamon, I trusted you with my very life. You have deceived me for years, though we shared food and drink and shelter together... though we traveled together to far-off lands. You played the fool to Mersyankh's ambitions and twice nearly succeeded in killing me and casting all of Kem into chaos."

By now Butehamon was gagged and held by two of Kagemni's guards. "Bind him and take him away!" Meni commanded. Then he turned to Kagemni. "I choose prudence over shrewdness in this case, Kagemni, for we can have neither a traitor in our midst nor have him available to our enemies. Yet I dare not risk a public execution for his betrayal, wish though I could, for that would be the rightful lesson for all to see. I ask of you a difficult task. Have Butehamon meet with a tragic end... and his entire crew along with him... every one of them."

I was astonished at the ease with which Meni read the nuances of the current crisis, took command of it and how easily Kagemni transitioned to his leadership. He left Meni's quarters with Butehamon and his soldiers through the rear of the compound, the route guarded by his most trusted men.

Thus it was that two days later we received the tragic news that Butehamon and his entire crew drowned in an unfortunate boating accident during military training. Their swollen bodies, or what was left of them after the crocodiles had their fill, were found scattered downstream along the banks of Mother Nile. In a gesture that those within the Court believed to be a moving tribute, Butehamon and his crew were buried with military honors. Prince Meni presided over the rituals and gave a moving speech that acknowledged Butehamon's role throughout much of his childhood. A few suspected the truth of what had transpired, but Mersyankh, Ihy and Neter-Maat could say or do nothing without their own betrayals being made public.

The incident with Butehamon solved one problem, but created another. Sixty days had already passed between Scorpion's death and his burial, as was the custom. Soon the thirty additional days of grieving would also be over and it would be time for the new King to be crowned. Each day, Ihy could be seen leaving the compound to meet in secret with those handfuls that formed their cabal.

This forced my hand. In the week following Butehamon's death, I brought the Prince to the Temple of Min to have him circumcised and shaved, to ritually purify him in preparation for his coronation. While one priest restrained him around the chest, the Chief Priest knelt before Meni and cut his foreskin, saving it in a jar of resin so that he would be made whole again at death. Meni cried out only at the moment of the cut.

"Is the pain better today?" I asked Meni on the third morning after his circumcision. Several times each day I treated the incision with a concentrated liquid made from juniper berries, followed by an unguent to soothe the wound.

"It improves every day," he said casually. I noticed that he had a large papyrus scroll unrolled on the table in front of him. He had drawn two curving lines down the center. On each line he had drawn several circles and next to each he had inscribed a picture word.

"Come help me with this, Anhotek," he said, motioning me closer. I saw that he had drawn a map of Mother Nile, from Ta-Sety to The Great Green. The circles were the names of villages along the river that we had visited together or about which he had knowledge. "I only know of Dep in the marshlands of Lower Kem. Where would I place Ahnpet in relation to Dep?"

"Here, along the coast to the east," I said pointing to the approximate spot.

"And where exactly would Kherdasakh be?" he asked. This time I pointed to a spot to the south of where Mother Nile splits. Meni dipped his writing brush and drew a circle and named it. So we spent the next hour, naming all the villages I knew along Mother Nile, in the oases, and along the desert trading routes.

"You are worried about the recent attacks by the Ta-Tjehenus?" I asked him.

"That and the Lower Kemians... and the coronation... and I know not what else. Does it ever end?" he asked me.

"Only when your body is prepared for the final journey and perhaps not even then. Until that time, the work of a leader is never finished."

"Is it too late, then, to crown Neter-Maat the King of Upper Kem?" Meni asked wryly.

"If we were wiser that is probably what we would do. Then we could journey to Meruka's village in Ta-Sety to live the rest of our days in peace and contentment." I sighed.

"Just today Kagemni told me that Mersyankh sent messages to King W'ash. She probably presses him to attack our northern border. The Ta-Tjehenus are raiding our meager grain reserves and taking our people captive for slaves. I fear that if King W'ash's forces join them, Neter-Maat may yet be the next King."

"If King W'ash succeeds in conquering us, Neter-Maat would be lucky to be his sandal-bearer," I replied. "And do not think that Mersyankh does not know this. They may wish to place Neter-Maat on the throne, but they would never pray for King W'ash to conquer Upper Kem right now."

"I had not thought of it that way," Meni replied thoughtfully.

"It has always been thus, Meni, that when a King of Upper Kem dies, our enemies push against the edges of our land to gain territory. The Ta-Tjehenus seek to expand their own influence, to gain resources that we usually have in such abundance. When they do not fight us, they fight King W'ash. I do not believe we have to fear an alliance between the two."

Again, Meni considered what I had said. "Let us assume that what you say is true. What if we were to launch an army here, along Mother Nile's west bank and have them march to the oases? As they establish control, we also launch an armada of ships downriver. At the split, the armada divides into two, one sailing down this tributary here and the other down here. Then, all three armies form a pincer, like the claws of a beetle, all meeting here at Dep," he said, tapping his finger on the circle representing King Wash's seat of power. "What do you say to that?"

I sat back, staring at the map as he waited expectantly for my response. "And what would the purpose be of taking such an action?" I asked softly. He threw himself back in his chair and opened his eyes wide.

"What are you asking me, Anhotek? Is it not obvious? If we are successful, it would mean our warring would be over. We would control the marsh dwellers. We would finally achieve peace."

I stared at him hard, before speaking. "To conquer the marsh dwellers, and thus to unite all of Kem is a noble goal, one that has eluded every mortal King of Upper Kem. But if that is the goal of this exploit, then you should truly consider instead fleeing to Ta-Sety, or better yet, to Setjet, to live a simple life with your sweetheart. In your eagerness to prove yourself, do not be blinded by the same mistaken ambitions that drove your father.

"Hear me out, Meni. Your vision is to unite Upper and Lower Kem, yet to what purpose? Unification must be guided by more than war and peace. Boosting trade would also boost the people of Lower Kem and elevate them to the higher state of living that we enjoy in Upper Kem. A united Kem would control the critical trade routes that would allow us to sell our goods and import the luxuries that our ruling class so enjoys. That in turn employs our tradesmen and women to weave our finest linens, to cast our famous pottery, to craft our delicate gold jewelry."

"You are right," Meni responded, nodding his head vigorously. "I... I sometimes focus on one objective and do not think of the other options available to me."

"Oh, I would disagree with that. You have the ability to consider all manners of options. What you must depend on your advisors for are to bring you other undertakings to consider. Then you must create the priorities that will achieve each one in its rightful turn.

"In this case, I agree that unification must be accomplished first. But recognize that it will take enormous resources to maintain order over such a vast land. The forces of chaos will prevail unless you make the people content. Trade is one way to do this, but we must also provide other means to their contentment."

"Such as?"

"Such as building roads to improve their daily lives. Or building more granaries to store grains to be distributed during times of famine. And building temples with a network of priests that can resolve disputes, explain the King's laws and collect taxes."

For a long time Meni sat quietly. At one point he closed his eyes and I supposed from the fluttering behind his eyelids that he was comparing my suggestions to his own grand vision for Towi.

The rest of that day, Meni and I sat in deep conversation, punctuated at times by Meni or me writing notes or making lists. We discussed who we could trust to propel the vision forward and who we would need to watch carefully. The next day, too, we continued our discussions, this time focusing on the coronation ceremony, which I had begun to plan for the first day of the new moon, only two weeks hence, to keep Mersyankh off balance.

Despite Mersyankh and Ihy lurking as an unknown presence in our plans, those two weeks were a busy time, and for most of it my heart felt light. The tasks that the gods had placed upon my shoulders were a blessing in another way, too. They distracted me from one awful fact, one that otherwise would have been impossible for me to face at that sensitive time. In two weeks, Prince Meni, miraculously birthed under the wings of Horus, would be no more.

Truly, his succession as King would thrust upon us unimaginable burdens to make his vision for Towi come to life. It took all my powers of concentration to not become consumed by the many implications of his ascension. But, there would be one burden that would be lifted from my shoulders when the Chief Horus priest placed the White Crown upon his head, a burden that I almost always treasured, but at times resisted.

Now it would be up to the new King to write his own scrolls documenting his reign, telling his truth, as the words of the gods moved his heart and hand and brushes. In this one task, above all others, I knew he would excel, for I, Anhotek, Chief Scribe, father to the son I loved, had taught him well.

# Book II

# NARMER

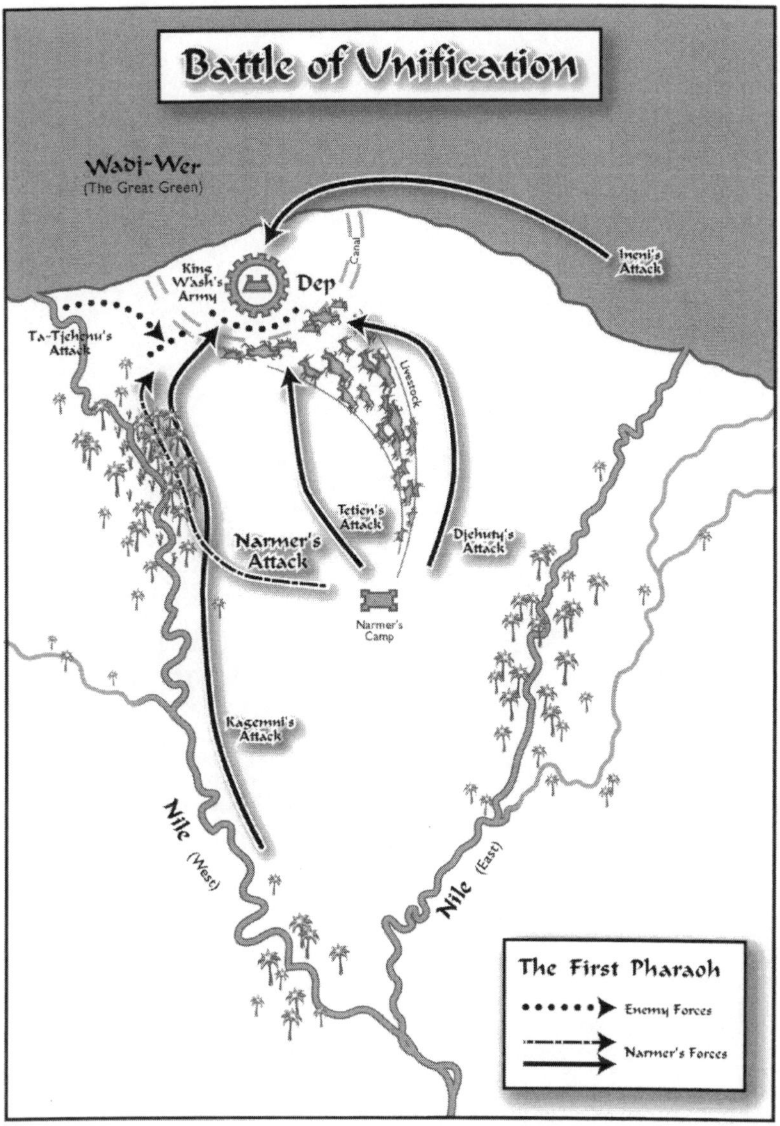
Battle of Unification
Wadj-Wer
(The Great Green)
Canal
King Wash's Army
Dep
Ineni's Attack
Ta-Tjehenu's Attack
Livestock
Tetien's Attack
Narmer's Attack
Djehuty's Attack
Narmer's Camp
Kagemni's Attack
Nile (West)
Nile (East)
The First Pharaoh
Enemy Forces
Narmer's Forces

# SCROLL THIRTEEN

## *Ascension*

A month had passed since the coronation. The palace was a beehive of activity and dear Anhotek the queen bee. He scurried about the manicured grounds, his limp more pronounced than ever, entertaining emissaries from foreign lands, planning with Kagemni and Kaipunesut, arranging meetings where my attendance would be helpful to advance trade or to approve a building project. I worried about him for he had recently celebrated his fiftieth birthday and his wrinkled, leathery skin and his paunch seemed to grow more pronounced by the month. His bald head made him appear even older.

The faint light from Ra's orb cast a pink glow in the eastern sky. Roosters crowed and donkeys brayed. This was the only time of the day when I could be assured of some quiet time to reflect and to write down on the holy papyrus parchment the truths my eyes had witnessed. Anhotek had advised me to take such time for myself, and I was glad to do so, for so much had occurred both before and since my coronation.

It had rained for an hour or two on each of the three

days before the coronation, a rarity for Upper Kem. Anhotek was concerned about it raining on the day of the coronation itself, for without a doubt that would have been a bad omen. Fortunately, Ra rose that day into a bright and cloudless sky.

The ceremony was held at the Temple of Horus in Nekhen, for that is the city of the falcon god and the home of the most powerful priesthood in all of Kem. The previous day Anhotek and the Chief Priest conducted a purification ceremony to prepare me for ascending to the throne. They anointed my shaved body with holy almond and sesame oils that were blessed by Horus, whose spiritual essence dwelled in his statue, hidden away in the temple's innermost sanctuary. The Chief Priest then crushed six seeds of the ben-ben tree and gave it to me steeped in hot water.

I had never before experienced the effects of the ben-ben seed, although I learned that day that the priests purify themselves with it prior to the Heriu-renpet celebrations for the New Year. Within the hour, the ben-ben seeds worked their foul magic and for the rest of the day I could not roam more than a few cubits from the latrine. So violent were my cramps and diarrhea, I worried that I might be forced to accept the crown of Upper Kem from the latrine. To be sure, there were some in Mersyankh's retinue who would have thought that seat a fitting throne for me.

But with Ra's blessing, instead I awoke feeling excellent and lively and was greeted by a most wondrous sight. The recent rains had caused the desert surrounding Nekhen to bloom with every manner of wildflower, some mixed among the low-lying green grasses of the savannah and others apparent in every valley and crevice of the desert foothills. In was as if the gods had sprinkled seeds everywhere and life birthed itself anew. White and purple, gold and blue comforted the eyes and impossibly sweet fragrances filled the air and pleased the nostrils. Everyone's spirits seemed buoyed.

Thankfully, Anhotek shielded me from many of the distractions related to the coronation. When he came to me that morning, he had already arranged its every detail, from the procession to the crowning. But not even Anhotek could have entirely prepared me for the spectacle that unfolded throughout the day.

After lining my eyes with kohl and painting my face with red and blue rouges, the priests dressed me in a newly woven pleated linen tunic, so fine and shear it felt like nothing touched my flesh. Anhotek then fitted me from head to toe with gold, lapis lazuli, turquoise, carnelian and other jewels. Even my sandals had gold thread woven through the reed sole plate and jewels were sewed into the thong pieces.

Peasants, traders, craftsmen, and the wealthy and powerful had come from all over Upper Kem for the coronation. Emissaries arrived from as far away as Ta-Sety and Babylon, as much to take full measure of me as an adversary as to honor my ascension to the throne. My tent was one of hundreds that were pitched on the rocky plateau overlooking Nekhen. An undulating blanket of people stretched deep into the desert, up the foothills and all along the green banks of Mother Nile. Nearly all were dressed in the white of purity and celebration, waving their arms and jostling for a better view. My first impression was that I beheld a field of white grasses swaying in the wind.

As I exited from the tent, the people began to shout my name, first a group near me, then others to the right or left or below us, until my name was no longer recognizable and instead became a steady noise that filled the ears completely. Wine and beer flowed freely, some provided by the Royal estates and some by the merchants who celebrated being soon able to transact business again.

Climbing onto my chair platform, I turned to face the crowds, crossing the crook and flail over my chest. A huge cheer erupted from the crowd. I sat on my chair and the procession to the temple began, led by fifty shaved priests, all dressed in the purest white linen. Behind them a large group of musicians played a lively processional, weaving melodic phrases from the lutes with trills by the flutists. Ten drummers kept the beat and behind them twenty or more dancers plied their craft, their sistras rattling suggestively with the provocative movements of their hips. The gossamer linen tunics they wore were so sheer they hid not a curve or feature of their most pleasing bodies.

I had always been inspired by the Temple of Horus, for it was truly a holy place, from which all legitimate kingly power derived. As a child I felt dwarfed by the huge Babylonian cedars that framed its entranceway, each greater in circumference than a full-grown man could wrap his arms around. Pennants now flew atop each of the four posts. Yet, as the procession approached the temple, the temple seemed far smaller than I remembered.

The double row of priests that had accompanied me split into two and now lined the entrance. At the head of the line, standing on the temple steps, was the Chief Priest. Anhotek walked by my side, accompanied as we were by a steady drum beat. The priests turned their backs to us and raised and lowered their hands to quiet the crowds that surrounded us. Soon, any noise we heard came only from the drums and the murmur of the distant onlookers.

"Whom do you bring with you, Anhotek, great Horus priest and Chief Counsel to the Royal family?" the Chief Priest ritually called to us as we stood before him.

"I bring Prince Meni, son of King Scorpion, to claim the throne of the Land of the Lotus," he said, standing erect and pointing his staff toward me.

"Because your hearts are light, Anhotek, you may bring Prince Meni to the innermost sanctuary, so that Horus alone may judge whether he is the rightful heir to the throne." The Chief Priest turned and walked inside the temple. Anhotek removed his sandals, but as I was about to do so, he stayed my hand. The assistant to the Chief Priest walked forward, knelt before me and removed each of my sandals. Then Anhotek and I followed just behind the Chief Priest. Behind us the assistant walked, carrying my sandals in one hand and a water bowl in the other.

The Chief Priest picked up an incense burner and waved it back and forth as we walked through the outer corridor. The puffs of smoke and sweet-smelling incense immediately brought to mind my childhood days, when Anhotek would place me in an incense tent to forestall my shakes, which by time I was fully grown had diminished in number.

The inner sanctuary was a large room, lit by candles. Incense burned from pots at the four corners of the room. Sand was sprinkled on the mud-brick floor and swept evenly, so that none may enter it save under the watchful eye of the Chief Priest. In the center of the room stood Horus, his gold falcon head sitting atop his human form. His bejeweled eyes looked down upon all who entered and I immediately felt a chill creep up my spine. Horus' manifestation filled me with awe and dread.

The assistant knelt again before me. He gently held my foot, placed it in his lap, washed and wiped it. Then he repeated the procedure on my other foot, stood and left with my sandals. The three of us then entered the sanctuary. A small fire burned in a brazier in front of Horus. Next to the brazier was a large stone altar, with various instruments set upon it.

"Horus, I bring before you Prince Meni, the heir of your servant, King Scorpion. The Prince brings you a holy sacrifice, that you may judge his fitness to become King."

The Chief Priest then called out to other assistants and he and Anhotek met them at the side entranceway amidst much commotion. In a moment the two of them walked in leading the temple's sacred bull, a huge black beast whose haunches reached to my shoulders. He had been groomed and purified with flax oil for the occasion and his hide shined to perfection. They solemnly walked it to the altar and placed its head into a copper yoke to keep it still. It was so docile, I knew at once that it had been given a special brew to sedate it and I pitied the poor animal's fate.

"Horus, guardian of Nekhen and the Kings of Upper Kem! Behold Prince Meni's ka in his holy bull incarnation. As he leaves this world, so too shall he be reborn as our new King!"

Anhotek handed me my sword and, lest I think too hard about the task and falter, I immediately brought the blade above my head and with all my strength I sliced cleanly through the beast's neck. He grunted as he fell with a thud upon the brick floor. Blood spattered everywhere and began to spurt in great rivulets from the animal's head and neck. Anhotek placed a basin on the floor under the head to catch as much blood as he could, while the Chief Priest immediately slit the beast's chest. He placed his arms into the carcass up to his shoulders and extracted the heart with a small ceremonial flint knife with an intricately carved ivory handle that had been commissioned for the coronation. The immense heart still beat strongly. He examined it carefully, smelling it and turning it over and over, his hands and robe now soaked in its crimson blood. He touched the tip of his tongue to a drop of blood on his finger.

"It is a strong heart," he said confidently, as he placed it into the gold basin that Anhotek held out to him. "It is perfect."

"I agree," Anhotek said, leaning over to examine it.

"Behold, Horus, Prince Meni is dead!" the Chief Priest exclaimed loudly, holding up the basin. "His heart is strong. His heart is pure. His heart is perfect. His heart is light. May our new King reign until he is aged beyond number. May he serve you proudly and bring credit to our people." He placed the basin on the altar, in front of the holy bull's head.

Anhotek stepped forward and, as he had instructed me to do, I kneeled before Horus. "Behold, Horus!" he called out in his priestly voice. "Here before you kneels the new King of Upper Kem, Land of the Lotus, greatest of the Two Lands. We dedicate his name to you for all eternity, for he shall bring credit to you and his people. Behold King Nar-mer!"

The name sounded strange, for once Anhotek and I had decided upon it, we had not mentioned it again for fear of Ihy casting a spell upon it. Until he called out my name, only the two of us knew what it would be. I had chosen Nar for the immense fighting catfish that lived within Mother Nile's womb, for if there was ever a symbol of my land, the giant, tenacious catfish was surely it.

Anhotek had chosen the name Mer, for to him the chisel

was a symbol of permanence, emblematic of the role given to me in my dreams by Horus himself, to carve the future of Kem. I was to be both the tool and the message.

Now the Chief Priest came close to me, so close that his mouth covered my nostrils. Seven times did he breathe out my name— Naaaaarrrrrmerrrr- and seven times did I breathe it in. My name filled me. With each breath I could feel it swirl into the spaces of my ba. Thus was I reborn as King Narmer, the catfish and the chisel.

Immediately, the two of them instructed me to remove my clothes and they cleansed me of the blood and dressed me again in fine linens. All my jewelry was removed, to be given as alms to the temple priests. Anhotek had commissioned even more exquisite jewelry to be crafted for the occasion, which he now placed upon my body. Once I was dressed, he turned to me solemnly.

"King Narmer, before you lays the challenge of leading your people along a just and difficult path. Take, then, the crook and flail and cross them over your chest as an oath to Horus." As I did so, he placed the White Crown of Upper Kem on my head. I remember clearly feeling the weight of the land upon me at that instant. In the space of a moment or two, images and fears passed through my heart, of Neter-Maat and Mersyankh, of Ihy and Butehamon, of Kagemni and our army, of the peasants and the merchants, of the Ta-Tjehenus and King W'ash's army in Lower Kem.

Anhotek immediately led me away from the inner sanctuary and out to the rear of the Temple, where the Chief Priest had just announced my rebirth to the crowds. When my eyes adjusted to Ra's disk, the sight overwhelmed me. Below me were tens upon tens of thousands of people. Upon seeing me they fell prostrate on the ground, even the Chief Priest and then Anhotek, the man who I cherished above all others. Not a sound could be heard for several minutes, except for the shuffling of the people, as if the waters of Mother Nile had been transformed into a human wave. My heart filled with love for my land and its people. I ached to have El-Or by my side.

Slowly, the Chief Priest stood and called out. "Praise

your King! Praise King Narmer!" The people below me stood and began to chant my name. Keeping my hands crossed on my chest, I turned purposefully this way and that to acknowledge their adoration. Then my eyes met those of Mersyankh and Neter-Maat and my blood ran cold as the water in Mother Nile's depths. Neither of them called out my name in praise, yet none would have seen that save me. Instead, they acknowledged my rule with stares of hatred. Behind those stares I saw not resignation, but tight-lipped defiance. And that, that above all, my heart still ponders at quiet morning times such as this.

My musings were interrupted by Apehty, one of my new servants, a priest from the Temple of Horus who was sworn to the allegiance of Anhotek. "I am sorry to bother you, King Narmer, but Kagemni is here. Shall I arrange for morning foods?"

"Yes," I said, snapping back from the despair that filled me when I thought of Mersyankh, Neter-Maat and Ihy. "Have Kagemni come in."

"King Narmer! Good morning!" Kagemni said as he entered, stopping to bow.

"Stop that!" I said to him. "I've told you before not to bow to me."

"Sorry, Narmer, but I need to keep in the habit of doing it or I will surely forget some time when some bastard dignitary is here. And how will that look?"

"It is of no consequence to me," I said. "What is the news from the border?"

"The situation with the cursed Ta-Tjehenus has worsened, the brazen swine! They raid our oases. King W'ash's soldiers raid the villages on our northern border. Yesterday I heard that last month they captured two villages and took many of our people as slaves."

"And the priests report that people are refusing to pay taxes," Anhotek said as he entered my quarters. "Good morning, King Narmer... Kagemni," he added, bowing slightly to each of us. "Matters are deteriorating quickly. We must do something."

"I agree," Kagemni added.

I knew inside me that they were right, that enough time had passed since Scorpion had died and that the forces of chaos tested my rule.

"Narmer, if I may speak of a sensitive issue?" Anhotek asked me. "With Kagemni here?"

"Of course you may," I replied "You two are my closest advisors."

"I understand that you have expressed the desire to send a messenger for El-Or and her family to… to make her your Queen. And you know that I… both Kagemni and I support that. However, it is my strong conviction that you should delay the marriage until after Inundation, so that you may clear up these military matters."

I sat for a moment absorbing his advice. "I… I know that your counsel is good… both of you. And it is true that I have been hoping to delay the war until after my marriage." I walked to the window. Below the palace, farmers were tending their crops. It was the end of planting and if we were to wage war, it would need to be now, during Proyet, although I dreaded marching and fighting if the war dragged out to the heat of Shomu.

"Alright," I said, suddenly feeling weary. "I will delay sending for El-Or so that we may begin planning for the excursion. Kagemni, I want your thoughts on logistics."

"Happily. I can have the army ready to leave in a few weeks."

"Not that fast!" I replied. "I want to plan the campaign first… in detail. Let us meet each day at this time for an hour or two. Once I feel confident of our battle strategies, you can plan the logistics in earnest."

The expression on Kagemni's face confirmed that he did not like having to undertake a lengthy planning process. Yet he did not object and he left to plan his recommendations for the next morning's meeting.

"How do the expansion plans proceed?" I asked Anhotek as soon as Kagemni left.

"More or less as we expected. Mersyankh acts as if we are killing her by the construction on the other side of the palace. Her servants have already begun to move into

Scorpion's old quarters. I imagine that being relegated to the older section is at the root of Mersyankh's objection. Still, we are making good progress. Your new quarters should be ready within a year's time."

"I am sure Kaipunesut will be relieved to have me away at war, to… to not have me looking over his shoulder every day."

"He is a loyal subject. He takes great pride in the expansion. The project puts people to work and speaks of abundance. Our people need that expression of… of confidence in the future."

Anhotek's reassurance pleased me. Throughout the next two ten-day cycles, Kagemni and I met every morning, sometimes with Anhotek, but as the days passed mostly without him. I interpreted this as a sign of his contentment with my views on mobilization and battle strategy. Kagemni, however, did not share Anhotek's confidence.

"Your position sounds fine… in principal," Kagemni said to me one day, speaking to me in that condescending tone that I hated. "But, in practice it will not work."

"But, how can you say that when you admit that you have never tried it!" I protested in frustration. "We have been through this argument again and again." I threw myself back in my chair and could only wonder about the bonds that he and Scorpion had forged in their battles to unite Upper Kem.

"Look, Narmer, I will do whatever you command." He also leaned back in his chair, his elbows on the armrests and his fingers crossed before his massive chest. "But, moving piss ant clay soldiers around is not the same as a real battle. You will never move groups of soldiers from here to there like some damned toys to… to fix your mistakes. Yes, warfare peaks the spirit and creates bonds between men that cannot be equaled. But battles are also terrible things, full of blood and spilled bowels and hacked limbs. It is full of uncertainty and… and terrible confusion. Your plan to lure them into charging our center is good, but when the enemy charge comes, it will not be as you think. Soldiers defecate on themselves as they run in panic, friends are hacked to pieces, heroes arise. You can only plan to a certain point, then a soldier's training and experience take over. Circumstances change by the minute and experienced soldiers can adapt, can... can turn setbacks into victory."

I remembered when I was a boy, Anhotek telling me that to be locked into a position without considering the consequences born of experience was a terrible flaw in one's character. He never needed to elaborate, for I saw that flaw each time I was in Scorpion's presence. Yet, I felt pulled by my own righteous convictions. This made me uneasy.

"You are right, Kagemni. My fighting experience is limited to the unfortunate event in Kherdasakh... hardly a battle in any soldier's eye. We will do as you suggest in this expedition, for I have much to learn about the conduct of war. However, I will now sit with your generals in the war council. I want to learn about provisioning and disciplining the army and all manner of details related to waging war." Kagemni visibly relaxed.

"But, I will also tell you that the very thought of killing other men who walk our own land as we do, who are fathers and sons like us... it disgusts me. Yet our enemies test us to the breaking point.

"I swear to you now, Kagemni, that this warring will stop, and the sooner the better. We will pursue this war without mercy, this I promise to you. I will put at your command every resource we have available, for without victory, without uniting our divided land we will never achieve our destiny. That is what I believe and that is what shall come to pass. This I swear as an oath to you, my trusted friend."

Kagemni stared at me, his mouth part open, taking full measure of my ba, and I believe that at that instant he did not find it lacking.

Thus the next month passed quickly, as affairs of state and training with my soldiers took all my time, such that I fell asleep each night, exhausted, but content. Yet, as the eve of our departure was upon us, and all of Tjeni buzzed with anticipation and all manner of rumor, I still felt an emptiness inside me. I missed El-Or.

As Ra set in the sky that very night, I wrote to her by candlelight, lamenting that our marriage would be delayed, but promising my love to none but her. Then, as if possessed by the spirit of Hathor, I wrote to her as follows:

> A year it is since I last saw you, my sister,
> And I am feeling ill.
> My limbs are heavy, I forget my body.
> If the shamans come, no remedies will cure me,
> Even the priests know not the cure.
> There is no name for my disease.
> Only your name can put me on my feet.
> The coming and going of our messengers
> Is what revives my heart.
>
> More beneficial to me than any remedies you are, my sister.
> More important are you to me than any medical papyrus.
> My salvation will be when you come here to Tjeni.
> When I see you, then I will feel well!
> When you open your eyes, my limbs feel alive again.
> When you speak, then I am strong.
> When we embrace, you drive away all evil from me.
> But, you have been gone for too long, my love.

With the rising of Ra's disk, we took off from Tjeni amidst great fanfare, blessings from the priests and the blowing of many rams' horns. More than two hundred and fifty ships were outfitted to carry five thousand men, and fifty more ships carried donkeys and supplies. Another four thousand men and their supply retinue would march along the west bank.

Wives and lovers cried and waved to the men as we set sail. Even Anhotek wept seeing me and Meruka leave. As we pushed away from shore he stood stooped slightly on the hill in front of the palace, his arms outstretched, making the hand gestures of blessing. This would be the first time in my life that I would be away from him for more than a few days.

Although Kagemni strenuously objected, I gave him charge of the four thousand land troops that were to consolidate the villages along the west bank, before striking off to the west to reclaim the Shedet oasis. I took command of the boats, since of the two of us I was far more comfortable on Mother Nile and also more knowledgeable of her moods, skills that by the gods' cruel joke I attributed to Butehamon's teaching. As a compromise, I agreed that Ineni, Kagemni's most trusted officer, would accompany me and be responsible for my safety. Despite the fact he had but one arm, the other having been amputated by Anhotek to save his life, he was a valiant warrior and had even learned to use his feet to good advantage in battle.

For the first few days of our journey, crowds lined the muddy shores in disbelief, for never in their lifetimes had they seen the King's army massed in such force. The boats took hours to pass a given spot and both children and adults cheered us on and wished us well. Using a detailed papyrus map that Anhotek and the priests of Nekhen and Tjeni had made for us, Kagemni and I had laid out the villages that required our attention. These we alternated, so that as the land army stopped and secured the allegiance of one village, the water-borne forces would leapfrog them and go to the next. So the entire first month passed with the only difficulties being the trial courts that I held at various places to punish spies or petty warlords who tried to coerce their villages into paying tribute for protection from the Ta-Tjehenus.

Another disturbing issue arose at each of the east bank villages that served as take off points for the desert trade routes to Setjet and Babylon. Traders spoke to me of the extortion they were required to pay for warlords to accompany them through parts of their journey. I knew I would need to deal with this issue once I returned from battle.

It is an odd thing commanding an army, although I did not think for a moment that the soldiers truly accepted me yet as their commander. They looked to Kagemni as their leader, as they had every practical right to do. Sometimes a lone soldier or even small groups of them, gazed toward me from adjoining boats with a strange look in their eyes. Did they question whether I was a true warrior like Scorpion? I, too, wondered if I was ready to lead men to their deaths in battle, but I knew that I had no choice in a matter that was heaved onto my shoulders by the gods.

At the end of the second month after leaving Tjeni, our entire army reached a tiny village on the east bank, opposite the oasis of Shedet. To this point we had not encountered any armed resistance. The war council suspected that spies had long ago warned of our approach and only the most foolhardy enemy would dare challenge us without an equal force. However, we were getting closer to the delta with each passing day and soon King W'ash and his Ta-Tjehenu allies would run out of room to hide.

We rested the armies for three days, time enough to also restock provisions. I agreed with Kagemni's request to distribute large rations of barley beer and wine and to allow the men to enjoy the services of those women who had accompanied the troops from Tjeni.

On the morning of the fourth day, Kagemni led his troops due west to Shedet, fully expecting trouble. The oasis lay in the middle of the desert, several hours march west of Mother Nile. Further west, beyond its lush green carpet of grasses and its life-giving lake, lay nothing but the destructive forces of the desert. After ten or more days of waterless travel, constantly chased by Anubis' minions, one reached the land of the Ta-Tjehenus, a miserable, barren land, according to Anhotek and the Chief Priest.

I stood on a hill overlooking Kagemni's army. Even as I watched, he split his forces into three units, to confront whatever opposition they might face. Once they emerged victorious, Kagemni and his troops were then to travel north to the delta, crossing the west tributary of Mother Nile at the shallows of Merimda. Once there, he would march straight on Dep, forming the western pincer in our battle strategy.

Although my troops could have rested several more

days before leaving, to allow Kagemni to complete his work, I instead commanded that we sail downriver, for I saw an opportunity to take corrective action to protect Wat-Hor, the Way of Horus, the most important trading route to the eastern lands. I had discussed this with no one beforehand, but I was determined this action was necessary as a symbol of my power to the people of Lower Kem and of the lands with which we traded. Wat-Hor was also the route that El-Or's family used most often in their travels to and from Kem.

In two days time we reached the lush water plains where Mother Nile splits into the five-forked tongue of a serpent. There we anchored. We were now deep into King W'ash's territory, yet we saw no sign of enemy soldiers. This worried my officers. I called for a meeting with Ineni and he drew his boat near and boarded mine.

"I am sending you and some men on a mission," I started to say, and his face reflected his surprise. "We must secure Wat-Hor from the thieves who prey on our traders. How many men will it take to secure it?"

"But... but I am pledged to your protection, Narmer. I gave my oath to Kagemni."

"It should not take long, Ineni. Ten days... a little longer at most. If Kagemni were present I feel certain he would agree with this strategy. Since we are here already, we should take advantage of the opportunity the gods present to us." Ineni was distressed.

"I take responsibility for this decision," I continued. "However, if it were Kagemni himself standing before me I would command him to do the same."

The following day, Ineni took five hundred soldiers with him, a mixture of spearmen, archers and swordsmen, and marched due east, there to follow the path of Wat-Hor to the very border of Setjet. He also carried messages with him destined for El-Or and Me'ka'el. With Ineni and his troops gone, we continued our sail northward.

No sooner had we entered the main eastern tributary than the differences between Upper and Lower Kem became noticeable. No longer did cliffs or high dunes encroach on Mother Nile. Suddenly the earth opened into a verdant sea of dark green grasses and lush trees. Birds flittered and chattered all around us, while hundreds of egrets and herons waded just beyond the reach of our boats. The eagles of the delta soared overhead, screaming to one another of our coming. That day we watched, spellbound, as a majestic male eagle swooped down in front of our boat, its reddish and black wings spread wide, its talons outstretched, and plucked from the water a perch the size of a grown man's forearm. As the men behind us cheered, Meruka said in a bold voice that this was a good omen.

Meruka later defended his interpretation by explaining that the eagle sees far, so that the omen bode well for a future day, not that one. As it was, the cheers we had heard behind us were not for the eagle's exploits, but shouts to action. From both sides of the river, groups of enemy archers suddenly stood up and loosed their deadly arrows on several of the boats. Before our soldiers could react, the enemy disappeared into the cursed grasses from where they had sprung. As I considered what to do I thought of Kagemni and my clay soldiers.

One man lay dead on the deck of a nearby boat with an arrow pierced through his eye, his hands still grasping the shaft. Twelve other soldiers lay wounded, several seriously. One older soldier looked straight into my eyes and grimaced as he broke off the shaft of the arrow that was lodged between his ribs, knowing that attempting to pull out the barbed head would have been far worse than leaving it in and risking a slow death from pustulence.

So it was that we had our first experience with King W'ash's army, although it was far from the last. Before another ten day cycle passed, I would have my first taste of battlefield war. For the unspeakable horrors inflicted upon us, and for those we wrought upon our enemies, I would later pray to Horus with all my being that it would also be my last.

# SCROLL FOURTEEN

## *Unification*

Nothing stirred, save the men swatting the infernal mosquitoes that beset us night and day. Every man was covered with red welts and oozing sores where they had scratched their skin to shreds. Many of those sores festered with all manner of afflictions and Meruka and his assistants worked from the moment they awoke until they fell onto their blankets at night applying unguents to heal our soldiers and creating potions to ward off these demons.

Rumors began to circulate that these black clouds were sent by the evil magicians of Lower Kem. Another said that the mosquitoes were the bits of skin that came off when the serpent Apep scratched himself in the underworld. Our very conversations were reduced to a few words, squeezed in between hand-waving to keep them away, slaps to one's body in hopes of killing one, rubbing them out of our eyes, and every manner of curse. Even the act of breathing often became one of inhaling and then spitting out these vile creatures.

Since I had no experience in battle, I felt it important to set an example through my behavior. That did not come easy. It was but a few months ago that I was still able to complain to Anhotek and receive his sympathetic ear. Now I had to bear mosquitoes and vermin, leeches and pains of the body silently. I felt the loss of what once was and will never be again.

At the moment we stood on a hummock of soil overlooking the dry plain leading to Dep, for the land of Lower Kem is flat and marshy as far as the eye can see and there are no purchases one can use to gain a fair overview of the land. This situation had been used by King W'ash's soldiers to their advantage for the past seven days. Whenever we turned a bend in the meandering tributary, or stopped for a respite from the heat and dew, the enemy unexpectedly arose from the rushes or from behind palm trees and rained their arrows upon us. To counter their strategy, we abandoned several boats and assigned the soldiers to walk along the banks to protect the rest of our convoy. This also slowed us to a crawl, since the soldiers had to slog through the serpent-infested wetlands to make headway.

After only a few hours patrolling the banks, often wading through water up to their waists, the men became fatigued and we were forced to swap troops. During the second day of watching our slow progress from my boat, I jumped into the water myself, amidst great cheers from soldiers in the adjoining boats. Immediately, my Guard jumped in after me. We took our turn on patrol and I still recall the feeling of stepping off firm ground into Mother Nile's mucky silt, the fertile mud oozing through my toes as I tried to gain enough footing to push myself forward. In an hour, I was exhausted. That night, I issued an order that the men on patrol were to have extra rations and beer and I wandered our encampments, sharing in the feelings of camaraderie.

On the third day of these maneuvers, just as we were in the process of transferring patrols, a series of war cries suddenly erupted just after the first group of boats passed a constriction in the river. From thick stands of reeds on either bank, archers with reeds bound to their bodies to better camouflage themselves, stood suddenly to launch their cursed arrows. As our men tried to protect themselves from the volley, the enemy spearmen charged and threw their missiles. Amidst the confusion, and before my officers could send in reinforcements, the enemy slaughtered twenty-two of our men in the space of a few minutes, some of them hacked to death. It was the first time we had met King W'ash's soldiers in hand-to-hand combat and, although we killed many of the attackers, we gained respect for their battle skills that dreadful day.

The incident also made me question my decision to send Ineni to secure the Wat-Hor. Having five hundred extra soldiers in these circumstances would not have mattered, but Ineni and one hundred of his hand-picked infantrymen, along with a similar number under Kagemni's command, had been training for the past year in hand-to-hand combat using many of the techniques of Anhotek's martial arts discipline. Kagemni named this unit the King's Guard.

In this matter Meruka's counsel was invaluable, for the Ta-Setys often engaged in tribal warfare that used small bands of men in close fighting. Meruka's technique with his dagger and the small leather shield he wore strapped to his left arm was without equal. However, Ineni had taken fully half of those trained troops with him and I feared facing W'ash's soldiers without them. I was also beginning to appreciate Kagemni's admonitions regarding the difference between theory and practice in war. When theory breaks down due to the harsh and ever-shifting light of the battlefield, only experience and training can illuminate new paths.

And so, insect-bitten and weary in spirit, my officers stood with me to finalize the strategy for our assault on the walled city of Dep, which lay in the distance. Squinting to keep the insects out of our eyes, we could not discern any obvious fortifications or assembly of troops. But we also knew that our ability to detect their deception was poor, indeed. For days now, we had sent our scouts north to determine where W'ash's troops were massed and west to obtain knowledge of Kagemni's whereabouts, but so far we had no information on either.

For another seven days we waited for word from Kagemni, time the men used to rest and replenish our stores. I walked among my soldiers every day, talking with them, training with them, even helping Meruka administer his potions. By now he had developed a potent and foul-smelling mixture that would keep the mosquitoes from biting and his assistants were kept busy mixing enough of it to pass among the men. I had refused to use it until enough was produced for each man. This one action gained the respect of all the soldiers, so that when I joined small groups in the evening for beer, I was warmly welcomed. In the space of six days, sitting around many fires until late in the night, I learned more about the everyday trials of my countrymen than I had for all my previous life.

On the evening of the seventh day, a messenger arrived telling us of Kagemni's victory over the Ta-Tjehenus in Shedet. Their resistance was lighter than expected, in all no more than a few hundred men. Kagemni's pincer strategy had worked well and the men in his King's Guard quickly punched through the enemy line and doubled back to surround the enemy. Once in Kagemni's stranglehold, the enemy surrendered and Kagemni took many for slaves.

Kagemni's plan to cross Mother Nile at Merimda and march on foot to Dep from the west was thwarted by the same marshy conditions we had faced. So, he sent his soldiers both upriver and down to commandeer as many boats as possible and then sailed down the westernmost tributary. They rested just a day's march from us, southwest of Dep.

With Kagemni's army now in position, we hastily convened our war council and finalized our plans. When all was set that night, I dispatched two messengers back to Kagemni advising him to be ready to march three days hence. And so, as Ra's disk rose in the east on the third day, our army moved out to begin the assault on King W'ash's stronghold.

My forces were divided into two. The main force of

four thousand soldiers moved out across the lush farmland. Under our feet, the black mud of Mother Nile was soft and fertile, yet thankfully sturdy enough to support both men and supply donkeys. Farmers, warned of our approach, hastily left their plows and thousands of cattle and goats in their fields. Our soldiers felt ill at ease in this strange land and we warily advanced in two columns, each with four men across.

The remaining soldiers still under my command I divided into five expeditionary forces of one hundred men each. These units I sent ahead and to the left and right of us to scout enemy troops and to defend our flanks. The expeditionary forces were further divided into ten units, each one lead by a soldier of the King's Guard. The Guards wore a leather breastplate and were armed with dagger and sword. A replica of Meruka's small leather shield was strapped onto their arms. We had, however, improved upon the design of the shield by affixing a round copper plate in its center, with the picture-writing of my name, the catfish and chisel, etched into it.

When Ra had just begun his descent in the sky, a messenger raced back across the field we were crossing to advise us that King W'ash's forces were massed outside the city's walls, prepared to stop our advance. He estimated that no more than five thousand soldiers protected the southern, eastern and western parts of the village, but that they occupied the strategic high ground upon which the city was built. The northern flank was protected by the waters of The Great Green.

Taking the counsel of Tetien and Djehuty, Kagemni's most senior generals, we made camp for the night and sent messengers to Kagemni to do the same. They returned soon to inform us that Kagemni's army was but an hour's run to our west. I instructed the priests to slaughter and butcher one cow for each twenty-five men and that night we feasted as we would have before a festival.

Kagemni would rally his troops prior to the battle, a talent that made his men follow him even unto their deaths. With a pang in my heart, I realized that I had never learned this skill from him or Anhotek. That oversight now plagued me.

I slept fitfully that night, beleaguered by the wretched insects, but also by the realization that my dreams for Kem now stood balanced on the knife-edge of a single battle. Yet, I also believed that Horus would not have given me such a responsibility without the measures to fulfill them.

The next morning I assembled the officers from each of the units of archers, spearmen, swordsmen and pages and walked with them away from our troops, to a point where we could see the assembled forces of King W'ash in the far distance. The smoke from their fires formed a haze that blew upon the breezes of Wadj-Wer to our encampment. With my officers forming a half-circle around me, I paced along their line and gazed long into each man's eyes. Only a few were younger than me. Many were easily twice my age of eighteen years. A peacefulness settled into my ba. I saw a measure of myself, my own fears and the exquisite excitement of battle fever, reflected in their eyes.

"You men... you good and worthy soldiers of Upper Kem, hear me out!" I called out to them in a strong voice. "Each of you has heard of my birth under the wings of Horus. And from Kagemni's own lips you have heard how Horus delivered me up from the desert on the disk of Ra. Yet I would be lying to you now if I did not tell you that I fear the battle ahead, for we fear what we do not know and most of you... no, every one of you has more experience in battle than do I."

By now the men were trying to keep their eyes on me, but they strained to see if the reaction of their fellow soldiers to my candid words was the same as their own. "I am your King and I know that you would loyally follow my orders, even unto your death. And surely, before this day is over, some of you will pass from this world to the next. Yet, I will tell you this. Through my holy shakes the gods themselves talk to me and show me great visions. They have revealed to me the glorious day when the Two Lands are united into one mighty nation. Think of it! One land stretching from Wadj-Wer, near which we now stand, all the way to Ta-Sety... and perhaps beyond." My gaze swept the men again and I could sense their excitement.

"To each of you I make this oath. That I will fight side-by-side with you in this battle as fiercely as the gods will allow me," I said, pulling my dagger from its sheath and holding it out. "All I ask is that you do the same and together we shall emerge victorious. If you die valiantly in battle, I shall grant you a warrior's funeral and a mastaba filled with all you will need in the next world.

"But, if you emerge from battle alive... ah, then you will have grand rewards... rewards befitting men who will be the leaders of a united Kem, for from among my officers... from among you loyal soldiers will I select men of strong ba who will help make these swamp-dwellers proper subjects of Upper Kem!"

The men stood speechless, for never had they heard of rewards extending beyond rations and plunder. Now they saw how their efforts could bring pride and riches to their families.

"Rally your troops, then!" I yelled and also withdrew my sword from its sheath and held it high. "Lead them with valor! Bring pride to your name and your land!"

Every man withdrew his sword and also held it high. "Praise Narmer!" one of the men shouted, waving his sword. "Praise Narmer!" Soon each of the officers yelled the same. I dismissed them and they ran back to their troops, eager to proceed.

I lingered for a moment, dagger in one hand, sword in the other, looking across the plain at W'ash's forces. In the distance five thousand of his soldiers stood poised to resist our advance, to cut us down like stalks of emmer wheat in order to protect their homes and farms, their wives and children. If ever I felt weak in my resolve, doubtful of the gift that the gods had placed onto my shoulders, this was the moment. With a sadness in my heart, I turned to walk back to my army.

As I descended the hummock of land, a mighty cheer rose up from the army. Every man raised his dagger or sword, spear or bow, mace or ax to the sky. "Praise

Narmer!" they screamed and their shouts filled my heart with strength. I held my weapons high above my head and turning to my officers I instructed them to begin the march on Dep.

For an hour we marched under Ra's burning disk, each passing minute bringing the city of Dep and our enemy more clearly into view. They were staged in dense groups on a gently rising plain upon the top of which the tall mudbrick walls of Dep could be seen. Messengers ran continuously from the front to the rear, bringing me details of the troop concentrations and their weaponry, which Tetien and I factored into our plans. In the far distance, to our left we could see Kagemni's men advancing in similar fashion. We were now so close, we could smell the smoke from their campfires and the pungent sweat of an army of men carried on the humid, salty breezes coming from Wadj-Wer.

I ordered our army to halt and called for Haankhef, my most trusted messenger, my oldest and best friend from Tjeni who was but two years younger than I. He had sailed with me and Anhotek on several occasions and was one of only a few friends that could defeat me in my favorite game of Senet. I instructed him to deliver a message to King W'ash himself, and no one else, offering him attractive terms if he were to surrender. Under the protection of my pennant, Haankhef removed his sword and ran steadily toward the enemy camp.

As we waited for King W'ash's response, Tetien and Djehuty ordered the men to rearrange themselves in their battle units, two major groupings representing the center and eastern flanks, while Kagemni took care of the west. Within each grouping, the bulk of the soldiers were infantrymen, employing swords, daggers, axes and maces.

Each infantry group was flanked by two units of archers, consisting of at least one hundred men each. Spearmen marched at the head of the infantry columns, while immediately behind them were the swordsmen, then the King's Guard. Thirty of the King's Guards were assigned to no other purpose than my protection and they took up their positions around me.

As the units assumed their final form, a group of eight priests from the temple in Dep appeared in the distance, walking down the rolling hill from the city. Four of them carried a small wooden, curtained bier, while the others carried poles that flew pennants with King W'ash's symbol. They shook with fear as they approached to within one hundred cubits of our troops, then hastily lay down the bier and ran back whence they had come, holding their robes up high to scurry faster.

I asked Meruka to investigate the contents of the bier and within a few minutes he returned to me in disgust to report that it contained the head of Haankhef. I felt as if an enemy's dagger had pierced my heart. I could not imagine Haankhef dead, his fair smile no longer fortifying me, our arms never to be wrapped around each other as we walked and swapped stories of our inflated exploits with women.

Worse still, Meruka reported that Haankhef's private organ lay before his head, the foulest of insults. Without all his body parts Haankhef's would wander for all eternity without reaching the afterlife. No clearer message could have been sent by the gods for what it was I must do.

I stormed to the front of the troops, incensed. "Look!" I yelled out, pulling aside the curtain, but unable to bear the pain of gazing upon Haankhef's sweet face myself. "Look, all of you good soldiers of Upper Kem... at what King W'ash thinks of you!" Some of my officers in the front lines who knew Haankhef gasped.

"King W'ash is a swine! He has insulted the gods themselves by using his sacred priests to bear such a foul message. He alone will bear the costs of such depravity. Together, men! Together let us take Dep and unite all the people of Kem under Horus, the falcon god!" A huge cheer rose up from the army and the officers rushed toward their units. In a moment we marched off, the raging anger of the soldiers barely restrained by their training and discipline. As they passed me, they saluted and cheered and raised their swords or spears in tribute. I answered by holding my sword high, but in truth I did not even remember what I had just said. Instead I felt a heavy weight on my heart and wished nothing more at that instant than to be able to collapse into Anhotek's arms. My King's Guard caught up with me and surrounded me and together we marched toward the enemy.

A dozen or more messengers walked along behind my Guard, waiting to relay battle instructions to the various field commanders. Behind them a large group of priests from the Temples of Horus led a pack of donkeys. Many of the priests were also shamans and had been trained by Anhotek and Meruka in the treatment of battle wounds. Behind them, hundreds of donkeys carried goatskins filled with water and bags full of breads and honey.

The two infantry groups split further and further apart, the eastern flank, led by Djehuty now several hundred cubits ahead of the center. To our left, Kagemni's army was also ahead of us. I sent a message to the commanders and the archers ran forward to assume their positions at the flanks of each group. If I were one of King W'ash's soldiers, I thought at that moment, I would be wetting myself in fear at the terrifying display our army presented. The archers stood, tense with readiness. Next the spearmen took positions between the archers, ready to charge once the volley of arrows was loosed. Behind them the swordsmen, axmen and mace troops stood, most of them protected by leather and copper shields.

A silence settled over the masses of men, a silence so thick and fraught with the egg of chaos it cannot be described justly, but can only be acknowledged with silent nods by those who have experienced its awfulness. Men barely breathed. My throat felt so dry I could not even swallow. The front line soldiers stared intensely at the enemy, who like them stared back, creating invisible yet powerful threads that the gods would soon yank together to weave the tapestry of our futures.

My senior officers looked toward me, as I stood staring toward the enemy masses and I prayed that my own men would not notice my knees trembling. I raised my sword slowly into the air. Every officer stared at me from every recess of the field. I quickly brought my sword to the ground.

The air around me chattered with the sound of wooden arrows tapping against their rests, followed by the twang of the nocks against the goat gut strings. Then a moment of silence as the archers drew back their weapons and aimed. Then the whistling of the bows as six hundred arrows pierced the air. Then the sound of the arrows pounding off enemy shields. And, finally, the sound of enemy soldiers screaming in agony as arrows penetrated their flesh, all in the space it took the archers to reload their bows.

Immediately, the archers let loose their second volley and simultaneously our spearmen charged across the remaining one hundred cubits to assault the enemy along three fronts. Their fierce battle cries pierced the air and the enemy slowly stood to repel their advance. Suddenly, as if in a nightmare, dozens of our men began disappearing from view, yet not a single arrow had yet been loosed, not a single sword yet drawn by King W'ash's men.

Tetien grabbed my shoulder and focused my attention on an irrigation canal that ran around the perimeter of the village, but several hundred cubits away from it. The enemy had cunningly disguised it with bundles of tall rushes and mats of grasses. In the eagerness of our infantry to prove their mettle, dozens ran heedlessly into the ditch. We watched, helpless, as the water frothed with fury. King W'ash's men had filled the canal with crocodiles and they feasted savagely on our hapless soldiers, fighting with each other to tear mercilessly at their victims' flailing limbs. Those few soldiers who tried to scamper out of the ditch were cut down quickly by the enemy's arrows and spears. In a few minutes the charge was over. More than a hundred men were lost, most torn to pieces by the savage crocodiles. A great cheer arose from the enemy and they banged their shields with the butts of their swords as they laughed and mocked our attempt.

My heart fell to my feet and I felt all color drain from my face. I looked to see my clay soldiers suddenly wearing confused expressions, silently pleading to me with their eyes to pick them up, to reconfigure them in smart rows, to pronounce my cunning strategy that would triumph over the enemy with no further bloodshed. As I watched my childhood games fade into a desert mirage, our archers saw the futility of their volleys and gradually desisted. The infantry saw no immediate way over the canal and so retreated in confusion under a rain of enemy arrows, cursing their fortune and their short-sighted leaders. The unit commanders looked to their officers for guidance.

In minutes a runner from Kagemni's command arrived with a message for Tetien. He listened to the boy, then turned to me while raising his hands to summon two of his officers. When they arrived, he spoke hurriedly. "Kagemni suggests we form teams to bring all the reed boats in our fleets to the canal and fill it with them. Then we may be able to cross atop them." The officers thought for a moment and nodded in agreement.

"It will not work," I said. "They will see what we are attempting before we are able to dump many boats in. They will surely pick off our men and set fire to the boats. That will demoralize our men even further. It is too risky.

"However, Kagemni's suggestion offers another option. Think on this, Tetien." I began to explain my tactic and he and his officers grew more excited as together we refined it. In a few minutes we sent a messenger back to Kagemni with our plan.

Two units of infantrymen ran back toward our landing area and began to move toward our position the immense herds of cattle and goats we had passed. Kagemni's men did the same. Soon, thousands of cattle were being driven forward by our soldiers, more and more soldiers joining the chase as they caught on to our plan. They ran the ill-fated beasts with shouts and the pointed ends of their spears until, one by one and in small groups, the animals fell off the canal embankment into the water, mooing and bleating in terror. Some goats tried to jump over the canal, but none made it. Our archers stood on the embankment, taking turns shooting the helpless animals and protecting their comrades from the enemy's archers. The water again boiled with the frenzy of crocodiles, only now the water was solid crimson.

From where I stood I could see the enemy pointing to our efforts in fear. In a few hours, with the supply of livestock exhausted and the shallow canal filled nearly to the top, I ordered that as many of our supply donkeys be killed as would be needed to fill any gaps.

By time this was accomplished, two supply pages ran up to advise me of the status of the next part of our plan. Tetien had counseled all the unit commanders on what they would be expected to do. As they regrouped their soldiers, I instructed the pages to bring forward their creations.

The masts of dozens of the smaller boats had been pulled and sawed into one cubit lengths. These were quickly lashed onto the masts of the taller boats, forming rungs, so that nearly sixty ladders were thus quickly built to lay across the canal. Many of the ladders were wrapped in dried reeds or rawhide laces or burlap to create a bridge that we could cross.

The enemy was ill prepared for the sheer number of crossings we had prepared. When I gave the signal to advance, only twelve units marched to the canal with their bridges plainly in view. Quickly King W'ash dispatched entire units to focus their defense on those vulnerable crossings. As the men were about to lay down the bridges, others of our units ran forward and placed bridges thirty cubits apart. Tetien and I could see confusion take hold of the enemy. At my command, all bridges went down at once and a swarm of men began crossing under the protective rain of arrows from our archers. Tetien left my side to be with his troops as they fought for control of the center.

At first the enemy fought fiercely, cutting down our brave soldiers with their arrows and spears. Hundreds of men on both sides of the canal lay dead or wounded, their pitiful cries mixed with the rallying shouts of battle. But once the King's Guard raced across the canal in the second wave of attack, slashing with their swords and fighting man to man, we could see the enemy's resistance begin to fail.

On the eastern flank of the battle, Djehuty had pushed

the enemy back nearly to Dep. Rather than continue forward, he turned his units to the left and fought to penetrate the enemy's center from the flank.

On the western flank, Kagemni's unit made steady progress against W'ash's soldiers. My attention was drawn to a ram's horn that blew a series of three short bursts from a parapet on the wall that ran around Dep. Suddenly, the enemy facing Kagemni's men moved to reinforce the center columns which were fighting Djehuty's flanking maneuver. Despite the hideous scenes that confronted me, I smiled at W'ash's miscalculation of Kagemni's troops. He would soon flank them from the west and decimate W'ash's men.

True to my expectation, I watched Kagemni raise his sword and rally his troops. The enemy fell back and toward the center and soon a thousand of Kagemni's infantry were in hot pursuit, the sweet taste of victory on their lips.

How fleeting are the gifts of the gods when men make assumptions about their intentions. No sooner had Kagemni turned toward the east when another series of blasts from the ram's horn pierced the battlefield. Kagemni's men could never have known what was happening, for they were descending a hill, mowing down the enemy with their swords and axes and maces. Suddenly, from the west, a terrible series of war cries filled the air. A horde of Ta-Tjehenus, two thousand or more strong, descended from their hiding place in the northwest. At the same time, more men poured forth from within Dep itself. Kagemni's men were completely surrounded.

There was no time to debate what actions were needed. I called to my Guard troops and together with the three hundred infantrymen they commanded and that we had held in reserve, we ran across the field at full speed to assist Kagemni. Once across the bridges we cut to the west, stepping over the hacked bodies of my fallen countrymen. The smell of battle enveloped us, a thick, overpowering, foul stew of body odors and sweat born of fear, of urine and the rank stench of disemboweled corpses.

I overcame the urge to gag by spitting upon the ground, then instructed the senior officer to take two hundred men and reinforce the center column, while I took with me ten of the King's Guard and the one hundred infantrymen they commanded. Together we sprinted to the west to outflank the Ta-Tjehenus, who were pouring onto the battlefield.

We ran along the bank of the western branch of Mother Nile, slashing with our swords at branches and the grasses and rushes that sought to slow us. The air was so hot and humid I was already feeling the effects of our run. The commotion we made attracted the attention of a Ta-Tjehenu tribal leader and he ran with a group of his men to meet our advance. They were dressed alike in black tunics and some wore silver breastplates. Every man had his face painted with black stripes, to instill fear in their opponents.

In seconds, they were upon us, slashing at us with the curved swords for which they were known. They came at us so quickly, the soldiers of the King's Guard who were still assigned to protect me were not even close to my position. I heard a terrible war cry to my right and a long shadow crossed mine. I turned to see a Ta-Tjehenu attacking me directly, clicking his tongue as he screamed and charged.

I remembered Kagemni's admonition never to look into your enemy's eyes, lest in that momentary connection you waver for even a second. The Ta-Tjehenu lifted his sword high while still a few steps from me and without hesitation brought it down upon my neck. I stood my ground until the last possible moment, then turned, stuck out my foot and tripped him. The tip of his sword stuck into the soft ground where I had stood and as he tripped, the blade turned face up and he fell upon it, slitting his own belly. His war cry suddenly changed to a pitiful wail as he rolled off the blade to see his entrails fall from the bloody gash. He clutched at them, as if to undo the damage that would soon send him to the afterworld, then looked into my eyes before collapsing, face first, onto the ground. The stench from his unformed feces assaulting my nostrils made me feel like I would vomit.

I turned again to my right to see one of my infantrymen pointing a dagger in front of him to fend off an enemy soldier. The enemy advanced slowly, sword drawn, determined to make his kill. As he drew his sword back to thrust it, I slashed at his exposed neck, and his half-severed head rolled sideways onto his shoulder as he instantly collapsed. My infantryman looked at me with much reverence, since he had briefly tasted the bitter waters of Anubis' river.

In those first few minutes of engagement we had decimated the enemy, with only a few of our men sustaining minor wounds. When I looked around I saw the unmistakable figure of Meruka, his twisted locks pasted to his head from sweat and dust, running his sword through the clan leader. I knew not that he was even with the troops I had quickly assembled, but I felt thankful that he had followed me.

"Meruka!" I yelled above the din of battle that still raged only a hundred or so cubits from us. He turned and held his sword high when he saw that I was of one piece, then ran to my side.

"You have done well, my King," he said, breathless from battle. "The men…

"It will all be for nothing if we do not come to Kagemni's aide," I said, cutting him off and looking for high ground from which I could assess our army's fortunes. "These Ta-Tjehenus are like wild beasts."

Meruka dropped his sword and scurried up a tall palm tree that stood at the edge of the battlefield. As we waited, my troops assembled near the tree, and the unit commanders surveyed their losses. In a few moments Meruka clamored down.

"The Ta-Tjehenus are pressing Kagemni's army from the west, not more than two hundred cubits ahead of us," he said pointing to my right. "W'ash's soldiers are attacking from the north. Kagemni's and Tetien's forces are squeezed together. Djehuty is in heated battle on the east flank. He is cut off from Kagemni and Tetien."

Meruka's eyes told me that the situation was not favorable. I looked toward the King's Guard, all of whom were blood-stained from battle. Some wore leather breastplates that had already been cut by the enemy's swords. Young pages ran amongst them with water skins.

"Pinhasy!" I called to the head of my guard. "Gather the wounded together here. Place ten infantrymen here to guard them. Leave two pages to serve them. But, if any have breastplates in good condition, swap them with those whose breastplates have been damaged. Be quick about it!"

As soon as Pinhasy was done and I had quaffed half a skin of water myself, I addressed our small band. "We go now to help our brothers," I called out so that my voice would carry over the din. "We attack from the flank and so carry the element of surprise. We will attack in two columns of six across, with my guard in the center, just as we have trained." I looked around, catching the eyes of as many men as I could.

"This is the battle that will truly test your good name. Before Horus, all I ask is that you fight hard and valiantly. If we must die, let it be as warriors, so that our families whisper our names in tribute for all time. We fight together for the glory of Kem!" I turned and raced to the edge of the field. Quickly the columns formed around me, the spearmen in the front and outermost layers. Twenty-five of my Guard still lived to fight and they surrounded me. Meruka was on my left side and Pinhasy on my right.

In front of us the battlefield was littered with the contorted bodies of the dead, with men screaming in pain from their gaping wounds, with a Ta-Tjehenu sitting on his haunches, silently holding his leg that had been severed below the knee, with limbs and torsos and heads, as if the gods had scattered them as seed to grow new crops of warriors and all that was needed was to have the farmers plow them under.

"Give them the command!" I said, awarding that honor to Pinhasy.

"In Horus' name, charge!" he screamed and with that we quickly dived into the currents of chaos that swirled around us. In less than a minute we had reached the outer flanks of the Ta-Tjehenu enemy. By the time they even realized our presence, it was too late. Our spearmen ran through dozens of them while their backs were still turned. The swordsmen plunged into the fray while the spearmen pulled their weapons from their victims or instead abandoned them and drew their daggers.

As our infantry engaged the enemy, it slowly exposed my King's Guard to the action. I stood ready to fight, but each time an enemy soldier charged us, Pinhasy or Meruka would strike him down. I turned this way and that, constantly on alert for attackers. Just then a group of fifty or more of King W'ash's men rushed from the village to attack us.

"Watch to the north, men!" I shouted. "Pinhasy, we must gain the high ground or be condemned to the swamp-dwellers controlling the battle!" We braced for the enemy's arrival, but all the while I scanned the battlefield for a clear path to the village. A group of men stood on the roof of a building inside the wall and shouted orders below.

In the fever of battle time itself stretches to the limits. So does the ability of the body to persevere despite lack of food or water. Yet the senses of the body are heightened to threats made upon it. So it was that although I was distracted by my search for a way to the summit of the hill, I initially ignored a spearman coming straight for me. Pinhasy and Meruka were crossing swords with the enemy. At the last moment I felt a shadow block Ra's rays and turned to see an enemy soldier take the spear back along his side, just before thrusting its serrated, ivory tip into my gut.

With the spear tip only two finger-widths from my gut, I whipped myself sideways to my left and vigorously thrust the point of his spear away from me with my shield. But, it was too late to avoid completely. I felt the searing pain of the blade rip through my side and glance off my rib. The enemy soldier was well trained and held tight to his spear. That was his undoing, for my pivoting maneuver threw him off balance. As he twisted to his right, I ran through his sternum with my sword, thrusting it cleanly into his heart. He died instantly.

I reached for my side to stem the flow of blood, but immediately an enemy swordsman rushed me. Unlike the Ta-Tjehenu, he approached warily, circling to my right, attempting to compromise my maneuvers, for he had just seen me strike with my right hand. As he approached close to my body, he turned fully around and swung his sword viciously, holding fast to the hilt with both hands, aiming at my neck.

I ducked his blow and as I lunged at him I tossed the hilt of my sword from my right to my left hand and thrust it through his abdomen. At first he did not know what had happened to him, but then he dropped his sword and grabbed for his midsection. He stood on his toes and grabbed tight onto my sword, as if by keeping it from moving he could bear the pain and live thus forever. Instead, I forcefully withdrew it. But his nearly severed fingers were of no concern to him now, for his eyes that had locked tightly onto mine told me he had begun his journey to the afterworld. He fell to his knees and began to choke on his own blood before falling on his face.

My maneuver caused the wound in my side to open up further and when I grabbed it, I felt clumps of dirt and sand inside. I looked around for a bandage I could cut from the tunic of a dead warrior, when I saw Meruka engaged with sword and dagger with two infantrymen. They sweated and grunted as they hacked at him fearlessly, but with no finesse. They were less than a cubit from me and I ran my sword through the ribs of the one closest to me. His companion made the mistake of taking his eyes off Meruka to watch his comrade fall amidst the sounds of air sucking through his severed lung. In a flash, Meruka slit his throat with his dagger.

"The high ground!" I shouted to him. "Follow me!"

"Wait!" he protested, staring at my bloody side. But I was already off. Over the war cries and moans of agony from the wounded, he yelled for Pinhasy and the remainder of my Guard. As I ran forward I caught the familiar movements of a figure to my right. Kagemni fought bravely, perhaps a dozen cubits away. We had thinned much of the force of the Ta-Tjehenu and Kagemni's men were now engaged mostly with King W'ash's soldiers.

My King's Guard troops fought to form a line on either side of me. We engaged bitterly for an hour, gaining a cubit here, then losing it, before gaining it again. The land, once a barley farm, now lay trampled, stained red with the blood of its people and ours. At one point, as I fought with an enemy even younger than me, I slipped on a severed hand, one that still gripped its mace, bits of skull now baked onto its shiny black surface.

We were now so close to the summit, I could see and hear the men on the parapet who called orders to the officers below. One portly man wore a long white tunic and had a long, bushy beard. I assumed from the descriptions I had heard from Mersyankh's own lips that it was King W'ash himself and at that moment I did not hate the man, but saw him simply as he was, a man determined to defend his people, even though he could have prevented this very battle. The resistance of his forces was weakening in front of us but on the eastern flank Djehuty's troops were being moved back toward the canal. Yet nothing would be gained by going to his aid so long as King W'ash controlled the vantage points. Despite our desperate thirst and weariness, we fought on. My limbs and back ached and every swing of my sword now took conscious effort, so fatigued were my arms from fighting and killing.

With no more than forty cubits to go before we reached the walls of the city, the ram's horn sounded again. I looked up to clearly see the young page who blew it, but he blew looking away from the battlefield, toward the interior of the walls of the city itself. A feeling of foreboding crept into me.

The gates to the village opened slightly and from inside poured forth a multitude of soldiers, swords drawn. From where they came I knew not, for Tetien and I had estimated that we had already counted more than eight thousand enemy soldiers by time I left with the King's Guard to join the battle. It was clear that King W'ash had placed his fate, and that of all Lower Kem, in the outcome of this one battle and we, so haughty in our opinion of our superiority, had misjudged his strength and cunning.

My wound and exertions had me close to collapsing. I could not imagine how the older soldiers must have felt then, seeing King Wash's reinforcements pour into battle. Perhaps experienced soldiers learn to pace themselves better in combat. If so, I knew not how, for when an enemy advances toward you with the sole determination to lop off your head, I know not how to respond except with all your cunning, skills and strength.

Yet, here we were, facing an onslaught of fresh soldiers. In that instant I called to mind Anhotek's training, his prompts to act, not think, to enter a space that allows the god-spirit to flow, to relax the muscles and not be deceived by the pain messages of the body. At once, the noise of battle that so irritated my nerves became like the rushing of Mother Nile through its grasses. The men that flew through the gates of Dep transformed into patterns of color and light that dance and swirl upon the ripples of its waters. I breathed in deeply and assumed the defensive position that had been ingrained in me by Anhotek. Suddenly, my sword became light and I could no longer feel the numbness in my fingers from clenching tight to its hilt, nor the intense pain of my battle wound.

As I awaited the enemy's arrival, I heard the horns of Ra himself blare in the sky and I knew that if I were to die then it would be in the altogether peaceful state that I now found myself in. I only wished the same would be true for Kagemni and Meruka and for all my loyal soldiers of Upper Kem who were to meet the same fate, until we met again in the afterlife. In that state, I never did see or feel the enemy descend upon us. Like drops of dye in a bowl of water, I watched them sink toward us, then swirl back amongst themselves in curlicues and dissipate. And then, it was over.

# SCROLL FIFTEEN

## *The Palette*

"Why are we still dealing with these nomes?" I asked. Anhotek sighed in frustration. I had just moved into the elaborate new section of the palace and stood by the large portico in my quarters that overlooked Mother Nile. Below me, farmers moved along their fields of emmer wheat, barley and flax, swinging their serrated-blade scythes to and fro in a rhythmic motion. Behind them their wives and children gathered the wheat and stood them in sheaves to dry.

"In another lifetime I would like to be a farmer," I said, turning to Anhotek. This morning he looked particularly old. His tunic hung on him in an unsightly manner, his cheeks sagged and pillows had formed beneath his weary eyes.

"The nomes are important, Narmer, particularly the ones governing Lower Kem. This system will strengthen your rule, so that you will not need to continuously fight battles to keep the Two Lands under your command."

"I know, I know!" I said, altogether impatiently. As I turned to sit down, the scar in my left side, where I had been speared during the battle of Dep, tugged at my insides. I winced in pain.

"Does it still bother you?" Anhotek asked in his fatherly voice.

"It is nothing," I answered, waving my hand dismissively. "It just pulls every so often."

"Do you…"

"Do I rub in the oil and honey twice a day, as you instructed me to do?" I filled in for him, laughing. "What does the esteemed Anhotek think?"

"I think you are impertinent, you always were impertinent and you will die impertinent!" he grumbled. "That is what old Anhotek thinks."

"Then let us move on. Who do you suggest for this… which nome are we talking about?"

"The territory that includes Dep itself. It is very strategic. The governor will need to keep rebellions suppressed and he will also need to establish strong trade relations with Upper Kem and with the lands to the east. The army there will need to be in constant readiness to repel raids from the Ta-Tjehenus."

"May they be cursed for all eternity!" I spit out, laying my hand on the scar. "I would rather we devote attention to wiping them from the face of the land!"

Anhotek half-closed his eyes and breathed in deeply and just watching him do so made feel my imbalance. "I am sorry," I said softly. "Go on."

"I suggest that Kagemni be appointed to govern the nome surrounding Dep. No one could hold that territory better than could he," Anhotek said.

"I am surprised that you would suggest him for such a post," I countered. "He is much too valuable to me to have him so far away."

"He is also getting older, Narmer. He is but ten years younger than I. He deserves to live out his years in relative ease."

"Of course he has earned that… and more. It is that I cannot spare him at the moment. I depend too much on his military advice. Perhaps in a few years. But, even then, I cannot imagine that he would want to be put out to chew his cud. That would not be Kagemni."

Anhotek picked up the papyrus scroll that lay before him and scanned his list of names. "Who, then, would you suggest?"

"I would prefer to appoint Ineni to the post," I said.

"Ineni!" Anhotek said, smiling broadly. "Old, one-armed Ineni. He is not even on the list. Narmer, you never stop surprising me!"

"So, you disagree?" I said, although I wish the words had not come out sounding so laced with disappointment.

"No! To the contrary, I think it a wise choice. I like Ineni immensely and... and I trust him to the highest degree, as does Kagemni. But he has no administrative experience."

"Ah, you have never commanded an army, dear teacher. It is not children's play. Ineni has led his men well. That takes great skill in governing. And forget not that every soldier of Upper Kem owes his life to his actions on that fateful day in Dep... even I."

Anhotek fidgeted in his seat. "What, you think I exaggerate?" I said standing up before him. "You have heard grand descriptions of our battle last year, Anhotek, but I have never told you of this detail before. You will know why I would place in Ineni's hands, over all others, the fate of Lower Kem.

"We were so eager that day, so full of vitality and hope... our plans so carefully laid, our forces apparently so overwhelming. Yet, when our men ran into the cunning of King W'ash at the canal, it was as if the gods had sucked out every breath of wind from a mighty sailing ship. Yet we overcame that obstacle thanks to the cunning of Kagemni and..."

"And yours, too," Anhotek interrupted. "All talk of your capable decisions regarding running the cattle into the canal."

"Yes, and my cunning, too," I agreed. "Then came the deception of the Ta-Tjehenus. And even then we were able to rally our men and overcome their surprise attack to our western flank." I turned to the open portico again, taking in the tranquil scene, while the smells of death and the images of destruction that faced me that fateful day flooded my mind.

"Ra's disk had begun to settle when we fought to the very walls of Dep. King W'ash's strategy of holding men in reserve to demoralize us was cunning, indeed. I remember rays of light dancing before my eyes and at that moment I thought... I thought of you," I said turning to Anhotek. "Yes, even until this very moment I did not recall what it was that calmed me. But, that was it... I thought of us meditating in the eastern desert together and... and a calmness infused my ka and time itself seemed to halt. I no longer heard the sounds of the battlefield.

"Oh, I was weary at that moment, Anhotek, standing there in front of those walls. My body and heart were heavy. But when I entered the meditation, my ka lightened. I watched as King W'ash's soldiers streamed from the gate. Then I heard the ram's horn blaring and I imagined it to be the horn of Ra, it sounded so distant. W'ash's men seemed to stop and then they turned around, back toward Dep's gates. They never raised their swords against us, as if Horus himself had intervened on our behalves.

"Then I saw the soldiers around me begin to cheer and chase the enemy and slay them, as I collapsed to my knees. Meruka picked me up. From around the walls of Dep came Ineni and three hundred of his men, but they were rested and well trained. It turned the winds of battle to our favor and from then on through the night we routed King W'ash and his entire army. We crushed the Ta-Tjehenus." I sat down next to Anhotek, nearly out of breath from retelling the story.

"That is a wondrous tale," Anhotek said, patting my hand with his gnarled fingers. "I have always told you that you would be protected by Horus' wings, Meni." My heart skipped a beat at Anhotek's use of my birth name.

"It indeed was the work of Horus, for how was Ineni to know that he should return to us by sailing from Ahnpet to Dep?"

"Well, he had completed the task you set for him of protecting the Wat-Hor. An excellent decision on your part, I might add."

"Yes, he had done well, although I wish he had left only one hundred men to continue to guard it, rather than two hundred. But, what made him decide to return to us by boats? He is an infantryman, not a sailor. Even he has been unable to tell me what possessed him to do so."

"Whatever it was, it gave our army the element of surprise."

"Oh, indeed it did! They never suspected that we would attack from Wadj-Wer. It was inconceivable. With their backs turned, the King's Guard troops under Ineni's command scaled the walls of Dep and the remainder of his troops reinforced our eastern and western flanks. It was a delightful sight when they appeared. It lifted us all up!"

Anhotek and I sat together quietly and I thought back over the past year since the battle of Dep and all that had transpired since. My ka felt full.

"What is next?" I asked.

"There is not much time left this morning, for the emissary from Babylon is here to reaffirm his country's warm relations with us. Today I will report to you on what Kaipunesut and I have planned in terms of trade and supply routes within Kem and from Kem to the lands east and south of us. We must decide about taxes, for as we speak the harvest takes place."

"The crops appear more abundant this year," I said, pointing to the wide swath of black land below us.

"Thanks be to the gods for that!" Anhotek said, holding his hands open toward the heavens. "Since the crops have yielded well, tax revenues will increase this year. I suggest we build a series of large grain storage facilities throughout the land, so that we can distribute from the stores during times of famine. This would be a boon to the people."

"Yes… yes, of course," I responded. "That is a good idea. Make it so, Anhotek." He nodded and made a few scratches with his pen on the papyrus scroll.

"And one last decree I will need before we discuss trade routes. When I traveled to Nekhen back when… when we had the trouble with Ihy and Mersyankh casting spells, I felt it… how shall I say this?… prudent to insure the loyalty of the priests of the Temple of Horus. So, I promised them that after you ascended to the throne you would do some grand things for the Temple… and for Nekhen itself."

"Such as what?" I asked, curious that Anhotek would not have mentioned this to me before.

"I promised to enlarge the Temple, to… to relocate it actually to a larger complex within the town. And, if you will allow me…" he said, reaching for a scroll that lay next to his chair, "here is a drawing that Kaipunesut sketched for the new compound." He unrolled the document before me.

"This is not an enlarged Temple," I said. "It is a city!"

"No, no, no! This is the city of Nekhen," Anhotek remarked casually, grabbing another scroll and unrolling it before me. I stared and stared but the sketch made little sense to my eyes.

"Perhaps you are in error, Anhotek, for Nekhen is most certainly not a walled city!" I remarked, looking up. It was not until my gaze fell upon the sheepish look on his face that his scheme began to unfold. The sly mother fox was testing his kit. I leaned back in my chair.

"Explain this to me, Anhotek, my teacher, for you surely have lessons for me still hidden in your tunic regarding deception." I swear that in my entire lifetime I had never seen Anhotek blush, but he turned a dark crimson then. He opened his mouth as if to speak, to explain away his actions and I wish I had enough willpower to have kept a straight face. Instead, I burst out laughing.

He stood up, indignant and gathered his scrolls as if to leave. "Sit! Sit back down, you sly desert fox!" I said, trying to compose myself. But every time I became serious, even the slightest glance at him caused me to lose my control once again. He sat there as if a spear was stuck up his rear.

"Can we afford such an indulgence?" I was finally able to ask in a serious manner.

"Yes," he replied stiffly, not looking at me.

"And this will mortar our relations with Nekhen and with the Horus priests throughout Kem?"

"Nekhen is Horus' birthplace. It is the source of power for every King of Upper Kem. Since the time the gods walked the earth, the Temple of Nekhen has legitimized every King's rule. For that reason alone it is worthy of expansion. But, there were other reasons for my commitment."

"And what would those reasons be?" I asked. I knew he would not volunteer that information. I had learned my obstinacy from him, Kagemni once scolded me.

"I had to plant the seeds so that your vision might blossom when you ascended to the throne. The Horus priests are the most powerful in Kem. They are the most numerous of all the sects. They can be found throughout the land. Your rule over a united Kem will require an entire class of priests, a group we could use to best advantage."

"Use, as in spying for us?"

"That, yes, but more than that. Kaipunesut and I have been developing plans for a special priestly group about which I shall report to you at a later date. But for now, think of the Horus priests as extending your ears throughout Kem and even beyond. They can be a way to check on the accuracy of the reports from the governors of each of the nomes. They are all literate and could write marriage contracts or agreements between merchants. They could resolve petty disputes. Upon your order, they could distribute grain reserves and collect grain taxes."

Everything Anhotek said was true, but left unsaid was the fact that he, as both a Horus priest and my Vizier, would clearly control the sect with his generosity in my name. Yet I could not begrudge him that. In truth, whatever Anhotek did, he did for my benefit and for that of our beloved Towi.

"Is that what these buildings are?" I asked, pointing to the scroll that outlined the Temple complex.

"Yes, these here are the granaries. Over here is an administrative building, to be used for Royal purposes, such as when you visit Nekhen and hold court. And here, in the center of it all, is the new Temple of Horus." Anhotek seemed pleased with the plans.

"Will the other sects expect the same treatment?"

Now it was Anhotek's turn to lean back in his seat. "Vision has genius to it, Narmer. Visions are bold. But they cannot move a people forward without tangible accomplishments. Ideas alone do not persuade the masses. The people will follow the vision of a leader only if they see that vision embodied in their everyday lives. Better irrigation systems mean more food in their stomachs. New and protected trade routes mean more jewelry on their necks.

"I leave later today to travel to Nekhen," Anhotek continued. "How would you have me deal with this?"

"Make the project in Nekhen happen," I said. I detected the trace of a smile on Anhotek's lips.

"And now one final matter," Anhotek said, rolling up his scrolls as he spoke. As I have said before, the thickest walls of a palace are more porous than burlap when it comes to keeping secrets."

"Ah, I know that well by now, my good teacher. And so what have the trained ears of your spies uncovered this time?" Anhotek leaned forward and lowered his voice.

"One of my best placed spies informed me of a conversation that she overheard between Mersyankh and Ihy. It is... sad. I suppose that is the best word I can use for it."

"Sad is not a word I would easily apply to Mersyankh's actions. Evil would be more like it." Anhotek grunted.

"It is wise to remember, Narmer, that evil is nearly always defined by the most self-righteous among us. And I, for one, would rather confront evil eye-to-eye than have to deal with it through the stench of the self-righteous." I was struck by my mentor's brutal candor.

"Stench? Well, it is also wise to remember, my revered teacher, that you speak to the King of the Two Lands!" I tried to keep a straight face.

"What I see before me is a man whose soiled swaddling cloths I changed!" I could no longer contain myself and we both laughed heartily.

"So, what is so sad about your spy's observation?" I continued as we regained our composure.

"Apparently, Ihy was delivering a message to Mersyankh from a cousin in Lower Kem, who counseled her to be patient within our Royal Court."

"Oh, yes. A strong suit of hers, no doubt," I said, sarcastically.

"Nonetheless, she was enraged and became quite agitated toward Ihy, who was only the messenger. She complained about not having chosen this lot for herself, and that is certainly true, Narmer. Scorpion's death and the subsequent events were surely not in her plans."

"Not in her plans until Neter-Maat was named heir to the throne," I quickly corrected.

"That may be true, but there is more to this story. At this point, she lamented their fate at the hands of the gods and wondered aloud at why they were being so tested."

"So tested?" I again interrupted. Anhotek sighed and leaned back in his seat.

"From our position, Narmer, your vision for Towi is right and hers obviously flawed, but a wise leader must look at the situation from his adversary's perspective, too. To Mersyankh, the correct path for Towi was to be united, too, but under King W'ash rule. With her limited powers here, she is confused about how best to proceed, perhaps even frightened by the choices she faces. A year ago, she had unlimited power nearly in her grasp.

"Yet it is the next part of her conversation with Ihy that bears scrutiny, for if there is ever a future opportunity to form an unholy alliance with that woman it would be well to bear the following in mind. She began to cry then, according to my spy. She wrung her hands and wept. Her words truly were ones of a mother seeking the best for her son, her only child."

"You suggest that behind that mut's face there lives a loving mother? Please, Anhotek, take pity or I shall heave up my midday meal." I said, disgusted.

"If you learn nothing else from me, my dear son, know this, that the day you doubt even the basest woman's capacity to defend her nest from those who threaten it, that is the day that you would do best to surrender your throne." I pondered Anhotek's animated words.

"And one more thing," Anhotek added, pointing at me. "Mersyankh sobbed aloud to Ihy about Neter-Maat's limited abilities, of his shortcomings in intelligence, which of course she blamed on Scorpion's ba. That is a sad thing, indeed, for a mother to feel about her son. I cannot imagine how painful that must be to her."

"You almost sound sorry for her," I said, surprised.

"Oh, sorrow is too simple a word, Narmer. If a lion in your menagerie was gored by a water buffalo you might pity the noble animal's fate, but you would hardly embrace it to lessen its pain. Mersyankh's ka is surely deeply wounded, but that only serves to motivate her more when she feels threatened. Her ba compels her to strike out at such times like a venomous viper. That is her nature. It is good for a leader to understand such wounds, in hopes of controlling such an adversary in a time of crisis, but to also be on guard against the strike."

I could not doubt Anhotek's counsel, but I knew I would need to understand better how to use such information to the benefit of my rule. I felt certain that even now Anhotek was making a note to himself to pursue such lessons with me.

"And Ihy?"

"What of him?" Anhotek asked, looking up.

"Are there lessons we can learn about him?"

"Ihy is my problem but, yes, there are lessons I have and continue to learn from him… many, in fact." Anhotek gripped his staff tightly, placed his elbows on his knees and looked down, his brow furrowed in thought.

"Ihy is a powerful shaman and in his rightful place his powers would be magnified. Yet, his fate brought him here. My heart aches for him, for he serves a difficult master with his dark arts, all the while shielding himself from the light that Meruka and I and the Horus priests serve. If you cannot serve Ra, you must serve the serpent Apep, and the cost of that service is dear." The pained expression on Anhotek's face at first surprised me, but as I thought about it, I understood the respect Anhotek had for worthy opponents.

"Ihy is a loyal servant, and I admire him in this. His fate is cast and none but the gods know where that will lead, yet he shoulders his burden without complaint." We talked for a few moments more before Anhotek left.

With Anhotek and Meruka gone to Nekhen, I had several pleasurable days to indulge in re-reading El-Or's letters to me and in imagining our future days together. Her words elevated my spirits, but also made me miss her all the more. It was as if her ka had illuminated her loving thoughts onto the papyrus and when I read them they warmed my heart.

> I found you, my beloved.
> My heart was exceedingly happy.
> We said to each other, 'I shall never leave you.
> My hand is in your hand.
> I walk with you.
> My heart is with you in all the lovely places.'
> You have placed me foremost among all the women of your land.
> And I know that you shall never break my heart.

Yet other of her passages made me laugh, for although El-Or was smart enough to have learned how to write our picture words quickly, she sometimes used them awkwardly. Such it was when she wrote:

> When your hand is in my hand,
> my body trembles with joy.
> My heart is exalted,
> because we have the runs together.

I hoped that she instead meant that her heart was exalted

because we walked together.

In twenty days, Anhotek and Meruka returned from Nekhen, having left Kaipunesut there to continue work on the various projects. During the time they were gone I had received various emissaries and had continued my habit of meeting regularly with Kagemni. Our main concern with our army since the battle of Dep was in reinforcing their numbers. In all we lost three thousand men that fateful day, whether through their death on the battlefield or through the infections that ravaged their bodies in the days and weeks that followed, despite the efforts of the healers that Anhotek and Meruka had personally trained. Another one thousand and six hundred men had lost limbs as a result of the battle, so that we lost nearly half the entire force that left Tjeni that bright and hopeful day.

Despite the losses, recruiting efforts were going well, in no small measure due to the honors we bestowed on those who had sacrificed themselves on the plains of Dep. Throughout the land, elaborate funerals took place and at Kagemni's suggestion, and with Anhotek's approval, I decreed that the rations of the men who had been killed would continue to be dispensed to their families for a year. Of those who lost limbs, Kagemni retained nearly one hundred to train new recruits, while more than double that number were now employed in the Royal workshops. An even larger group served as supervisors on the Royal agricultural estate outside Tjeni. Anhotek also made arrangements with the priests of the Temples of Horus to employ some of these men in various temple tasks.

The day after Anhotek and Meruka returned from Nekhen, Meruka arrived early in the morning in my chambers. I was shocked at his appearance.

"What... what have you done to your hair!" I shouted to him from across the room. Every vestige of hair on his head had been shaved clean and his head anointed with flax oil. It shone brightly in Ra's light.

"I will explain in a moment," he said smiling.

"Anhotek put you up to it, did he not?" I asked, looking around to see if Anhotek was hiding until the two of them saw my reaction.

"He is not feeling well," Meruka responded. "The journey was filled with many activities. He is tired and his head hurts from the travels. He has asked me to brief you."

The day was a beautiful one, like most days in our fair land. The sky was a deep blue and a few thin, wispy clouds could be seen in the far east. By now half the fields were stripped of their crops.

"I worry about him," I confided in Meruka. "He is aging."

"We all age, Narmer. Our beloved Anhotek approaches the setting of his years," Meruka said matter-of-factly.

"How... how can you say that with so little feeling?" I asked.

Meruka looked at me questioningly. "I have deep feelings for Anhotek, but to you he is a father and the bond between father and son runs deepest of all. The soul only borrows the body for a short time. After death it moves on to another body. Anhotek's spirit is strong. I will surely see it again in this world after he passes."

Meruka's words brought him comfort. But on nights when I was alone, I found it painful to think of future days without Anhotek by my side. It was one thing to be King and to have people follow your commands. It was another to have the surety of wisdom that propelled those commands. Although I would hardly admit it to others, I often waited until Anhotek spoke before making a decision.

"And what of your visit to Nekhen?" I asked.

"Before I describe that, on the voyage back to Tjeni, Anhotek made mention of your herbs. Is your supply still plentiful?"

"I noticed this morning that it is lower than usual. Anhotek usually replenishes it well before this."

"I have heard stories of people outgrowing the shakes. But, with Anhotek so busy, I will replenish the jars in the next day or two, just to be safe. Do you have enough to last that long?" I nodded.

"Anhotek also mentioned that you have not been sleeping as well in recent months. Do you take extra herbs on such days?"

"Not usually. I just..."

"You have grown much in the past year, Narmer. We considered increasing your herbs for that reason alone. But when you do not get enough sleep and the responsibilities and worries of being King do not relent, you must take more herbs. I will talk with Anhotek about that today and we will make a decision." I knew it was no use complaining to Meruka of how tired the herbs made me feel, nor mention how many times recently I had missed taking a dose, to no ill effect.

"That will be fine," I said. "Now tell me of your trip to Nekhen... and who robbed you of your hair locks."

"We... I was given a big surprise," Meruka said, rubbing his bald head. "No sooner had we arrived then Anhotek took me to the Temple of Horus and they made me a Horus priest. I... I still do not know what to make of it."

"That is a great honor!" I exclaimed. "I have never heard of a foreign-born becoming a Horus priest. You are well respected in Kem, Meruka."

"I do not feel worthy of such an honor," he said, distraught.

"Do you feel that Anhotek felt any more worthy when your father made him a shaman of your tribe?"

"Perhaps not. I... I think that sometimes we grow into a role for which we are destined. You are right. I have served Kem for many years. I have learned much from Anhotek. It may be time for me to embrace this new role." But neither of us spoke of why Anhotek would have chosen this time to raise Meruka's status.

"In any event, the shaved head is very becoming. It makes you look more... more priestly."

"Hmmm," he groaned.

"And were the priests pleased with the plans for the Temple and the city?" I asked, reaching over to pick some grapes from a bowl. Meruka eagerly took a bunch when I passed the bowl to him.

"They were very happy," Meruka said, smiling. "Kaipunesut's plans made their eyes shine." I laughed, thinking of the pleasure giving such a gift would have been to Anhotek. We sat together, munching on grapes, bread and honey.

"Anhotek also wished me to tell you that we commissioned Meri-ib to carve a special palette to commemorate your victory over Lower Kem."

"Who is Meri-ib?" I asked.

"Anhotek considers him the finest stonemason in all of Kem. I have seen his works and they are exquisite. Very finely detailed."

"And this palette?"

"It will be a large ceremonial palette. Anhotek desires to circulate it among the temples in Upper and Lower Kem for a year, then put it on display in the courtyard of the Temple of Horus in Nekhen. Kaipunesut, Anhotek, Kagemni and I have worked on its design for several months now. Here, I brought with me the sketches that Kaipunesut has drawn." Meruka opened two scrolls and laid them out on the table before me.

"It is drawn in its actual size," he added. The palette itself seemed to be nearly the shape of the delta. The drawings contained so many detailed scenes, Meruka sat silently as I absorbed its content.

"These are amazing drawings!" I said, looking up at Meruka. "It... it appears to tell the entire story of the battle of Dep."

On the top section of each side the picture words of my name were carved in the center, the catfish and below it the chisel. On the reverse side of the palette I was depicted wearing the crown of Upper Kem, holding an upraised mace in one hand and the hair of King W'ash in the other, about to smite him.

"But I never use a mace and W'ash was dead when we found him," I protested. "And he was a great deal fatter."

"I was there with you when we found him," Meruka reminded me. "The meaning is symbolic of your victory. You see, here above W'ash's head is Horus in his falcon form grasping the symbol for the land of the papyrus and the head of W'ash in his talon. That shows that the falcon

King of Upper Kem has dominion over Lower Kem and its people.

"And each of the papyrus stalks represents a thousand fallen enemy. That is a clever statement," I noted. Meruka appeared excited that I was catching on.

"Right here, above the slain Ta-Tjehenus, I should like Kagemni's symbol to appear to honor him for his contributions."

Meruka smiled. "It shall be so," he said.

On the front side of the palette I stood triumphant, holding a mace and the ceremonial flail. I wore the crown of Lower Kem. "Is this Anhotek who walks in front of me?" I asked.

"Yes, and in front of him your trusted officers and officials who are now governors of the nomes."

"That is good. Anhotek has not looked so fine in many years. But these bodies... what are they?" At the right edge of the palette were the decapitated bodies of ten soldiers.

"They are the Ta-Tjehenu tribal leaders who were wounded or captured during the battle. You agreed that we should cut off their heads and private parts and send the heads back to their lands." I recalled agreeing to Tetien's suggestion the day after the battle, in part to send a message to the Ta-Tjehenus and in part as retribution for what they had done to my childhood friend, Haankhef. There were so many decisions to be made after the battle and I was so weary with fatigue, it was not until this moment that I recalled the incident that was now memorialized on the palette.

"I will need to think about whether or not this should be included," I said, pointing to the scene, which in retrospect sickened me. I had given the order and it was done, without my ever having to bloody my own hands. "What are these things?" I asked.

"The two wild creatures in the center are being held by leashes. Anhotek says this symbolizes the taming of chaos. Their heads being intertwined represent the unification of Kem. In the center a cup is formed within which we will grind cosmetics for Royal events."

"Superbly done," I remarked. "It ably demonstrates Kaipunesut's craft."

"He is indeed a craftsman," Meruka agreed. "On the bottom you are in your Apis bull form, trampling King W'ash and the walled city of Dep. Thus the palette will glorify your conquest for all eternity. Anhotek plans to include the palette in the Sed festival. Your deeds will be told and retold for all generations to come."

The creation of legends is a curious matter and I wondered if other great leaders ever felt that events simply overtook them. I had hardly planned for the battle of Dep to play out as it had. I wanted to quell the raids that W'ash and the Ta-Tjehenus made into our lands, so that Kem could be united. Yet, what had transpired had fit neatly into the vision that the gods had visited upon me in Ta-Sety many years ago and several times since.

At that moment Panehsy announced his presence. "I am sorry to disturb you King Narmer. I have an urgent message for Meruka." I looked from Panehsy to Meruka and I saw something pass between them, a glance, a flicker of recognition.

"What is it?" I asked, suddenly concerned.

Meruka looked at me with sadness in his eyes. "It is Anhotek, I fear. Speak, Panehsy."

Panehsy looked uncomfortably at me, then returned his glance to Meruka. "He is burning with fever, Meruka," he said nervously. "He... he is delirious."

# SCROLL SIXTEEN

## *Immersion*

We raced down the dimly lit corridors from my residence to the old section of the palace, where Anhotek's quarters were located, our sandals slapping loudly against the mud-brick floors. My heart raced with all manner of terrible thoughts.

Meruka instructed me to wait where I was until he had assessed the situation, but I could not sit patiently awaiting word of Anhotek's fate. Meruka slowed to a walk as we neared Anhotek's quarters. He took a huge breath and exhaled slowly, centering and grounding himself for the diagnosis that he would be required to make.

As we entered his quarters, I could hear Anhotek's voice, deep and sounding as if he had sand in his throat. He tossed about his straw bed and only by laying his body across him was Surero able to contain him.

Meruka went immediately to Anhotek's side. "He is drenched in sweat, yet his eyes are open," he commented as if he were discussing Anhotek's symptoms with another shaman. "His pulse races."

"He complained of a severe headache," Surero said,

regaining his breath as he stood on the other side of Anhotek's bed.

Anhotek looked terribly thin and frail. The bags below his eyes hung heavy and his eyeballs were sunk deep in his skull, dark black rings encircling them. He was pale, despite his high fevers. Even standing a cubit from his bed I could feel the heat being thrown from his body.

"What... what is it?" I asked, looking at Meruka in desperation.

Meruka stared deeply at me then. "Narmer, I do not yet know what ails him. But, it will take me twice as long to find out if I must babysit you at the same time." Meruka's words cut me, but they were also right. I stepped aside.

Meruka immediately knelt by Anhotek and grasped his hand. "Anhotek, can you hear me?" For a moment Anhotek stopped his tossing. A drop of sweat fell from his earlobe onto his bed. His eyes stared at the roof, but he gave no sign of understanding.

"How long has he been in such a state?" Meruka asked turning to Panehsy and Surero. The two looked at each other.

"Perhaps a few hours," Panehsy volunteered. "He complained first that the headache was getting worse. Then he complained that his muscles hurt him."

"He began to shiver as if he were cold," Surero added. "He said he was tired and lay down, pulling his blanket over him and asking me to bring him another. Then he began to sweat and toss. In the past hour he started to murmur things as he rolled around."

"What did he say?" Meruka asked.

"Nothing I could understand. Words... just words," Surero responded.

"Did he have a bowel movement?"

"No," Surero answered.

"Yes," Panehsy said. "Last night. He complained that he must have eaten something that disagreed with him. He did not say anything further, but I assume his stool was loose."

"Has he eaten?"

"Nothing," Panehsy said.

"I offered him food, but he refused," Surero added.

Meruka closed his eyes. "Did he take any medicines?" he asked, his eyeballs rolling around behind his lids, as if he were reading a papyrus scroll.

"None in the past day.... not that I saw," Panehsy answered first.

"Last night, when he complained that his head ached, I saw him mix a potion," Surero said. "I asked him if I could help, but he refused."

Meruka pulled down Anhotek's eyelids, all the while speaking to him to soothe his distress. He picked up Anhotek's hands and examined the fingers. Finally, he stood up and came over to us.

"I believe he has the mosquito illness," Meruka said, gravely.

"The... the mosquito illness?" I repeated, alarmed. "Wha... how?..."

"When we were in Nekhen there were reports of people who were afflicted. Traders from Ta-Sety said that this was a bad year in their land for mosquitoes. They have had several years of drought and this past year the rains brought a plague of mosquitoes. This happens."

"What can you do? Will... will he survive?" I asked.

"I will do everything I know to cure him. The mosquito illness is common in my country and we have ways to treat it. But, I would be lying if I said it will be easy. Anhotek is old and frail. He must fight a difficult battle."

What could I do then? The King commands and others obey, yet at that moment I felt as powerless as a bull with a nose ring. I looked back at Anhotek, who once again tossed and murmured nonsense words. My heart felt like it was rent open. My eyes become wet. Without the others there, I would have fallen to my knees praying for Horus' help once again.

"Please, Meruka, for all our sakes, cure him. Make him well again. Do nothing else but care for him. Anything you desire for his care will be yours."

Meruka looked into my eyes again. Waving his hands

behind him to move Panehsy and Surero away, he whispered to me. "You know he loves you, too, Narmer. On the trip to Nekhen he prayed for you. He spoke of his concern for the burdens you bear."

"Please, do not talk as if his days are numbered! Treat him with all your skills. I will call for the Chief Priest of the Temple of Nekhen to come here with all haste. We will do all we can to rid him of this plague." I turned to Panehsy and instructed him to leave immediately for Nekhen with a detachment of my King's Guards. Then I left Anhotek's quarters.

I wanted to run then, run to the comforting waters of Mother Nile, to find my old boat, to sail the gentle breezes peacefully to the east bank and disappear once again into the solitude of my beloved desert mountains. But I could no more do that than run to my residence, for a King, I had already learned, is his own most miserable slave.

I walked deliberately, my muscles tense from their containment. Word had spread that Anhotek lay ill. Servants stood against the walls and lowered their eyes as I passed, but a few glanced back up too soon and I noticed how they looked at me with pity.

As I entered my quarters I gave the guards orders that no one was to disturb me. I ran to the wall that defined the edge of the garden, the most private space in my quarters, and collapsed. There I sat, hunched over, and cried. I cared not for my eye makeup or my linen tunic. More than anything else I wished to be held, to bury myself in Anhotek's chest, the smell of his body as familiar as my own, his hand caressing my hair as he comforted me. Then the improbable image of Scorpion comforting me flashed into my heart and I bunched up the hem of my tunic, stuffed it in my mouth and screamed.

For the next three days, I slept little and even then fitfully. I visited Anhotek at all hours and he was the same, no matter what remedies the weary Meruka tried. Panehsy and Surero bathed him with cloth soaked in cool Nile water. Steam tents were erected to sweat out the poisons from his body. Every manner of potion was administered to no avail.

His temperature remained high and he raged delirious.

On the morning of the third day I sat by his bed, holding his hand and talking to him as Meruka had suggested, while Panehsy fed him a broth of vegetables and fowl to strengthen him. He looked up at me as if for a moment he recognized who I was. Then his eyes went blank and he vomited over his bed sheets. Meruka shook his head and I left, my heart heavy with despair. By now the servants who saw me approach avoided me for fear of witnessing the pain in my ka that I made no effort to hide.

At my quarters, I was shocked to see Ihy, dressed in his leopard skin tunic, standing near the guards. I had not seen him in a month or more and even then just for a moment. When he saw me, he straightened himself by holding tight to his staff.

"May I have a word with you?" he asked, in a voice altogether pleasant. The last thing I wanted was to have to deal with another of Mersyankh's complaints, which is what usually brought Ihy to request an audience.

"Go ahead," I responded and crossed my arms on my chest.

"If it pleases the King, not here," he said respectfully, tilting his staff toward the guards. I weighed his request for a second. "It concerns Anhotek," he added. I waved him into my quarters.

I ordered Ahpety to bring us morning foods and for the first time since I had known him, Ihy and I sat and broke bread together. He made no attempt to engage in business immediately, but instead talked of his healing practice with some of the families of the Royal house, which I had allowed him to continue after I ascended to the throne. He avoided speaking of Mersyankh or Neter-Maat.

When we were done eating and as we sipped barley beer, Ihy finally got to the point of his visit. "I have heard that Anhotek is worsening."

I did not ask Ihy what the source of his information was, for Anhotek had taught me that in a palace the walls are thin and full of holes for prying eyes.

"His condition has not worsened, but it has not

improved either. He is very ill," I replied as calmly as I could.

"May I speak freely?" he asked. I looked at him and felt something inside me scream 'No!'

"Speak as you wish," I finally said

He sat forward in his chair. "I know he has the mosquito sickness, Narmer. At his advanced age, not improving is the same as worsening. Each day the illness demands more and more of the body, until one day it demands more than it can provide and the next world beckons sweetly."

"I suspect there is a point to your visit, Ihy, other than so crassly lowering my spirits," I said sarcastically.

He leaned back in his chair and nervously passed his staff back and forth between his hands. "There is. I wish you to allow me to treat Anhotek."

Nothing that Ihy might have said to me could have shocked me more.

"Wait! Before you refuse my offer, please hear me out. In Lower Kem the mosquito illness is very common in some years, even becoming a plague. I have lived through many such plagues. I have seen every treatment imaginable.

"I do not mean to speak ill about Meruka's skills as a healer. But, he is from the south, where illnesses are different. The dark-skinned people of Ta-Sety are not affected as badly by the mosquito illness as our peoples, so Meruka may be at a disadvantage.

"And there is a final factor, of which I am loathe to speak. However, I will do so and allow you to judge its truth in your heart of hearts." Ihy first looked down, took a deep breath and then stared intently into my eyes.

"The mosquito illness is a dark illness. The person sees not and hears not. It brings out the inner demons of men and women and they twitch and sweat and toss about as they confront them. You have seen it, so you know that to be true.

"Who better than me to battle the demons of darkness? Every healer, every shaman bases his practice on either the dark arts or those of the light. Neither is right, neither is wrong. Each must be used wisely. That is why I urge you to allow me to treat Anhotek. I can help him, but I must act soon, before he weakens further."

I was speechless. I stared at Ihy, into the inky-dark pools of his eyes. They were impenetrable. I felt bewitched by his words, yet in my heart I knew that there rang a truth that I could not deny.

"And what is in it for you?" I found myself saying.

"Ah, the question of questions! Anhotek has trained you well, King Narmer. Here it is, then. Right now we are in a weakened state, me and Mersyankh and Neter-Maat. We fought hard against your ascension, despite the odds against us succeeding, and we lost. But Mersyankh is persistent, if nothing else. For that I give her much credit. She... she holds out hope yet that she and Neter-Maat will at least have positions of power within the Royal court."

I was unsure if Ihy's words added to the intoxicating effects of the barley beer or if he was slowly weaving a web of deceit, like a crafty spider enticing his unwitting prey. Either way I felt myself being drawn in.

"In any case, the gods have cast my lot with Mersyankh. We are outsiders and after your victory in the battle of Dep worth less than the dirt beneath your feet. We are cut off from our own power, from our own people.

"So what do I gain from treating Anhotek? Redemption of a sort. Prestige. Acknowledgment that my powers are of some consequence. But the real question, Narmer, is the one I believe Anhotek himself would counsel you to ask. What do you gain by my treating your mentor? If I fail, you have someone to blame, a sacrificial goat. And with my position diminished, Mersyankh becomes far less a threat to you. And if I succeed you have your teacher back. But you will also have laid the first building stone of an alliance, a healing of the festering wounds that resist any shaman's ministrations."

I poured over Ihy's words to find the cracks in his logic, the tiny crevices where deceit and subterfuge might hide. The implications of his offer were enormous.

"I will acknowledge that what you say is intriguing, Ihy.

Surprising, but intriguing. You obviously have confidence in your powers and I respect you for that. I have heard from others in the Royal court that your healing skills are rare." He bowed his head at my acknowledgement.

"Nothing would please me more than to see Anhotek well again. He is old, but until now he has been vigorous, and I thought it was the will of the gods that he live many more years. I will take your offer under advisement."

"Time is ...."

"And I will send you my answer before Ra's disk sails into the west." With that, Ihy bowed his head, stood and turned to leave my quarters. But, before he exited through the twin columns, he turned.

"I thank you for hearing me out. You are not... what I mean to say is, you have become a... a worthy man."

"Worthy man or worthy opponent?" I asked wryly. Either would have been a compliment coming from Ihy.

As soon as he left, I sent Ahpety for Meruka, making it clear that he should come only when he felt able to leave Anhotek. But, within minutes he was in my quarters.

"I thought it best to come immediately," he said as he entered. "Because of Ihy's visit."

"Is nothing private in this palace?" I asked, frustrated. Meruka did not answer and we stood in uncomfortable silence until I sprawled onto my reclining couch, staring at the roof above. Unlike the old palace, the roof over the new section was solid, made from mud spread over wood slats that had reeds woven between them. Each room had a rectangular section of the roof that was elevated and had places cut out for light and air to enter. I found the effect of Kaipunesut's design altogether pleasing to my eyes.

"Is it true that when a man of Anhotek's age does not improve, it is the same as getting worse?"

"All healers are aware of that," he replied with disdain. "Is that what Ihy said?"

"Yes... yes he did. He... Ihy offered to treat Anhotek." Meruka sat still on the chair and did not betray his reaction. "He claims that he is very experienced in treating the mosquito illness. He says..."

"Yes, I know what he says," Meruka said softly.

"He told me that the mosquito sickness can be treated best with the dark magic that he practices. I... I do not know what to do," I said, sitting up.

Meruka stood then and walked slowly to the portico that overlooked Mother Nile. He watched the scene below for a long time, then straightened himself before returning to me. He pulled his chair close to my couch.

"Meni," he said so gently I looked up at once, "I can see the pain that afflicts you. I, too, love Anhotek, but not like the love that you two share. Sometimes the most difficult thing we can do is surrender our power to the gods, to give them the time to work their own magic.

"Let me remind you of the day on the banks of Mother Nile, when you had your first big vision. Anhotek could have medicated you. He held the powder right there in his hands. But, you shook your head and he loved you enough, he was wise enough, to trust the gods to do their work, although he knew the terrible risks.

"Ihy possesses great powers. I do not deny this. But, if you love Anhotek... that... that is foolish of me to say. What I mean is you must trust your love for Anhotek and do for him what he himself would choose to do. Allow me to continue to heal him, for I know in my heart of hearts, that he would rather pass from this world in light than continue to live due to Ihy's powers of darkness."

Then Meruka picked up his huge black hands, the hands that had wielded sword and dagger with such ferocity that the enemy in Dep scattered at his very sight, and he cupped my head in them. He touched his forehead to mine and prayed, first in a whisper so soft I thought he was trying to tell me something. Then I realized that the language he spoke was his tribe's.

At first all I felt was the pressure of his strong hands, steadily increasing. Then I felt a buzzing between my ears, as if my head were a hive of bees. Then the buzzing became a swirl of color and light and sound that built in fervor, until I reached up and grabbed Meruka's muscular forearms. Soon serenity infused my ka and we sat together, rocking slowly back and forth. I was transported then to a realm that I had only experienced in my dreams, a place of solace and light, where my ka floated as freely as a cloud, and in this lightness I knew what it was I must do.

"You have great wisdom in your heart," Meruka said to me as he left. "You will do what must be done. I will follow your command."

"When the Horus priests arrive, what then?"

"We will conduct a powerful healing ceremony. I have done all I can for Anhotek's body. Now we must minister to his ka."

"I wish to be present for the ceremony," I said.

"With your presence, the healing magic will surely increase. We will call you when we are ready, perhaps as early as tomorrow."

That afternoon I sent Ahpety to Ihy's quarters with a message I personally wrote, to thank him for his offer, but also advising him of my decision to be true to Anhotek's ba. I asked Ahpety to await a response to my scroll.

"But, my King, he gave me no response," Ahpety said upon his return, "other than to say that the decision was what he expected. He... he dismissed me with a wave of his hand."

"And he said nothing further? Was... did he seem upset?"

"I could not tell. Forgive me, master, but I am a Horus priest. It gives me gooseflesh to be in his presence. I cannot bring myself to gaze into his eyes. I... I am sorry."

By evening Anhotek had sipped a broth and held it in his stomach. I felt hopeful for the first time in days and retreated to my quarters late in the night, when the palace was quiet. I had finally fallen into a fitful sleep, full of demons and spirits, when I felt someone shake me. I spun from my bed, alarmed, and knocked poor Surero on his back. He scurried to his feet. "Come quick, Narmer. Anhotek is... he..."

I pulled on my kilt and ran down the corridors far ahead of Surero, who pattered along as fast as his tiny feet could go. The fear in my heart was so great, I expected to see Anhotek lying lifeless on his bed. When I entered his quarters, I saw Panehsy holding down Anhotek's writhing body and Meruka frantically erecting a vapor tent. Candles were lit throughout the quarters.

"Here, take this end!" Meruka shouted at me. I grabbed the coarse linen end he offered and wrapped it around the frame he had constructed.

"What is it?" I asked, alarmed. Anhotek looked awful, pale, and sweating. Even his paunch had retreated and his ribs now protruded.

"He has suddenly worsened," Meruka replied, while mixing the potions he would need to minister to Anhotek. Then Meruka stopped in the middle of grinding a leafy material. The mortar clinked against the side of the pestle. He lifted his nose as if he were sniffing vapors in the air. He turned his head slightly from one side to the other and his eyelids fluttered so that all I could see were the whites of his eyes.

"There are demons in the air, Narmer," he whispered, coarsely. "Dark, powerful demons are entering our world from the afterworld. They..."

Gooseflesh rose along my spine, my head felt light and my heart beat hard in my chest. "Oh, please merciful Horus, not now!" I heard Meruka say. "Protect his head from the shakes!" I think he shouted, although by now his voice came from far, far away as I retreated to a land that, despite his potent magic, he would never know.

Meruka's booming voice became a drum that beat in my ear as I swam under the thick waters of a huge river, escaping from... I knew not what it was, but I felt its sinister presence standing on the river bank behind me. I could not breath, yet I knew I must somehow get to the other side of the river or drown. Yet, I did not fear the drowning. I felt torn between the sweet seduction of the water and my desire to reach the far shore. At that moment I knew not which I would choose. The deep water beckoned with its tranquil promise of serenity, the drums now joined by a chorus of singers and the melodious notes of flutes.

Stop swimming, Narmer, the waters beckoned. Stop struggling. Free yourself from the obligations that weigh so heavily upon your shoulders. My arms stopped pulling, then. My feet stopped kicking. I surrendered to the song of the waters and released my ka to the sweet ether that enveloped me. I tumbled effortlessly and the sensation seemed vaguely familiar, undeniably comforting.

I looked up to see a shimmering figure kneeling on the far shore. It held out its hands towards me and I could not decipher whether they offered me help or asked for it. I followed the hands and arms to its shoulders, a drawn out journey of time and spirit. I traveled as does the fingertips of a blind beggar, up the neck and to the figure's featureless face. I was drowning, but my ka gazed upon the eyes that had so many times penetrated to my essence. It was as if a bolt of lightning had been loosed by the gods into my heart. I began kicking and pulling frantically. It was Anhotek. For the first time, he was asking for my help.

My hands reached out from the water and when we touched our kas became one. Only then, even after all the years we had spent together, after all the joys and heartaches, did I truly understand the pure love that flowed between us.

Suddenly I felt my legs being pulled back under the waters, foul-smelling waters that now frothed with hatred and bitterness, fed by dark powers that emanated from the opposite shore. I fought against being sucked in, but the more I resisted, the more powerful the dark forces became. I knew in my heart that I would soon lose the battle and both Anhotek and I would drown in the sinister brew.

I felt Anhotek's grip loosening. I looked back toward him and saw that rather than letting go his grasp, he was bending, as a willow tree bends toward the water. I wondered at this strange vision, until I understood his message. Yield and you will be strong. Many times in my training Anhotek had uttered those words.

As I yielded to the forces that pulled me under, I felt an ever stronger connection to Anhotek's ka. Love, caring, compassion radiated from him as from the light of Ra's disk. Our kas entwined and I slipped from the grips of the evil spirits that grasped me from below. Now the waters turned as clear as those of my favorite spring in the mountains of the Eastern desert. A beautiful chorus, in a harmony that reverberated throughout my ka, emanated from all around me.

So it was that I awoke in this existence just as Ra's disk rose in the sky. My first sensation was of a chorus of voices, singing in harmonic rhythms that were more beautiful than ever I had heard, than ever I could have imagined. I opened my eyes and all around me men dressed in white tunics stood, joined by their hands, heads bowed. Sweet, melodious chants poured forth from their open mouths. The Chief Priest of the Temple of Horus in Nekhen stood next to me holding my left hand. My right hand was folded over Anhotek's, who lay beside me, his feet by my head. Meruka kneeled next to Anhotek and held his left hand. Meruka's own right hand grasped that of another priest, so that we were all connected in an unbroken circle.

I blinked my eyes to clear them of the haze of my journey. I turned my head to my right and beheld Anhotek's blessed eyes staring back at me. A weak smile appeared on his lips and that was all I saw for the next few minutes, for my eyes immediately blurred from my own tears. Anhotek squeezed my hand then and I squeezed his back and I remember thanking Horus himself for his boundless mercy. For all the times I had cursed being born under his wings, I would have endured ten times the burdens to have been able to serve as his instrument in saving my beloved Anhotek.

Meruka then fussed over us for the longest time and when he felt that Anhotek and I were safely back from our journeys, he agreed to allow the Chief Priest to leave with two high-ranking assistants. They returned in an hour, stating that both Ihy and Mersyankh were missing. Neter-Maat, however, snored soundly in his bed. Whatever Mersyankh had plotted, she was cunning enough to have done it away from the palace grounds.

One of the priests withdrew from his tunic a series of

scrolls upon which were exquisitely drawn figures, the details so fine each and every person depicted was immediately recognizable. I sat up, still tired and headachy from my shaking and the herbs I had been given. At once I saw the figures of Ihy, Mersyankh and Neter-Maat, dressed regally and drawn in a huge size. Neter-Maat wore the crook and flail and the crown of Upper Kem. I stood next to him, but in a size that was small in comparison, my hands out to my sides, bowing low toward him. The huge drawing of Ihy showed him wearing a mask of Anubis and carrying his staff, while a smaller Anhotek stood on the side of him, his staff snapped in two. Below Queen Mersyankh stood a much smaller Meruka, bowing low. From the wide eyes of the priests, I could see that there was something about the pictures that I did not understand.

"It is part of a magic ritual," the Chief Priest said. "Part of very dark ritual. The… the figures are given life through magical incantations."

"This explains much of what has happened the past day," Meruka added.

"He is a powerful shaman," the Chief Priest continued. "But he has not been trained as a Horus priest. He invoked a mighty spell on you and Anhotek, but in the end his power could not hold sway over both of you at the same time."

"What happened last night?" Meruka asked me softly.

"He was immersed in Ihy's magic," Anhotek said. It took me a moment to understand the humor in Anhotek's remark and we immediately began to laugh until my head pounded and Anhotek began to cough. For the rest of the morning Anhotek and I related our various stories. The priests interrupted us constantly to ask questions, to compare notes with each other and to marvel at how similar were Anhotek's and my experiences.

During the afternoon meal, we discussed what to do about Ihy's attempts on Anhotek's and my life. In the end we decided that since Ihy's magic in this instance was to no avail, we would not risk disruption in the Court by accusing him. Unification was too recent, and still too fragile, to confront Mersyankh's and Ihy's treachery. However, the Chief Priest wrote a series of scrolls regarding the incident and had each one stamped and sealed by his assistant to bear witness against Ihy at some future occasion. Anhotek and the Chief Priest discreetly instructed their spies to determine who was helping Mersyankh and where they had held their ritual.

I was interested in seeing what my own reaction would be to seeing Mersyankh or Ihy again, for though in my mind I had thought of various ways to handle it, I could not be sure what might happen in the passion of the moment. Anhotek had suggested that I pretend as if nothing had happened, for it was certain that no one who was present in Anhotek's quarters that night would betray what had transpired. By avoiding any mention of it, we would be showing that evil pair that their plotting and magic were of no consequence.

As it happened, I did not have to wait long. Ihy and Neter-Maat were hardly seen at all in the palace over the next two days. But, on the third day after our ordeal, Mersyankh's vanity forced her hand. She apparently felt that too much time had passed since her last complaint to me over the construction of her new quarters. She sent her messenger to me with a request for an audience. I responded that I would see her immediately, a response that she and Ihy must not have expected.

"I am at the end of my patience over the matter of my new quarters!" Mersyankh announced as soon as she entered. She was dressed in a fine robe and laden with gold jewelry set with carnelians and turquoise on her neck, arms and legs. She had lately resorted to having her servant apply her makeup too thickly to attempt to hide her wrinkles, so that I looked upon her with a certain degree of amusement.

"And how are you today, Queen Mersyankh?" I asked, while pulling a bunch of grapes from the stem in the bowl to the side of me. "And you, too, Ihy?"

He tilted his staff and held it so that his hand blocked his eyes from my view. "I am well, King Narmer. And you?"

"Oh, I am fine, today. I had a headache a few nights ago… a minor ache. But, today I feel quite well." That was the extent of my acknowledging Mersyankh's and Ihy's evil actions.

"Well, I am most certainly not well!" Mersyankh said, crossing her arms over her chest. "There are constant delays in my new quarters." The degree of her frustration could not have been due solely to construction delays.

"Perhaps Ihy has a potion or incantation that can help," I suggested, staring straight through Mersyankh. "I mean for your not feeling well as a result of the delays."

"You… that…that is impertinent!" she hissed back at me, dropping her hands to her sides in balled fists. "I am the Queen and I have the right to expect…"

"Mersyankh… perhaps…" Ihy tried to interject.

"Do not interrupt me, Ihy!" she said, pointing her finger at him. "The least Narmer can do is to expedite the building as… as a matter of respect. Is that asking too much? I have not even seen Kaipunesut's drawings yet!"

"Ah, yes," I said, matter-of-factly. "I meant to say something to you before this, Queen Mersyankh. I will do what I can to speed up the construction, but right now… I am reluctant to even mention this… but Kaipunesut is involved in another major project… very important… in Nekhen. He will be gone for several months, I fear. Shall I have him assign one of his capable assistants to draw up the plans for you?" I knew this last point would be like a hot skewer going through her flesh.

Mersyankh became even more enraged. Her face flushed red and the muscles in her neck tensed and stood out. "You know full well that I want only Kaipunesut to draw them!" she shouted, stomping her foot. "I cannot understand why you…" she said pointing directly at me, her long, gold-painted nails shimmering under Ra's rays.

At that moment, Kagemni's page approached Ahpety, who immediately came to my side and whispered in my ear. I held up my hand to silence Mersyankh, which only infuriated her more. Her face was crimson next to her white robe.

"Queen Mersyankh, I must apologize for cutting short this important meeting," I said standing up. "Kagemni has just returned from Lower Kem and, well, you know how troublesome the Lower Kemians can be. I must attend his briefing. But, we will reschedule this meeting... perhaps soon." I turned and left, her face still red.

"Why did you not say something!" she exploded at Ihy as soon as she thought I was out of earshot. I smiled as I walked down the corridor to the small room that I used to meet with my council.

"You owe me a full damned week's worth of fine barley beer!" Kagemni said as I entered.

"That and more!" I replied. We hugged tightly. "It is good to see you back safely, my friend."

"I understand that it was less safe here than with the army in Lower Kem. What..."

"More on that later, Kagemni," I said, waving off his question. "First tell me what the situation is like in Lower Kem."

"Basically good. The trade routes are protected by our troops. Trade flourishes. The farmers complain that they pay their taxes because their crops stand for all to see, but that the damned traders hide their gains and are taxed little. In the eastern region of the delta the priests report a tax protest. Neither farmer nor trader pay any taxes."

"We have not fought a great war to have this happen," I said, standing. "We must increase the treasury to pay for the many projects we now undertake to benefit the people."

"What do you propose?"

I paced for a moment while I thought. "Anhotek predicted that we would see tax protests from the delta within the year, that they would surely test our resolve to unite the Two Lands. Soon I will appoint a governor of that nome... to administer the law and taxes. But I will tell you this, Kagemni. We cannot take this lightly. All people must pay the taxes I decree. If anyone does not, whether in Upper or Lower Kem, they will be treated the same. I will have them killed and their property seized. I will set an example that the people will remember for a long time."

I turned to Kagemni, then. "Take Neter-Maat with you, Kagemni. Put down this rebellion… and quickly. It is time he sees what efforts it takes to collect the taxes that support his mother's excesses. He will see what the bloody work of a real army entails."

# SCROLL SEVENTEEN

## *An Uneasy Alliance*

"We call it The Houses of Life," Anhotek said, opening his arms to encompass all who sat around the large wood table. He sat at my right side and around him sat Meruka, the Chief Priest of the Temple of Horus at Nekhen, Kaipunesut and Kagemni.

It was nearing the end of Inundation and Anhotek and Meruka had been able to spend large blocks of time working on their various plans and proposals. Anhotek and the Chief Priest would often walk along the high paths above Mother Nile, conferring, sometimes accompanied by Meruka. Kaipunesut would scurry back and forth from these meetings to the building projects he supervised, his eyes focused on the ground in front of him, a series of scrolls always tucked under his arm. He constantly urged his supervisors to push the farmers to work harder, for he knew he would only benefit from their labors for the three or four months that the Inundation covered their fields.

In the past year since his illness, Anhotek had improved greatly, although he still retained a haggard look about him. His clothes hung poorly and his cheekbones were more pronounced. Yet his many projects brought him outdoors more, so that his color was healthier and his activity seemed to revive his spirits considerably.

"Why must we have these Houses of Life? What do they do?" I asked, looking questioningly at the men. They, in turn, looked toward Anhotek.

"Unification poses complex challenges. The Houses of Life will add a structure that will make governing a unified country easier. Right now there are temples to our many gods throughout Kem. Each has its local following. Some areas are served well by temples, other areas have none within a day's walk. Yet our people are a religious people. They seek to do the right things and to live a life in harmony with ma'at.

"To rule effectively, we must create a strong, central priesthood that is able..."

"A Horus priesthood, I assume." I interrupted.

"Narmer, we have discussed this before," Anhotek said, sighing. "The Horus priesthood is already the most powerful in Upper Kem. It has legitimized every King going back to the god-Kings that walked the Two Lands. The Temple of Nekhen is revered even in Lower Kem. Those are the facts. We are trying to use the resources we already have to create the vision of a united Kem that we now all share."

"I only... go ahead, Anhotek."

"We are not saying that there should be only one priesthood. There are temples, like the Temple of Min and the many Temples of Isis, and groups of priests that trace their lineage as far back as the beginning of time," the Chief Priest added. "It would not bode well for us to cast their beliefs aside, not even those who worship Apep. What we are saying is that the Horus priesthood would represent the official views of the King.

"Within each Temple of Horus, we would establish a House of Life, but no more than one in each nome. The scribes at the Temple of Horus in Nekhen would make copies of all important scrolls. The Houses of Life would then serve as repositories for all our ritual texts, for medical information, for our laws. They would disseminate the King's decrees, such as what interest rates are allowed during times of famine. Or they might announce a special visit by the King for the Sed festival." Anhotek nodded toward the Chief Priest.

"Within each House of Life," the Chief Priest continued, "we would appoint one priest to be the official scribe. This setem priest, as we call him, would maintain all the ritual texts. He would research laws, draw up marriage and business contracts. When a woman sues for divorce, he would then be able to divide the marital property fairly. He would have at his command all the knowledge that preceded him, not just for religious practice, but also for administering the nome, for keeping ma'at strong."

"Since they would be proficient in reading and writing the picture words," Anhotek added, "they would also help the governor keep receipts for taxes and records of important events like births and deaths, or special business arrangements between the Royal court and local merchants."

"Bringing Upper and Lower Kem under tighter control of the King," I said. "That is indeed desirable." Anhotek and the Chief Priest smiled and glanced at each other, for the proposal was mostly the result of their work. "But will not the priests of Lower Kem resist? I think, particularly, of those loyal to Ihy."

"Undoubtedly they will," Anhotek responded. "The people of the delta are not as familiar with the Horus priests. They mostly worship Wadjet, the cobra goddess, or else are shamans or magicians of the dark places, like Ihy. But, as you know, the delta is... it is an unusual place. So much water and marshland separates one town from another. Their power is scattered. They have not developed lines of priests who pledge their allegiance to one Temple. That should make our job easier."

"And, whether they initially support this plan or not," the Chief Priest added, "they have at least heard of the Temple of Horus. They respect our exalted position. No matter what other of our gods they serve, they fear the might of Horus, the falcon god of Nekhen."

"The delta priests who become Horus priests will benefit from the material goods they will accumulate from tutoring the sons and daughters of the wealthy," Meruka said. "That is a powerful way to counteract Ihy's allies. A growling stomach holds few allegiances."

"Yes, I see that," I remarked. "But new temples will need to be built… more priests trained. How will we afford this?"

Again Anhotek spoke up. "There will be enough resources in the treasury to accomplish this… and more. And there is another benefit to the plan that we have not mentioned. The temple complexes we plan to build, thanks to Kaipunesut's skills, will include granaries. A portion of the taxes collected as foodstuffs will be stored there, to be distributed as needed during times of famine. This will add stability to your rule, Narmer, and the rule of all your descendents. The people will take well to such acts of kindness and generosity. They will be more amenable to paying taxes when they see how it benefits them during times of need."

"That and the persuasions of Kagemni's army. Still, this is quite an ingenious plan, my good men," I said and they all smiled and nodded. "Another question. Will these setem priests also hear disputes between aggrieved parties?"

Anhotek looked at the Chief Priest and shrugged his shoulder. "I… I am not sure. We have not discussed this specifically. We wanted first to gain your approval to move ahead with the planning. We could explore this."

"I especially find these boundary disputes after Inundation very tedious, Anhotek. It seems like every day during Proyet I listen to these petty disputes. The stakes get buried by mud and then they get moved by one party or another and soon they are ready to kill one another. See if these priests of yours can readily settle such disagreements."

"Perhaps they can also serve as the measurement supervisors," Kaipunesut offered. "Since they will read and write, they can enter the measurements on a scroll and refer to them whenever a dispute arises."

"Brilliant!" I called out, slapping my hand on the table. "That is an excellent idea. Alright, then. You have my blessing to go ahead with the planning. Are we done?"

"Yes," Anhotek replied, after glancing furtively at the Chief Priest and Kaipunesut. "Until ten days from now." Everyone stood. Kagemni left to return to his field commanders, while Kaipunesut hurriedly left with several papyrus scrolls of his architectural plans tucked under his arm. Meruka and the Chief Priest walked away, engaged in an intense discussion.

"Your ba appears light today," Anhotek said smiling. "To what can we attribute this unusual event?"

"Either you tease me or else your mental abilities are declining," I replied, trying to appear serious.

"Ah, the sweet effects of love yet linger. You are hopelessly smitten, my dear King Narmer."

"Oh, Anhotek!" I replied, in no small measure happy for his acknowledgement of my state of grace. "She is so beautiful. The ten days we spent together in Inerty were like a taste of the afterworld. Her warmth... the smells of her body intoxicate me like no beer or wine could ever do. We sat for hours in the evenings, staring at Ra's flaming disk descending over the desert dunes, just... just holding hands, her head on my shoulder. I can almost feel it there now," I said, touching my left shoulder gently.

"I venture that her hands were not all that you touched," Anhotek remarked wryly.

"Many is the time you explained to me the charms of a woman, dear teacher. Yet... yet ill prepared was I for her perfumes. Her scents are captivating. Once I touched and smelled her sweet treasure, I... I was overcome by a heated passion such as I never imagined I was capable of."

"Yet, you did not plant your seed within her?" Anhotek asked with alarm. "We have spoken of this before!"

"No. No I did not. But I would have, had she not been so versed in the womanly arts. I was so stiff, I could not think of anything else but filling her womanhood. She caressed it in such a way that it exploded forth its seed in... in another special place. It was... satisfying in its own way."

"Oh, I see," Anhotek responded. "That is a good sign, Narmer. She is comfortable with different ways of pleasuring you. Many women are not so giving. But, she loves you, as you do her. That anyone who sees you two together can readily observe." He sat silently for a moment.

"And would she praise your lovemaking to her friends as enthusiastically as you do hers?" he asked me, in his most fatherly tone.

I hung my head in embarrassment for a moment. "Perhaps not the first time or two. I… I was too heated. It was not what I expected. I mean, the pleasure was far greater than I imagined. I… I could not control it.

"But, after a few times I think she might speak enthusiastically about me to her friends. She guided my hands ever so lightly, until I learned what pleases her and then she yelled with pleasure."

Anhotek smiled broadly. "You have always been an eager student… when you are interested in the subject at hand, so to speak." At that, we both laughed.

"But you have not come to speak to me of the art of making love to a woman, my dear teacher," I remarked, recalling the looks that passed between him and the Chief Priest and Kaipunesut.

He smiled. "Not much passes your eyes unnoticed." He drew himself up and groaned at the pain in his knees, until he bent them to restore their vigor.

"There is yet another matter that the three of us have discussed. We are not ready to bring a plan for your consideration, yet I feel we must advise you of our thinking. If you disagree strongly then it would be better to abandon it at this early stage."

"It sounds serious," I commented, rising to refill my cup with water. As I poured, I saw across the river a group of fishermen struggling to attach their nets to poles set deep into Mother Nile's mud. As her waters receded day by day, the fishermen set weirs and nets across the flood plains to trap the river's abundant fish. Behind the group of men, large masses of fish flapped in the shallow water. I smiled thinking what heroes these men would be to their families that very night when they brought home their impressive catches.

"It is serious, especially when you bind it together with the Houses of Life proposal." He began to pace, as he always did when organizing his thoughts. "We suggest moving the capital..."

"What?" I said, throwing myself back in my chair.

"Please, Narmer, hear me out," he continued, but my mind was already racing with fear and anticipation.

"The gods give a leader a vision, then they taunt him with the timing of it. You have already started down the path toward your vision for Kem. The battle of Dep was thrust upon you, yet you rose to victory and now unification is yours. Unification!" he said, curling his fingers into a fist. "Think of that! Scorpion defeated Nubt and finally unified Upper Kem. But unification with Lower Kem eluded your father and his father's father before him. Now you have achieved that noble goal. With the new roads that are being built, trade already flourishes and Kem prospers. Your agricultural estates produce crops in abundance here and in the delta. As they prosper, you will be able to create and sustain the institutions that are needed to govern the Lands of the Lotus and Papyrus.

"But, a new vision must also be tangible. The people must see and feel its power. If you continue to govern from Tjeni, the people of Lower Kem will eventually grow resentful. Their wounded pride will fester. No matter how powerful the Temple of Horus, the King's power will seem remote from their lives.

"That is why we suggest a new capital for a united Kem. There are too many power conflicts between Nekhen and Tjeni and Nubt here in Upper Kem, and Dep and Shedet in Lower Kem. We need a new city, a grand city such as has never before been imagined." Anhotek stopped to gauge my reaction. I felt overwhelmed, frightened.

"Where would this city... this new capital be?" I asked timidly.

"I do not say this lightly, Meni..."

"It has been a while since you have called me by my

birth name," I interrupted.

"Oh, I am sorry! It just comes out of my mouth from time to time."

"I do not mind, Anhotek. Not at all. It always brings back fond memories. But, I interrupted you," I said, although I would much have preferred to continue recalling our days sailing upon Mother Nile than have to deal with the matters of state.

"Yes, yes. We have thought of many sites, but the one that stands out is just south of the place where Mother Nile forks. It sits on a ridge. There is a tiny, nameless village there now."

"On the west or east bank?"

"The west bank."

"I believe I know the very site of which you speak! It sits on a small rise and the land around it is rich with crops. There is a temple there... a small one. You can see it from Mother Nile. We provisioned there on our way to the battle of Dep."

"Yes, that is the place. The priest there speaks highly of you. There are several advantages the site offers, aside from the obvious political ones. It sits very advantageously to monitor and control river trade between Upper and Lower Kem. It has pasturage available on the east bank and has a very broad flood plain to allow for an extensive Royal estate. But, best of all, it sits at the edge of the most heavily traveled route to the Wat-Hor."

"Near the northern entrance to the Way of Horus!" I exclaimed, jumping from my chair. "That is wonderful, Anhotek! Magnificent! El-Or will be overjoyed at hearing of this. Her relatives would eliminate weeks of desert travel. They would be able to visit her without undue hardship." I hugged Anhotek then and was reminded of how thin and frail he had become.

"However, this decision raises many complex issues," he said, pulling away from me. Leaning on his staff, he walked back to his chair. I pulled my chair next to his.

"Most important is the issue of your marriage. I know this weighs heavily on your mind, Narmer. Love always seeks to express itself fully under Ra's light." I felt a rushing sound in my ears and my heart beat wildly, for I had thought of my marriage to El-Or many times in the past year.

"The Chief Priest and I have consulted the gods over this. Meruka, too, has consulted his Ta-Sety gods for their counsel. We have all come to the conclusion that the signs are not favorable at the moment."

"Then why did you play me like a fish after a worm?" I protested angrily. "If it is not meant to be, then why put it forward?"

"I did not say it was not meant to be. It is far better for a ruler to be advised of issues well before they become a crisis." I shut my eyes and breathed in to calm myself.

"We ask that you be patient. Wait for one year from this Proyet. Waiting has many advantages and also a few perils. It will give us time to plan a glorious ceremony, which El-Or deserves," Anhotek said in a measured tone. "The new Temple of Horus in Nekhen should be completed in one year's time, so that we can combine the decommissioning ceremony of the old temple with the commissioning of the new temple. Once that is done, El-Or could join you and the first official ceremony in the new temple would be your royal wedding. Proyet is an auspicious time for a royal wedding. Just as the Black Lands burst forth once again in green, so will your marriage grow and your seed blossom within El-Or's womb."

I sat quietly, my hand under my chin, thinking on Anhotek's words. He was correct, of that there was no doubt in my mind. Yet, the pain of meeting El-Or again for short periods of time, then separating, seemed too painful to bear.

"And the perils of waiting?"

"It gives Mersyankh a chance to plan and plot alliances with the houses of power in Lower Kem."

"Is there not a way to do away with her and her evil twin?" Anhotek squirmed in his seat.

"There are ways," he surprised me by saying. "There are always ways to accomplish ones desires. But they may not be the best route to take in the long run. When a man stares intently at his feet when he walks, he risks falling off a precipice."

"You speak in riddles again."

"From the looks of things in Tjeni, your rule looks secure, the future sweet. But in the land of the marsh dwellers, the mud is thick indeed. To do away with the problems within your palace's walls would foment unforeseen challenges to your rule."

"It's better a known adversary than an unknown," I said, nodding, repeating Anhotek's own teaching.

"We may not know all the ingredients that those evil two add to their stew, but we know enough to detect them in the kitchen, as it were." For a moment we sat, each silently contemplating the effects of Mersyankh and Ihy on our lives.

"Alright, Anhotek. The wedding will be held a year from this Proyet. Make it so." Anhotek seemed relieved.

"Planning will start after Proyet, for to do so before then would invite mischief from the gods... and others." I nodded my approval.

"Another item we must discuss... regarding the Royal treasury. There is enough money in the treasury to sustain the Houses of Life project and the new Temple of Horus and the road building and even the building of the new capital. However, the costs begin to grow worrisome. And we have not even discussed the need for expansion of the irrigation canals all along Mother Nile."

"And that is sorely needed," I added.

"Yes, if we are to expand our crops and the trade and taxes they bring. I have not discussed this with anyone else, not the Chief Priest, not Meruka, no one. But, it is an idea that I have been thinking about."

"Go ahead, then. I am eager to hear your thoughts."

"The extended royal family has benefited from the increased trade. The pottery works in Nekhen have become famous throughout Kem and even into Setjet and Ta-Sety. The breweries outside Tjeni make the finest barley beer in all the land. Men have become wealthy from the protection and stability the King's army has afforded them."

I agreed, for the relatives of the royal family had expanded their residences as the palace itself expanded.

"I am thinking that we should encourage these wealthy businessmen to put some of their own wealth into carefully chosen Royal projects. That way we can spread the huge cost over a larger group. Businessmen could curry favor with the Court. It would enable those who have accumulated wealth to ascend to a higher social rank, to positions of power and prestige. Such far-seeing people could be rewarded with Royal titles or special treatment in trade of certain commodities. They might be granted the honor of placing their tombs in the Royal cemetery. It would give such people powerful motivation to support the King's rule during times of crisis. I want your permission to discuss this with a man I know well. His name is Anedjib."

"I have heard of him. He is a portly man, correct? I met him once, when he came to our ship to oversee his porters who were loading grain."

"Yes, he has enormous stores of grain, which he buys from our farmers and then sells to traders from Setjet. Yet, his access to the Royal court falls far short of his means. He is but one example of the kind of person I am thinking of involving."

The next week Anhotek arranged a meeting among the three of us. I could hardly believe the man that accompanied Anhotek was the same one of my memory some ten years before. It was as if Anedjib had swallowed another man whole. So fat was he that he walked with a waddle, as if he were a duck walking on a muddy shore. The skin behind his chin hung down in great folds.

I sat upon my throne to receive him. We had rehearsed our strategy beforehand, for it was widely known that Anedjib was a cunning negotiator. He shuffled toward me, his gaze cast upon the floor and he bent as far as he could, although I doubt he moved more than a hand's width due to his wide girth.

"Come, sit down here," Anhotek said.

"Ah, yes, thank you Anhotek. May the gods look upon

you only with favor… you and King Narmer," he said, still not looking at me. He collapsed into the chair, which creaked under his weight.

"I apologize, my dear King. It is… I have been told that it is an affliction that I have," he said, not able to look Anhotek in the eye as he spoke those words. "I eat like a bird, yet I have swelled like a corpse floating on Mother Nile. I sweat like a jackass, too, as you can see." I could hardly believe how Anedjib ran his mouth.

"Would you like a drink to cool you?" Anhotek waved his hand for Ahpety, who poured a glass of water into his cup. As he reached for the cup, he turned to Anhotek.

"Might you have some barley beer? Oh, forgive me…that is so rude of me. Forget my ravings… please. This water will do just fine," he said and raised it to his lips.

"Ahpety, bring our guest some barley beer," I called out. "Make it our finest… from our own brewery."

"Oh, my King, blessings upon you!" he said, trying to bend at the waist. Instead, his chair groaned as if it would break apart.

As Anedjib drank his way through an entire pitcher of beer and devoured an assortment of cheeses and breads, we discussed the irrigation canal project and the granaries.

"What do you anticipate the projects will require? In terms of gold, I mean?" he finally asked.

"We will pay for most of them. But, we seek three thousand debens of gold from people such as yourself."

"Three thousand!" Anedjib gasped, nearly choking on the handful of grapes he had just packed into his mouth. "Three thousand? Did I hear that right?"

"That is correct… each," Anhotek responded without blinking.

"Each? Did you say each? Anhotek, that is a lot… a very lot of gold. That is…"

"Anedjib!" Anhotek interrupted. "That is a mere fraction of the grains that you could convert into gold from your granaries in Tjeni alone. No! Do not attempt to protest, for we are now quite aware of your holdings. Had we but known of your successes before now, we would have amply increased the King's treasury just through your fair share of the taxes." Anedjib winced at the implication of Anhotek's words.

"I... I see," he said, wiping his face with the sleeve of his tunic. "Yes, yes, yes. I can smell a good investment when I see one. Let me see. Three thousand debens. Between my investment and those of other businessmen I will also bring to this project, I believe we can work a deal. I am sure of it!"

And so, without my having spoken a word, other than ordering food and drink for Anedjib, an uneasy alliance began that day that would have enormous implications for the future prosperity of our land.

# SCROLL EIGHTEEN

*I Whispered Her Name*

Looking back, the time passed quickly. For more than a year, I was occupied by the unpredictable affairs of state. In a single day there were meetings after meetings, building plans to approve, policies to develop, new laws to craft, disputes to settle, small rebellions to put down and the constant awareness that Mersyankh, Ihy and Neter-Maat lurked in the shadows, waiting, manipulating, testing the boundaries of my good will.

But at that moment my ka felt at peace, for I sailed on the waters of my beloved Mother Nile. I stood at the bow of the Royal barque, alone, recalling the creation myth that Anhotek had told me many times when I was young. Only a few hundred cubits in front of us was the Island of the Creation, where the very egg of life emerged from the waters of chaos. That holy place always raised gooseflesh on my skin, for every time I neared it's lush presence I felt a strange sensation, as if the spirit gods that still dwell there tugged at my ka. Now the boat tacked toward the west and before me, stretched as far as I could see in any direction, was the glorious city of Nekhen. We had arrived for two weeks of ceremonies that would culminate in my marriage to El-Or. I breathed the deep, slow, cleansing sen-sen breaths again and my ka felt balanced. Ma'at was strong.

Thousands of people lined the shore to welcome us. A double row of priests, dressed in clean, white tunics stood facing each other from the boat landing, up the grassy embankment and to the temple itself. Each one held a new red pennant with the sign of Horus emblazoned upon it.

I stepped onto my gold-lined carrying chair in the center of the boat and Meruka placed the white bulbous crown of Upper Egypt upon my head. I looked straight ahead, as I had been trained to do by Anhotek, my face unexpressive, as if I were being pulled by the rays of Ra alone. In fact, it would have been difficult for me to look any other place, for the glint of the gold that decorated my hands and arms, my legs and chest would have certainly blinded me.

As the ram's horns blared news of my arrival, throngs of people ran down the slippery embankment or crowded upon the grassy ridges to catch a glimpse of their King. I hated these tedious, officious ceremonies, but at the same time I felt the pride of my lineage, a line of Kings who had descended from the god-Kings themselves. It made me shiver despite the already oppressive heat.

For the rest of the morning, Anhotek and the Chief Priest finalized the details of the twin ceremonies that would take place the next day. That afternoon, I sat in judgment for the disputes that had arisen since my last visit to Nekhen and could not be resolved by other means. If nothing else, the painful process of listening to the earnestly aggrieved parties increased my resolve to speed the formation of the Houses of Life and I said so to Anhotek.

In the evening, Anhotek and Kaipunesut had arranged a party of sorts, at which Anedjib waddled around, singing the praises of the Royal projects that over the past year had already added to his prosperity. Dancers and musicians performed and wine and beer flowed freely. Cakes and sweets lay heaped upon the tables that surrounded the old temple grounds.

It was clear to me that our idea of sharing the risks and

benefits of paying for these costly projects had worked, although during the first six months, when their investments went in only one direction, all we heard from Anedjib and his partners was whining and complaining. Now their investments were paying off handsomely and their trade had increased threefold in this, the beginning of the second year since we had first collected their gold. Anedjib and his colleagues had recently begun to purchase quantities of luxury goods coming from Ta-Sety, Setjet and Babylon on their return caravans and selling them to the wealthy. In this, it was reported, they could not keep up with demand.

The next morning, we held the decommissioning ceremony for the old Temple of Horus, most of which had already been disassembled. As the Chief Priest chanted the blessings of gratitude for all that Horus had done to protect Nekhen and all of Upper Kem, I placed the first clay jar filled with offerings into a large pit that had been dug in the courtyard. Each of the priests placed their jars of honey, dates, frankincense, flax oil, myrrh, barley and other foods, so that if Horus were to first visit the site of his old temple he would not lack for sustenance. Anhotek and Meruka then placed a scroll into the pit, advising Horus of where the new temple was located.

"This is an uneasy time for all of Kem," the Chief Priest said to the gathering, "for until the new temple is dedicated, Horus the falcon god has no earthly home. Let us adjourn to the new temple, which King Narmer, son of Horus, has built."

The priests scurried to pick up their pennants and to line up along the route. Only a few hundred cubits separated the old temple from the new, but our view was blocked by the four-cubit high, double mud-brick wall that now encircled the center of Nekhen. The base of the wall was wider than the top, so that from where I stood, its graceful lines swept far into the distance.

From atop the wall, a man blew three long blasts on the ram's horn, followed by a series of short ones. Kagemni's men took positions on either side of the gates to keep back the crowds. Kagemni himself led the King's Guard at the head of the procession. My chair-bearers lifted me up and marched toward the huge wooden gates that were now swung open.

As we passed through the gates, a huge cheer erupted from the crowds. They shouted their blessings at me, poor and rich alike, and threw flowers at the feet of my chair-bearers, so that soon they walked ankle-deep through colorful petals. Before us, along the wide avenue, lay the new Temple of Horus in all its imposing glory. My immediate impression was that here was a temple worthy of its namesake.

Four immense poles, carved from the trunks of cedars imported from Setjet, framed the front of the temple. Atop the poles colorful pennants fluttered in the warm desert breeze. The outer pennants had the symbol of Horus emblazoned in white upon a deep red background. The inner pennants had my name, the catfish atop a chisel, emblazoned in white upon a blue background.

The new temple was shaped similarly to the original, but it was at least three times as large. Huge mud-bricks made up the walls, but they were painted with vibrant colors, an architectural first by Kaipunesut, who loved to create new designs. I wondered how he convinced the Chief Priest of the necessity for such a bold display.

The doors to the temple opened into a large courtyard, which easily held two hundred or more people. Trees and plants were everywhere and a pond, circled with plants, took up a quarter of the area. Just being in the courtyard engendered within me a feeling of peace and contentment.

The commissioning ceremony itself was a simple affair, attended only by the most senior priests, as well as Anhotek, Meruka and myself. We had all been ritually purified at sunrise and our entire bodies shaved. Unguents were then applied to kill any remaining lice and to heal their incessant bites.

Once the offerings from the Royal family to Horus were made, Anhotek and the Chief Priest surprised me with two items. The first was a gift of the ceremonial palette carved by Meri-ib, the very same palette that Meruka had shown me in a drawing more than two years ago. I had only thought of it once during all that time and assumed that it was a minor work, relegated to a corner of some temple. But, here it was before me, carried to my elevated chair by two of the Chief Priest's assistants.

It was much larger than I had anticipated, nearly a cubit in length and perhaps a third as wide. The stone upon which it was carved was extraordinarily smooth and of such a color as I had never before seen, a dark gray, with a greenish tint when Ra's light illuminated it just so.

The scenes of the battle of Dep and the unification of Kem were so detailed and so exquisite, I could not speak for several moments. I just stared at the palette, trying to understand the story told in its images. The main scene showed me, wearing the crown of Upper Kem, smiting King W'ash. Horus was perched in domination on the papyrus symbol of Lower Kem. After several minutes had passed, Anhotek nodded his head and the men turned the stone palette around, so that I could see the reverse side.

My eye was immediately drawn to the intertwined necks of the serpents of chaos that created a circle upon which cosmetics could be ground. But, it was the register above them that drew my eye, for there was an unmistakable image of me walking in a procession, led by Anhotek. My attention was drawn to the object upon my head.

"The palette, it... it is a wondrous achievement. But what is this?" I asked of Anhotek, pointing to the crown pictured upon my head.

With the words just out of my mouth, Anhotek motioned for another assistant, who brought forward a jar containing kohl. As the priests tilted the palette to a horizontal position, Anhotek removed a pinch of kohl, dropped it onto the center of the palette, added oil, and ground it to a paste. He carefully applied it to my eyes and stepped back. When I opened my eyes, the Chief Priest raised his hands and all the priests in attendance began to hum, a penetrating harmonic tone that raised and lowered in pitch every few moments.

"King Narmer, son of King Scorpion the Second, son of King Falcon the Second, son of King Lion, son of King Crocodile, son of King Falcon, son of King Scorpion, son of Horus," he intoned in his sing-song voice, "you have achieved what no King has done since Horus himself walked the Two Lands." He motioned to his assistant, who carried a pillow, upon which rested the same crown that topped my figure on the palette. It was at once familiar, yet strange, and the contrast unbalanced me.

"King Narmer, you and your heirs from this day forward shall wear the double crown of the Land of the Lotus and the Land of the Papyrus," he said, pointing to each component of the combined crown. What first seemed strange, now seemed so obvious. I glanced at Anhotek and knew at once this must have been his doing, for the political genius of combining the two crowns was immediately evident. The Chief Priest moved forward and placed the red and white crown upon my head.

The heat of the day was upon us already and I had not had much to eat for the morning meal and perhaps those two factors could explain the dizziness that overwhelmed me such that I feared I would have the shakes at that very moment. My head swirled and I gripped the arms of the chair. Behind my eyes patterns twirled like eddies of pollen caught in the currents of Mother Nile, red and white, lotus and papyrus. But soon the patterns straightened and became a ribbon of green and it stretched and stretched, as far as the eye could see. I knew then with certainty, for I could see it in the inner vision of my heart of hearts, that my boyhood dream had become real. Mother Nile flowed uninterrupted, through one land, one people, from Abu to Wadj-Wer.

"And that is what I saw," I said later that day to Anhotek, when we had a chance to rest in the shade. We had toured the temple complex and I inspected the granaries, where priests sat and weighed and recorded the tax grains that local farmers brought into the walled city.

"That is a good sign, Narmer. Horus still protects his

people through you." He then poured us cups of barley beer, a special concoction that the brewers of Nekhen gave to the Chief Priest as offerings to Horus. No finer beer could be had in all the Two Lands.

"Have you decided on her Kemian name?" Anhotek asked.

"I have... or I should say we have," I corrected myself. "Would you like to hear it?"

"I would, but I will not until five days from now, perhaps on the day before your wedding. I do not wish any magical spells to be cast, for once uttered, the name will be cast upon the winds of the spirit world for our enemies to retrieve." While I might have gazed at him with a skeptical eye in years past, his battle with the mosquito illness was still too fresh in my mind. I did not argue, but simply nodded my head in agreement.

"When is El-Or due to arrive?" I asked. My insides buzzed like a bee with anticipation of her arrival, our wedding, and the delights that I now imagined in exquisite detail would follow.

"Kagemni left this morning with a contingent of King's Guards to meet her caravan along the Wat-Hor east of Tjeni. They plan to march in double-time. I imagine she will arrive in a few days. I can see you are eager."

"Is it that apparent?" I asked. Instead of answering, Anhotek laughed, such as I had not seen him do in a long time.

During the ensuing three days, Anhotek, Meruka and Kaipunesut met with me frequently to finalize the wedding ceremony and all that would follow. By now a steady stream of dignitaries had begun to arrive from all over Kem and Ta-Sety, Setjet and Babylon and lands even on their far borders. Tents of every color and manner were set up throughout the grasslands and low hills surrounding Nekhen. A delegation even arrived from Ta-Tjehunu, laden with gifts. We debated for many hours before deciding to return them all, along with a small replica of what was now known as the King Narmer palette. The pain of their involvement in the rebellions leading up to the war of unification and their treachery at the Battle of Dep were still too fresh in our memories. The scene of the decapitated and emasculated Ta-Tjehenus represented on the palette would be as clear a message as we could possibly send.

It was during one of our meetings on the fourth day since the dedication of the new temple that a messenger arrived with an urgent message for Anhotek, who left for nearly an hour. When he returned, he seemed pale. "Excuse me, but I have an urgent message for the King," he said nervously.

"What is it?" I asked. "You look alarmed."

"My King, I know not how to tell you this. I... the caravan... El-Or's caravan has been attacked. Me'ka'el has been found... his body... he was murdered!"

"What?" I screamed. "What are you saying, Anhotek?" A rushing sound filled my ears and my heart pumped as if in battle. "Where is El-Or?"

Anhotek hung his head. "They... they have not found her yet," he said, his voice barely beyond a whisper.

"What do you mean they have not found her?" I ran to Anhotek and grabbed his arms, looking into his face. "What... what are you saying?" The look he gave me then, a look of pain and utter despair, I will never forget.

"The messengers gave me only sketchy details. She is missing, that is what we know, El-Or and Sara both. The caravan was not at the appointed place when Kagemni arrived, so they ventured east onto Wat-Hor. They found the caravan had been attacked. Me'ka'el had been killed. Kagemni's troops are searching for El-Or and her mother now. Knowing how upset you would be, he promised to send runners every day with news. He has requested more troops be sent immediately."

I let go Anhotek's arms. My legs shook badly and I stumbled back toward my chair. Meruka met me half way and helped me to sit. "But, how... who committed this barbarous act?" I asked, feeling a pain deep in my heart. Meruka looked at Anhotek with an indecipherable expression.

"We do not know yet. We may never know. But lately

Meruka has been troubled by dreams of Mersyankh's treachery."

"What?" I yelled in a rage, standing back up. "Is that demon so vile... so brazen that she would try kill my beloved? Send for them... immediately! I will be done with them! I will kill them both!" Neither of them moved.

"It is not Ihy," Meruka said softly. "I would be surprised if he knew anything about this evil act, aside from sensing that demon spirits swirled about the land." He spoke with the same assurance that I had come to respect.

"What about Mersyankh... and Neter-Maat?" I asked angrily.

"All three arrived here days ago, as cheerful and bright as Ra himself," Anhotek answered. "Mersyankh has hosted one party after another, currying favor with the wealthy businessmen. If she is at the bottom of this, it is undoubtedly cleverly disguised and will not be easy to uncover."

"And so... what? You are resigned to accept whatever mischief she schemes to beset upon us?" I was infuriated. "I have had it with her!"

"That is not what I am saying," Anhotek responded. "You must calm down, Narmer, for what is needed here are clear heads!" I spun around angrily and paced heavily to the other side of the room.

"Our teacher is correct, Narmer," Meruka suggested. "We will get our spies to uncover this plot, if indeed it is Mersyankh's doing. It might simply be a raid by thieves."

"Unlikely," I responded. "Ineni safeguarded Wat-Hor years ago. There have been few reports of thievery along Wat-Hor ever since he left the gutted carcasses of a few tribal leaders tied to acacia trees along the route."

"That is true," Anhotek said with deliberate calmness. "I suggest we wait for Kagemni's return and a full report. In the meantime, we will employ all our resources to find out if Mersyankh was involved, and if not she, then who may have been."

"Then I will be among the soldiers to come to Kagemni's aid," I said, hunting for my sword. "Prepare for me to leave!"

"No!" Anhotek said firmly. I shot him a severe look. "That is foolish. This could be a trap, Narmer. In fact, the more I ponder this, the more possible that scenario becomes. Perhaps they kidnapped her to lure you to your death. You have no heirs yet. If you perish, Neter-Maat becomes king."

Again I felt my legs shaking and sat down, holding my head in my hands. "I…until I see her standing before me, I do not know how I can live. I must act or I will go crazy."

Anhotek shuffled next to my chair. "Sometimes the most courageous action a King can take is to not act, to allow his trusted advisors to act in his behalf. You have proven yourself a great warrior, Narmer, but there is nothing you can do that exceeds Kagemni's abilities. You must trust that his love for you, and for El-Or, propels him toward noble actions. He will not rest until he finds her."

I did not sleep at all that night, but paced my room in the temple sanctuary, alternating between cursing Mersyankh and praying to Horus to intervene. It was during the afternoon of the following day that Anhotek entered my room. He clutched a small scroll tightly in his right hand and leaned heavily upon his staff that he gripped with his left. I could see from his eyes and his body that he, too, had spent a sleepless night. I looked from him to the scroll and back.

"What… what is that scroll that you hold?" I asked with fear in my heart.

"It is…" he started, then extended the scroll toward me. I grabbed it and opened it as I walked toward the light of the small window. It was a note from El-Or assuring me that she and her mother had survived the attempt on their lives. I devoured every picture-word she had written. The rhythm of her words and the ring seal impression at the bottom of the scroll convinced me of her safety and also of her despair in losing her beloved father. I looked up at Anhotek with a mixture of relief and sadness.

"Kagemni is with her now," he continued with a sigh. "She will be safe from this point onward. Horus has answered our prayers."

I sat down heavily and offered the chair opposite me to Anhotek. My knees shook. "The wedding... Me'ka'el's burial?" I stammered.

"The wedding must be postponed, that is for certain. However, I imagine that Me'ka'el has already been buried, for it is the custom of their people to bury their dead immediately."

"When will she arrive in Nekhen?"

"They will be here two days from now, probably near sunset. Our spies are on alert to see what Mersyankh's reaction will be. Kagemni sends word that El-Or's mourning period is one cycle of the moon. I suggest that we schedule the wedding to take place immediately after and that we stay here during that time. The city of Horus is the safest place to be right now, surrounded by the army and by our priests, who would willingly give their lives for you and the future Queen. There is much we can do while we are here."

Before dawn on the second day, I was awakened by Anhotek's gentle rocking and as I opened my eyes, for a fleeting instant, I felt as if we were back on Mother Nile together. When I came to my senses, I jumped from the bed, anticipating terrible news.

"Quickly, Narmer. Get washed and dressed. But, be quiet, for we must sneak out of the temple alone."

I washed my body, rinsed my mouth and brushed my teeth with an acacia twig. I wore a plain tunic and my leather belt and sword. Together, we walked out of the complex quietly, where we were met by some attendants with a simple carry chair.

"Where are we going?" I asked.

"To the river," Anhotek whispered.

"I do not need a carry chair. It is a quick hike," I protested, pointing at the four men who waited, the poles at their feet.

"It is not for you," Anhotek whispered, embarrassed. He shuffled toward the chair, climbed up and together we walked toward Mother Nile.

As we approached the river, with Ra feebly lighting the desert sky, I saw a few small fires and a large contingent of soldiers. Anhotek ordered the chair to be put down and we walked the last fifty cubits together, his arm hooked in mine. The first to greet me was Kagemni and we hugged and kissed each other like long-parted brothers. I whispered my gratitude to him over and over until he took me by the arms and, smiling, gently pushed me down the embankment toward the shore. Upon his signal, the soldiers surrounding El-Or's boat moved a respectful distance away, holding the hilt of their swords high on their chests in tribute to me.

A graceful figure stood on the deck, silhouetted by Ra's disk rising in the east. The orange light shimmered through El-Or's white linen gown and the gentle curves of her body were revealed in all their sensuous glory to my eyes and I was forced to stop for a moment to catch my breath. In all my days, I had never seen such an intimate sight. It filled me with such longing, I gasped and my eyes filled with tears. Her hands were clasped together, as if in prayer, but when she saw finally that it was me, she opened her arms wide and rushed to the edge of the boat. I ran to her then and scooped her into my arms and hugged and twirled her around and kissed her passionately and tasted her sweet tongue on mine. Even the cheering of the soldiers, quickly silenced by Kagemni, did not detract from that magical moment, but only added to the bond that I felt with my soldiers. That morning Horus' wings spread wide and enveloped us all.

Despite her grieving, that afternoon El-Or came to my quarters to share the mid-day meal with me. She wore a burlap tunic, torn at the sleeves and hem as a sign of mourning. She wore no makeup, but looked beautiful to me as we sat on the balcony of the palace, overlooking Mother Nile.

"When shall I meet with the Chief Priest and Anhotek regarding the wedding?" she asked me while we waited for Ahpety to serve us.

Her question took me by surprise, for I had instructed everyone entrusted to care for her not to mention the wedding preparations while she yet mourned. "You need not concern yourself with that now," I answered softly while holding her hand in mine atop the table. "There is time."

"It is sweet of you to protect me this way," she said smiling and stroking my fingers with hers. "But, if I am ever to understand your beliefs and customs, as I must, then I wish to start immediately. The wedding is close at hand and I have much to learn."

Her words warmed my heart. "Thank you, " I said, staring into her eyes and feeling my heart filled with love. "I... we all grieve the murder of your father. It... it is a blemish on our land that he should have been killed on our soil."

"No! Stop talking like that!" she insisted. "My mother herself reminds us that my father was blessed with advanced years, far beyond most mortals. We should more regret his absence from his only daughter's wedding than his passing to the next world." Her eyes welled up with tears at this thought.

Over the next ten day cycle, El-Or met several times each day with the Chief Priest or Anhotek or both at once. They taught her our people's beliefs and wedding customs and discussed every manner of wedding preparation, from what foods to serve to the actual sequence of activities that would lead to our holy union.

For my own part, I was intent on finding out who was behind the attack on El-Or's caravan. Kagemni dispatched a detachment of troops to retrace their route, seeking more information from the desert dwellers and posting guards to protect the rest of El-Or's family who were traveling to the wedding. The Chief Priest sent messengers to every temple and shrine near to the incident to make inquiries. And I made it known through my diplomatic channels that anyone who provided information to us would be suitably rewarded. All this was done discreetly, for we did not want others to suspect that El-Or had been attacked. The reason we gave for the wedding delay was Me'ka'el's death from old age. However, for the next month nothing beyond what we already knew emerged to see the light of day.

For one thing, Meruka and Anhotek determined that Ihy was unaware of the attack, although even with my respect for their shaman abilities I did not feel confident in their conclusion. Still, I agreed with Meruka's belief that Ihy would have been far more likely to invoke evil spirits than plot such a brazen attack.

So, our suspicions fell upon Mersyankh who, once we announced the delay, had left Nekhen hastily and returned to the palace in Tjeni. Anhotek's spies reported that she was in the foulest humor they had ever seen and that Neter-Maat would disappear for days, each time brought home by his guards in a drunken stupor from the house of a prostitute. Five days after Me-ka-el's murder, several lesser priests were found dead near the scene, their throats cut. Yet nothing we uncovered at that point showed us what her role was in the attack on the caravan. Anhotek and Meruka convinced me that unification was too fresh in people's minds and my rule still too untested to risk a confrontation with Mersyankh that might render apart that fragile union. They counseled me to bide my time, but to be wary.

As Kagemni told it, he had followed the Wat-Hor to a mountainous pass. There he found Me'ka'el, his man servant and two of our soldiers who were assigned to guard them along Wat-Hor, all of them run through with a sword, as if the work was hastily done and the evildoers sought to flee as quickly as possible. After searching for a day longer, they found El-Or and Sara hiding in a mountain cave, littered with bat guano and ibex scat, their servants and a group of four of my King's Guards protecting them. One of the soldiers was gravely wounded and died as they transported him down the mountain.

The soldiers could not identify their attackers, except to say that they appeared to be foreigners and wore their hair in the braided style of the Ta-Tjehenus. Our soldiers had circled El-Or protectively and Kagemni learned they had fought bravely and driven off the attackers, then retreated to the cave for fear that the enemy would return. And so our investigation temporarily ended, until after the wedding, when I told Kagemni and Anhotek we would continue it.

Thus the month of mourning passed quickly and soon Nekhen was again a beehive of activity. On the night before the wedding, a group of dark black men arrived at the temple and were escorted to my chambers by the Chief Priest. When Meruka looked up, he leaped from his chair, for here was one of his many brothers and a few more of his relatives, arrived with many wedding presents, among them a precious female leopard cub, orphaned at birth and raised by Atuti's family.

We talked for hours, recounting our adventure in Ta-Sety and all that had transpired with their tribe since. Although most of the descriptions of events in Meruka's village caused us to laugh, especially Atuti's problems with his three wives, the news of Sisi's death fell upon us like a dark cloud. Upon his deathbed he had asked that Meruka receive his shaman bag and all his medicine tools. As he unwrapped them, we all cried tears of sadness and joy.

At long last Ra's disk rose into a cloudless, blue sky on our wedding day. For seven days prior to the event, one for each of the seven manifestations of Hathor, I was forbidden to see El-Or. The Horus priests took us through seven days of ritual purification, which included a day of fasting in preparation for a visit to the Temple of Min, the goddess of fertility. I found it difficult to concentrate on the ceremony there, knowing that El-Or sat in an adjoining room, praying to the goddess that her womb would be receptive and fertile to my seed. When the day was over, the Chief Priest carved my name on the statue of the goddess, so that her fertile ka would enter me.

An hour before sunrise on the day of the wedding, El-Or's procession left her compound near Mother Nile and made its way toward the temple. I could hear the ram's horns blaring and the musicians beginning to play. The steady din of the crowds rose to a roar. The Chief Priest reported that the population of Nekhen had swelled tenfold over the past few days. His priests estimated at least a half-million of my people were here to celebrate the wedding, although he believed the number to be far greater, even double. No one had ever seen so many people gathered in one place.

It took nearly an hour for El-Or's entourage to finally reach the gates of the temple, where the Chief Priest met her and escorted her through the outer courtyard and into the inner courtyard, where she awaited my arrival. One of his assistants ran to our quarters to summon us.

"Remember, do not be nervous," Anhotek counseled me, nervously. He gripped his staff tightly to quiet his tremors. He turned his gaze to my face and squinted hard. "You look like a... a god."

His observation was accurate, for I had seen my own image in the large silver mirror. My face was crafted with the finest quality cosmetics from Kem and Setjet and Babylon. My eyelids were painted with green malachite and my eyes lined with black kohl. Gold threads were woven into my hair. I wore a pleated white linen kilt with a braided gold waist band. My chest was covered in gold jewelry of exquisite craftsmanship. Gold bracelets with turquoise and carnelians set within them adorned my arms and wrists. My toenails were painted in red ochre and my sandals sparkled from the gold threads and jewels that were woven into the thongs.

"We must go," Meruka said softly to us. "Ra rises to bless you."

We had but a short distance to go from the Chief Priest's quarters to the temple itself. But we took a route that wound through the streets of Nekhen, so that as many of the people as possible could claim to have seen and been blessed by me. Although the King's Guard kept most of the people away from our procession, enough managed to break through their ranks to touch my carry chair and ask for my intercession with the gods for a sick child or spouse. Others heaped praises upon me and still others threw flower petals.

Finally, we reached the Temple of Horus and after suitable ceremony, I was led into the outer courtyard. My heart fluttered wildly, for I had not seen El-Or for the required seven days of purification and I longed to gaze into her eyes and to again feel the touch of her soft hands in mine.

As I entered the outer courtyard, I could see her entourage on the far opposite side. Sara stood beside her and, along with a column, blocked my view. At a signal from the Chief Priest both processions moved slowly to the inner courtyard from opposite directions. I tried to keep my gaze straight ahead, but at the moment that El-Or stepped down into the inner courtyard, I caught a glimpse of her, a glimpse that took away my breath. Gracefully, she stepped with her toe pointed down, her hands gently supported by a woman servant on either side. The sun shone through her gossamer gown, revealing her ample breasts, an uncommon trait in Kemian women, and her shapely, yet delicate figure. She continued walking along the courtyard path to meet me at the entrance to the sanctuary.

In another moment, our two processions met and each person preceding us parted and lined up on either side of the sanctuary doorway until only El-Or and I faced each other. Still, she stared appropriately at the floor until, at the command of the Chief Priest, I held out my hands to her. Then, as she took them in her own she looked up at me, her lids rising slowly, revealing her deep brown eyes, as if she were all too aware of their seductive power over me. But, how could she have been thus aware, for if she knew how completely she was able to strip me, her lover, the King of all Kem, of any semblance of power with just her eyes, would she have still pierced me so with her gaze?

I continued to stare at El-Or, struck by her simple beauty. I found out only later that she had insisted on no makeup at all, but was finally persuaded to use a small amount by Sheftu, the maid servant Anhotek had given to her when she first arrived in Nekhen. Her eyes were slightly accented with green malachite and outlined in kohl and they sparkled with the reflected light from the jewels that adorned her hair and neck.

The Chief Priest snapped me out of my daydreams and we turned, my left hand holding her right and together we moved to the alter in the inner sanctuary. This was the first time she had ever laid her eyes on the living Horus and I could feel her hand trembling in mine. I squeezed it gently to assure her, but she averted her eyes from Horus' powerful gaze.

"El-Or!" the Chief Priest spoke to her from behind the alter. "Do you willingly sacrifice your ba to ascend to be King Narmer's wife?" He was dressed in his white tunic and red robe and upon his head he wore his white cloth cap, embroidered with Horus' falcon image.

"Yes, I do," El-Or replied.

"Do you promise to support your beloved, King Narmer, through the many difficult times that will surely arise during his reign?"

"I do," she said.

"And, do you love King Narmer with your heart and ka?"

El-Or turned to look into my eyes. "Oh, yes. Very much!" she whispered. The Chief Priest and I smiled at her eager response.

"Do you willingly promise to raise your children according to the customs and practices of Kem?"

"I do."

"Do you swear these things as an oath before Horus himself?" El-Or swallowed hard and cast her glance above the Chief Priest, toward the bejeweled eyes of Horus.

"I do," she said firmly.

"Then it is time for the transformation. What name have you two chosen for the Queen of all Kem, wife of King Narmer, with whose holy presence you will share the throne throughout eternity?"

We turned toward each other and looked into each other's eyes for a long time. My heart felt full.

"Neith-hotep," she said simply, turning back toward the Chief Priest.

"Neith-hotep!" the Chief Priest echoed, nodding his head. "Neith-hotep." The name rolled gently from his tongue and he seemed genuinely pleased. Anhotek, who stood at the Chief Priest's side, smiled broadly and nodded his approval. It was the first he had heard the name we had chosen, for above his own curiosity he feared the Evil Eye and all other manifestations of the dark forces that had become part of our lives since Ihy had joined the Court.

Yet neither of them were aware of the efforts that El-Or and I had put into choosing the name. There was no day that we were together since her decision to wed me that we had not spent considerable time discussing the name through which she would be born anew. In the end, we decided on Neith, to honor the goddess of abundance, for whom my own mother had been named. But it was El-Or's idea alone to pair the goddess Neith with the word for peace, for she told me it was her fondest wish for our children to grow up in a land of prosperity and peace. And so my beloved Neith-hotep, Queen of Kem, was to be carried into this world on the wings of Horus, my god-protector.

"And you, King Narmer, Ruler of all Kem, Wearer of the Crowns of Upper and Lower Kem, do you promise to love and care for your beloved, Queen Neith-hotep, for all eternity?" the Chief Priest asked of me.

"I do."

"Will you share with her your ka and plant within her the seeds of Kem's future?"

"I will," I answered with much anticipation.

"And in wedding Neith-hotep you agree to respect the beliefs of her people and treat her mother as you would have your own?"

"I do."

The Chief Priest's assistant brought forward a living dove, wrapped tightly in white linen so that only its head peeked out. He held it out to El-Or, who slowly breathed her former name into its face. Then, so quickly and deftly I hardly noticed, the Chief Priest twisted its neck and held it up to Horus.

"Thus El-Or has departed this earth. We ask that you guard her ka in her journey to the afterworld, mighty Horus. Unite her ka with her father, Me'ka'el, friend of Anhotek." I glanced to my side to see tears welling in Neith-hotep's eyes. We stood in silence for several minutes to respect El-

Or's departure from this world and to honor the memory of her father.

"It is time for the Whispering of Names," the Chief Priest said solemnly, interrupting our thoughts. He turned us to face each other and clasped our hands together. From behind Horus arose four poles and pole-bearers. A large sheet of white linen was fastened to each pole, emblazoned in blue with Horus in his falcon form, perched on a branch. Two of the men stayed behind Horus, holding their poles high, while two others moved forward, creating a protective tent over Horus, the Chief Priest, Anhotek, Neith-hotep and me.

The Chief Priest nodded to Neith-hotep and she moved so close to me not even a sword's width separated us. I lowered my mouth to hers, wanting more than anything else in this world to kiss her soft lips. She stood in front of me, her face upturned, her eyes closed, her brow furrowed expectantly. I closed my eyes and breathed out my name in a long whisper. "Naaarrrmmmerrr," I breathed into her mouth. She breathed my name in deeply, inhaling with it a part of my ka. Then, still holding one of my hands in hers, she circled around me, until I felt her other hand gently grab mine and she came full around and stood in front of me once again. It felt as if she had wrapped something around me as she circled, yet when I opened my eyes for a brief second nothing physical enveloped me. Six more times did she breathe in my name and circle me and by the end of it I was light-headed and certain that I was entwined in a cocoon of her sweet love, an altogether pleasant sensation, as if I had drunk the finest Babylonian wine.

Now it was Neith-hotep's turn. I gazed down upon her as she turned her lovely face toward me. Before Horus himself I swore that I had never seen anyone whose beauty ran so deep. Before she began, I took three deep sen-sen breaths to center my ka and to enter the meditative space. She breathed out her name slowly, and so softly I had to focus my mind to hear it and I knew then that she did so purposely so that none but me could hear the sensuous promises that were carried on the currents of her voice.

With the sen-sen breaths I imagined the sounds emanating from her mouth, carried on the wings of Horus to my own. They swirled into my chest and the instant they reached my heart they were no longer sounds, no longer just a name. Instead, Horus blessed me with a gift above all others. He gave me a part of Neith-hotep's gentle ka.

There are no words I can write to describe what I experienced while I breathed in and circled my beloved. Anhotek, in retelling the tale over the years insisted that I did not walk, but floated around the Queen, that he saw my ka emerge from my body as a spirit presence and slowly dance entwined with Neith-hotep's. The Chief Priest, upon his death bed in that very sanctuary years later, swore that he watched Horus himself raise his arms uncertainly toward our kas, as if by touching them he might experience the joy of what he himself had created. Of none of these can I vouch for. What I felt during that ceremony still causes me to tremble with wonder. Yet this I know for certain, that the gods themselves brought us together to unite our kas for all eternity.

None could say how long the Whispering of Names took or when it was done. No one counted whether or not I had completed seven circles of my beloved. None could even remember whether the Chief Priest completed the ceremony by reminding us to reflect back upon it at times when our love for each other faltered. No matter, for through it I finally came to discover the greatest truth of all.

There were times when I gazed upon Neith-hotep years later, when she stood alone on the portico of our quarters silhouetted by Ra's disk, when she tenderly suckled our son, even when I saw the torment in her eyes during the unspeakable horrors that Mersyankh later wrought. At those times and others I knew the deeper truth, that the celebration of our enduring love never really ended, it had only begun that day we stood before Horus. For it was at those times that I truly whispered my beloved's name. I Whispered Her Name.

# SCROLL NINETEEN

*Ma'at*

At this moment I hardly needed Anhotek to remind me of my blessings. It was our fourth month of sailing down Mother Nile since our wedding, a journey combining our wedding celebration with the Following of Horus. Events within the Court, and the War of Unification, as the battle over Dep had come to be known, had long delayed the Following of Horus ceremony. Horus priests throughout Upper Kem complained that the people suffered from not seeing their falcon god, or more accurately his representative in this existence, the King. I laughed over what the people might say if they knew how un-godlike I felt.

Neith-hotep and her mother fished from the Royal barque. They laughed over the tiny perch they caught, but also over the manner in which Big Mafdet pounced on the shiny fish as they lay flapping about on the deck. Day by day we could see the graceful leopard grow in height and length. She ate ravenously and her weight now exceeded that of a child. But she still displayed kitten-like behavior. After much discussion, we decided to name her Mafdet after my constant companion during my childhood.

I reclined on my couch, smiling at Neith-hotep's and Sara's daily visit and wondering for the hundredth time what it was that I had done that the gods would favor me with such a jewel as Neith-hotep. Her sparkling ba radiated goodness and infected everyone's spirit with joy who came into her blessed presence. As a youth I compared myself to the laborers who toiled along the banks of Mother Nile and saw that I was fortunate in worldly possessions. But I would happily have traded that wealth for even one year of the many happy family scenes that I witnessed. Now, I had what I had only dared dream about. But my heart pained, for who knows what plans the gods have for our lives? Too much joy is a cause for worry, Anhotek used to say.

Ra's disk slowly inched its way toward the western hills and Sara hugged Neith-hotep goodbye and bowed slightly toward me with a smile. I waved back to her, feeling the fullness of her happiness and wondering for an instant what it would be like to be hugged by my own mother.

"Will you and the Queen be ready for the evening meal soon, my King?" Ahpety asked, interrupting my thoughts.

"In an hour would be fine," I answered. Neith-hotep waved to her mother as I walked up behind her. Her perfume, a subtle blend of lotus essence, smelled divine. She turned at my approach and smiled.

"I am so happy right now!" she said, pulling me closer and taking my hands into hers. "I never imagined that life could be so content." Her light blue gown fluttered slightly in the warm evening breezes that were just now blowing in from the desert.

"Nor I," I said, my heart so full with love for her I felt my throat constrict. She would have hugged me tight to her bosom, had we not been surrounded by other boats in the Royal fleet. Mafdet rubbed herself back and forth along our legs, her long tail swishing from side to side. "Would you like to bathe together before the evening meal?"

After the sailors checked the shore for crocodiles and then set up our privacy tent, I removed my kilt and eased into Mother Nile's cool embrace. I kneeled up to my chest in the shallow water, bracing against the gentle current, all the while staring at my love undressing. Facing away from me, she pulled up her gown, slowly revealing her legs, then her rounded bottom and then the sinuous curves of her back and neck. When she turned toward me, my eyes were drawn toward the magic triangle formed by her full breasts and the patch of dark hair that surrounded her womanhood. I felt my rod stiffen with yearning.

"Dare I enter the water?" she said coyly, wading out ever so slowly toward me, her hips swaying as her legs propelled her forward. "Or would I be better to take my chances with the crocodiles?" When she came directly in front of me she knelt to hug me.

"Ouch! What is this weapon that you hold?" she whispered, laughing and grasping my manhood in her hand and sending a current through me as if I had been jolted by a lightning fish. We laughed and then she rolled onto her side and swam a few strokes away, before turning on her back. Her nipples stuck straight out and the area surrounding them was dark and puckered from the cool water. I clucked my tongue at her.

By the time we had finished our bath and swim, I was heated to a high passion and as we dried ourselves, Neith-hotep leaned toward me and kissed me deeply, her tongue darting in and out of my mouth for the briefest of instants. She was as inflamed as was I. We left the privacy tent and climbed back on board, my manhood nearly painful with exquisite anticipation.

"Your evening meal is ready," Ahpety said, pointing to the covered stern where we usually ate our meals and where benches were now set with steamed fish, fresh fruits, baked breads, cheeses and wine. Our mosquito tent had already been erected and our beds prepared. "Anhotek said he wishes to speak with you later this evening."

"I... uhhh... we... that is, the Queen and I... Neith-hotep and I are... we are not feeling that well, Ahpety," I said, with a wink of my eye. He placed his hands together as if in prayer and bowed.

"I see. I will leave out the food, should you and the

Queen... recover later this evening. And what shall I tell Anhotek?"

"Tell him that we are retiring for the night. I will talk with him first thing in the morning." Ahpety bowed deeply, his arms outstretched. He soon left in his skiff, along with the captain and crew.

Finally, we were alone. I picked up a palm twig and crushed it between my teeth and quickly brushed them. Then, sucking on a mint leaf, I entered the tent, where Neith-hotep sat combing her hair with the hand-carved elephant ivory comb that was one of her wedding presents from Meruka. After a few strokes she reached out and picked a grape from the bunches that sat in a clay bowl to her left and the strap of her thin gown fell from her shoulder to reveal the gentle curve of her breast.

Even after four months of enjoying the indescribable pleasures of her body, I still marveled at my good fortune. Entranced, I took the ivory comb from her hand and continued to stroke it through her silky hair. The scent of the lavender oil with which she had anointed her hair teased me, carried on the breezes that fluttered through the tent. I combed lazily, although my attention was now focused on the curves of her neck, which had always captivated me, even from the first time I laid eyes on her in Me-ka-el's tent.

When I could stand it no longer, I leaned down and kissed her neck gently, at the place where it formed a hollow. I breathed in her delicate perfume as my lips touched her soft skin and the gooseflesh immediately rose along her shoulder and arm. She reached up her hand and loosed the straps that kept on her gown and I watched as the fine, white linen tumbled softly over her aroused nipples and down into her lap.

I held her cheeks in my hands and brought my mouth to hers. I could taste the sweetness of the grapes still upon her lips and then, as she offered herself up to my desires, also upon her tongue. Our hearts fluttered wildly with anticipation. I felt like mounting my beloved in a heated passion, but I also wanted to prolong the pleasure as much as possible. Suddenly, Neith-hotep giggled.

"What is so funny?" I asked.

"This!" she answered teasingly, grasping my manhood lovingly in her hand. "It... it is as if it has a life of its own!" she added in amazement.

I laughed with her. "Sometimes I think so, too! Whenever I look at you it awakens and springs to attention."

"Oh, is that what it needs? A little attention?" With that she slid off the bench to her knees and slipped my swollen manhood into her mouth, lifting the most sensitive part with her stiffened tongue. The feeling was so intense, if a Ta-Tjehenu arrow pierced my heart that moment, I would have risen straight to the next world. After only a few minutes I could take no more and I lifted her up. She stood in front of me, her gown at her feet, her dark nipples before my lips.

No man who walked the Two Lands that night could have been more fortunate than was I. The boat rocked gently and the tent enveloped us like the wings of Horus, may his name be blessed. Neith-hotep's most secret treasures beckoned me. As we kissed and caressed each other, she gasped in pleasure and her entire body shuddered.

"Please," she whispered, pulling away from me, yet holding my face between her soft hands, her lips so close to me I could feel her warm breath as she spoke. "I cannot stand any more! My legs are shaking!" She took my hand and guided me toward the bed.

Neith-hotep lay back on the bed and raised her hands to coax me down. All that Anhotek had told me about a woman's love for her man, about the secret pleasures she willingly shares with her lover, had proven true and at that moment I felt thankful for his patient guidance. Yet I could never have suspected that the actions he described, ones that as a boy at the edge of manhood whet my imagination and often my bed, were far, far more wondrous in the embrace of the woman I loved. If our understanding of the afterlife is similarly limited by our lack of experience, then achieving it is worth all the suffering we endure in this life, for it must be beyond any treasure, beyond any pleasure imaginable.

At that moment, suffering was far from my mind, though. I braced my knees on the wood frame at the edge of the bed and slowly I inched myself into Neith-hotep and, moaning with desire, she dug her nails into my back. The candlelight was reflected in the sheen of sweat on her cheeks. I leaned down on my elbows and kissed her mouth and neck and gently rolled her nipple between my lips and teeth. My body sensed that she was close to the heights of heaven. Finally, she arched her back and screamed, a deep, throaty sound that emanated from her ka. She rose and fell in time with her pleasure.

When I look back on the times that we made our most passionate love, when time or circumstances brought us together as one to unite our kas and liberate them through the pleasure of our bodies, I knew that Neith-hotep was none other than a gift sent to me from Horus, my brother. For on those special occasions, as the time for the height of my pleasure infused my ka, I felt as if I stood at the edge of a precipice in the red and blue mountains of the eastern desert. I felt the flush of Ra's warmth upon my face and body. And once I spilled my seed, I fell from the heights and soared like my falcon brother, through the canyons, over the mountains and along Mother Nile herself. I could never decide which was the more pleasurable, the sexual release or the soaring of my ka afterwards.

With Neith-hotep's spasms of pleasure, I threw open my arms at the edge of the precipice and shot my seed into her, over and over until, spent, I sank onto the bed next to her. As she tenderly stroked my hair, I soared over Kem, content beyond all imagining. Ra's warmth flowed through me and rained down upon my land and my people. Thus we slept, deeply entwined in each other's arms.

In the morning, after we had bathed, I escorted Neith-hotep to her barque. I noticed that Sheftu looked at me, then cast her glance downward and turned away from us once I came aboard. When I returned to my boat, Ahpety also acted strangely.

"Is it me, or is something amiss here?" I asked Anhotek when he had boarded for our morning meeting. He, too, only smiled.

"Well?" I persisted.

"Yes, well indeed. That is how I would consider your performance last evening. That is how all of us in the procession would consider it."

I pondered Anhotek's words and tried to recount the events of the previous night.

"As for myself, I did say to Meruka that I believed you were not aware of the candles lit within your tent. Others that observed your performance were not so sure," he added, smiling wryly.

"Oh, for the love of the gods!" I said, burying my head in my hands. "Was it... were our shadows...?"

"Yes, they were. Projected onto the tent as if for a child's shadow play, yet... most certainly not suitable for children's amusement."

"How embarrassing! This knowledge... this will surely embarrass poor Neith-hotep to the point that she will become a hermit."

Anhotek stared at me with his fatherly love and pride, then laughed. "No, I have arranged it that no one will mention it to our unsuspecting Queen. Even Sata is in agreement. But, I must say that had I known about its effects beforehand, I might have arranged for you to intentionally put on this display of your virility."

"What are you saying?"

"Your soldiers and priests are quite impressed with their King's sexual prowess. Several commented about Horus in his bull form. I would say they were quite prideful. Your behavior last night may kindle a peak of childbirths when your soldiers return to their wives."

I forced myself to smile as Anhotek laughed, although I worried that Neith-hotep might still hear of our carelessness and be less inventive when it came to our sexual enjoyment.

"In any case, it is a good thing for the people to see their King as virile. Next to being a fearsome warrior, nothing pleases the people more than knowing their King is also a good and fertile lover." He paused to take full measure of my response. "May we continue with other business?"

For the rest of the morning we dealt with the many issues that affected Kem, from the construction of the new capital, to Mersyankh's attempts to bribe several young Horus priests in Lower Kem.

"I will be leaving for perhaps one or two ten-day cycles," Anhotek remarked towards the end of the morning. "We.. the Chief Priest and I, are developing a census system so that we are able to account for all the people in a given area of the land."

"Toward what purpose?" I asked.

"To maintain rule over a unified Kem," Anhotek answered. "If there is growth in the number of people in one area, we can anticipate their irrigation needs or temple construction projects. We will also be able to anticipate tax revenues."

"I see," I responded, thinking whether now would be the best time to raise an issue with Anhotek. "Since you will be away, let me seek your counsel on a matter that weighs on my mind." I stood to pace as I presented my case. "I have been thinking of what duties to give to Neith-hotep once we are done with the Following of Horus procession. She is smart and very quick to assess a person's ba. I trust her judgment in these matters."

"I would agree," Anhotek added, nodding his head.

"I have been thinking that your time is better spent with the affairs of state and with developing the Houses of Life. I should like to appoint Neith-hotep as Overseer of Architects, to help plan and carry out our many building projects." Anhotek raised his wrinkled brow and leaned on his staff with his gnarled hands as he looked over the water.

"This is in no way a reflection on your good work, Anhotek... of course, you recognize that. I merely wish to take advantage of all Neith-hotep's gifts."

Anhotek breathed deeply and stood as tall as his hunched frame would allow. "I am getting old, Narmer.

That is true. It is not as easy for me to juggle the many demands that have been placed upon me." He turned to me then and stared at me with a look that was difficult to interpret.

"I would be most honored to train Neith-hotep in the matter. It would be a wise choice to name her Overseer of Architects. You can trust her."

I looked hard at Anhotek, for it would have been my last wish to be the cause of any disrespect. "You are right. I can trust her, as I have always trusted you. I have been blessed by the gods to have people in my life who shower me with their love."

Anhotek smiled at me then, not an easy smile, but one restrained by his own thoughts and doubts. There were things I wanted to say, feelings I wanted to express to him, but the time was not right. He needed to think on the implications of our discussion. To force the issue would cross the line toward disrespect. After a few more words, he gathered his pride and left my boat. He rejected Panehsy's outstretched hand as he cautiously stepped aboard his skiff. To see him so bent over was not easy for me.

In two more days our procession neared the splitting of Mother Nile in Lower Kem. By now the harvest was nearly complete and throughout the land grains from the abundant crops were being stored in the King's warehouses located in the Temples of Horus. Everywhere we looked, it seemed as if a new temple or granary was being built.

People stopped their work and lined the shores to catch a glimpse of our boats and cheered me and their new Queen. They threw flowers before us, in some places so thick that it seemed like we sailed upon a carpet of color, not a drop of water visible between the hulls of our boats.

Late one afternoon, as Neith-hotep and I talked and drank wine together, our sails thudded to fullness with the first cool breezes of evening coming off the desert. After leisurely rowing along the shore for many hours, the captain took advantage of the breeze and ordered the crew to sail out toward the middle of the river, around a jagged point of land that had blocked our view downstream. Neith-hotep looked up and gasped, nearly choking on her drink. I, too, coughed when I turned and saw the impressive view of a large city overlooking Mother Nile where before there had been nothing but a tiny temple. It was Inabu-hedj, the city that Anhotek and Kaipunesut had planned as the new capital, its high white walls commanding a majestic presence over Mother Nile.

As Anhotek and the Chief Priest had planned it, this was to be our final stop in the Following of Horus procession. I was to hold court in the temple to settle local disputes, as well as inspect the construction projects within Inabu-hedj. Anhotek had sent Meruka ahead to make arrangements.

We ate our morning meal aboard the boat and left immediately for the city. Neith-hotep rode on her chair, but I insisted that I walk, for I wanted to feel what would soon be the sands of our new home beneath my feet. Meruka awaited us at the spot that was to be the entrance to the new city, wearing only a plain white kilt that contrasted handsomely with his black, muscular body. We greeted each other warmly and as Neith-hotep got down from her chair, I noted that he eyed her from head to toe, probably checking whether my seed had yet been planted within her. He was not the only one whose eyes lately betrayed his curiosity.

That entire morning we walked the length and breadth of Inabu-hedj. Several buildings were left partially completed, waiting for Inundation to arrive with its ready supply of laborers. Yet it was easy to see the overall plan of the city, including its tall walls and ramparts for its defense. Inside were granaries, gold and jewel storehouses, houses for members of the Royal family, Royal workshops and a grand Temple of Horus with its House of Life library. However, the city was planned around our palace, a huge structure like none our Lands had ever seen.

Meruka showed us the palace plans, drawn by Kaipunesut on papyrus. Throughout his presentation Neith-hotep's eyes were wide with excitement. She frequently interrupted him with questions he could not answer, and he deferred her until Kaipunesut's return from the stone quarries in a few days. We both knew that her mind had already conceived of more than a few changes.

That afternoon I held court to settle the several disputes that had arisen since unification and that the local priests were not able to resolve. I suggested Neith-hotep attend the session, since there was little else for her to do and I had come to value her intuition with people.

So far, Anhotek's plan for the Houses of Life had generally worked well, with many of these disputes being settled at their earliest stages by the most senior priests. However, the further we traveled away from Tjeni, the greater were its flaws.

The third case I heard that day concerned a wealthy landowner near Inabu-hedj, in the region of the delta just north of where Mother Nile splits. The case was brought by an adjoining farmer, a peasant man, his spine bent from stooping and carrying heavy loads and who had long since lost his teeth to the sandy bread and harsh conditions wrought by poverty. The case at first seemed easily resolved, a land dispute based on the annual surveying of the lands after Inundation, and I wondered to myself during the deliberation why it should have festered so long.

On the one side, Sekhem, dressed in the finest cloth and jewelry, told his story and brought as his main witness Osorkon, the local priest who was in charge of surveying. He, in turn, brought with him his surveying scrolls.

"So, you see, King Narmer, it is really only a matter of this peasant farmer envying the hard-earned gains of Sekhem, who has toiled his whole life to raise his lot to make his family proud and benefit his King," the priest, a portly man summarized. He smiled at me and then at Sekhem.

"Hmmm," I pondered. "Tell me, Osorkon, does this happen often? These land disputes, I mean."

Osorkon did not hesitate to reply. "Oh, yes, master, this type of accusation happens frequently." I stole a glance at Neith-hotep and her eyes twinkled with excitement as she anticipated my next moves.

"Will you be so kind as to allow me to see your scrolls?" I asked Osorkon as pleasantly as possible, holding out my hand.

"Yes, yes, of course," he replied, falling over himself to race forward. He pulled them from his long leather pouch and stopped before my raised platform. Looking down toward the ground, he handed them to me.

"But, my master, those scrolls are…" Wenamun protested through his toothless mouth. His clothes had been washed as best they could, but even his wife's best efforts could not mask the stains and rips.

"Silence!" I shouted at him. "Do not speak until I have asked you to!" I noted Osorkon's smug smile. To his credit, Sekhem stared straight ahead. Poor Wenamun cowered and shook at my command.

For several moments I studied the scrolls. Neith-hotep and Meruka stood behind me to review them over my shoulder. Neith-hotep bent down to whisper to me, pointing to two places in the text, one on each of two scrolls, then wiggled her finger slightly from one to another so none but Meruka and I could see. I nodded discreetly to assure her that I indeed understood, yet it was difficult for me to accept that she had uncovered something that had completely escaped my eye. Meruka then reached over and bent the bottom edge of the scroll and whispered several things in my ear.

"You keep excellent records, my trustworthy priest," I said with honeyed sweetness. "It appears quite clear that you have documented Sekhem's case." Osorkon look at once relieved and stood tall, the fat from his midriff hanging over his tunic belt.

"Wenamun, it appears from this," I said pointing to the scroll on my lap, "that you are an opportunist, taking advantage of Mother Nile's precious gifts to steal another man's land. What do you say in your defense?"

Wenamun was so frightened he could hardly speak, his words forced from his pursed lips in whistles. In exasperation, he turned to his wife, who came to stand beside him, then bowed low to the ground before me.

"If I may speak?" she said softly, her pale blue, tattered gown looking for all the land like the sad remnants of her wedding gift.

"You may, but be brief and, above all, truthful," I warned, pointing directly at her.

She looked at me for a moment before beginning, then cast her glance down to the floor in respect. But in that moment her gaze pierced my ba.

"My name is Senay, my King. I have borne three children to this man," she started slowly, pointing to Wenamun. "I know him to be truthful and hard working. He has never beaten me. He loves our children and has always provided food for our house, even during times of drought, even if he must take to the desert mountains to hunt." She wrung her hands together as she spoke, unsure of how she should proceed.

"I am a farmer's wife, a lowly peasant. I do not even know what the boundaries of our land are. I help in the fields when needed, doing as I am told. But, I know that Wenamun would never lie, that... that this little piece of land was his father's and his father's father's for as long back as our village memory goes."

"Then how do you explain this?" I asked, holding up the scroll. She blushed.

"I... I do not know, my King. I... we cannot read or write the picture words." She looked at her husband, who stood as if dumbstruck, just staring at the ground. "Perhaps the good Osorkon made an error, or..."

"My King! Look at them... you can see..." Osorkon protested.

"Now it is your turn to be silent!" I said firmly to Osorkon. "Continue, Senay."

"It may be an error," Senay repeated, not looking at me, "or perhaps it is that..."

"Senay," I interrupted. "Come closer. That is right. Now, bring up your eyes to meet mine." She again blushed, only this time a deep crimson. As she raised her eyes, still keeping her head bowed, the deep wrinkles that lined her face were accented by the harsh sun that shone through the temple's doorways. Unlike her husband, she still had a few teeth in the front of her mouth, although they were worn nearly to the gum line. Her hips were wide from childbearing.

"Do not remove your gaze from my eyes until I am done speaking with you. Do you understand?" She began then to tremble with fear.

"You speak now to King Narmer, son of King Scorpion, son of King Crocodile, son of Horus. Now I command you to speak your truth. You are under the King's protection." I squinted my eyes to peer deeply into the ba of this strong woman. "You do not believe these to be errors, do you?" She shook her head. "Yet I cannot make your case for you."

A long moment passed before Wenamun stepped forward to defend his wife. One glance of rebuke from me was all it took for him to step back.

"Speak woman!" I commanded her. She shifted from one leg to another before answering.

"No, this... this happens every year. After every Inundation under King W'ash's rule, the surveys made Sekhem's lands bigger and ours shrink."

"Only your land?" I asked.

"No. This... this has been happening to all the farmers in the village... for many, many years. Some were left with so little land they abandoned their farms and became fishermen or traders or... whatever else. Then Sekhem buys their land for the taxes that are owed, although... although some say he does not even pay the taxes." Osorkon fidgeted nervously as he listened to Seney's account. "We celebrated your victory over King W'ash, hoping for a change, but..."

"And do you have any records that show your land boundaries?" I persisted.

"None, master. We are peasants, we..."

"Then I am perplexed as to what to do, Senay. Here are wonderful records that our fine priest, Osorkon, has carefully kept over the years. There can be no disputing these figures." Osorkon and Sekhem nodded arrogantly, anticipating their victory in my court. I sat quietly for several minutes, then began to wrap the scrolls tightly, as if to place them back in Osorkon's bag and render my judgment.

"One more item, Osorkon. You mentioned earlier that these accusations have arisen before. I am curious. How often has Sekhem prevailed as opposed to the peasants?" Osorkon looked toward Sekhem, who shrugged.

"I have no idea, master. I... I do not recall."

"That is very strange, Osorkon. A man with your attention to detail, not knowing what the results of legal disputes are within his region. Would you not agree?"

Osorkon was now in a state of agitation. Sweat began forming on his upper lip. "It is only that I do not have my records here with me, King Narmer. I would be happy to consult them and..."

"No, it is not that important, my loyal priest. Just give me an estimate. No, not even that! In the many years you have served here, can you give me just one example of where the peasant in the dispute has won his case against Sekhem? Just one will suffice." Now I noticed that even Sekhem was beginning to sweat.

"I... I cannot, King Narmer. I am... it is that..." Osorkon's breathing was coming in shallow breaths now.

"Well, allow me to continue along a different line, my dear priest. You are such a meticulous scribe. Every row and column here is neatly arranged," I said, pointing to the rolled-up scrolls. "Very excellent writing, even to the point of writing the picture words quite small so that you will not waste even a scrap of papyrus. That is to be commended, Osorkon."

By now the desperate priest had no idea where I was heading with my inquiry. "Thank you, my King. Thank you," he said bowing his head up and down.

"Is papyrus paper plentiful in your temple?" I continued. Osorkon wrinkled his brow, as if trying to comprehend my inane question. "Do you have trouble understanding my question, good priest?"

"No, no, I was just... I was not certain why you asked

that odd question… I mean, not that the question was odd. I did not mean that at all, King Narmer. What I meant was…"

"Osorkon, let me give you, a religious, pious man, a piece of advice. Allow me, your King, descendent of Horus, to ask the questions and you to provide candid answers. Does that seem like a fair bargain to you?"

"Oh, yes! Yes, master. Yes!" He would have continued repeating that and bowing had I not interrupted.

"Then answer my question. Is papyrus paper plentiful here?"

I already knew the answer to that question. With the harvest so plentiful and every extra laborer pressed into the construction of Inabu-hedj, the priests throughout the region found papyrus paper in critically short supply.

"No, it is not. It is exceedingly scarce."

"Then perhaps you can explain this to me," I said deliberately while unrolling the scrolls again. I motioned for one of my guards to approach my chair to hold one end of the papyrus.

"Come closer, Osorkon, for I have need for your wise counsel. Here the writing stretches in neat columns from edge to edge, top to bottom. Yet on this second scroll your writing only occupies two-thirds of the scroll. And here again, on the third page it stretches over every piece of the papyrus surface. Would you not say that it is strange that you would waste such a large expanse of paper?" I looked up to see Osorkon wide-eyed with terror.

"And another curious thing… most curious of all. At the bottom of this second page, below all this blank space, I notice a smudge… there… right there along the very edge," I said pointing. "It is hard to detect, Osorkon, is it not? Take a careful look, my humble servant, and tell me what that might be?" Osorkon tried to steal a glance at Sekhem, but his eyes could not rotate far enough in his head. He sweated profusely and his tunic was now stained through the chest. He stood frozen in his spot.

"Allow me to guess at what this might be, Osorkon," I said, standing up, but careful to position myself so as to prevent him from making eye contact with Sekhem. "Could it be that you wrote these papyri in vegetable dye ink, the kind that dissolves with the use of oil? Could that smudge be ink that somehow escaped your eye? Could it possibly be that you changed the previous survey results and began anew on this third page?"

"Tell me, my dear Osorkon!" I said in my most commanding tone. "Tell me the truth and I shall spare your life! You shall have no second chances!"

Immediately, the priest fell to his knees and hands. "Please, mighty King Narmer, ruler of Upper and Lower Kem. Please, spare my life, for... for I was forced into a deal with the demon Apep himself!"

"And who conspired with you?" I asked as calmly as I could.

"It was me," Sekhem said haughtily, stepping forward. "I bribed the poor bastard."

By now both Wenamun and Senay were transfixed, uncomprehending what unfolded before their eyes. Senay arose and held tight to her husband's powerful arm.

"What you did is against our laws," I said matter-of-factly.

"Whose laws?" Sekhem responded with such arrogance, it took every bit of self-control I possessed to refrain from striking him down. Osorkon looked sideways, unwilling to believe Sekhem's disrespect and fearing that it worsened his own position.

"I am as good as dead now, anyway, dear King Narmer, so you might as well hear what your own advisors will not tell you. We Lower Kemians will never accept your rule. Never! You are nothing more than a temporary invader. In the end, we will prevail and cast you and your people out like old wash water," he said dismissively. Some in the audience gasped at his remarks.

"Silence! All of you, or I will have you removed from my court!" I turned my gaze back to Sekhem. To his credit he did not flinch.

"Like anyone in the Two Lands, you are entitled to your opinion, Sekhem. But, like everyone else, you are also obliged to act in accordance with our laws, however much you may disagree with them or feel they are beset upon you. But, know this, Sekhem. You are mistaken. My victory over W'ash was destined by none other than Horus himself. Your arrogance blinds you from seeing that.

"And, you are wrong about being put to death, for I shall spare your life, although in future years you may wish I had not been so generous. Instead, you will live, dear Sekhem. You will live to see that unification is not some desert mirage. And in sparing your life, you will provide me with a means to mortar my rule."

I turned to the captain of the guards. "If these two speak again, even one word, fill their mouths with rags and bind them." Immediately the captain ordered two guards to hold each man. I turned back toward Senay and Wenamun.

"I decree that you shall have back the land in dispute and three times that amount... no, ten times that amount from Sekhem's holdings that immediately adjoin your farmland." Meruka hurriedly wrote my decrees. Senay and Wenamun looked at each other in disbelief, then faced me again.

"What you have done is bravery of the highest order. When the laws are fairly applied, ma'at rests like a comfortable blanket upon our land. Tell this to the people of your village. And tell those who have been aggrieved by Sekhem's treachery in the past to come forward to also make their claims.

"Meruka, you will supervise the cleaning of the temple here. I wish it purged of all the vile filth that has soiled this land. And, you, Osorkon," I said pointing directly at him. "What you have done is the foulest of insults to man and god. You have abused your priestly role and with your own hands have stolen from our people. You have lied to Horus and to me, his heir. With your own hands, you have inscribed your lies onto holy papyrus paper. Therefore, I will see that you never again defile the priesthood. Before this day is done you shall have your hands cut off and be cast out of the priesthood. Meruka, make it so!"

Osorkon was too dazed to respond, but just looked pitifully at me as if I had spoken a foreign language. As two of my King's Guards dragged him away, he wet himself.

"As for you, Sekhem, I have a special fate in store. You have wronged the gods that protect our land. You have upset ma'at. You will witness with your own eyes how mistaken you are about the future of Kem. Meruka, arrange for all of Sekhem's lands to be properly surveyed and then… confiscated… every last parcel." I looked deep into his eyes as I said those last words. This time he could not prevent his eyelids from fluttering.

"You cannot do that!" Sekhem whined. "You are not…"

"Guards, gag him!" I said firmly. As two of my King's Guards held him, another rushed forward, ripped off Sekhem's tunic and stuffed a section in his mouth, before gagging him. When they were done, I continued.

"Meruka, make certain that any claims against his lands by the farmers in the village are properly judged. The remaining lands will become part of my Royal estates. As for you personally, Sekhem, I will not tolerate your arrogance and disrespect. Captain!" I called, turning to Rekhmireh, the captain of my King's Guards, who had served first with Kagemni, then under my command in the battle of Dep. "Cut out Sekhem's tongue so that from this day forward none shall bear the burden of his arrogance!" Neith-hotep stared upon my face with disbelief.

"But I am not yet done with you, Sekhem," I continued, surprised at my own anger over the matter. "You have disrespected the sanctity of the King's rule. From this day forward, your name will be stricken from the records, as if you had died at childbirth. Under penalty of being rendered mute themselves, none shall again call you Sekhem. From now on your name shall be Mesedsuhor, 'he who Horus hates.' Meruka, make this so." Amidst the shocked murmuring of the court, I rose and left the chamber.

# SCROLL TWENTY

## *Desert Wisdom*

"Shhh!" I whispered, holding a finger to my lips and lowering my palm to the ground to get Anhotek's carriers to stop moving. They were ten or more cubits behind me, along a boulder-strewn, mountainous trail in the eastern desert, three days march east of Tjeni. It was mid-morning and Ra's disk began to heat the rocks fiercely, so that it felt like the inside of a baker's oven.

I arose from where I was crouched behind a giant, round boulder to peek at the ibex we had been tracking for the past two hours. He was a large male, easily weighing more than me, his tan coat perfectly matching the light brown rocks that surrounded him. He circled on a flat rock slightly above and to the right of me, outside a watering hole that was hidden in the mountain cave below it. His horns stuck up straight from his head, then curved slightly toward the back. Immediately, I crouched back behind the rock and placed an arrow onto the nock on the string of my bow until it clicked. I took a deep breath to calm my heartbeat.

In a smooth motion I stood, all the while pulling back on the bow and swinging it over the rock toward the ibex.

In those few seconds he had turned his body toward me, so that he presented only a small target. I could not aim for his head. Anything but a direct penetration would just deflect off his hard skull. The only possible shot was to his neck and without hesitation I aimed for it and let loose my arrow.

As it flew through the air, the beast turned to jump away and the arrow lodged on the inside of his front leg. He bellowed as he leaped away, out of sight.

"Ha! You missed him again," Anhotek laughed from his chair.

"Damn him!" I cursed, slumping back against the rock. It was the second time I had missed killing the spectacular animal that morning. "He moves too damned quickly!"

"Ahhh, I was hoping you would not say that!" Anhotek sighed. He struggled out of his chair and hobbled up the path toward me, leaving Mafdet straining on her leash with the servants, who did not seem pleased to be left alone with the grown leopard. When Anhotek reached me, he placed his staff against the rock and eased himself down next to me with a grunt.

"Why is it that I sense a lesson coming on?" I teased him.

"My dear Narmer, you are too full of yourself sometimes," he said smiling broadly. "It is good to remind yourself from time to time that even though the throne you sit upon is exalted above all others, you still sit on your own behind!" Even I had to laugh at Anhotek's sense of humor and between laughs I drank from his water skin.

"We have talked of this before, Narmer. If it is simply you against the animal, you will almost always lose. To be a successful hunter you must think as he does, anticipate his next move, to…"

"That sounds fine in principal, Anhotek, but when I am actually hunting it is different. There is a… a…"

"Pressure inside to make the kill?" I nodded. "Then that is archery practice, not hunting," he added. We sat in silence for several moments, passing the goatskin of water back and forth.

"You know, Narmer, the desert nomads, like Baba…

you remember him?" I nodded again. "Well, Baba and the men of his tribe hunt the ibex with rocks." I arched my eyebrows at such an absurd suggestion.

"No, I am serious. They will hunt with spears if they are pressed to by hunger. But, most of the time they hunt with rocks, for only a hunter who can do so is worthy of that title. In my youth I accompanied them many times."

"But, how is it possible?" I asked, turning toward my old mentor.

"They consider the ibex a member of their tribe, like Meruka's tribe thinks of the antelope. They believe each animal harbors the spirit of a recently dead person, who has come back to nourish the tribe. As children they spend hours observing the ibex, tracking it, putting on headdresses with horns and playing like they are the animals.

"I have watched as two or three men hunt the ibex," he said, stretching his hands out before him as if placing the imaginary men. "They approach it from opposite sides. They know each mountain and they understand the animal's fears and its plan to escape and... by simple movements of their body, they confine it to a single place." He leaned from side to side as if to show me.

"When the trapped animal turns to flee one way, they adjust their bodies and it stays put, frozen, its muscles tense. Then it thinks to run the other way and they move accordingly, with every moment inching closer and closer, until one or the other man raises his rock and throws it."

"And they are able to accurately hit it in the head?" I asked, incredulous.

"Throughout their childhoods, they practice their accuracy by throwing rocks at an ibex skin stuffed with clumps of dried acacia weeds. But, the most wondrous thing is that many times they might only hit it in the neck or on the shoulders. But, by the time they do that, the animal just drops anyway. It is as if it is so tensed from waiting, so fearful even the slightest touch topples the beast."

"It dies from fright alone?"

"Perhaps. Their legends say that if the men prove worthy hunters the ibex willingly sacrifices itself for the good of the tribe. The person-spirit within it has tested the living hunters."

I sat for several moments contemplating Anhotek's words. "This is good information. I will try to learn more about the ibex..."

"No matter what animal you hunt, ibex or other," Anhotek corrected me. "Like the rails we hunted together on Mother Nile."

"True enough. But for now, I have wounded that poor animal and must put him out of his misery. As is, his pain will spoil the meat." I stood and offered a hand to Anhotek.

"No, go alone. I need to rest in the shade, then the servants will carry me back to camp." My heart ached for Anhotek, for nothing would have given him, or me, more pleasure than to continue the hunt together. I squatted before him, supported by my bow.

"I will be the ibex," I said, smiling. He seemed genuinely pleased. Once I left it was not hard to track the animal by its trail of blood spots. I could also see that he was favoring the wounded leg. In one steep passage he missed his jump and small rocks and sand lay scattered about where he had scurried for his footing. Nestled in a crevice was the fletching from my arrow.

As I rounded the next bend, I saw the ibex just below and ahead of me, panting from lack of water and shaking with fear. I pitied the majestic animal, for if ever the gods put an animal on land for a purpose, it was for the ibex to climb and run on these tortuous mountain paths. I knew that I could take him in an instant with my arrow, for he stood broadside to me, unaware of my presence above, thinking himself protected by the sheer cliff that rose above his head. Instead, I nestled down in a crevice and observed him.

The heat from Ra's disk caused his right foot to stick to the ground as the blood dripped from his wound. He would lift it every few minutes and reposition it, all the while attempting to lick the wound with his tongue, which was not nearly long enough. Then he would moan for a moment and look to his left and right, before putting the foot down solidly. As the moments passed, his right shoulder began to twitch from bearing the extra weight on his front quarter.

I contemplated how to bring him down, for to not do so would condemn him to a painful death and would not be looked upon favorably by the gods. He had three escape routes. One took him straight out over the edge of the rock upon which he stood, leading to a steep drop. I decided at once that if he were startled, he would choose that route only as the last resort. His leg was too painful to withstand a punishing jump.

Being on his right side, I felt certain he would not take the path that would come toward my position. The only escape route that remained was the well-worn path that disappeared gradually around the cliff to his left.

I quietly laid down my bow and arrows, then leaned over and picked up a large, smooth, rounded rock that lay within my reach. I hefted it in my hand until the purchase felt balanced. I breathed in deeply, eyes closed, imagining the force of my throw, its trajectory and its effect on the ibex. I waited until he placed his foot anew and then, in one smooth motion, I stood and let loose the rock, aiming for a point half a cubit in front of him.

As soon as he saw me stand, he calculated his options, but weakened by his injuries, he hesitated for an instant. Then he bolted to his left. The rock hit him just behind his right ear and he toppled immediately. I jumped from my vantage point and rolled to my feet, then pulled out my dagger from its leather scabbard and leaped the few steps until I was quickly upon the stunned animal. Holding its head by the horns, I quickly punctured his thick fur and slit his throat. He tried valiantly to rise up as I did so, but I leaned on him with all my strength, my cheek tight to his muzzle, so that I smelled upon his breath a mixture of fermented forage and fresh blood. In a moment he shook with the final dance of death and I laid his head softly upon the hot rock. His eyelids were still open and as I reached to close them I felt a warmth flow into my ka. I offered up a prayer to Anubis for his ka to journey quickly to the next world, where I prayed he would wait for me, to live his eternal life among my Royal menagerie."

"You were right," I said to Anhotek later that afternoon, "about hunting the ibex." Mafdet slept off her meal, a huge cut of the hindquarter of the ibex. She lay no more than a few paces from us, her pale yellow chest rising and falling in shallow breaths. Every so often her snoring woke even herself and she looked around for an instant or two in amazement before gently laying her spotted head back into the sand. Her tail twitched in spasms against the merciless biting flies.

"It is not often I am right anymore," he said softly, and I had to turn toward him to see if he was serious. He looked at me for a moment before smiling awkwardly.

"You know I do not think that, Anhotek," I replied. We sat in the shade of a large rocky outcropping at the base of the mountain. "There is so much to be done and you have been away much of the time. I must also rely on the counsel of others now."

We sat, not saying anything for several moments. The silence of the desert was broken only by the muffled voices of the servants and soldiers on the other side of the mountain. I wondered what Anhotek was thinking.

"It is good to be away with you," I offered, feeling a lump rising in my throat. "It... it reminds me of when we used to travel together. I miss those days." Still Anhotek sat quietly, his legs crossed, his ancient wood staff, carved with symbols that I would never understand, lay close to his side. I tried to recall ever seeing him without it and could not.

"Why so quiet?" I finally asked.

"It is hard to say," he responded after a while, looking straight ahead at the mountainous desert landscape, his voice almost a whisper. Across the wide, dry valley from us stood one of the blue mountains that the nomads believed harbored their god spirits.

"We have time," I said, smiling at the words that over the years together we would use to give each other permission to talk. He looked into my eyes then, one of his infrequent, but deep stares that he used to measure my ba. The skin below his eyes were exceedingly wrinkled and hung in bags, like soft pillows. Yet his eyes still burned with intensity. It was always a strange sensation feeling that stare, but now, perhaps because of my age, I was more conscious of its effect on me. For the few moments that our eyes met I felt as if our kas were connected, that something flowed between us, something that if I were to reach out I could touch and hold. As soon as this awareness came to me, it was over and Anhotek cast his glance back out toward the desert.

"It is a strange experience, getting old," he started. "I wanted so much to join you in the hunt today, to… to cast off this tired, aching body and run up the trails together with you."

I shook my head in agreement. "That is funny, for I wished the very same thing."

"I am nearly sixty years old. I have outlived all but a very few of my friends." His eyes looked sadder than I had seen in a long time. He turned toward me.

"I have accomplished more in my lifetime, Narmer, than I ever thought possible. My visions as a youth… they would never have come true were it not for Horus' gifts, both to me and to you. When he gave you the gift of seeing the future, it put Towi on the path to greatness. Every day our land grows stronger. Our people are better off than they have ever been."

"Only in hindsight does that appear true," I commented.

"Such is always the case," Anhotek continued. "Only strong, wise rulers who have a vision for their people are able to make the difficult decisions that will craft that vision. When you ruled against Sekhem and Osorkon in Inabu-hedj last year, who was to predict that it would make you a hero among the common people in Lower Kem? It worked because you listened to the rightness within your heart. That was a big lesson for you." At the time it seemed as if my decision was fraught with difficulties. Neith-hotep, for one, hardly spoke to me for days, saying that my ruling against Sekhem and Osorkon was excessively cruel.

"There is a matter that I must bring to your attention,"

he started. I suspected that what was to follow would be the issue that had troubled him for this entire trip. I wondered whether he had arranged the trip knowing that he would have uninterrupted time to present some pressing matter to me.

"The situation with Lower Kem is not stable," he continued. "Your judgment in favor of Wenamun was a wise and just one for the common people. But, it has incited discontent within the wealthy and powerful."

"I do not wish to hear this, Anhotek. He is a thief... an evil man. He is fortunate I did not have him killed."

"Of that, there is no doubt, Narmer. And confiscating his land for the peasants and your agricultural estate will be a continuing lesson for all of Kem. Yet, if we were to look closely at every deal of a wealthy man, whether for land or for wares, there is a good chance that at least one of them would not meet the test of our laws or customs." Anhotek's words were certainly true. Yet what leader likes to know in his heart that beneath the house of his rule there exists rot that undermines its very foundation?

"I am sure there is a point to your ramblings," I suggested.

"Indeed, there is. I believe you need to consolidate your support with the wealthy class in Lower Kem. I have thought long and deeply about this and have even discussed it with the Chief Priest, although only with him," he said, staring at me intently. "We believe it will soon be advisable... perhaps even necessary... for you to choose a second wife... from the houses of Dep."

Had Anhotek lifted his staff and struck me over the head, it would not have been a greater shock to me. It felt as if he had cut me open and yanked out my heart with his bare hands.

"How... how could you even suggest such a thing? I will not hear of it!" I looked away from him in utter disgust. My throat burned with the taste of bile. Just the thought of betraying my beloved was more than I could bear. I shook my head to rid it of such a thought. But, the more I tried to dispel it from my head, the more it plagued me.

"I am going for a walk!" I said, standing up. Immediately Mafdet sprung to attention, looking intently from me to Anhotek.

"Wait, Narmer, you must listen…"

"No, I must leave… now. I am feeling unkind thoughts and… I… I will be back in a while." I took off and Mafdet joined me, trying to rub her head against my knee as I passed. I reached down to pet her behind the ears and at once my ba calmed, although only a little. But, it was enough to cause me to change my mind.

"Will you walk with me?" I asked, turning toward Anhotek, who sat hunched over as if I had struck him.

He looked up and considered my offer for what seemed like a long time. "If you can tolerate my presence, then yes, I would be honored." He picked up his staff and pulled himself up by it. He adjusted his medicine bag around his shoulder and we took off, Anhotek shuffling on one side and Mafdet prancing on my other.

"I am sorry to have brought the issue up without warning," Anhotek said, nearly out of breath, when we had walked nearly a quarter of the way around the base of the mountain. By now it was late afternoon and Ra's disk began to cast the acacia trees in an orange light, their gnarled branches creating demon images from their shadows.

"I cannot understand why you would bring this up at this time," I replied, still wounded from his suggestion. "You always have my best interests in your heart, but this… it feels like I am a stranger to you if you would suggest I take another woman as my wife."

"Narmer, listen carefully, for in all your life in this world you will have none other more dedicated to you." He hastened his walk and stepped into my path to stop me. "I swore an oath to Horus upon your birth that I would serve you to my death. But even I serve many masters. Yes, you are my main devotion, but I also serve Horus. Without him we would not be here talking. And we both serve Towi. Her interests must come first. Always."

Despite my anger, I would never think to question Anhotek's loyalty, either to me or to our land. Although his suggestion sickened me, I felt I must hear him out.

"Explain to me your reasoning," I finally said.

"Never before has Towi been unified under one ruler. But, the houses of Dep are still strong. Mersyankh's own family is still powerful and they know full well of the rivalries between you and Mersyankh and Neter-Maat. There are small groups of wealthy landowners and traders who will support them, if given a chance, who now fear your rule only because of your judgment against Sekhem and the might of your army. But nothing binds two houses together like a marriage between them."

"We... we have only been married for little more than a year, Anhotek," I pleaded. "I love Neith-hotep with all my heart and ka."

"Who better than I knows that?"

"I have not yet even planted my seed in her."

I thought I detected the twitch of a smile on Anhotek's face. "There is an old tale, Narmer, of the farmer who lovingly plants his seed in his rows, worried, worried, worried over whether they will grow at all. As he plants, he thinks of all that can go wrong... drought, flood, pestilence. Yet he is so focused on the empty rows ahead, he does not see that behind him tiny sprouts are already breaking through the fertile soil." He hesitated while the picture he painted formed in my mind. "Neith-hotep is already with child," Anhotek said matter-of-factly.

"What? How would you know?"

"She herself may not know it yet," he said. "There are things that a shaman knows, certain signs."

I knew better than to question Anhotek's medical judgment. I looked up into his eyes.

"You look as if you have seen a mut spirit. This would be good news, Narmer. By the time we are back in Tjeni, she may know she is with child. But, if she is, you must let her surprise you with the news." I hardly knew what to say. At the moment I simply felt overburdened with information.

"Let's sit for a while," Anhotek said. I quickly surveyed the base of the mountain and pointed to a suitable spot to sit, where a series of flat rocks looked inviting. As we approached the rocks, I walked quickly ahead in order to move one rock close to another so we could continue to talk. But, as I reached for the rock, Mafdet suddenly jumped from my side and pounced so quickly, I was startled. Then, in the next second, she screeched in pain, a howling wail that only a large cat can make.

At once I knew what had happened. She pulled her paw away and out flew a scorpion, still whipping its hideous poisonous tail into Mafdet. As soon as she shook it loose, I squashed it with my sandal. But Mafdet was still screeching and trying to bite and lick at her paw. She was so crazed, spinning in circles, I felt powerless to do anything.

Anhotek hobbled to us, quickly assessing the situation. "We must act quickly," he said, stripping off the top part of his tunic and handing it to me. "Wrap Mafdet in this... quick, quick... and hold her tightly."

Anhotek dumped the contents of his bag in the sand, looking for the proper medicines. "Curses upon me!" he said, kicking the sand. With a grunt he grabbed his flint knife and knelt next to me. Mafdet was already panting in shallow breaths and every so often she would resort to a screech, pulling her lips back to bare her sharp teeth.

"You will need to wrap her, so I can cut her and allow the poisons to run out."

"Wrap her? A full-grown leopard that is agitated? How?" Only then did the folly of Anhotek's own words appear to him. He thought for a second or two, then stood and held up his staff, slowly rotating it until the carving of a scorpion that was near its top faced outward.

"Narmer, place your foot atop the scorpion's body, as you did when you crushed it." I immediately did as Anhotek instructed.

"Oh, Ra, come to Mafdet, whom King Narmer loves, whom the evil scorpion stung in this lonely place. Hear her anguished cries that reach to the very heavens. Harken on your way. The sandal of King Narmer, son of Horus, has trampled the scorpion demon, as Isis herself did with her son Horus when he was stung. Settle Mafdet's spirit, so that we may minister to her."

Throughout his prayer, Anhotek waved his staff back and forth. He sang the words in a low voice, the tone and pace varying in a way I did not understand. But Mafdet did, for she soon relaxed and settled down on her haunches and began to lick the site of the sting. As Anhotek repeated the prayer two more times, he nodded to me and I sat next to Mafdet and held first her good paw, massaging it, noting that she kept her knife-sharp claws inside. Then I gently grabbed the paw that was stung. She turned her head to me, staring at me with her feline eyes, as if to reassure herself before placing her care into my hands. I then took both her paws into my hands and stretched them out until they were in my lap and she lay down on her side next to me, panting, her head on my thigh.

"I must cut her," Anhotek said, squatting in front of us, holding his ivory-handled knife. Mafdet's eyes darted from me to Anhotek. "You will need to wrap her. A scratch from a leopard's claw can fester."

"She will be fine," I reassured Anhotek, not certain myself why I said so. He looked at me and nodded. He took Mafdet's paw into his hand and took some time to place his thumb and fingers just so. I could see from the whites of his fingertips as he worked that he was applying pressure with them and her sharp claws appeared and disappeared each time he pressed and let go. When he was satisfied he quickly sliced into the thick, black pad and squeezed to get the blood to flow into the sand.

"May Mafdet live and the poison die!" Anhotek recited. "I have been sent by Horus to cure the suffering Mafdet. Here, the poison dies, its fire drawn away by the hot sands."

Mafdet only winced when she was cut, trying to withdraw her paw from Anhotek's hand. He let her move it slightly, then pulled it back toward him as he chanted. When he was done, he removed the wax stopper from one of his medicine jars, poured out a thick substance onto a small piece of linen bandage and applied it to Mafdet's wound. Then he wrapped her paw tightly.

"Now, we must wait," Anhotek whispered. He looked

around us. "Soon Ra's disk will begin to set and your King's Guards will come looking for you."

"They will probably bring a sledge or chair with them anyway," I said. Anhotek smiled now, taking my hint.

"I will be fine walking," he offered. Thus we sat waiting, the two of us, Mafdet's head on my lap, my hand stroking the soft hair of her neck. The circumstances brought back a vivid memory of a hot, humid day, long ago, when Anhotek and I sat together in Scorpion's palace with my tiny cat, the first Mafdet, on my lap. My thoughts ran uncontrolled, from those days when one scorpion's presence loomed large in my life, controlling everything I did, to the present, when it was but a desert mut, an annoying and dangerous presence that had little day-to-day impact on my life. Yet the thought of my trampling the scorpion troubled my heart.

Within five days, we were all safely back at the palace in Tjeni. From that point forward, Mafdet would never leave my side, even taking to sleeping at the foot of our bed. She also became agitated or aggressive toward any manner of vermin that ventured into her presence. As we walked the palace garden one day soon afterward, a harmless little dung beetle ran across our path. Mafdet leaped at it, yet did not pounce on it with her paws. Instead, she surrounded it, growling menacingly, her teeth bared in a ferocious pose just off the ground. Soon the helpless beetle continued on its journey and Mafdet simply jumped out of its way.

On the day we arrived from the desert, within the first few minutes, Neith-hotep ran radiantly toward our caravan and hugged me to her tightly. It was the first time since our wedding that we had parted for any length of time. I was surprised at how much I had missed her body nestled in my arms. She grasped my hand joyfully and led me immediately to our chambers.

"I have wonderful news to tell you!" she exclaimed, beaming as radiantly as she had the day we were married. Her cheeks glowed with color and her eyes sparkled.

"I am with child!" she said, jumping up and down. I smiled and hugged her to me, although at that moment I wished that I had not known of her condition in advance. As we held hands, I looked at her abdomen, but could see nothing that had changed. It still had only her womanly roundness to it.

"Are you certain? How do you know this?" I asked.

"I am certain. There are some things a woman just knows," she said. Yet to this day, I do not know what the signs were that Anhotek deciphered to realize that Neith-hotep was with child even before she did herself.

But, once word of the pregnancy spread, excitement grew within and outside the Court. The nobles, the servants, the merchants, all were happy to hear the news that their King was not only virile, but fertile. Neith-hotep herself encouraged the fervor by commissioning Kaipunesut to plan an addition to the palace in Inabu-hedj for the first of our children.

Within two months, Anhotek came to me with additional news. He had tested Neith-hotep's urine three times with emmer wheat and our child was to be a boy. Now all the Court was in a frenzy of enthusiasm and joy, knowing that there would be an heir to the throne and that ma'at was strong throughout the land. All, that is, except Mersyankh. She and Ihy withdrew so that their presence was missed at nearly every Court ceremony or celebration. She reportedly fumed when she heard that Kaipunesut had been charged with building a nursery before he had completed her new quarters and I secretly sent a message to Kaipunesut to urge him to work with all dispatch to complete Mersyankh's project.

The first part of Neith-hotep's pregnancy was not easy for her. Each morning she awoke with the heaves and by mid-day she experienced a malaise that kept her in bed, sleeping, most of the afternoon. Sheftu, who had two of her own children, did not seem concerned. Anhotek, however, believed it best to take a series of precautions.

Two months after our return from the desert, on a cool evening, I came into our bedroom to see Neith-hotep pacing back and forth, agitated. By now her stomach was beginning to swell ever so slightly. As I approached to hug her, she turned to face me.

"I cannot stand it any longer!" she nearly hissed at me. "I... I feel like... just look around," she said, opening her arms. "It is like... I feel like..."

Not knowing what to do, I wrapped her in my arms and squeezed her toward me, thinking that she desired some physical assurance from me. At first I thought she was cuddling deeper into my arms, but she was instead trying to push herself away and I let her go.

"I feel confined enough already!" she yelled at me. "Look. It is like a temple in here... or have you not even noticed? There are statues of Heket and Hathor everywhere. Incense burns all day. Anhotek visits me three... four times a day to recite prayers and to examine me. If he cannot come, he sends Meruka or Panehsy. It is maddening!"

I stood there, struck dumb, for my lovely Neith-hotep had never before raised her voice at me. She was highly agitated and I did not know what to do, how to react to her ramblings. I glanced about the room, yet it did not appear to me like a temple. And, the incense, in fact, appealed to my senses.

"Well, what have you to say?" she demanded.

If there was one thing that Anhotek had taught me about women, it was to say nothing at such times that would make the situation worse. I just stood there, like a mud-brick pillar, staring at the woman who up to this point I felt I had known. I searched about furtively for signs that she had indulged in wine or barley beer, but there were no such indications.

"Are you feeling well?" she asked me. "You seem like you are struck dumb. Does what I say not make sense to you?"

"Oh, no, I am not saying that!" I responded, although if the truth be told I could not make sense of any of it. "I just..."

"Good. For a moment I thought you would think I am being difficult." She sat with a sigh at the foot of the bed. Mafdet, who sat at my side, her ears pinned back, looked up at me sheepishly and for a second I wondered if I looked the same.

"Come here," she whispered and I started toward her before I realized she was motioning to Mafdet, who sauntered over and lay down across her feet. She petted her absently. Not knowing what else to do, I went to the water pitcher instead and poured a cup.

"Will you talk to Anhotek about it?" she asked.

"Of course I will," I said, nearly sputtering the water from my mouth. I would gladly have done anything to stop this madness, although I had no idea what I should talk to Anhotek about.

In two days, Meruka returned from Inabu-hedj and he and Anhotek came to see me to report on the excellent progress that Kaipunesut was making in the new capital. The project was helping relations with Lower Kem. Many of the local farmers had been hired to do the work and local merchants were benefiting from the construction activities.

"This is good news," I said. "Let us lift a cup of good barley beer to celebrate!"

"It will be the showplace for our land," Meruka said with assurance, "and a model for all other lands." We quaffed our cups at his words.

"There is a matter I must raise with the two of you," I said once our chatter had stopped, "...regarding Neith-hotep." They fell silent immediately and Anhotek eyes became wide, as if expecting terrible news.

"She... frankly, Anhotek, she complains that you fuss over her too much... that you both are making too much of her being with child." Anhotek looked surprised and even hurt.

"But, she is feeling ill... she complains of fatigue and..."

"Is that unusual for a woman at the start of her pregnancy?" I asked.

"No, but she is the Queen and... and I..." Anhotek's words trailed off as he realized, as we all realized our predicament. We sat quietly, each of us holding our cup in our hands, each of lost in thought.

"I, too, am frightened," I admitted. "I think often of what my life might have been had my mother lived. Not that I cast any blame, Anhotek," I quickly added, turning to him. "I trust you more than anyone else in my life. I know you did more than anyone else could have done. Hemamiya recounted how it was you alone who brought me back from the dead."

"Wish that I could have done the same with your mother." He looked away for a moment, his eyes filled with tears. "I... I loved her dearly."

"Anhotek, if it were up to you and me, we would smother Neith-hotep in our love. We both need to consider her wishes in this matter."

"She is from Setjet," Meruka said. "She is wider at the hips. Not as wide as Ta-Sety women, but wider than Kemites. She is strong. She will be fine." He smiled then, a wide smile that showed his pure white teeth.

After a few moments, Anhotek sat tall in his seat. "I will adjust, then. I will not be so... so attentive."

"There is one other matter," I ventured, knowing that I risked hurting Anhotek if I did not approach this delicately. "The Queen, being from Setjet, is used to having a woman... a midwife... tending to a pregnant woman. She feels as if you are more her father, Anhotek, as you are to me. She..."

"Say no more," he interrupted, holding up his staff, his hand shaking. "I will arrange for the best midwife I know, a woman named Takhaa-en-bastet, to see her soon. Takhaa is also a healer. She is revered in her village. We have worked together before."

"I still want you to supervise her care," I added. "It is just that we must adjust to what Neith-hotep's people are accustomed to... make a compromise, as it were." If Anhotek was insulted by my requests, he did not show it. But he appeared tired when he later left my quarters, followed by Meruka.

"Did Kaipunesut give you any drawings to show me?" I called out after Meruka as he passed me. He turned to answer and I winked at him and motioned with my finger for him to stay.

Whether or not Anhotek noticed my gesture I never

knew, but he half-turned and smiled at me before shuffling on. I still wonder whether he knew what I had planned or whether, perhaps, he was acknowledging my mastery of the political arts. The end result was the same. I had Meruka to myself for a few more seconds.

"I need your help, Meruka. His hand tremors worsen. Please...think of a way to wedge yourself into Neith-hotep's care." Meruka looked deeply into my eyes for a moment, then nodded, but said not a word.

# SCROLL TWENTY-ONE

## *A Sweet Drop Of Rain*

It was not more than a week after Anhotek's sixtieth birthday celebration, a lavish affair attended by his many friends from throughout the land, and even some of his enemies, when Neith-hotep woke me in the midst of the night to tell me that her birth waters had flooded and that the birth pangs had begun. Her face was contorted with pain and I hurriedly put on my kilt and called to the guards to bring Anhotek at once.

Grasping her abdomen, Neith-hotep lay back down on the bed, groaning, her nightgown already soaked in perspiration. All I could think to do was force her to drink water, which she did in copious amounts as I supported her head. In a few moments, Anhotek hobbled in, looking painfully serious, holding his staff in his right hand, his left arm supported by Meruka. Behind them walked Takhaa-enbastet, barefoot and wearing her simple hemp robe, the only one of the three who smiled. She was Meruka's age, but a full cubit shorter than him and nearly as heavy, making her portly figure somewhat comical.

"Make way for the mother duck!" she said, waddling as

she did past Anhotek and placing her basket of instruments and potions on the table next to the bed. Neith-hotep managed a warm smile when their eyes met.

"Anyone call for Sara?" she asked in the peculiar lilt of her native village. I shook my head. "Well, do it!" she demanded, unimpressed as she was with power. "A birthing woman needs her mother's help. And be quick!" she added, clucking her tongue twice at me.

The room was already a beehive of activity. With hours to go before Ra would rise in the sky, candles were quickly lit throughout our quarters. Supported on one side by Takhaa and on the other by Meruka, Neith-hotep hobbled slowly to the bed in the small, but airy birthing room that had been furnished next to our bedroom.

In one corner, facing out toward the room, was the birthing stool, its comfortable caning woven through a solid wood frame. The seat was in the shape of a semi-circle, to allow for the delivery of the baby and the back was slightly reclined to aid the mother in pushing out her baby. The legs of the stool were set into holes drilled into four large stones, so that it was elevated and allowed the healer or midwife to stand in front of the mother and guide the baby out during the birth.

Around the room sat tables of fruits, nuts and drink for the gods, and for the shamans and women in attendance, as was our custom. There was also a small bed to allow Neith-hotep to rest between contractions. Next to the bed were two tables, where Anhotek, Meruka and Takhaa quickly laid out their birthing tools. Behind the tables stood various handmaidens, all directed by Sheftu, ready to bring water, clean sheets or whatever supplies would be needed. All seemed ready as Neith-hotep entered the room.

"I will examine her," Anhotek said nervously as soon as Takhaa and Meruka had eased the Queen onto the bed. His hands shook as he reached for his tools.

"What for?" Takhaa asked rhetorically, as she sat on the bed, holding Neith-hotep's hand, while her other hand rested lightly on her abdomen. "She has already had two contractions since we arrived. The baby is nearly ready."

"What...?" Anhotek began to say, taken aback by Takhaa's dismissive comment.

"Honey," Takhaa said turning to Neith-hotep, as if Anhotek had not spoken, "why did you wait so long before calling for us?" She picked up a linen cloth as she spoke and gently wiped Neith-hotep's forehead.

"I... I wanted to be sure. I did not want another false alarm." Just then another contraction began its mounting cycle of pain and Neith-hotep arched her head back into her pillow.

"Two minutes," she said, almost under her breath, but loud enough for Anhotek and Meruka to hear.

"That is too fast!" Anhotek said in a near panic. He stepped toward Neith-hotep. Immediately Takhaa stood up and placed herself solidly between the two.

"Let us talk," she said, as she hooked Anhotek's elbow with her arm and led him away from the Queen's bed. "You, too, Meruka." The three huddled together in a far corner. I joined them as soon as I saw Sheftu take Takhaa's place next to Neith-hotep.

"The birth is normal, Anhotek. You are too worried..." she started to say.

"She is the Queen," Anhotek objected. "We must do everything to assure that the birth goes well."

"It already does," Takhaa replied, looking into his eyes. He was too agitated to look back into hers, searching within his own heart for anything that might go wrong.

"Takhaa is right," Meruka added. "Her build is more like my people than yours. She has already borne most of the birth pangs with no help at all."

"Allow me to do my job," Takhaa continued. "If there is any difficulty, you and Meruka are here to oversee. Go use your priestly knowledge to pray for the gods' help." Anhotek stood, hunched over, considering her words. In a moment, he walked to Panehsy, who waited just outside the birthing pavilion, and whispered instructions to him. A few minutes later, Panehsy returned with an altar, incense and a leather bag that he quickly emptied containing statues of Heket, Hathor and Horus. At that moment, Sara arrived.

From the bed, Neith-hotep called out in pain. "Something is happening!" she screamed. Takhaa turned quickly and lifted Neith-hotep's gown. She nodded her head and Sara came to Neith-hotep's side and bent down to kiss her daughter, who looked up at her, her eyes wide with fear.

"Quickly, Sara, bring her to the chair!" They lifted Neith-hotep by the arms and she shuffled to the chair and collapsed into it. "Bring two stools!" Takhaa instructed. Once Neith-hotep's feet were propped up on the stools, Takhaa yelled. "Now, push... hard!"

With her knees nearly to her chin, Neith-hotep began to push, her face turning purple from the effort. When her breath ran out, she panted several times, before drawing in again, holding her breath and pushing. The servants were so excited they jumped up and down, waving their fists to keep from clapping them together. Anhotek had lit the incense and was offering prayers to Hathor to hasten the birth of our baby. Meruka stood behind Takhaa, waiting in case she required his assistance.

I noted these things that happened only in thinking of them afterwards, for at that moment I was transfixed on another matter altogether. For between my beloved's legs, from the sacred place that for so long now had provided me the most intimate of bodily pleasures, I saw a miraculous sight. A head began to emerge, a dark-haired head, misshapen, wet, elongated, but a glorious and beautiful sight to my eyes.

"Good! Push! Push!" Takhaa was calling out, but her voice now seemed far, far away. The baby's entire head was out now, cradled in Takhaa's loving hands. Tears welled in my eyes and my breathing came as shallow gasps as I witnessed the miracle of my child's birth. Nothing that had happened to me in my life, nor anything that would yet happen, would equal the wonderment I felt at that moment.

"Quick, get Anhotek!" Takhaa yelled, sending my heart plummeting to my feet. My legs shook fiercely as Meruka grabbed Anhotek and nearly lifted him to the birthing chair. Takhaa pushed Anhotek under the Queen and in a sudden gush of water and arms and legs, Anhotek held our baby, his hands supported by Takhaa. The baby's body was blue and purple and wrinkled as a ripe plum. And deadly silent.

As Anhotek held the lifeless body, Takhaa tied off and cut the cord. While she tended to the birth of the placenta, Sheftu brought an alabaster vase in which to place it. Meruka, lifted the baby from Anhotek's hands by its feet and held it upside down as Anhotek put his fingers in its mouth to clean out the mucus. Once he was done, Meruka slapped the baby on the feet. I could feel everyone in the room holding his or her breath. Then the baby sucked in a chest full of air and let out the loudest, most melodic cry I ever heard, a sweet music that filled my very soul and sent shouts of joy flying across the room. Tears poured from my eyes and my legs felt so weak I thought I would collapse to the floor.

Meruka come to me then, as if in a dream, holding the new Prince. The contrast between the tiny, white Prince and Meruka's huge, black hands was something to behold. He handed the Prince to me and I marveled at how perfect he was, how little each of his fingers and toes were, how tiny was his manhood. Without knowing how it was I got there, I found myself standing next to my beloved, both us of crying. She now held the Prince and he suckled her dry breast contentedly until, exhausted from his ordeal, he fell asleep, her nipple still half in his mouth.

It is surprising to no end how life goes, how we walk upon our individual paths, travel on our journeys, thinking at any moment that we know who we are. We imagine that we are capable of making judgments about the characters of our friends or family. But, when I looked upon my beloved at that moment, I knew that I truly saw her ba for the first time, and not just a beautiful woman, or my passionate lover, or a dutiful daughter. As she and the Prince slept for a few moments in the birthing chair that morning, with Ra's light just beginning to illuminate the sky outside, I saw Neith-hotep for the first time as a mother. There could be no doubt in my mind that her destiny was fulfilled, that the future of our land was great, that ma'at was stronger than I had ever before known in my life. I leaned down then and kissed her lightly on her lips and she awoke with a start.

Later she would tell me that it was not my kiss that startled her, but a dream she had that she walked in the desert with our son, her throat parched, the forces of evil pressing in. She prayed to Horus for help and in that moment the sky opened up and she felt the first sweet drop of rain hit her cheek.

Yet when she opened her eyes, it was my face pulling away from kissing her and she saw a second tear drop from my eye onto her face and through it Ra's light sparkled, making it appear as a jewel. And so Anhotek interpreted her dream and my tears as a strong omen, a continuation of Horus' protection over my son and our land. That is what I remembered of that day. That, and the pang of fear, as I gazed lovingly at my son's peaceful face and recognized that along with my greatest joy, the gods had also visited upon me my greatest vulnerability. The images of Mersyankh and Ihy crossed my mind and I felt a cold chill run through my ka.

I forgot my fears over the next few weeks, as one after another the celebrations over the Prince's birth went on without end. Neith-hotep's recovery was swift and within a few days her breasts became engorged with milk and our baby suckled contentedly whenever he became hungry. Despite Anhotek's suggestion, Neith-hotep insisted on nursing without the help of a wet nurse. Anhotek reminded her that her people did not have a class of princes and kings, but nothing he could say would dissuade her.

After much discussion, we agreed that we would combine the Prince's Naming with the dedication of Inabu-hedj, for Anhotek always believed that to combine important ceremonies magnified their magic with the gods. Once word of our plans got out, it seemed as if no one in the Court could talk of anything else. Even when I sat to judge a difficult dispute, where a priest was accused of stealing gold from the Royal treasury, as soon as it was over one of my aunts approached me to ask if she was to be invited to the dedication ceremony. Minutes later another relative asked me the same question. By the time the dedication arrived, I was sick of the entire matter and wanted nothing more than to be settled into the new palace and to put the entire event behind me.

Neith-hotep on the other hand, became more and more absorbed in the plans as she recovered from childbirth. Several times I entered our quarters and found her suckling the Prince while discussing the guest list with Anhotek or arguing about the foods that would be served.

Finally, word came from the priests on Abu Island that the river had crested and Akhet was nearing its end. Anhotek hastily arranged the Hunting of the Hippopotamus ceremony to celebrate Mother Nile receding and ma'at being restored to Towi.

We rowed in an orderly procession to Nekhen in three boats. Meruka and I had convinced Anhotek that if he did not stay behind to continue with the planning, Inabu-hedj would never be dedicated nor the Prince named. This was the first time in more than thirty years that Anhotek had missed a Hunting of the Hippopotamus ceremony and everyone seemed tense from not knowing how the gods would react.

The new Chief Priest, the son of one of Anhotek's late friends, met us at the dock with an entourage of Horus priests and escorted us to the Sacred Lake. The temple's menagerie of colorful ducks, geese and tall wading birds occupied most of the water. But one corner of the lake was empty of birds and there rested the enormous beast.

When I first laid eyes upon the hippopotamus my heart fluttered, for it was huge. Its two eyes were above water, stuck atop a massive head that was easily the width of a grown man's outstretched arm. Its body stretched the length of two men laid head to toe.

"He is the embodiment of chaos," the Chief Priest whispered. "Be careful once you let loose your spear." I nodded, only half-listening to him at that moment. My attention was focused on the beast, watching his rhythmic breathing, the way his huge eyes surveyed the crowd standing on the shore, the subtle shifting of his body as he plotted his escape routes. The Sacred Lake was shallow throughout and he would be unable to dive down as he would were he still free in the protective bosom of Mother Nile's cool, deep waters. He snorted nervously.

"Harken, oh Horus of Nekhen!" the Chief Priest called out as he raised his staff high in the air. The crowd immediately quieted down. "Mother Nile's waters now recede. Yet chaos still abounds throughout the Two Lands. Mut spirits roam." He stopped to take the pulse of the crowd, which was transfixed on his words. The giant hippopotamus was becoming more agitated. He moved his head slowly in a wide arc to try to better understand what was happening around him.

"This hippopotamus killed one of our priests. He is a mut disguised as an animal. Through King Narmer Horus will restore ma'at to our Lands."

The crowds burst into a mighty cheer. Without taking my eyes off the beast, I stepped onto the wide barge before us. At the same time, my soldiers mounted the two barges on either side of me, their spears at the ready. Ahpety handed me the ceremonial spear I was to use, a well-balanced length of hardwood cut from the forests deep in Ta-Sety, with an intricately carved silver spearhead mounted on its tip.

In front of us the beast snorted so forcefully, great puffs of spray erupted into the air. As the barges spread out, he ducked his head briefly below the surface. My gaze never left him. In fear, he desperately searched for a way to escape under the water. The embankments surrounding the Sacred Lake were too steep for his short legs, for the gods created the hippopotamus so that the waters were its best protection.

The pole-bearers pushed us ever closer to the frightened animal. When we were twenty cubits away, it lifted its head out of the water and opened its jaws wide to let out a mighty bellow. At that moment my soldiers lost their merriment, for the immense jaws of that powerful beast could easily break a man's spine in two. Again it roared its fearsome warning. The pole-bearers looked toward me for guidance and I pointed my spear to urge them on. When we were but ten cubits from the animal, I held up my hand and the barges on either side of me stopped.

"You men stay here to block his escape routes," I cautioned. Alone in my barge with my pole-bearer, as our ritual demanded, I nodded my head for him to continue.

The beast backed himself toward the high bank as far as he could without his rear end coming out of the water. He wiggled his backside, bracing his powerful rear legs into the muddy bottom to affect a charge.

"Come directly toward him," I whispered to my pole-bearer. "Slowly, though... very slowly."

I raised my spear and when we were but three cubits in front of him, he raised his body up from the water and let out the most fearsome bellow I had ever heard. Had I been immersed in the waters of eternal damnation I could never have imagined a more terrible cry. He wiggled his head back and forth for a second as he screamed, before beginning his charge. I watched his backside muscles intently. The instant he set them to charge, I heaved my spear with all my might into his open mouth.

The mut of the underworld froze time at the instant the spear tip penetrated the giant's flesh. His eyes opened wide in panic. He reared up onto his hind legs and tried unsuccessfully to shake the painful barb from his mouth, but it was seated too solidly. He bit down and the spear pole broke in two. The end flew from his jaws and nearly hit one of my soldiers standing in the barge to my left. Then, as if he had sucked in the breath of all foul spirits in the land, he charged straight for my barge.

I immediately shoved my pole-bearer off the barge with all my might, toward the waiting hands of two of my soldiers in the barge to our right. As I saw them reach to grab the boy, I felt a power beneath my feet such as I had never experienced. In the next instant, I wondered to myself why my soldiers should be upside down and below me. I flew from my barge as if propelled by a dust devil.

In the next moment, I fell with a huge splash into the Sacred Lake on my back and neck, so forcefully my head burrowed into the muck of the bottom. It tasted of bird and hippopotamus dung and worse. I quickly pushed myself out and broke the surface. At least a dozen of my soldiers had run from the shore and had dived into the water to rescue me, their spears at the ready. The soldiers on the two remaining barges battled mightily with the enraged hippopotamus. Between the two barges I caught a peek of the beast, spears sticking out of its body in every conceivable place. He churned in the water valiantly, his blood turning the water crimson. By the time I waded to shore, the beast was subdued and nearly dead. I walked along the shoreline amidst cheering from the crowds that ringed the Sacred Lake, yet my gaze was still focused on the mortally wounded animal. As I approached what I expected to be his lifeless carcass, he turned his head around and his eyes met mine. I stopped dead in my tracks. The beast's jaws opened and closed, as if he were trying to speak to me and I had the terrible feeling that he was warning me of something foul and evil. Then, he closed his mouth slowly and his head sank beneath the waters.

The Chief Priest ran up, smiling and congratulating me. My soldiers held their spears high and yelled in attribution, singing my praises and bragging of my prowess. The evil mut had been exiled from Towi and ma'at restored, the Chief Priest pronounced over and over to the crowds and though I listened to his words, other messages raced through my mind, unsettling ones. Despite the omen, thanks be to Horus, I did have enough presence of mind to make it clear to the Chief Priest that I would not look with favor on the sacred hippopotamus being quite so large in future years.

Had it not been for the celebrations that followed, I would have left Nekhen that minute and sailed straight back to Tjeni, to Neith-hotep and the Prince. The more I thought on the matter, the angrier I became with myself for leaving a weakened Anhotek to protect my wife and son from the powerful evils of Mersyankh and Ihy. Their recent excuses for not attending Court functions were hardly credible. I had not laid eyes on them for weeks. And while reports of foment circulated widely in Lower Kem, our spies could not link any of the incidents to Mersyankh or Ihy.

Until we reached Tjeni, until I held my beloved in my arms and checked on my son's safety, it must have been exceedingly difficult for any of my soldiers to be in my presence, for I was short-tempered and overly demanding. Every time a boat appeared on the horizon, I could feel my body tense until it passed, each time saying a silent prayer to Horus that it not be a messenger from the palace bearing bad news. At one point during the sail, Meruka tried to talk about preparing for the plagues of Shomu, but I could not focus on the matter and ended it quickly.

Throughout the journey north, I kept to myself and ruminated about the affairs of Towi, of Anhotek's deteriorating health, of Kagemni's advancing age, of the choices Anhotek discussed with me for a second wife. These were problems that plagued me greatly and had hidden in the dark places of my heart. By time we approached the palace, I had begun to develop a plan to deal with these issues, albeit one fraught with many difficulties.

Once we arrived in Tjeni, my worries about the Court appeared to be ill-founded. The next morning, after a night spent in the comforting embrace of Neith-hotep, I convened a meeting of my most trusted advisors.

"The planning for the dedication goes well," Anhotek reported first. "With the sacrifice of the hippopotamus, all is ready. We leave in two weeks time for Inabu-hedj."

"And the ceremony... what will it involve?" I asked.

From a long leather pouch, Anhotek removed a small papyrus scroll. He reviewed its contents before responding. "We will begin with the dedication ceremony," he finally said. I felt a certain sadness for my teacher then, for in years past he would have recalled every detail of the plans from his memory.

"The Temple of Horus and the House of Life within it must be dedicated first to impart holiness upon the site. Then you will circle the walls of the city, to wrap it within

Horus' protective powers, and dedicate it as the capital of all Kem and the site of the King's palace for all eternity." Anhotek paused for a few seconds. "Knowing your dislike for these ceremonial events, we have crowded them all into one day."

"Good," I said, nodding to the others.

"The following days will be ones of celebration and libation. Emissaries will arrive from all neighboring lands. On the seventh day after the dedication we will have the naming of the Prince."

"At the temple in Inabu-hedj?" I asked, surprised.

"Yes, it will be the first official ceremony after its dedication. It is a good omen. The Prince's eventual coronation will, of course, be in Nekhen."

"Yes, of course." We waited for Anhotek to continue, but he sat and stared vacantly, as if no one else was present in the room.

"Are there any other urgent matters?" I asked of the others, trying, in part, to cover for Anhotek's lapse.

"There is a matter I wish to bring to the King's attention," Kagemni said. I looked to my Chief General and felt a pang of regret that the gods afford men such a brief time in this world. The muscles of Kagemni's once feared rock-hard body sagged with age and his notorious barrel chest now showed more rib than muscle. Yet he still projected a fearsome figure, if for no other reason than his formidable reputation.

"Go on."

"There is the matter of Abu Island. We recommend building a fort and temple there."

"But, why? There is no more peaceful site in all the Two Lands than Abu Island. The people there are hardly a threat."

Kagemni looked toward Meruka and Anhotek. "It is to protect our land from my people," Meruka said, his head held high and proud.

"From... what?"

Kagemni continued. "Anhotek has always pleaded that we be cautious about Ta-Sety. They are an advanced people.

We recruit among them for mercenaries. Right now there are only minor skirmishes over our border. The fort would be a show of power. It would provide an early warning if the Ta-Setys, or tribes to their south, were to invade our lands. It would also serve as an advance supply outpost if we were to need a staging area for war."

"But we are on friendly terms with the Ta-Setys. How will they react when they see us building a fort? It may provoke them to war," I protested.

Anhotek stirred back to life. He sighed deeply, such that we all fixed our attention on him. "Yes, it is a paradox," he started. "They are our second most important trading partner. They buy our grains to feed their people. But our wealthy class has become much too dependent upon their ebony and ivory. Their ostrich eggs are indispensable, if we are to believe the nobles in Nekhen. And then, there is their gold. I can foresee the day, certainly not in our lifetimes, when we might require their gold to pay for building roads and temples and new cities to house our people.

"Trade builds good neighbors, but it can also lead to conflict. If we approach this project wisely, we will avoid the Ta-Setys seeing the fort as a threat."

"There is another matter," Kaipunesut added. "We could build a device on Abu Island to measure the height of the flood each year. Then we could better estimate the harvest. That would be a very useful planning tool."

I weighed their words for several minutes. Visions of my youth, mingling with the humble villagers and fishermen of Abu Island filled my mind. I recalled my first foray into Ta-Sety, when I met Meruka and his brother, Atuti, who still visited us from time to time. Most of all I recalled Sisi and my promise to him of many years before. I knew then what I must do.

"You present good arguments for the fort and temple," I began. "The first task of any leader is to protect his people. But, I also have sworn an oath to Meruka's father, whose spirit still dwells in his son." I looked full into Meruka's eyes and his cheek quivered with emotion.

"You may begin plans for a temple. The device to

measure floods would be most welcome, too. But, out of respect to Sisi and Meruka we will not do anything to provoke our Ta-Sety neighbors. Instead, we will send a delegation to Ta-Sety, headed by Meruka, to strengthen our trade and our good name with them." Anhotek had a faint smile on his face at my decision. Meruka's chest swelled with pride. Kaipunesut's quill swiftly made picture words on his tiny papyrus scroll. "Make preparations to leave after the dedication of Inabu-hedj," I said turning to Meruka. He nodded and I saw his eyes filled with water.

"Now, I have some matters to discuss," I continued. "In the past many weeks, I have debated in my mind how to plan for the administration of Inabu-hedj. All the nomes now have governors except for the region around Inabu-hedj. I have decided to name Kagemni the governor there."

Kagemni shot back in his seat and nearly toppled over. "Me? A damned governor?" He looked around at the rest of the council, dumbfounded. "Have you drunk too much already this morning, Narmer?" But no one else's eyes reflected the humor he saw in the situation.

"I... I'm a damned soldier!" he protested, in a near panic. "I'm not going to kiss anyone's backside to get their agreement to anything!" He paused to frantically collect his thoughts, as we watched in some amusement. "I hate attending celebrations, let alone host one." Finally, he turned to me. "I will not do it, Narmer! I would rather you put me to the sword for insubordination than make me the damned governor of a damned nome!" He sat back and crossed his arms over his barrel chest, refusing to look anyone in the eye.

I let silence fill the space between us for many minutes before speaking. In the meantime, Kagemni constantly rustled in his chair, huffing and snorting and folding and refolding his arms. No one dared look at him. "May I speak in my defense?" I asked after a suitable time. He made a gruff sound with his throat.

"I am not asking you to give up your position as Chief General of the King's Army, my dear friend. I need you, now more than ever." He twisted in his seat, not looking at me.

"With Inabu-hedj soon to be our new capital, I will need my most loyal soldiers nearby as a show of power for the Lower Kemians. You will have all the help you need to arrange public functions. Most ceremonies and celebrations will take place through the King's palace and so you will only need to make an occasional appearance." He shrugged his shoulders, but still did not look at me.

"There is another matter that weighed upon my decision, Kagemni. You are the most experienced army officer in all of Kem. I need you nearby for counsel when the need arises, not at the far flung borders of our lands. You fought valiantly for Scorpion and by my side at the battle of Dep. It is time, my dearest of friends, to turn over field command to a younger man of your choosing."

I could have said more, but did not. Kagemni was a man of few words and I respected that in him. Like all people, his strength was also his weakness and he was now rooted in obstinacy. He needed to juggle my words within his heart and thus dull their sharp edges. Like the loyal soldier he was, he would follow my orders, like them or not.

"That is all I have for this morning," I said, already feeling exhausted. "Is there anything else?" Everyone shook their heads, but continued to stare at the floor. "You may go," I said.

"I will do it!" Kagemni suddenly burst out. "I damned well do not like it, but I will do it!" I smiled at him warmly then, in recognition of our friendship, but also as a testimony that the soldier within him would not allow the meeting to end without acknowledging the command of his superior.

"Thank you, Kagemni. I know you will do what I ask and do it well. I will not have to worry about my back with you in Inabu-hedj."

"You are damned right! But, you had better follow my advice concerning your protection!" he added crustily.

"I will, my loyal friend," I said, and got up and hugged him. He squeezed me hard and pounded my back vigorously. "Damned governor! You must have caught some illness in Nekhen!" he added as he let me go. As the rest stood to leave, I turned to Anhotek.

"Stay for a moment, Anhotek," I said as he attempted, with difficulty, to get up. "We will share a bit of fine barley beer together before the morning is over." He sat back down with a groan, as if his limbs ached from the effort. I poured the thin beer into each of our alabaster cups.

"That was well done with Kagemni," he said as soon as he had quenched his thirst. "You have learned the art of diplomacy well."

"Thank you, but if I do excel, it is due to your teaching."

"A teacher can do only so much if the pupil has little talent, Narmer. It makes me proud to see the man you have become."

"Well, we shall see how good my diplomacy skills are, for I have yet a matter to discuss with you." He began to smile, then broke out into a full belly laugh and put down his cup lest he spill it.

"Ah, I have been waiting a long time for this discussion, although I must admit that I expected it well before your… your… promotion of Kagemni."

"You know me better than that, dear teacher," I said, catching his mischievous mood. "Promoting you, as you call it, without your knowing my intention before even I did, would be impossible. So, tell me how we handle this matter, for between you and me I lay my skills aside and speak to my father only from my heart."

"I have thought for a long time on this," Anhotek offered, reaching back for his cup and then gazing at me. "It is my wish that none other than Meruka take my place when I leave this world." There! The subject that I had dreaded bringing to my mentor for so long had been handled by him so deftly, I accepted it as the gift it was surely meant to be.

"He is not born a Kemian, but his god-given magic is stronger than any man. He is loyal to you and to Towi. And, he is a strong Horus priest. The priesthood trusts him and that will be important to you when I depart. But… but most important of all is that you trust him."

Anhotek's last words made my throat close, forcing tears into my eyes. I took a long drink from my cup. "I do. We are each of us your sons, yet never rivals for your affection. I agree with all you have said. Should we elevate him soon?"

"I hope not!" Anhotek laughed, "for I plan to walk upon the sands of Towi for many years to come. I am old, but the reasoning of my heart has not completely left me yet."

"No, I did not mean to replace you as Grand Vizier or Shaman to the Court," I countered. "Should we use the ceremony in Inabu-hedj to improve his positioning within the Court?"

"Ah! Yes, that is a grand idea," Anhotek said, and I knew then that we could fool each other no longer about his decreased usefulness to my rule. "Yes, let us create an elevated title for him. Yes, yes."

"Shall I name him Chief Scribe... or perhaps Vizier to Neith-hotep?" I suggested cautiously. "That way he would exercise his power in the Queen's behalf. He would be a visible symbol of power for all to see."

"And Mersyankh?"

"As usual she will be angry, she will yell and scream and protest until I am sick of her all over again."

Anhotek considered my words. "Except that soon she will live in Inabu-hedj, surrounded by her family and their power base in Lower Kem."

"There is no power in Lower Kem but I," I said more officiously than I had wanted.

"If you believe that, then I have taught you little and your reign will not last long, my son. Never underestimate Mersyankh and Ihy. Every day Ra's disk burns bright, but the blackness of chaos waits patiently for the night. Remember these words and they will serve you well."

"You are right. We will talk more about our plans and how to deal with those two powers of darkness. Now it is nearly time for the mid-day meal and a well-deserved rest. Go in peace, Anhotek." He started to get up by himself, but he could no longer put enough force into his staff to help himself. He held out his hand and I pulled him to standing.

"Old age has few redeeming virtues," he sighed.

"Your presence in my life is virtue enough... to me, anyway," I said from my heart. I hugged him tenderly and felt his frail body in my arms.

As he began to leave, he turned back toward me. "And what about Tawaret?" he asked. "We need to give her family a response. Our delay borders on disrespect already." Tawaret was the woman who had emerged from Anhotek's discussions with the powerful families of Lower Kem as the ideal candidate for my second wife. I had tried my best to avoid direct involvement in the discussions, since I felt torn by my loyalty to Neith-hotep.

As Anhotek described her, she was dark-haired, very short and, in his opinion, would end up being as fat as her ample mother. Yet she had alluring eyes and a pleasing, if docile, ba.

"Yes, yes, go ahead and arrange the... the... wedding." I had trouble spitting out that word. "What would it entail?"

"As much or as little as we would have it be, considering that this is a new venture for the Two Lands."

"Then make it as little as needed to appease, yet honor, Lower Kem. Frankly, I worry about how this will settle over my one true beloved."

Anhotek turned and put his hand on his chair to further support himself. "And with Mersyankh, too. Allow me to develop a plan. I will have Meruka talk with Neith-hotep. She is more likely to listen to him than this old man." Anhotek breathed in slowly.

"At any event, I am tired. I will work on this plan soon, so it can be done as quickly as possible and be put behind us and not fester."

As soon as he left, I walked to the adjoining wing of the palace, lost in thought, reviewing the entire morning's events. In our quarters, Sheftu had set out a table of nuts and fruits and roast duck. Soft music filled the air. Neith-hotep sat on the portico, the Prince asleep in her arm, her nipple still in his mouth. A small drop of milk ran down his contented face. Just a few cubits away, three women sat next to one another, one picking at the strings of her lute and the other two deftly fingering their flutes. The lute player finished singing her lullaby as I arrived and all three musicians left.

I sat next to Neith-hotep and kissed her neck. She smiled warmly, handing me the baby to hold while she placed her breast in the halter under her gown.

"Did it go well?" she asked.

I stared at our baby's face for a few seconds before answering. What thoughts ran through his head, I wondered? Had the gods already drawn a map of his life for him to follow? Would he live long enough to be the next King of Kem? Would it still be united under one rule? My mind raced uncontrolled.

"It went better than we expected," I responded, the smell of the Prince's sweet milk breath wafting to my nostrils. "The new leadership will soon be in place." The tone of my words reflected my sadness.

"It must be hard for you... terribly hard," Neith-hotep whispered, hooking her arm through mine and leaning her face on my shoulder. We both watched the baby sleep in peaceful contentment.

"It seems not so long ago when life was simple... when I sailed the peaceful waters of Mother Nile with Anhotek."

"It is not easy ruling a people. But you do it well, my love," Neith-hotep said, squeezing my arm. "The people love you. You have a passion... a love for the land and its people. That is at the root of all your decisions. Kagemni knows that. Meruka knows that. And Anhotek... it is he who taught you to love. For that I will be eternally grateful." At that moment, my ka felt full with pride and love and I could not believe my good fortune in having such an understanding woman with whom I could share my ka.

Oh, how the gods laugh at we mortals, for it was not six months later that I sat in the palace at Inabu-hedj with Anhotek. "So how do you define eternity, dear teacher?" I asked of my mentor. He immediately saw the bite to my query.

"Well do I remember you asking me such questions, Narmer," he answered cautiously, "but then again you were but a boy of perhaps six or seven years." He grasped his staff and tapped it lightly to the brick floor a few times. "So tell me what is really plaguing your heart."

"Alright, here it is then. After all those years of study with you, I finally know exactly how long eternity is!" Anhotek screwed up his brow. "Yes, it is exactly six months." I took a swig of barley beer from my cup. "And, I learned that bit of true wisdom from you… albeit indirectly."

"Hmmm," Anhotek responded, obviously confused.

"Yes, I say this because approximately six months ago, my dearest wife… oh, excuse me Anhotek, I forget that I must specify which wife nowadays… my dearest wife Neith-Hotep told me that she was eternally grateful to you for having taught me to be so loving. Now that, due to your brilliance, I am married yet again, allowing me to be even more loving, my dearest wife… Neith-hotep, once again… is no longer grateful. In fact, quite the opposite. So, I have learned that eternity is exactly six months in duration." With that I sat down with a flourish.

Indeed, as he had promised, Anhotek had developed the plan to cement our relations with Lower Kem more quickly than any of us could have imagined. Since the entire Court had moved to Inabu-hedj for the Prince's naming and the dedication of the city, Anhotek felt we should arrange the wedding on the heels of those celebrations. The locals were only too happy to accommodate and rushed into the fray lest I should change my heart.

The wedding itself was a simple, yet elegant affair, more a tribute to Anhotek's planning than to any loving relationship between Upper and Lower Kem. He designed it so that Neith-hotep would not have to be present for the ceremony itself, and even judiciously placed one of his calming potions into her sweetened water each day leading up to the ceremony and for a few days afterward.

Tawaret, may Horus bless her innocent young heart, looked radiant amidst the pomp of the ceremony, which was attended by every dignitary from Lower Kem. By now such high events were commonplace in Upper Kem, but Lower Kem had never witnessed such a spectacle. I call it simple, but in reality it must have appeared extravagant to the eyes of Tawaret's family and friends. She wore a gown made for her by Upper Kem's most desired dressmaker, one that minimized her thick thighs and emphasized her small breasts and thick, dark nipples. It was bordered with gold threads that contrasted nicely with her dark hair. She wore her long hair pinned up with gold stays studded with bright orange carnelians, her curls tumbling out of the bun and down to her shoulders, a most pleasant distraction. Her eyes were indeed seductive, although they had little effect on me, such was the pain I felt in wounding my one true love. Tawaret was an eager talker, perhaps too eager, but her youthful enthusiasms did make her enjoyable to be with.

However, the days around my wedding to Tawaret and the months since were painful ones for Neith-hotep and me, for she saw the marriage as a betrayal and none could convince her otherwise, although we tried. Oh, Horus, how we tried!

"Please, my love, try to see it from my perspective. I..."

"No, I do not see it such and I will not see it such, now or ever!" she replied, her arms folded across her chest and her lips set in a most determined manner. Suddenly she turned to face me.

"You can send Meruka again to try to persuade me, or even the cursed Anhotek who I believe put you up to this, or... well, it makes no difference. What you fail to understand," she said, pointing her finger directly at me, "is that what you did is an insult. It is a sign of disrespect to me and my people."

"But, it is no such thing, my love, it is..."

"Which love, today's or tomorrow's? When you tire of me, will you dip that insatiable monster into her all-too-willing sanctuary?" she yelled. "Or will you whisper words of love into her ear, too? Will you call me Tawaret one night in the heat of passion?" With that she stormed out of the room and I knew it was useless to try to discuss this situation with her calmly.

Yet every attempt at reasoning with my beloved failed. One night we were again discussing the situation and I was trying to only listen, as Anhotek had many times suggested.

"It is how I was raised," Neith-hotep was explaining. "My people have come to believe that one woman for one man is the best way for a people to survive. If a man takes another wife, we look upon it as shaming his first wife. I… I do not know what a woman of my tribe would do if such a thing happened."

At that point Anhotek entered with a scroll that needed to be signed before an early morning meeting with a Babylonian wine merchant. "Oh, I am most sorry, my children. I can see you are discussing something important," he said as he turned to walk away. "I will return in the morning."

"No, do not go," I made the mistake of calling after Anhotek, hoping that he might use his magical powers in this dispute with Neith-hotep.

Poor Anhotek looked from me to Neith-hotep and back. Like a caged bird he perched meekly on a chair, nervously fidgeting with his staff. No one said a word and soon the air was thick with tension. I felt I had no choice but to start.

"Anhotek, Neith-hotep and I were discussing the marriage to Tawaret and how it was a necessity to strengthen a united Kem. She, however, feels it is a sign of disrespect toward her. We have been over this again and again and I was hoping you would have something to add that might help her to understand."

"Excuse me, my King, my Queen, but I thought this matter had already been settled. In any event it is already done."

"If it were settled, my dear Anhotek," Neith-hotep said icily, "then why do you suppose it was necessary to place your magical potions in my drink every day during the week of wedding events?" Anhotek's fingertips were white upon his staff. He looked down and blushed.

"Oh, do not blush so, Anhotek, for I willingly drank your foul brew the better to tolerate my shame!" At this she began to cry. I had never before seen my love so angry or so upset. For many minutes we sat silently, my insides twisted, until my beloved was able to regain her composure.

"Dear child," Anhotek began softly, "I know that my counsel has wounded you terribly. And, yes, though you suspect it in your heart, I tell you here now that though your husband protects me, it was my counsel that mortared the houses of Dep and Nekhen with this marriage." Anhotek's admission caused Neith-hotep's shoulders to relax and she leaned back in her chair, nodding in angry agreement.

"Many is the time I sat with your father," Anhotek continued. "Me-ka-el was one of my dearest friends, as you well know. He allowed me to hold you when you were still nursing at your mother's breast, Neith-hotep."

"And what has this to do with this abominable marriage?" Neith-hotep snapped. Anhotek's voice and mannerism was beginning to have an effect upon my beloved, but she was too angry to allow it full reign over her ka.

"It has this to do with it," Anhotek answered calmly. "I know the stories of your ancestors that Me-ka-el told me around the campfire. Many of them had more than one wife. I did not think..."

"No, you did not think! Obviously. Those ancestors lived many generations before us. We have learned from their mistakes as the great rulers of Kem learn from theirs. We have carved ourselves out to live differently from the surrounding tribes. My people no longer believe in many gods or in many wives." Neith-hotep arose and paced toward the portico, then spun around.

"And did my father also tell you of the problems these many wives caused, the jealousy, the plotting against one another for favor, the... the hatreds they created within the family? Or how they turned one child against his half-brother? No, I am sure that was conveniently left out.

"It is... it is as if a man thinks that his conquest over many women somehow makes him greater than he really is, that planting his seed in many women elevates him in the eyes of other men. Yet, he soon realizes that his is a fool's gain, when he must mediate constant bickering and unhappiness in his household. And that is the truth that is told in the women's tents."

In my entire life I had never seen Anhotek at a loss for words, but now he sat in his chair, his hands shaking, his eyes closed, as he breathed in not only the words, but also the emotions that Neith-hotep had just given voice.

"This has all happened too fast," Neith-hotep continued. "Much too fast." In the next room, the sounds of Hor-Aha crying penetrated the darkness and immediately Neith-hotep's breasts began to leak milk, staining her halter and gown. "I have already written to my mother," she said, holding her head high. "It has been far too long since I have seen her. I plan to leave with Hor-Aha shortly to stay with her in Setjet." I was shocked to hear of these plans without Neith-hotep having involved me in them.

"Visit or stay?" I asked, afraid of my beloved's answer. I felt as if I sat far away, observing my tiny self in this discussion, powerless to change the events that were now unfolding. Neith-hotep turned to me and I could see the pain in her ka by the way her eyelids flickered and the way her tears welled yet again.

"Visit or stay?" she repeated so softly I strained to hear her. Then she wrapped her arms across her breasts to hold back her sweet milk and began to quietly sob. In an instant, she turned and left the room.

There was nothing we said that night nor the next days that changed her heart, nothing in my entreaties of love, nor in Anhotek's magic that dissuaded her from leaving the palace. In just five days she was gone, and with her a piece of my ka was ripped from me.

# SCROLL TWENTY-TWO

## *My Son*

"Can we get back to business, my friends? These meetings drag on so long," I said, exasperated, as Kagemni and Rekhmireh, Chief General of the Army, finished exchanging war stories during our break. "I have another meeting shortly."

The council waited for me to provide further explanation. When I sat silently, Anhotek, Meruka and the Chief Priest glanced at each other questioningly, but said nothing. Kaipunesut gazed absently out the portico toward Mother Nile. He had aged so poorly he more resembled a long, bent stick than the vibrant man he once was.

"So, what is next?" I asked. No one stirred.

"Anhotek!" I shouted, so loudly I awoke Mafdet from her nap and she sprang to attention by my side, the hairs on her back standing alert to danger. "What is the next item of business?" Anhotek fumbled with the piece of papyrus that held the agenda for our annual council on the status of Towi. He held it at arm's length and squinted at it as if on it were some indecipherable writing. His hand shook so badly, it made my heart ache just to witness it. The bags under his eyes hung heavy and he sat stooped over, his frail frame no longer able to support his upper body. At thirty, I was already in my middle years, but at age sixty-five, Anhotek was by far the oldest man in Inabu-hedj, or Tjeni or Nekhen for that matter. Those who revered him believed that the ka of the gods dwelled in his body and that he still lived to walk the land only to serve as their eyes and ears. Although I, too, respected my teacher, I did not believe such rumors, for if the gods depended on his failing eyesight and poor hearing to know what was going on with their creations, they were far less powerful than I had thought.

"Next month is the Blessing Over Mother Nile ceremony before Inundation," Anhotek said, his voice quivering with infirmity. His teeth were now yellowed and worn almost to the gum, so that he stumbled over the way he pronounced some of his words. Because of his famed oratory in his youth, I know this embarrassed him. Mafdet sauntered to the other side of my chair and sat down next to me, tilting her head until I petted her.

"We...ummm... have much to celebrate," Anhotek continued. "As Inabu-hedj has developed over these last... what is it now, five years? Trade along Wat-Hor has increased greatly. We export all the barley and emmer we can grow. The pottery from Upper Kem is in high demand throughout the lands to our east and south. The mines of the eastern desert produce gold as fast as we can extract it, and the Royal workshops create jewelry that is the envy of every land around us. The flax from your Royal estates produce the finest linen in all the lands and the flax oil is exported far and wide. Even though this past year the floods were not high, the granaries are still full and... and the Royal treasury grows nicely. The gods have looked upon us most favorably, my King."

"And imports?" I asked. Anhotek stared at me. "Imports, Anhotek!" I repeated loudly. "What about imports?"

"They thrive!" he answered as if amazed that I would ask him such a foolish question. "The wealthy... even some of the peasant shopkeepers, cherish the spices from the eastern lands. The marketplaces now are full of strange and pleasing aromas. The lapis lazuli and turquoise from the east are much sought after by our nobles."

"And the cedar wood," Kaipunesut interrupted, hesitantly. "I have come to depend upon it for our building projects."

"Speaking of imports," I said, picking up my wine goblet, "why is it that this wine from my estates cannot compare with its Babylonian rivals? Have we not been trying for years?"

"We do our best," Kagemni offered, raising his hands. "This winemaking is not easy… much more damned complicated than I had thought. Since I have taken on the responsibility for the Royal agricultural estates here, I have been…we have tried different grapes, different ways of planting… an unholy damned frustration."

"It is just that it tastes…" I said, looking at the cup in my hand.

"Like warm donkey piss! I know," Kagemni interrupted, waving his hand dismissively. "I have arranged for a delegation to travel to Babylon to speak with their vintners… to wrestle from them their damned secrets."

"Good luck!" Rekhmireh said, laughing. "The King may need to launch a war to wring such secrets from their tongues." Rekhmireh's thick neck sat on his broad shoulders and short body so determinedly, he gave the appearance of a great bull hippopotamus. Yet none under his command would dare confuse his comical appearance with any lack of authority. His compact build gave him awesome power with the mace. In the battle of Dep, and other skirmishes since, he distinguished himself as a brave warrior. By the time Kagemni chose Rekhmireh to replace him as Chief of the Army, our troops respected him highly, so that the transition was as smooth as warm honey.

"You are full of dung, Rekhmireh!" Kagemni yelled across my circle of advisors, pointing at Rekhmireh's chest. "One good defecation and that barrel chest of yours would deflate and we would see whether there is a neck under your damned chin!" With that, both Kagemni and Rekhmireh nearly fell from their chairs laughing.

"There is another item," Kaipunesut finally interrupted and everyone settled down. "The new temple at Tjeni is experiencing many delays in its construction. Each time I resolve one problem, another emerges. It..."

"There is dissension among the priests" the Chief Priest said while nodding his head toward Anhotek. "Our Semet priest there is old and the reports we have received indicate that he is having... ummm... difficulties."

I raised my eyebrows. "But... but why in Tjeni? It is our home." I noticed then that Anhotek and the Chief Priest threw each other a quick glance, then lowered their gaze to the floor.

"It is a long way from Inabu-hedj to Tjeni, my dear King," the Chief Priest said tentatively. "You have been absorbed in the affairs of state and... and with your family matters here in Inabu-hedj. Mersyankh, Ihy and Tawaret, spend their time now in the palace in Tjeni. It is to be expected that there will be... difficulties from time to time in Tjeni. Mersyankh knows well how to mix a poisonous brew."

I cringed when I heard the names of my two nemeses, although it pained my heart that the circumstances that the gods forced upon us made innocent Tawaret a victim of her family's exalted position in Lower Kem, as well as the object of such dissension between Neith-hotep and me.

In my heart I had always imagined my relationship with Neith-hotep as a comfortable boat that floated smoothly down Mother Nile's embracing waters. But as soon as Tawaret came aboard the boat was roiled in boiling waters. Storm after storm beset us and finally, on that fateful day now so many months ago, I watched from the portico as the vessels carrying my beloved, her retinue and troops from my King's Guard sailed away to carry Neith-hotep, with Hor-aha in her arms, to her mother in Setjet.

I had expected that, once she was away, Neith-hotep would realize that her action was too extreme, that she had gone too far in exerting her independent ba. And so, after the first ten-day cycle, I awoke with Ra's entrance into the world and watched his chariot depart each evening, expecting to spot Neith-hotep's ships plying the river toward the palace docks. But another ten-day cycle passed with no signs of my only true love, and yet another and another and another. Nor did any papyrus arrive from her. The days of sending each other love poetry had ended. We were, each of us, too stubborn, too angry, too confused to accept the other's predicament. It was foolish. I know that now, but at the time, the hurt I felt wounded me greatly.

My wound soon began to putrefy and its poison infected the people around me. Those who I loved most bore my displeasure. I was short-tempered. I sulked. I avoided making decisions, so that my advisors nagged me more and I was further ill tempered with them. And all along I went through great pains to avoid seeing or dealing with Tawaret and her advisors, such was my discomfort over their desire that I consummate the marriage.

Thus, I began to undertake a daily walk just before Ra's entrance to sort through my thoughts, even going so far as to take along a scroll and pens to help organize them. On the eve of the tenth day of each cycle, I began a fast that lasted an entire day. I had my Guard troops row me across the river to walk among my desert mountains and to meditate. The solace was good for my ka.

"You ask whether my walks have helped, and so I shall tell you," I said to Anhotek during one of our informal meetings in the shade of the portico one hot afternoon. I was eager to share my revelation with him.

"Would you like some?" I asked, offering him the bowl of grapes. His refusal only heightened my concern over how thin he had become of late.

"I have had an insight into our problem with Neith-hotep," I began. "It comes from considering these questions; what is best for The Two Lands and what is best for Neith-hotep and me?" Anhotek turned more fully toward me, gripping his staff between his knobby knees.

"You have taught me that we must always do what is best for Towi, no matter what its cost to any one of us and

I have tried to live my life with this wisdom in my heart. For that reason, I agree that a royal marriage between the houses of Dep and Nekhen was critical to mortar Unification and was ordained by Horus himself. Yet... there is something else I have learned from another teacher, my ka twin Neith-hotep. When the Queen is unhappy, the King is even more unhappy. Why this should be so is a mystery that is beyond my understanding, but it is so nevertheless. All the powers of mighty Towi that I control are of no consequence in light of my lover's discontent." A tiny smile began to form on my mentor's lips.

"And when the King is unhappy, the Court suffers and so does the business of Towi." I sat back, slowly swirling my barley beer in my cup.

"What do you propose to do about this revelation?" Anhotek asked. "There is no doubt that it is an eternal truth."

"Wait, there is more!" I started. "I remember once when we discussed my pending marriage to Neith-hotep you said that there cannot be two Queens in one palace." I stood, thinking again of these words.

"It sounds so simple, dear teacher, but truer words have never been spoken. What we have here is an impossible situation." Now I turned back to Anhotek.

"Therefore, here is what I decided, though I wish to expose this to your scrutiny. I want Tawaret away from Inabu-hedj. I wish for you to have constructed a large addition for Tawaret and her retinue adjoining the palace in Tjeni. That will limit the daily reminders of her presence, even when the Court moves to Tjeni for festivals. And, placing her in Tjeni allows us to more carefully watch her alliances."

Anhotek slowly tapped his staff on the brick floor, thinking through my plan. "I think this plan has good elements, Narmer. However, there is pressure from Tawaret's quarters to consummate your marriage to her. I cannot think how you can avoid this much longer. How do you account for that?"

"I have thought of this, too." I now paced back and

forth. "In fact this thought has caused me many sleepless times. I know there are men who willingly shoot their seed into any willing receptacle, but that is not me, Anhotek. By Horus' holy name, I have eyes only for my Neith-hotep. I will admit to you that there are times I would happily make love to her more times than she would prefer. Yet the thought of shooting my seed into another woman just to temporarily satisfy my desire makes me ill."

"I know that, my son," Anhotek said. "And ever was it so from the first moment you laid eyes on El-Or." Anhotek leaned back to take a breath. "This still leaves us with the problem of consummating the marriage to Tawaret."

"Yes, I know. And speaking with my heart, Anhotek, the truth is that I do not know that I can do it. What I mean is that I feel I would be able to perform, but I do not know if Neith-hotep will agree to this. And I plan to give her the final say in this matter." Anhotek turned nearly all the way around in his seat to be sure he had heard me correctly.

"I will convey to Neith-hotep my plans to relocate Tawaret, as well as certain assurances regarding my contacts with Tawaret. Once she is back in Inabu-hedj we shall together make a decision regarding consummating the marriage to Tawaret."

"And if she refuses to allow it?"

"Then so shall it be and we will have to make plans to deal with that complexity. Unification has never before happened, so what we do now has never before been done. There is no expectation. We lay the foundation for future expectations."

And so it was that I, the most powerful man in the Two Lands and in all the surrounding lands, sent a papyrus to Neith-hotep pleading my case. And then, I waited.

The Chief Priest's voice snapped me back to the discussion at hand. "It seems obvious that the delays in the temple at Tjeni might very well have been instigated by those evil two. We already suspect they are behind the recent sabotage events at the Horus temples in Lower Kem." I recalled that in each instance important administrative papyrus scrolls had been burned. My blood heated with thoughts of her scheming.

And yet, at quiet times, when my heart imagined Mersyankh's seemingly desperate actions, I felt as if I actually understood her frustrations, for the gods had placed upon her shoulders an impossible burden. She struggled, perhaps valiantly in her own heart of hearts, to overcome the obstacles placed in her path and to elevate herself, her son and, as she no doubt saw it, all the people of Lower Kem. Her youth, so full of beauty, so full of promise as Scorpion's wife, now withered slowly on the vine.

I often questioned my tolerance of her bold behaviors and at these quiet times it came down to this; despite her faults, despite her evil actions, I had always considered her a worthy opponent. That her vision of Kem clashed with mine was not of her making. She was but an actor in a larger play of the gods. But, so was I, and only the gods themselves knew the ending. Yet my clear vision of Kem's future always seemed to include her desperate plotting, anxiously watching at the edges of the play, waiting to make her grand entrance. Her presence only served to sharpen my vision, a role of which I am certain she was unaware.

Anhotek and I spoke of this when I was but a young man, soon after Scorpion's death. He explained to me how a warrior never excels on the battlefield until he has worthy opponents to sharpen his skills. I never forgot that lesson, and thusly I viewed my strong, but misguided stepmother.

"Send a high-level delegation to Tjeni immediately" I finally commanded. "Have them stay until these delays are resolved. It should be accomplished before Inundation."

"Agreed," Anhotek responded.

"And I would like you to lead it," I said to my mentor.

"I... I am too old for such a mission," he quickly protested. "My bones ache. I must complete the legal scrolls and... I... I hate long journeys any more."

My heart pained for my dear teacher. But, I believed that in trade for contributing to the aches in his bones, the trip would be good for his heart and ka. The priests and businessmen in Tjeni were fiercely loyal to Anhotek and would welcome a chance to entertain him. "I would like you to go, Anhotek. It is a short trip and the time on Mother Nile will be good for you. Meruka and Sennedjem will work on the scrolls in your absence. Take Kaipunesut with you. And I think you should also..."

Suddenly, I heard something scurrying across the floor of the room and a tiny voice yell: "Father, father, what is taking you so long?"

Prince Hor-aha ran toward me as fast as his five year-old legs could carry him and jumped into my lap. He wrapped his arms around my neck and I hugged him tightly to me as I rocked him back and forth.

"We are in the middle of a meeting, my little Prince, and..." I started to explain to him.

"But, Father, it is taking to-o-o-o long," he protested. I could see Neith-hotep standing toward the back of the room. "You promised you would take me fishing!"

"Ah, the mystery of the other important meeting has been solved," the Chief Priest said, smiling. "And who are we to keep the King from his most important duties?" He looked around at the other men, who smiled and nodded in agreement.

"Hor-Aha," I said, turning my son around so that he faced my council. "You must tell my friends about the tiny perch you caught when we fished together last cycle."

"It was not tiny!" Hor-Aha whined, turning to face me to see if I was serious. "It was huge, bigger than this!" he said, spreading his hands wide. "Even bigger than Anhotek's staff!"

"That is big, indeed, mighty Prince Aha," Kagemni roared in his deepest voice. "Even I would be afraid of such a fish."

"Me, too!" Rekhmireh agreed, pounding his chest loudly.

"Well, my bold little Prince," I continued, "I know where there are other such fish. I am almost done with my meeting. If you will wait for just a few more minutes, I will take you just as soon as I am done."

He looked at me then, Prince Hor-Aha, and it was as if my ka drank from the love in his eyes. Every time I looked upon his tiny, perfectly formed body, with his black braid hanging neatly down the side of his head, I marveled at the miracle the gods had visited upon Neith-hotep and me.

"Alright," he said, sliding off my lap. "But try to be quick. You all talk too much." Amidst the ensuing laughter, Neith-hotep came to retrieve our son, a broad smile upon her lovely face, and I again thanked Horus for her love and devotion. She had managed to overcome her objections to my marriage to Tawaret, although she did set some firm boundaries on how it might be expressed.

"What a perfect name for him," the Chief Priest said. "Horus' warrior. He is full of the fighting spirit."

"He is that and more," I responded, thinking back to that time five years ago when we wrestled with his naming. "You men heard his command. We must be brief, or I shall face both his disappointment and his mother's anger. What else is left to discuss?"

"A brief item," Meruka called out. "Our midwives and shamans have noted that more mothers appear to survive birthing and more children survive their first year. The priests report the people are happy about this. They see this as a sign that the gods look favorably upon their King." I smiled inwardly at this news, for I now knew how difficult it was for a woman to birth a child. I silently thanked Horus for this gift, a blessing that seemed to me no coincidence, for ever since we had named Prince Hor-Aha, the land itself seemed to have rejoiced. Anhotek believed that both mothers and infants benefited greatly from the extra stores of grain and the availability of many different foods in our markets.

As we all got up to leave, I called to Anhotek. "One thing more, dear teacher. I think you should also take Neith-hotep with you. The Prince will stay here with me."

"If Neith-hotep is to go with them, then Rekhmireh should escort them… with a division of soldiers," Kagemni said with authority.

"Make it so," I said, looking at Anhotek, although I knew that it would be Meruka who would arrange the details. Anhotek seemed pale and shaken by my decision, but he raised no further objection. In two days time I stood with Hor-Aha on the shore of Mother Nile, hugging Neith-hotep farewell, while the Prince embraced her thigh.

"Be careful of the evil two," I whispered in Neith-hotep's ear. "Heed Anhotek's advice if he should sense any omens. Promise?"

"I will," she answered, before kissing me softly on the lips. "And you, my little Aha, you take good care of your father while I am away. Make sure he does not work too hard."

"I will take him fishing on Mother Nile for a long time," he whispered, loud enough for me to hear. "He likes that. And he never works when he fishes," he added seriously.

I turned to bid Anhotek a safe journey, but he was already on board. As we stood waving to one another, Hor-aha held tightly to my leg. I felt a mighty urge to hug Anhotek to us, as if to form an unbroken circle. Instead, we looked into each other's eyes deeply, until finally he nodded and held up his hand, his fingers forming the Horus blessing over me and my son.

For two, ten-day cycles, Aha and I experienced the joys of being together without too many disruptions of the Court. We often slept outdoors on the balcony of his bedroom, his head resting on my arm as we watched the lights of the gods in the sky. One night I explained to him a simple story of creation and for the next few nights he asked questions about it incessantly, until my head spun with confusion over what I had or had not told him. My heart went out to Anhotek then, for the suffering he must have endured under my constant barrage of insatiable questions. Yet my frustration was rewarded each time when, in the midst of an earnest answer, I would hear Aha's regular breathing and I turned to see him asleep on his side, facing me, his body curled up next to my chest.

One of those evenings, as my heart swelled with the joy of my son sleeping beside me, I thought back to the day Neith-hotep sailed back to Inabu-hedj with our son. We had been separated for many months, yet I knew from our recent papyruses that we were each committed to solving the vexing problem of Tawaret.

Neith-hotep was much pleased with my decision to move Tawaret to Tjeni and with my promise to resolve this issue to her satisfaction before even seeing Tawaret again. She came to understand, perhaps through the guidance of her mother, how the fragile union between the Land of the Lotus and the Land of the Papyrus necessitated an equally tenuous union between its leaders. Thus, part of the agreement that Neith-hotep and I struck over the first ten-day cycle since her return was that I would travel to Tjeni to consummate the marriage and quell the objections of Tawaret's relatives and advisors.

When my beloved first suggested this, I felt like I had been shocked by a Nile eel. I had thought I would have to plot exceedingly well to get her to agree to my consummating the marriage. But then she explained to me what she would exact in return and I smiled inwardly. First, I was never to discuss the actual coupling, nor describe Tawaret's body, nor anything that transpired during that visit. Second, I was to return to Inabu-hedj and undergo thirty days of ritual purification, supervised by Meruka, before she would agree to lay together with me in the same bed. Finally, and most strangely, she insisted that during that purification period I empty my seed with my own hand at least seven times before she would allow me to enter her. If not for her own desirous nature, I feel certain that she would have insisted that I also place my member in boiling water to purify it before she would have consented to touch it.

Shortly after the twentieth day since Anhotek left, a messenger arrived from Tjeni with a note from Neith-hotep, assuring me that the conflicts at the temple were resolved and that the delegation would be leaving in a day or two. I looked at her note again and again, for it buoyed my ka greatly. Although Aha and I spent days at a time fishing and hunting and doing his writing lessons, I sorely missed Neith-hotep's sweet ba and her soft body cupped inside mine while we slept.

I was awakened the very next morning by the presence

of a spirit staring upon my face. As I cracked open one eye, I saw Hor-Aha standing next to me, completely unclothed, yet unmoving. I opened my arms and he pressed against me so hard, I knew at once that he was rooting for the comfort of his mother's breasts.

"What is it, my Prince?" I asked him. He did not respond. "Did you have a bad dream?"

"How can a person dream when he is not asleep?" he asked of me, in such a desultory spirit it made gooseflesh raise along my arms.

"It happens, little one. There are night dreams and day dreams. Each one carries a lesson with it." I let my words sit softly within him.

"This dream made me feel bad," he whispered.

"Did you see anyone you know in your dream?" I asked.

"No. It was a feeling... like when I swim in the waters of Mother Nile, only... only the coolness was inside me." As I was about to ask him a question, I felt his rhythmic breathing against my chest and I knew that he already slept in the security of my arms. But I took his bad dream as an omen. Suddenly, the face of the hippopotamus I had sacrificed in Nekhen appeared to me, his eyes alerting me to danger.

Thus it came as no surprise when, later that day, as we were about to sit down for the evening meal, a messenger ran into my quarters breathless to report that our ships were sighted close to Inabu-hedj. I made Aha finish his meal and sent him off to his room with Ahpety. I walked with my King's Guard to the shoreline to await the first ship, Mafdet at my side, her tail waving to keep away the flies. As I watched Neith-hotep's ship approach the landing, a terrible sense of foreboding fell over me like a veil.

My feet were rooted to the spot I stood upon and as soon as the boat was fastened, Neith-hotep ran across the deck to me and hugged me so tightly I thought my ribs might crack. I barely lifted my arms in response, so heavy was my dread. She pushed me lightly away from the ship and held my arms in her hands. She looked deeply into my eyes.

"It is Anhotek, Narmer. He… he is in a bad way."

Was there a mortal being who walked upon this land who could have expressed how I felt in that moment, or in all the moments that followed throughout the rest of my days? No. Not then. Not ever. I must have asked Neith-hotep what happened, for she began to relate to me the events of that horrible night, after she had sent to me the note assuring me that all was well. I heard some of her words, but I truly did not listen carefully, or perhaps at all, for on the horizon I saw a fleet of boats rowing at double-beat toward us. In a moment I made out Rekhmireh standing at the bow of the fastest boat, dressed in his full military uniform, urging on his men.

In a moment the boats came alongside the landing and upon Rekhmireh's deck I could see a reed platform, upon which a man lay, covered with a bloody blanket. There was much commotion on the landing and suddenly Meruka appeared beside me and Neith-hotep. I found it exceedingly hard to make out individual words and instead heard a whooshing and beating sound in my ears. Meruka helped me aboard Rekhmireh's boat and I nearly tripped on a rope as I stumbled toward the man on the platform.

If it was Anhotek, I would hardly have known, for his body was so battered it was difficult to recognize him. His arms were broken in so many places, they bent and bent again as they rested along his sides. His skin was a horrible patchwork of purple bruises and swelling. Someone had thoughtfully laid his staff alongside him and wrapped his broken and swollen fingers around it. As Rekhmireh's soldiers removed his blanket to move him, I could see that his legs were similarly broken and a piece of bloody bone as long as a man's hand protruded from his left shin. His nose was broken and bloodied and his face looked as if it had been hit squarely by a mace head. His skull was crushed on the right side and blood and hair were matted along the depression. I began to shake from the shock.

Meruka leaped ahead of me, knelt by Anhotek's side and leaned his ear against his frail chest while feeling his pulse. He lightly passed his hands over Anhotek's arms and legs. Then he looked up at me with a gaze I will never forget, a look of resignation and hopeless despair.

My knees buckled under me then, yet none came to my side to assist me, for what can a person do to help another so aggrieved? I fell to my knees and grabbed Anhotek's hand and his body sucked in a small breath of air, but it was only his body, for his ka seemed to have already vacated it. I leaned my head gently against his chest.

I cannot remember how we ended up back in the palace, but during that fateful night I dreamed an altogether pleasant dream. Anhotek and I sailed alone upon Mother Nile, the boat gently rocking to and fro. I awoke with a start, to find Neith-Hotep rocking me in her arms, and when I regained my senses, I wished for nothing more than to return to the dream that was to be no more. My heart ached greatly and tears welled in my eyes and ran freely down my cheeks. Neith-hotep stroked my hair.

"It is not your fault," she whispered. Yet my heart told me otherwise. Anhotek's feeble attempt to dissuade me from sending him to Tjeni filled my heart with pain.

Aha slept peacefully beside us. Neith-hotep said not another word to me. Her pained expression spoke for her. With a heavy heart I slipped on my tunic and walked to back to Anhotek's quarters.

Candles lighted every walkway in the palace. Although none slept more than a cat's nap that night, hardly a sound could be heard. As I passed servants, ministers and priests in the halls, they stopped and bowed their heads toward me, out of respect for the bond between me and my beloved Anhotek.

Only a few candles cast their feeble light in the room in which Anhotek lay. Meruka sat by his side, holding his hand. Panehsy and Surero wiped his face with cool washcloths. Fourteen Horus priests silently surrounded his bed, their elbows interlocked, their heads bowed, their hands clasped in prayerful meditation. The calming incense of lavender burned in the room, but none of Meruka's curative medicinal plants. This was not a good sign. The heaviness of death floated in the air.

I tapped one of the priests on the shoulder and he broke the chain to allow me to approach the one man they revered above all others, even above the Chief Priest. Despite the yellow light of the candles, Anhotek looked as pale as a spirit, yet serene. His right hand still grasped his magic staff.

By then I had heard the details of Anhotek's injuries. He had lost his balance while praying under the full moon and had fallen from a parapet atop one of the walls at the new temple in Tjeni. A pile of jagged rocks broke his fall, but bones throughout his body were broken.

"It is a miracle he has survived this long," Meruka whispered. "He wanted his ka to pass from his body at home."

I looked at Anhotek for a long time. His breathing was so faint and unsteady, I could detect it only when I concentrated on the hairs of his nose. "His body died when he fell," I said to Meruka. "Only his ka is whole." Meruka nodded, the water in his bloodshot eyes sparkling in the flicker of the candles.

I knelt by Anhotek's bed then, knowing full well that he felt no pain, while mine was unbearable. Every part of my skin felt raw, so that the very air in the room pricked me like tiny daggers. I gently cupped his left hand in mine and brought my face down to his gnarled fingers.

Oh, how cruel the gods can be at times! Through blurred vision I inspected Anhotek's wrinkled skin, his swollen joints, the spots of age that dotted the back of his frail hand. Who in that room could suspect what that hand had meant to me? I could still recall the sting of its fingers on my bottom when he caught me after I had toddled away from him on the banks of Mother Nile and nearly drowned. How many times had I watched the back of that very hand as his fingers pointed to this picture word or that one as he taught me to read and write? How many times did it reach out to grab my neck and pull me toward him to heal me with his hug? How often... how often did that gentle, loving hand stroke my hair as I lay in his lap?

It was as if I could feel his stroke again, so real were the memories. But the stroke I felt was not a memory. I looked up to see another gnarled hand stroking my head, ever so gently. There was no doubt in my mind, nor in any others that witnessed the miracle that night, that Horus gave me one last gift before taking Anhotek to the afterlife.

"Meni, it is you, my son!" Anhotek whispered. I looked into his smiling face and watched as his ka withdrew, first from his eyes. Then his head rolled to the side and his hand slipped gently from my head, never to be felt again. Those were the last words that came from Anhotek's lips.

No one moved then, or in the few moments after. I rested my head on Anhotek's chest, wanting to hug him, wanting him to hug me. Then the priests began a chant, so low in sound and pitch, at first I thought it was the gods themselves that sang. Slowly the chant became louder.

"Stop it!" I yelled, my voice cracking. Too late, I saw Neith-hotep standing next to Meruka, her hands held to her quivering lips, tears streaming down her face. Meruka came to me then, some say with his powers further enhanced by our mentor's ka. He placed his hand at the point between my shoulder and my neck and applied pressure. I tried to turn to look at him, but instead I blacked out. When Neith-hotep helped me from Anhotek's quarters a few minutes later, the priests' chants for the deceased had entered the many-part harmony that would accompany Anhotek on his journey. Their melodies ebbed and flowed through the hallways of the palace. I am thankful to this day for Meruka's kind gesture, for the rituals that Anhotek had lived and died for were quickly restored.

I do not remember at all what happened over the next few days or weeks. It was as if Mother Nile had skipped Inundation that year for me. People from far-off lands say that we Kemians live and die by the flooding and planting cycle of our creator river. For me, the cycle was broken forever that night.

I neither ate much, nor slept well for the next seventy days, as the Horus priests prepared Anhotek's body for burial, to join his ka in the afterlife. Neith-hotep later told me that I spent many of the days curled into a ball like a stray dog, in the corner of the portico, ignoring her, ignoring our son. Instead, she said, I stared for hours on end at the boats sailing back and forth along Mother Nile's wide expanse. Mafdet fed erratically and would leave my side only long enough to relieve herself. She would immediately return and curl up next to me and nudge me gently until I absently picked up my hand and stroked her head, as if she sensed that the very motion fulfilled some need deep inside my heart.

If I did spend my days thus, I do not remember them at all, for my heart was empty of all feeling except guilt and grief. I do recall some of those nights, though, times when the only relief from the pain I felt in my heart resided in unending pitchers of cheap barley beer.

The shamans will tell you that by the grace of the gods, people do not remember their pain, that only hazy memories, vague shadows of it remain after one heals. I, for one, do not believe that. I can feel the pain of Anhotek's departing clearly still today, even as I write these picture words of my story. Above all, I remember the pain of the guilt I carried in my heart, for I believed that it was me alone who had sent my father to his death.

# SCROLL TWENTY-THREE

## *The Scorpion Returns*

Mother Nile had begun to subside and wild grass seeds had already begun to sprout in the flood plains, dotting the black land with patchy green stubble. In my alcohol-fogged mind I hardly noticed. My days began long before Ra's rise in the sky, drinking cup after cup of barley beer and sharing the night sky with the mut of my soul. Once, when the light of Ra's disk lit the sky, Neith-hotep found me on the portico, soaked in my own urine. I yelled at her to stay away and later poured beer on my wet tunic to mask the odor, laughing all the while, until tears began to flow.

On the seventh day following the seventieth day since Anhotek's death, I managed to sit in my chair platform straight enough to lead Anhotek's funeral procession, although I cannot recall many of the details. Kaipunesut had designed and built an elaborate tomb, far more intricate than Scorpion's, for Anhotek's comfort in the next world. Meruka had arranged all of the fine points of the funeral and I was later told that during the long service the soldiers of my Guard held me up whenever I began to doze off. Such was the shameful tribute I gave to my beloved teacher and mentor. That the gods did not immediately strike me dead I can only attribute to Horus' protection, although he must have been grievously wounded defending my life against them.

During the Sealing of the Tomb ceremony, the effects of the alcohol had begun to wear off and my head pounded in the heat of the day. As the Chief Priest sealed the door with beeswax and Kaipunesut's workmen began to affix the bricks in mortar to prevent tomb-robbers, I felt the gods squeeze my heart so hard I wanted to heave up the contents of my stomach. I groaned and my trusted guards glared at me, certainly not with any more disgust than I would have looked upon myself, had I but the courage to do so.

As evening fell that night, when the barley beer had achieved its effects of drying my heart, Neith-hotep came into my quarters. I had not even bothered to cover my waste pots and the room stank of every manner of foul odor.

"I am busy!" I snapped as soon as I saw her, dressed in a hemp robe that was torn at the seams in mourning.

"I can see that," she replied acidly.

"Do not start with me!" I bellowed, pointing the hand at her that held my cup of beer and spilling part of its contents on the floor in front of me. For an instant I could not remember the woman's name who stood before me, although I knew I should and I ran through the names of Mersyankh and Neith-hotpu, before Neith-hotep's name settled in my heart. I refilled my cup with beer and drank a long gulp.

Neith-hotep removed a piece of my soiled clothing from a cane chair and sat down. I noticed her glance furtively around the room that was now my living room and bedroom, for I had not slept with Neith-hotep since Anhotek's death.

"Your heart is in pain, my love," she said softly, her eyes penetrating mine. "You blame yourself for Anhotek's death. Yet… yet it is not your fault."

"Of course. Not my fault… just as it was not my fault when I sent for you and your father."

"What does that mean?" she asked, perplexed, cocking her head to one side.

"I failed to protect him, too!" I said, quaffing the entire cup of beer. "The King of all Kem, unable to protect those he loves. It is ironic, is it not?"

"But, Anhotek was the proper choice to make things right with the dissenting priests. None other could have done the job. I was there. I saw it with my own eyes. You did the right thing, for the good of Kem."

"Do not talk to me of the right thing! Had I done the right thing, Anhotek would be sitting here now, enjoying the setting of his years. I could have sent Meruka or... or the Chief Priest of Nekhen. His job is to keep his priests in line!"

"Narmer, my love, you are being too hard on yourself. Please... please let me help you."

"You can help by leaving me alone!" I shot back, the spittle from the beer running down my unshaven face. She appeared smitten by my harsh words and hung her head, not able to look upon the mut that had stolen her lover.

"I have left you alone far too long," she answered, her brow furrowed in pain. "I pray each day to Isis to rescue her son once again from the venom that afflicts him. I..."

"Get out!" I screamed, jumping from my chair. "I do not wish to hear the dung you sling at me!" I raised my cup and threw it at the table next to Neith-hotep. It smashed into many pieces and Neith-hotep held up her hands as if to protect herself from my wrath. She stood up warily, for the first time shaking in fear of me. It was more than I could bear, seeing her thus, trembling before the evil spirit I had become. It had been weeks since I dared look at myself in a mirror, yet what I saw reflected in her eyes was clearer than any image I could see in polished silver. I rushed toward her, enraged.

If I had a deben of gold for every time I have replayed that scene in my heart, Towi's treasury would easily be more than the combined wealth of all the lands known to our traders. Horus is my witness that I meant to do her no harm. I know now, too late, that I was possessed by a power stronger than that of any man. And so, with my ba poisoned by alcohol, I pushed Neith-hotep. I pushed my beloved, not to hurt her, not to push her over a chasm wider than any man could reasonably expect to overcome, but to remove the reflection of that hideous mut that I saw in her eyes.

It is of no matter now, for what is, is. I pushed and she slid away from me, waving her arms as if by some valiant effort she could maintain her balance and stay on her feet and somehow erase what I had just chiseled into the very foundation of our relationship.

Her back hit the mud-brick floor first, then her head, but it revealed itself slowly to my eyes, as if the gods had restricted the flow of time, just to taunt me. Her body crashed into a table crowded with bowls of fruit and nuts. The legs of the table buckled and its contents spilled over her body. I watched, powerless, as she rose, so frightened her chest heaved in spasms, her robe soiled with splatters of fruits. Her eyes ran steadily with tears, but she drew herself up to regain her dignity and did not cry.

"I... do... not... know you... any more!" she gasped between breaths. "You... are not... Narmer. Not... the... Narmer... I love...or... that... I once loved. You are... Narmer... to... none that used to love you... not... not even to Hor-Aha!"

Perhaps it was the effect of Neith-hotep's words that penetrated to my ka, but the very next thing I saw was Horus himself laying on the hot desert sands, the stinger of a scorpion still embedded in his foot. I felt his pain, now spreading throughout his body, as he writhed in agony. It was my pain he bore, of that I am certain. Perhaps he even bore the pain of all of us affected by Anhotek's death. As Horus lay dying, he called for his mother, Isis, but she did not come. In the distance, a dark, powerful figure approached, looming ever larger. And, when I opened my eyes, Meruka stood above me, and next to him Panehsy. I was in our bed, in the bed that Neith-hotep and I shared, made sacred by our loving consecration.

"You have had the shakes," Meruka said quietly,

holding his hand on my shoulder to restrain me when I tried to arise. "You must rest now."

"But... I... I have not had the shakes since I have been a youth. Anhotek said I had outgrown them."

"The alcohol mut can do anything," Meruka answered, disgust written all over his face. "The most powerful magic is powerless against it."

Over the next ten day cycle, I slept most of the day and night, interrupted now and again by small shakes, Meruka later told me. As my ka battled the mut spirits within it, I wanted more than anything else to take a long drink of barley beer, to drown in its bitter warmth, to surrender to its seductive powers. But I was too weak to rise and seek it myself and I suspected it would be futile to ask it to be brought to me. Instead, Panehsy forced copious amounts of Mother Nile's healing waters into my body, until I passed water every few minutes. I knew not where Neith-hotep and Hor-Aha hid, but if the truth be known, I did not want to see them, so great was my shame.

At night, I was left alone, save for the King's Guards who protected me, more from myself than from any enemies, although I later learned that Meruka was truly fearful that Mersyankh and Ihy would use my weakened condition to do me even greater harm. Without the alcohol clouding my heart, the nights passed painfully slowly and I began anew to feel the ache of Anhotek's absence.

On one such night I dreamed the dreams of the damned. I walked and walked without end along the dunes and plains of the western desert, searching for something, someone, unsure of what or who it was. Yet I knew I must search on. My throat ached for water. Suddenly, I turned and in front of me was a black mountain with a cool spring set into its base and shaded by a rocky overhang.

I ran toward the tiny pool and as I was about to drop to my knees to scoop its pure waters to my lips, I saw a scorpion guarding it. My heart pumped in fear. No matter which path I took, the scorpion was between me and the pool, its stinger coiled. I raised my foot and was about to stomp it with my sandal, when I heard Anhotek's voice inside me, his voice difficult to understand, the words making no sense. The more agitated I became, the more unintelligible was his message.

Then I stepped away from the pool, closed my eyes and breathed in my sen-sen breaths to calm my ba. When I opened them, I saw the pool anew, its clear waters shimmering with the reflections from Ra's disk. I walked to the scorpion and knelt before it and marveled that such a tiny being could have such great power over a man, all because of a stinger no bigger than a sliver of fingernail. This was its nature, to defend itself with its poisonous barb, and in so doing it doomed itself to living a life of isolation. I reached down and calmly picked up the scorpion by its tail, its stinger still coiled, as I had seen the desert nomads do. It was powerless. It waved its two large claws and its feet wildly, but when I placed it upon my hand, it calmed down. Still holding its stinger, I controlled its destiny, but I also controlled mine. I walked away and released the scorpion under a rock, unharmed. Then I returned and drank from the cool waters.

I awoke with Meruka holding a cup of water to my lips. "You were thrashing about. Panehsy summoned me." I sat up and drank that cup and two more. Once I had quenched my thirst, I recounted the dream for Meruka, feeling strangely buoyant.

"What is the meaning of the dream?" I asked. Outside, Mother Nile's waters flowed swiftly, making a hissing sound against the sharp sedges and papery reeds.

In the dark, with no candles burning, all I could see were the whites of Meruka's eyes and faint reflections of light upon his bald head from the lights of the gods in the night sky. "It is a message from Anhotek," he responded, his deep voice solid, reassuring. I breathed in, trying to fathom in my heart what the message was. "A powerful message. Anhotek is safe in the next world," he said, nodding his head.

It is hard to describe what the effect was of Meruka's words, whether it was the finality of how he said it, or the thought that Anhotek's ka had truly crossed over to the afterlife and thus was irretrievably lost to me. But once he had spoken, without the poison of beer or wine infecting my heart, I felt lonely beyond measure, insignificant, lost. My tears flowed freely.

"Anhotek is gone from this world, Narmer. You must accept that." He reached over and grasped my hand.

My heart felt heavy. I hung my head over my knees and cried. To whom could I turn for firm guidance, when I debated the rightness of my decisions? Who would support me, even when the error of my action might be obvious to all? For what man could I live my life so that he would be made proud? Anhotek's words came back to me, that the loneliest day in a man's life is the day his father dies. In all my life, no truer words had ever been spoken. I felt their truth weigh down upon me, I felt the very air within the room, the desert air outside, the air of the heavens pressing down upon my heart and even my skin felt raw and pained.

We sat together, hand in hand, for many minutes, neither of us saying anything, both of us breathing into the silence more than we could ever have expressed in words. Finally, Meruka broke the silence.

"There is a difference between the religious beliefs of Kem and Ta-Sety," he said softly. "The Horus priests believe that we become immortal in the afterlife. In Ta-Sety, my people believe that our ancestors live forever, right here." He pounded his fist softly on his chest.

"Life is a cycle. The joys and bitterness of life mold the ka of our youth into our adult ka. If the gods grant a man a long life, his wisdom ka reunites with his child ka and we are given the honor of caring for him as an elder. When his aged ka and his child ka reunite, his journey to the next world will be an easy one.

"Each of our elders lives inside us, reminding us of our past, lighting the path ahead of us with their wisdom." Meruka put his large hand under my chin and lifted up my head so that I was forced to look into his eyes.

"I will tell you this secret, Narmer, for you are as close to me as my brother, Atuti. My father visits me often, whenever I am in need... even at other times. Anhotek is no longer of this world, but he lives inside you... and me... as surely as Mother Nile flows to Wadj-Wer." He withdrew his hand, but I continued to stare at his dark face. How long had it been since the two of us played, carefree, in the forests of his home? A lifetime ago? Ten lifetimes?

"I... I am so ashamed," I confided in Meruka. "Ashamed... and guilty." I hung my head again under the weight of my actions.

"You are guilty of only one error," Meruka said. "Falling prey to the seduction of alcohol to reduce your pain. Mersyankh and Ihy could not have plotted better vengeance. Once that path is chosen, though, all else follows."

"I can see that now. But it is an error with terrible consequences," I said, shaking my head. "I...I have acted grievously toward those who care for me the most."

"Terrible consequences, yes, but also unexpected blessings," he responded mysteriously, his voice deep and dark. "As for the wrongs you have done, you can make amends."

I wished then that Meruka was truthful and not merely using priestly words to make me feel better. But Meruka would never do or say anything that he did not believe. That alone gave me much hope.

"How do I make amends? I mean with Neith-hotep... with you... with Hor-Aha?"

"You have already started to make matters right between us. Keep your heart open and all else that follows will be right. For me, there is only one thing more I would ask, but for Neith-hotep and Hor-Aha there is much you will need to do."

"And for you?"

"Swear an oath to Horus that you will never again lift a cup of beer... or wine... to your lips."

Meruka might as well have asked that I swear to stop Ra's disk from setting in the heavens, so powerless did I, the King of the Two Lands, the great warrior of the battle of Dep, feel against the seductions of that warm, earthy brew.

"I... I do not know if... if I can do as you ask," I stammered, recognizing how my shameful protest betrayed my weakness and fears.

"Then think of this," Meruka said, drawing himself full up in his chair, as if to gather strength before a mighty blow. "The scorpion's poison still afflicts you." His words struck me as troubling images and I could feel the poison thick as honey flowing within me. Meruka later told me that my face radiated more light in that instant than a room of lit candles.

"The dream!" I said. "It..."

"Yes... a gift to you from Anhotek... a gift you could not have received had the poisons not infected your body and then been cleansed."

I knew instantly that Meruka was right. I thought then of the scorpion, of the only way of life it knew, his stinger always at the ready. I thought of the other Scorpion, the one that afflicted me throughout my childhood, of his ever-present stinger. My life had been dominated by Scorpion's presence, darkened by the deep shadows he cast upon my ba, his stinging barb forever threatening my path.

"I picked it up," I said tentatively, still attempting to make sense of Anhotek's message. "I picked it up with these very fingers."

"You did not need to destroy it. Anhotek told us this many times, that many barriers we face are there only because we choose to see them as such."

"Yes. Yes, that is true!" I answered, feeling my heart alive for the first time in months. "But, I always imagined Anhotek meant physical challenges, like defeating a much larger opponent in battle. Until tonight, even I did not know how deeply Scorpion affected even my heart."

"Then this lesson has been Anhotek's true gift. Scorpion's actions toward you were not borne of power, but of weakness. You can choose to allow them to rule your behavior or not, just as you chose to move the scorpion in your dream, instead of smashing it." Meruka leaned back again in his chair. I could only sit quietly and ponder all that had come to my awareness this night.

"There is yet another, deeper meaning to the dream," Meruka continued. "Perhaps I should wait, but my heart tells me to offer it to you now."

"Go ahead," I said, swallowing hard.

"The scorpion does not hate its prey, Narmer. It does what it does without malice. It is a creature created by the gods, the same as you and me." Meruka poured us each a cup of water, which we both drank before he continued. "This may be difficult for you to hear, but Scorpion... he loved you..."

"Stop it!" I responded angrily. "You have pushed your lesson too far!"

"Why, because you want to believe it untrue?"

"No, because I felt his venomous stinger my entire childhood! Me," I said, pointing to my chest, "not you!" Meruka looked at me for a long time, until I became uncomfortable under his stare.

"I am sorry," Meruka said, standing up as if to leave. "I... it is just that I thought you strong enough to hear me out. But, the alcohol has... I am sorry." He shook his head and turned toward the entranceway.

"No, do not leave!" I shouted after him. "It is I who should be sorry, for you speak to me from your heart. Please, Meruka, sit back down and tell me of your deeper knowing."

Meruka sat and as I looked past him the faint light of Ra's disk rose far to the east. "There is not a person that walks the land, nor... nor a god that roams the heavens that does not know of your love for Anhotek. Yet the alcohol so clouded your heart that you even disrespected his memory at his funeral.

"So it is with anyone who walks that path. Scorpion's drunkenness dried his heart and corrupted his ba. Perhaps what happened to Anhotek was destined to be. We both know he could have easily dissuaded you from sending him to Tjeni. Perhaps Anhotek and Horus, working together, created this play in which you were but an actor... to help you see the larger truth. Anhotek knew of Scorpion's love for you... and the pain Scorpion bore in his heart that he tried to quench with cheap barley beer."

We sat in silence until Ra rose in the sky and the palace began to bustle with activity. "I leave you now to travel to Tjeni," Meruka said, getting up from his chair. "There are urgent matters I must settle. I will return in one cycle, perhaps two. You have much thinking to do."

Meruka hugged me and left, giving instructions that I was not to be bothered, except by Panehsy. That day I slept on and off, alternating dreaming with much thinking. I was awakened frequently by Panehsy who forced me to drink water until I begged him to leave me alone. During the night I slept fitfully, aware of a pain deep in my heart that caused me to struggle for breath. When I awoke, not a person stirred in the palace and I walked to the portico to calm myself. Alone with the night sky, I began to sort out my dreams and my conversation with Meruka the night before.

"You were sleeping fitfully," a voice whispered to me and I jumped with fright. In the shadows, Neith-hotep stood, her arms folded on her chest. My heart raced with so many feelings, I could not speak. I had been sleeping naked and I instantly felt ashamed of Neith-hotep seeing me thus. I groped for the nearest chair and sat down.

"Would you like some water?" she asked, stepping forward into the light of Ra's silvery night disk. She looked as lovely to my eyes as ever, but her shoulders were slumped as if she carried a large burden.

"Yes," I answered, and she brought to me a pitcher of water and a cup, both of which she placed on the table before me. She did not pour the water.

"Would you like some, too?" I finally gathered enough courage to ask. My throat felt dry, as before battle.

"No, I am not staying. I only came to check on you." It was then that I noticed a boat on Mother Nile's bank, running lanterns still lit.

"Where are you staying? What?... I am confused," I said, feeling as if I were a small child again. I gulped my water and stared in Neith-hotep's direction.

"It is a confusing time for all," Neith-hotep whispered.

Even in the dim light I could see her muscles taut, her body uncertain of what to do.

"Have... have you been here to check on me before?" I asked. She hesitated a moment.

"Yes I have." This surprised me greatly, for so many nights I spent awake or pacing my room, our room, I would have surely noticed.

"Meruka has talked with you," I ventured.

"He has. But he did not tell me much."

"Did he tell you about my dream?"

"Only that Anhotek's ka visited you and... and that the message he sent might change things."

"For the better?" I asked tentatively.

"Can it possibly be for the worse?" she asked me, her voice so full of pain, my heart nearly broke.

"No, I imagine not," I said, my despondency evident in my voice. I sat quietly while she stood uncomfortably, her shoulder leaning against the doorway's brick pillar, her head gently touching. Her hair hung behind her, tied loosely in back with an ivory comb.

"Neith-hotep, I... I do not know where to begin... what to say. My shame overwhelms me. I have never felt so alone in my life." In the light of Ra's night disk, I saw a reflection of a tear on Neith-hotep's cheek. I hung my head in shame. I heard her draw in a quivering breath.

"You have been through a terrible grief, Narmer. I did not foresee how deeply it would affect you... none of us did." I thought long on her words and about Anhotek.

"Will you stay long enough to hear me out?" She shuffled about on her feet and I could see from the tension in her body that she debated whether to stay or run, as a man does on the battlefield.

"I will listen," she said, crying softly.

"I did not know until Anhotek's dream visit how deep was my loss," I continued. "I only knew that the pain in my heart at his death was beyond measure and I blamed myself for it. He was my father and my teacher and... and my closest friend." I looked up to see Neith-hotep shivering, her arms crossed over her chest to keep herself from shaking.

"All my life I have hated Scorpion. I have used his hatred of me to thrive. I looked upon his death as a freedom to be relished. This is the great folly of youth, to be so possessed by one's passions that they blind one from the truth. What I have seen... these past few days... is... is that I need not have carried that hatred with me all my life. He did not hate me, Neith-hotep. Can you understand that? He did not hate me. He just did not know how to show his love. Perhaps he thought me too fragile because of my shakes. Yet, his very actions toward me strengthened me, like metal forged in a fire.

"I know not if this makes sense to you, but... I have come to understand that I drowned my pain in barley beer because I grieved the loss of both of them, both my fathers... Anhotek and Scorpion." Tears flowed freely down my cheeks.

"What I did was terrible, horrible... what I did to you, to Hor-Aha, to Meruka, to... to Anhotek..." My head spun recalling the half-formed images of my drunken rages. "But, it is over now, Neith-hotep. It is over. I have sworn an oath never to hold beer or wine to my lips again. I... I would gladly do anything in this world to make amends to you."

By now Neith-hotep cried without control, her entire body sobbing while she held on tight with her left hand against the pillar, her right hand grasping a gather of her gown to her eyes.

"I felt so alone, Neith-hotep, so alone. I was in an abyss of my own making."

"You were never alone, you beast!" she screamed at me, advancing the few paces that separated us. "I was there for you! I rocked you in my arms! But, you... you pushed me away, like I was a harlot, like... like I was that other woman you married for convenience!"

Her words stunned me to inaction. My head throbbed and my entire body buzzed as if I had touched a lightning fish. "No, no! I love no other woman but you! Tawaret is a figure-head, that is all. Other than that one night, I... I have never even placed my hand upon her." I paced to the edge of the portico and turned toward her. She stood in the same spot, her hands over her eyes, sobbing.

"Neith-hotep, I cannot undo what I have done. I have hurt you beyond measure and for that I feel... I feel nothing but shame and disgust." I walked a few tentative steps toward her. "But I believe in my heart that Horus himself allowed me to fall to the depths, so that... it... it makes no difference what the reasons were."

By now I was so close to my beloved, I could smell her perfume carried on the gentle breeze. My heart told me to act then, but I was as frightened as I was before the battle of Dep, for in that battle I had only the death of my body to fear. I drew in my breath and slowly held up my hands to her shoulders and touched her. At first, she cringed, her entire body rigid.

"Neith-hotep, I know I have dishonored you. I have no right to call you my beloved, although as Horus is my witness, I love you more than I have ever loved another woman. I beg you to give me a chance to make it up to you... to reclaim what now seems lost. Give me a chance to redeem myself in your eyes."

I felt her muscles relax, if only slightly. Then she turned her face upward to look into my eyes. She stared for what seemed like an eternity, a penetrating stare that bared my ka, turned it this way and that, and left no dark places for a man to hide.

"I want to believe you, to have my Narmer back... the Narmer I knew," she finally whispered. But we both knew that the former Narmer was gone forever and that, for better or worse, the man who stood before her would emerge stronger or else plunge to the depths of degeneracy. I felt Horus' strength on one side, Anhotek's guidance on the other. I drew strength from knowing that I could control the scorpion's poisonous barb.

But my strength would be meaningless without Neith-hotep's love to support me. What is a man without a deep love in his heart, except a thin shell, hiding behind his bravado, fearful that others will find out his true fears and weaknesses? Uncertainty reflected itself back to me from

Neith-hotep's eyes, but also a glimmer of hope. Isis sent Neith-hotep back to me, to finally rid me of the poisons that had coursed through my body.

We stood together that night, my hands gently holding Neith-hotep's upper arms. We stood a long time, looking deeply into each other's eyes, delicately probing each other's ba. I felt blessed beyond imagining to have such a loving woman as my wife, as my lover, as the mother of my child. And so, after a few moments she collapsed in my arms and we held each other close throughout the night.

Over the following ten-day cycle I felt as if I had been reborn from the dead. There was much to do, many decisions that had been tactfully postponed during my illness. Kagemni was ecstatic at my return and he offered to hoist a cup of beer in my honor, only to realize his mistake and trip over himself to cover it up, before apologizing profusely.

Several days later, I was in the midst of listening to one of Kagemni's tales of how he had judged a dispute in his nome, with Rekhmireh at his side laughing heartily, when Meruka suddenly appeared at the door, Panehsy next to him. I noticed that he eyed me carefully before entering my quarters. I stood to embrace him, feeling warmly toward him and thankful for all he had done to heal me. As I pushed away from him, I noticed that he had locked his gaze with Kagemni.

"There is news to report regarding issues at Tjeni," Meruka announced. "I would ask that the King schedule a meeting of his council for tomorrow morning, as the first order of business."

"What issue is so urgent?" I asked.

"I ask that you grant my request without questioning me, for if you do I will have to reveal all I know and at this moment that would not benefit you... or Kem. I am tired from my journey. Tomorrow would be better for all." I was uneasy with Meruka's words, but trusted his judgment.

"Tomorrow then, immediately after the morning meal," I said, not taking my eyes off him. Meruka bowed and left and soon afterwards so did Kagemni and Rekhmireh.

All day and through the night I wondered about Meruka's strange behavior. After I had put Hor-Aha to bed, I talked with Neith-hotep about my concerns and asked that she be present for the meeting.

Shortly after Ra's disk rose in the sky, I heard the Court being prepared for the meeting. Chairs were assembled from all over the palace, and I began to feel more and more uneasy as the time for the meeting neared. Finally, just after the morning meal, Meruka walked into my chambers. Neith-hotep and I sat, eating a sweet bread and drinking an herbal tea that Anhotek had always favored when tensions were high.

"The meeting is about to start, Narmer. It would be good to have Neith-hotep present."

"I have already asked her to sit next to me for the meeting. Now, can you tell us what this is all about?"

"I beg your indulgence. You would be better off learning of what I found in Tjeni as the others find out. Then you will react with your heart."

And so we adjourned to the hearing chamber, where I usually held Court while in Inabu-hedj. Chairs had been placed around the room, in a semi-circle, with two aisles separating the three sections. All chairs faced my throne. Neith-hotep's chair was placed a half-step behind and to the left of mine.

When we walked in, Mafdet on my left side and Neith-hotep on my right, I noted that my entire Council was there, as well as several of my cousins, head priests and wealthy landowners and merchants of Lower Kem. However, I was surprised to see Mersyankh and Ihy and Neter-Maat, seated in the front. Reluctantly, they rose as I entered with the Queen. As they rose, Mafdet stopped for an instant, her body tensed, her head lowered. She stared at Ihy and Mersyankh and they at her.

"Be seated," I said after I sat upon the throne chair, noting that Mersyankh was already seated. Her aging, wrinkled face was formed into a permanent scowl. "Meruka has called this meeting. Proceed," I said with a nod of my head. Mafdet sat up straight at my left side, her ears perked and with her gold, bejeweled collar around her neck, looking like royalty herself.

"King Narmer has charged me with writing the holy papyrus scrolls recounting the accomplishments of Vizier Anhotek's life and a description of his tragic death. Yet, I have been... confused by certain... peculiar aspects of his unfortunate accident," Meruka began, at first staring nervously at the floor as he spoke.

"As you know," he said, pointedly nodding his head toward Ihy, "I just returned from Tjeni, to better understand the incident." I began to feel a lump form in my throat. If Ihy or Mersyankh were apprehensive, they did not show it, but stared straight ahead at Meruka.

"So, I gathered the stories of each of the people who in any way had anything to do with Anhotek that day and I noted some interesting things. I will share them with you, King Narmer, and with you men," he said, turning and nodding his head toward my Council, "and women." I could not recall ever seeing Meruka command a situation so completely

"Bring in Menmireh." Two of my King's Guards escorted a middle-aged priest into the chamber. He studiously kept his gaze upon the floor.

"Menmireh was the head priest at the Temple of Khenti-Amentiu in Abdju," Meruka said matter-of-factly, looking first at me, then the Council members. "He was transferred to the new temple being built in Tjeni to help train new recruits in preparation for its opening. Tell us what happened the night of Anhotek's death, Menmireh."

"There is nothing more to say," Menmireh responded nervously. "I have already told you, it was an accident. Anhotek tripped and fell."

"Yes, you did tell me that. But, Anhotek was a great man and I am responsible for writing the papyrus of his death. I only seek to... to understand this fully. What time was this?"

"We found him when Ra's night disk was full in the sky."

"Dead, or nearly so."

"Yes."

"From the fall?"

"Yes, from the fall... of course."

"Do you have any idea why old Anhotek would be out so late in the night?" Meruka asked, pacing back and forth, but gaining strength in his voice with each question.

"No." It might have been my imagination, but I thought I noticed Menmireh's eyes flutter nervously.

"But, in Tjeni, you told me he was praying."

"Yes, yes... he was praying. But I did not know that at the time. I... I found that out later." Menmireh was obviously nervous. He wiped his palms on his hemp tunic.

"So, tell me again how it was that you were also out at night, ready to help poor Anhotek?"

"I... we heard him fall and rushed to help him," Menmireh said, swaying forward, as if pleading his case.

"'We' meaning you and your assistant, Nakhtimenwast, right?"

"Yes, the two of us. We... we found him. First we heard him fall, then we found his body."

"Did he yell as he fell... was that what you heard?" Meruka asked.

"Yes. No, no, he did not yell. He just fell."

"That is surely odd, Menmireh, for Nakhtimenwast told me that what attracted his attention was that Anhotek let out a yell as he fell."

"Yes, perhaps that is what woke us, a small yell... a gasp. Then... then we came running to his aid." Menmireh rubbed his hands together and a dark stain from his sweat began to show through his tunic.

"But, there was no aid to be given, right? He was already dead or nearly dead?"

"Why do you keep asking me that question? I already told you he was dead," he said testily.

"Again, I am only trying to understand the situation better... for the sake of the holy scrolls. You see, dear Menmireh, your assistant Nakhtimenwast said to me that Anhotek let out a groan when you arrived. That would mean he was not yet dead, would it not?"

Menmireh was now frightened, his eyes open wide. In searching for an answer, he glanced sideways at Ihy, a mistake that did not escape my attention, or Meruka's.

"He was alive, but... but only barely. He was old. He... he had fallen from the parapet onto the rocks. It was... a... a terrible tragedy."

Meruka stopped pacing and turned to face Menmireh, their bodies no more than a cubit apart. Meruka's tall frame towered above the priest's, his dark black skin no longer vibrant as it once was, but now powdered with the gray sheen of age.

"What puzzles me the most," Meruka continued, his deep voice just above a whisper, "is that such an old man, who retired early every night in his declining years, should be out praying so late. Yet... and this also puzzles me, Menmireh... Anhotek's able assistant, Surero, reported to me that Anhotek was awakened just before his accident by a messenger, a very quiet messenger. Anhotek left his room immediately. Fortunately, Surero lay quietly awake and observed this."

The people in the room began to whisper to each other in hushed tones. Mersyankh and Ihy sat straight as spears. Neter-Maat turned this way and that trying to comprehend what was happening. He leaned toward his mother to ask her a question, but she poked him in the ribs and he sat up straight. Even Mafdet sensed something was amiss and the hairs on her back rose up.

"Do you know anything about this messenger, Menmireh?" The priest's body now shook with fright. His eyes were wide open, as if witnessing his own death walk, but unable to stop it.

"No," Menmireh croaked.

"From Surero's description, some say it was one of the initiates that you were training, a young man named Siatum. Shall I bring in Siatum to question him about...?"

"That is not possible!" Menmireh shot back too quickly.

"Why not, Menmireh?"

"He... he left the priesthood. He... he could not take the rigorous training." Menmireh's tunic was now soaked throughout. He rubbed his hands against his sides continuously.

"Well, we will get back to poor Siatum in a moment, Menmireh. I say 'poor' Siatum because he also had a terrible accident that night. Were you aware of that? He, too, had a fall, only he fell on a dagger that lodged between his ribs. Then, probably thinking Mother Nile would heal his wound, he dragged himself a hundred cubits to her banks and threw himself in. That is a coincidence of the gods, is it not, dear Menmireh? But, of course you would know that, since you are their servant," Meruka said sarcastically.

Meruka paced away from Menmireh. "One more piece of information before we get back to Siatum, who was found the next day, one leg eaten by crocodiles, but... amazingly still alive," Meruka said, turning around to face Menmireh. The effect on Menmireh was profound. He gasped loudly.

"But, as I said, more on Siatum later, my dear priest. For now I wish to tell you about Anhotek. When he arrived here in Inabu-hedj, barely alive, I found that blood had poured freely from each of his many wounds. Yet... and this is the strange part to a healer like me... the wound on his head, the wound that bashed in his skull, did not run at all. The wound was matted with blood and skull and brain and hair, but no bleeding. That... that is what I find most curious of all."

"Stop it!" I yelled from the throne, standing up, my body shaking with anger. Mafdet immediately bolted onto all four legs. She growled in a low, steady manner at Menmireh, arching her neck forward as if to pounce were I but to give her the signal. I stared at Meruka. "Stop this now for my blood boils over in outrage!"

"Please, my King, I beg you to allow me a few more minutes, for this evil stew has yet to thicken." We stood thus, staring at each other, until I felt Neith-hotep's arm upon mine, gently urging me back to my throne. Meruka bowed toward me and Neith-hotep and turned back to Menmireh, who now sat on his heels, bent over toward the ground, shaking like a reed with fear, whether from

Meruka's questioning or Mafdet's growl I knew not.

"Menmireh, it is all exposed now, all of it," Meruka said in his deepest, most powerful voice. "Tell us the truth now, or else be damned to the underworld for all eternity!"

On that memorable morning, inscribed afterwards in Meruka's scrolls as The Day of Truth, Menmireh, crying uncontrollably and rending his tunic, described the sordid tale of Anhotek's death. He told how he sent Siamun to lure Anhotek to the parapet and how Siamun had pushed him from the edge to make it look like an accident. Despite his old age, Anhotek miraculously survived the fall. As Menmireh and the other priests involved in the conspiracy debated what to do, Anhotek moaned. Menmireh picked up a rock and bashed it into his skull, silencing him. Surero came upon the scene shortly after, to find Anhotek still alive, although barely.

It was only left to determine who had arranged the plot on Anhotek's life, although none in my council had any doubt who the evil-doers were. Menmireh, to his credit, did not readily reveal the organizers. It took Kagemni and Rekhmireh two days to relieve him of his burden. They called me, along with the rest of my council, to the place where they did their work, for we all felt it was necessary for me to hear Menmireh's confession myself, so terrible would be the consequences.

The mud-daub hut they took me to sat at the edge of a military encampment, yet no soldiers could be found nearby, so horrific was Menmireh's screaming. When I saw him, or what was left of him, I knew that he had already abandoned his body and sought only to rectify his ka, to lighten his heart for Anubis' unerring scale.

And so, that very day, as farmers throughout Kem went about their daily business of planting their crops upon the life-giving black soil of Mother Nile, I summoned Mersyankh, Ihy and Neter-Maat to the Court chamber, where the only chair in the room was my throne. They stood below me, Ihy leaning on his staff, Neter-Maat standing tall, and Mersyankh, bedecked in her jewelry and makeup, her demeanor as defiant as ever.

I began by unrolling the scrolls that the Chief Priest had written many years before, when Anhotek had fallen sick with the mosquito illness and we had found Ihy's magic drawings, the ones that portrayed a huge Neter-Maat crowned King and me as his tiny servant.

"These scrolls reveal your treachery going back many years," I said to the three of them, while holding open the scrolls before Mersyankh's and Ihy's faces.

"Well, the King has been busier than I had imagined," Mersyankh said to Ihy in her high-pitched voice. Ihy closed his eyes and stood silently, as if he had already resigned himself to his fate and was trying to shut out her irritating voice. She then turned to me.

"We should have killed that charlatan back then… no, even earlier," she nearly hissed at me. "And you," she continued, pointing her bony finger in my direction, "you are alive and Neter-Maat not the rightful King only because of incompetence."

"Incompetence?" I asked her, trying to restrain my anger.

"That fool, Butehamon, could not even properly arrange to have you killed in Kherdasakh!" she whined at me. "And… and those incompetent soldiers could not even kill a defenseless girl on her way to Nekhen! Incompetents, all of them!"

Meruka stepped forward then, ready to respond to Mersyankh's evil tongue, but I held up my hand to stay him.

"I pity you Mersyankh, for you fail to grasp who has been the true incompetent."

"Is that what you think? Well, King Narmer, hear my words well. Often success is masked as failure until the very last moment. And do you know what I regret most of all, my dear stepson?" she continued with her venomous attack. "Ah, I can see not, for you still fancy yourself able to see almighty Horus' visions. In truth, your sight has been blinded by his wings that you hide beneath.

"So I will tell you my sincerest regret. It is that I will not live long enough to see you become weak, like your worthless, drunken father." My eyes blinked for but an instant at her affront, but she was too cunning to miss that.

"Oh, yes, mighty King Narmer. The Scorpion's stinger was as limp as wilted grass. He was a pitiful drunk, consumed by the abomination he was forced to call his son. And you... you have already taken the first steps along that path. You will become just like him."

To say that her words did not skewer me would be a lie. The room was deathly silent, waiting for my response. I, myself, searched my heart for the correct words. Yet until I opened my mouth to reply, I did not know what I would say.

"Thank you, Mersyankh, for you have, indeed, shaped my life. You sharpened the blade that Scorpion forged and that I used to become the King of a united Kem." The effect of my words was more severe than if I had smacked her with the back of my hand. Her eyes widened and she was about to reply, when I looked away from her and continued.

"Ihy, for your part in this continuing conspiracy, I order you put to death immediately." I nodded to Kagemni and he walked to Ihy's side, took his staff and handed it to Rekhmireh. With Mersyankh and Neter-Maat watching, Kagemni bent Ihy over a log, face up. Kagemni reached out to Rekhmireh for the executioner's sword, but I stepped between the two and grabbed the sword myself. I thought of my mentor's words to me so long ago concerning Ihy's loyalty, misplaced though it was, and I said a silent prayer to Horus to intervene with Anubis as I tightly gripped the hilt of the sword.

Kagemni looked into my eyes, nodded, and kneeled next to Ihy's head. As he held Ihy's head by the hair, Ihy's and my eyes locked upon each other. His face was wrinkled with age and he looked tired and, some later said, even relieved. I raised my sword and brought it down cleanly through his neck. His body twitched for but an instant.

Standing before Mersyankh, I broke Ihy's staff in two and ordered that his body and staff be returned to Tjeni and burned in his own fire pit, the same one he had used to great effect against Hemamiya. His head I ordered displayed in every village in Lower Kem that lay along the route to Wadj-Wer, before being tossed into its depths, along with Dep's rubbish.

Because Neter-Maat had served in the army without incident, Rekhmireh asked for permission to deal with him. The very next day, Neter-Maat was assigned to lead a small garrison of soldiers in a desolate outpost along Wat-Hor in Setjet.

As for Mersyankh, I could not bring myself to take her life. Against the advice of my Council, I banished Mersyankh from my Court, confiscating all her possessions, to live her life as a peasant in the small fishing village I had come to know as a child on Abu Island. Knowing Mersyankh, my punishment would, in many ways, be crueler to her than death. Never able to leave Abu Island, I felt safe that she would live out her days under the watchful eyes of the Horus priests at the new temple that stood upon the highest bluff on the island.

For years I questioned what had stayed my hand from ordering Mersyankh's death, whether it was that she remained one of the few living links I had to Scorpion, or whether it was due to the insights Anhotek had shared with me about her character, or perhaps it was for some other, deeper reason that the gods had not revealed to me. But, whatever the reason, one thing later became certain. My decision to spare her life was a grievous mistake.

# SCROLL TWENTY-FOUR

## *The Lesson*

"Is he not truly like his father?" Rekhmireh asked, smiling and poking me in the ribs with his elbow.

"If you poke me one more time, then it will be me and you down there," I responded good-naturedly, pushing back at him with my shoulder.

"And you know who would win that fight!" Rekhmireh answered back, trying again to poke me in the ribs. Instead, I grabbed his elbow and pulled on him and he toppled off his chair. Everyone in the reviewing stand looked at him, some pointing and laughing.

"He has had too much to drink," I said loudly, trying in vain to make myself heard above Rekhmireh's and Kegemni's laughter.

It was the seventh day of the festival of Proyet, a day when the military around Inabu-hedj assembled to witness the prowess of the elite King's Guard. Each unit in the army picked one man to represent them and he could select any one man in my King's Guard in hand-to-hand combat. The contests had been going on for a full day and the combatants were narrowed down to the five finalists who would show off their skills to their King. We were watching the third contest, pitting Hor-aha against one of my finest Guards, Wer-ka, the son of one of Tjeni's finest metal workers, who had inherited his father's large frame.

The two men circled each other cautiously, each holding a training mace, a straw- and grain-filled sack fastened tightly to a stick. Despite its laughable appearance, in the hands of a well-trained man it could deliver a blow that the recipient would not soon forget. The soldiers, some two thousand strong, were gathered on the fertile plain below the palace. They cheered wildly for the contestants, most of whom sided with Wer-ka.

Hor-aha was a full head shorter than Wer-ka, but he was also five years younger, and his fifteen year-old body was in peak form, his upper chest strong and sinewy and his midsection trim, their muscles taut and sculpted. But, he was also too full of himself, and as he postured in a circle, flexing his muscles, Wer-ka spun around and hit him on the side of the head and nearly knocked him off his feet. The crowds cheered wildly. Hor-aha staggered, shaking his head, his right foot nearly touching the edge of the out-of-bounds circle. He lifted on his toes to hold his balance. Wer-ka made the mistake of watching his footwork, rather than pursuing for the win.

Hor-aha acted as if he was still gaining his balance, when suddenly he spun around and landed a solid blow to Wer-ka's mid-section. As my Guard bent over, Hor-aha hit him on the back of the head with his mace, then swept him off his feet quickly with his foot, as I had taught him to do. With Wer-ka on his back, he stood over him, placing a foot on his chest, his mace raised high at the ready, in the victory stance. The crowds erupted wildly. Most cheered, but my King's Guards booed and hissed at him loudly, but in good spirits.

"He performed well today," I said to Neith-hotep as we ate our evening meal. "You would have been proud of him."

"I do not take pride in grown men hitting each other or… or practicing how best to kill a woman's husband or son."

"But, he may need to defend his wife or mother from invaders or thieves," I reminded Neith-hotep.

"You know how I feel about such matters," she said angrily, and I knew from her tone that it was best not to pursue the issue. She put down her cup and walked huffily to the railing of the portico and looked out over the black fields, just now beginning to show the first traces of the green that would soon blanket them. Below us, the farmers worked to catch the last rays of Ra's light, the remembrance of the past five years of famine fresh in their minds. Smoke billowed from hundreds of straw huts and mud-daub houses as wives, mothers and daughters prepared meager evening meals for their men.

I found that at times such as these, the wisest words I could offer were no words. Instead, I enveloped Neith-hotep in my arms. At first she was rigid as stone, but I simply held her tight and rocked her gently to and fro. In a few moments, I could feel her body relax.

"Do you have any idea how it encourages me when you get so... so prickly?" I whispered into my beloved's ear. She struggled briefly to get out, but from the way she pressed her buttocks into me I determined that she did not truly want me to let go.

"That is not always what you tell me when I challenge your behavior... or your decisions," she said coyly.

"Ah, but there is a difference between your anger and... and however it is that you act now. It brings out a passion in me."

"Forty years old and still you act like a young ibex buck. My friends tell me their husbands find little use for them any more." I smiled and she turned around and put her arms around my neck and kissed me then, passionately. Suddenly our mood was broken by a clucking sound.

"The King and Queen are at it again! Have you two no shame?" We turned to see our son standing at the entranceway, his body bruised and cut from his bouts, yet his chest swelled with pride.

"How...? You are supposed to be with your unit," I

said, my manhood suddenly as limp as a wilted lotus.

"Obviously, that is what you thought!" he replied with boundless enthusiasm and ran over to his mother, who hugged him tightly. Then he came over to me and we embraced warmly.

"You are all scratched and bruised," Neith-hotep said, her face wrinkled with concern. "Let me have Meruka look after you."

"No, I am fine... really. Just a few scratches, that is all." Hor-aha turned to me, his eyes wide with excitement. "Did you see that move I made on Wer-ka, father? He hardly knew what hit him."

"I will leave you two to discuss your childish battle stories," Neith-hotep said as she left the room. "Be sure to say goodbye before you leave tonight, Aha."

"Well, what did you think, father?" Aha asked immediately. I smelled beer on his breath from celebrating with his fellow soldiers. He poured himself a glass of water and sat on the nearest chair, without offering me any.

"You did well, son... very well. I am proud of you."

He hesitated, looking at me for a few seconds. "What?" he finally said.

"What do you mean, 'what'?

"Your voice does not reflect your words. There is something you are holding back. I did something wrong."

"No, not that I know of. You were... perfect. Your form was perfect." Yet Hor-aha was correct. There was something that did not sit well within me. "Too perfect, perhaps."

"Too perfect? How is that possible, father? That is like... like saying ma'at is too strong."

"You are right, it does not make much sense. But... how do I say this? There is a big difference between doing things well in training and doing well in battle. They are entirely different experiences."

"But you have prevented me from entering battle," he responded without thinking, an altogether frequent flaw in Hor-aha's ba. "I am the same age as you when you lead the mightiest army ever against Dep."

"I was two years older than you are now. With each passing year, my age in battle gets younger and my deeds magnified. That is one of the advantages of being King."

"Still, I have been trained by you and Kagemni and Rekhmireh. You saw today what I can do to even your King's Guards. I would like you to send me into battle, or at least a skirmish against the Ta-Tjehehus or... or the Ta-Sety raiders."

Aha was in his prime years and deserved the chance to prove his mettle. "I agree with your reasoning. I will speak with Rekhmireh... if you promise not to discuss this with your mother."

Aha's face lit up. "Are you serious, father? You are serious, right? Good! I will tell no one... and I will make you proud of my battlefield accomplishments."

"Just make sure you return alive and with all your limbs. As is, I will no doubt have to sleep in another part of the palace until you return." Aha chose to ignore that comment.

"And, when I return, I would like to speak with you about what my role will be in the Court."

"Aha, you are too brash! I am still alive and healthy... at least relatively."

"And I wish you a long and prosperous life, father. I just... you ascended to the throne when you were barely older than I am now. I would like to have more responsibility so that when the time comes for your passing, I shall be prepared. Meruka has tutored me. Kaipunesut taught me before he passed on. I feel ready!"

"I do not disagree that you are ready, Aha, or capable. It is just that you cannot do it all at once. You know, it is good to remember, from time to time, that although the throne you will one day sit upon is exalted above all others, you still sit on your own behind." I smiled inwardly at having finally said those words to Hor-aha, the same ones that Anhotek had said to me many times. "But I will speak to Meruka about this. We will develop a plan."

It is an odd thing, raising a child. We go through the difficult process of growing up ourselves and so think ourselves able to turn around and grow our children, as if one had anything to do with the other. Raising a boy, especially one born to as many privileges as Hor-aha, was not easy. Youth believe with all the passions of their ba that they are not mortal. They see with only one set of eyes, Anhotek used to say, eyes that only see forward. Adults have gained the use of the other set, the one that looks backward at life's experiences.

As soon as I awoke the next morning, refreshed from a night steeped in Neith-hotep's delights, I sent Ahpety to request Meruka's company for the morning meal. It was already late and Meruka arrived with a handful of scrolls, each representing a matter needing my attention.

"Put the scrolls away, Meruka, for I am in need of your counsel. Please..." I added when he held up the stack to object.

"About Hor-Aha..." I started to say.

"I heard."

"You heard what?" I asked, cocking my head to the side.

"That you are sending him off to fight with Rekhmireh against the Ta-Tjehenus."

"Horus!" I yelled out in frustration. "Give me the strength to not kill that boy!" I stood up to pace before Meruka's chair. "I did not promise him that, Meruka! I did not! He is impetuous, brash, disdainful..."

"Do you describe him or yourself?" Meruka said. Before my eyes, he began to laugh uproariously and pound his thigh. I tried to stay serious, but his words cut my defenses to the core and soon the two of us were curled up and slapping each other in laughter. Tears rolled down our eyes and each time we stopped, one of us would look to the other and we would again burst out in snorts of laughter. Ahpety came in to see if we were possessed by some demon spirit.

"It is a good thing to have someone who knows me so well," I finally said, wiping my eyes on a towel. "It reminds me that I do sit on my own behind." I arose and tried to breath in deeply, but my laughter-filled lungs rebelled.

"Speak with Ny-ankh. Persuade him to our cause. As Hor-aha's personal scribe, he should reason with him, calm him, make him less impetuous."

"He tries, my King. He tries as hard as humanly possible. But Ny-ankh is not Anhotek. And the present circumstances are not the same as you faced. Hor-aha has had a father who encourages him and a mother who indulges him."

And so we continued to deal with the challenges that Hor-aha raised, but also the various issues of state that Meruka brought with him that morning. After we had finished a meal of dates, cheese, heavy bread and goat's milk, Meruka put aside his scrolls.

"There is one more matter for your attention. I have waited to tell you so that I could check my sources for their accuracy. These are names that we have not had to deal with for a while," he continued, and from the manner of his voice I knew instantly of whom he spoke. "Neter-maat has finally married."

"Neter-maat?"

"Yes. It was an arranged marriage, performed before Inundation by a shaman near Wadj-Wer."

"Arranged by who?" The expression on Meruka's face was its own answer. "What? How did that mut arrange it from Abu Island? She is ancient... and powerless."

"Ancient, yes. As old now as Anhotek was when he passed to the next life. But, not powerless. Her advanced age apparently won over the hearts of a few priests on Abu Island. She persuaded them to be her messengers to her family in Lower Kem. I have since dealt harshly with the priests."

"This is incredible!" I said, sitting down hard in my chair opposite Meruka. "Mersyankh still stirs her evil brew. The gods have begun yet another act in our play." I tried to imagine how Mersyankh might look now. Perhaps she was stooped low to the ground. Perhaps disease had ravaged her face. But there was no doubt in my heart that if I saw her eyes again, I would recognize her without fail.

"To whom?" I asked Meruka, who looked at me

quizzically. "Who did Neter-maat marry?"

"A cousin. The daughter of a former local village leader in Lower Kem, near Wadj-Wer."

"And a relative of W'ash, no doubt."

"W'ash's niece."

"And so her evil potion thickens, does it not my dear friend? It thickens indeed."

"It does. Neter-maat is afflicted greatly by alcohol. He is drunk all the time, my spies report. Slovenly and slower than ever. But the marriage does put him in line to rule Lower Kem, should the latest rebellion succeed in casting you out of the delta."

"But the rebellion is being handled well, right?" I asked. For the second time that morning Meruka waited a moment before answering.

"It is being handled, Narmer. How well only the gods know. The Chief Priest tightens his grip on the Horus priests, but Lower Kem crawls with other sects, over which we still do not have tight control. Our spies do what they can."

"Is there a connection?"

"Does Ra rise in the sky every morning? At the time Anhotek was killed, Mersyankh and Ihy were scheming a major uprising. Their plans may very well have succeeded if we had not uncovered their foul plot."

"And for that I owe you a great deal." For a moment Meruka's seemed surprised by my comment.

"You do not owe me anything, Narmer, for what I did, I did out of love for you and my mentor… and my adopted land." He paused for a moment to allow his words to sink in. "But, old alliances die hard. It took Mersyankh several years to adjust to her life on Abu Island, to create new alliances, to weave a new scheme. The timing of Neter-Maat's marriage, the current raids by the Ta-Tjehenus, the tax rebellions… all of these events seem connected. They reek of Mersyankh's conniving."

"But, it has been ten years since Anhotek's death," I said, incredulous.

Meruka smiled. "Her ka is timeless, Narmer, as is her

ambition. But, she is old and I believe this will be her death rattle." I thought long on Meruka's words and had to agree with his counsel.

"I think that by reducing the taxes in light of the drought, we have removed one of the major irritants," Meruka continued. "The peasants, as usual, still support you. They see for themselves that we did the best we could with the grain stores. They lasted three years. This Inundation was better than last year's, so the crops will yield more. And we can count on the army. It is strong and loyal under Rekhmireh's command."

"W'ash's family... I should have struck them all down when I conquered Dep," I said in disgust. "And Mersyankh... I should have executed her with Ihy."

"Perhaps, but I believe this is a matter of time and succession. The wealthy families of Lower Kem have seen your might. You are the living conqueror. They do not like that, but they respect it. As you add years, people's eyes and ears turn toward who will succeed you. Hor-Aha has not yet established himself as Towi's future leader. When he does, they will accept the fact that your rule will last for many generations."

Meruka was right. By seeking to protect Hor-Aha from the stench of Court intrigue, of the wealthy petitioning for exceptions to laws that applied to all others, of attempts by the privileged to curry the King's favor so that they could more easily twist their blades when their kinfolks' backs were turned, I may not have served him well.

Over the next ten-day cycle, Meruka and I developed a plan that would expand Hor-aha's military skills and make him more proficient in the affairs of state, while attempting to keep his already swollen head from popping. In thirty days' time, with the land along both banks of Mother Nile bursting in green, even into the cultivated river valleys, I left the beautiful white walls of Inabu-hedj with a detachment of five thousand soldiers. Rekhmireh led the expedition, bound for Ta-Ihu, the northernmost oasis in Kem, a remote village in the Great Desert, west of Inabu-hedj. The Ta-Tjenhenus had attacked Ta-Ihu regularly over the past three years, recently extorting taxes from them in a brazen display that challenged the King's very authority. Meruka's spies reported that several of the local families had aided the invaders, in trade for lower taxes. However, he suspected more foul play and insisted on accompanying us. We left Kagemni and Neith-hotep in charge of the palace in our absence.

Hor-aha led his unit of one hundred swordsmen. For the first several days of our journey, I watched with pride as he drilled with his troops every night. His physical prowess was extraordinary, his ability to run at full speed, then turn on a knife's edge and thrust his sword against an enemy without losing his balance. His upper body, although sinewy, was powerful. Yet, he was also brash and many were the times during these maneuvers that he would have surely gotten his head crushed by a nimble opponent's mace. Rekhmireh would correct him and Aha would rectify that mistake, but the next moment he might attempt a different, but similarly reckless maneuver. That tendency brought a terrible fear to my heart.

Rekhmireh had arranged for his supply officers to have one thousand jars of thick barley beer and water ready for us at each encampment along our route, each one guarded by a small group of soldiers. This arrangement worked well until the tenth day, when an advance scout ran back to us to report that at the place arranged for our next camp, still two days' march from the oasis, the guards were found dead and every water and beer jar broken.

Rekhmireh immediately gave orders to ration water and he sent runners back along our route with orders to refresh the supplies, a task that would take many days. We both understood that our situation could turn grave. We could either sit and wait for the water to arrive, or attempt a forced march to the oasis, which would have water in abundance. After discussions with our top officers, Rekhmireh and I decided to march on and engage the Ta-Tjehenus.

Throughout the next day we marched quietly, each man knowing full well how the intensity of the desert could draw out of a man the full measure of his ba. The men were trained to understand that every excess motion, even a needless word or laugh, could mean the difference between life and death. Ra's rays seared the very sand beneath our feet, so that walking upon it, even with reed sandals, burned the soles of our feet. The soldiers marched, heads down, wearing only a tunic and carrying their water skins and weapons. Rekhmireh ordered all breastplates and armbands removed, to be carried in the rear by the pages. We left all donkeys behind, for we could not spare the extra water that the beasts required.

Later that day, a scout reported that the final water encampment before the oasis was also ravaged. Rekhmireh wisely decided to divert around the route so that the men would not be discouraged. The next morning, just two hours after Ra rose in the heavens, with our bodies severely drained, we reached the sandy plateau that separated the dry, barren desert from the lush, lake-fed oasis of Ta-Ihu. In the distance we could see its greenery, the heat of the desert's rays causing its image to shimmer before us. It was also apparent how Ta-Ihu got its name, Land of the Cattle, for great herds of the large beasts grazed in pockets all around the village. In this remote region the farmers were able to breed some of the finest cattle in Kem and the surrounding lands. With a determination borne of thirst and deprivation, we began crossing the hot sands that led to the oasis.

As we descended the dunes toward the valley floor, I was once again reminded how different are our imaginings from the realities of war. Before embarking on our march, bathed and refreshed, the young recruits thought they would arrive to fight in a similar state of alertness. How quickly a soldier's urge to battle subsides when he finds himself in such dreadful circumstances. It is only the mortar of leadership and discipline that can still bind such men into an effective fighting force. In that regard, we were fortunate to have a man like Rekhmireh, tutored under the wings of Kagemni, as the commander of the army. He walked among his men, at times taking me with him to help rally our troops. With one unit he would simply share a story that left the soldiers laughing and with another he would share his water skin. Whatever action he took, in every instance he managed to motivate his men to their utmost.

In another hour, we were close enough to Ta-Ihu to make out individual people in the town. Rekhmireh ordered the soldiers to retrieve their breast plates and ready their arms. Soon, a delegation of priests and officials could be seen leaving the village, slowly making their way toward our army.

Rekhmireh conferred with me and then ordered his men split into five large units of one thousand men each. Three of the units, occupying the central formation, were close together, with me and the King's Guard behind them. Far to the left and right the flanking units were dispersed. The sandy plain was silent, save for the rustling of men and equipment, as the entourage from Ta-Ihu reached us. After a brief discussion with them, Rekhmireh sent a messenger to me with advance notice of what had transpired.

Meruka appeared agitated after hearing the messenger's report and as soon as the delegation was escorted to us to continue their discussions, he began asking questions of the temple's head priest. In just a few minutes, despite their evasions, he determined that the priests and villagers had indeed supported the Ta-Tjehenus. I said not a word, but listened impassively to the entreaties of the priest to us to accept their pitiful offer of tribute.

I had not seen Meruka so agitated since the trial following Anhotek's murder. "This entire situation has the foul smell of deception and betrayal," he said, pacing before me. "I had not an inkling of something so rotten in our midst. I… I was fed wrong information all along and I did not seek to question it." Meruka looked at me then. "I am terribly sorry, Narmer. This situation is in large part my fault."

However, it was Rekhmireh who felt most ashamed, for he had not sought to establish a military outpost to protect our western lands, thinking that the battle of Dep would have lasted longer in the minds and legends of the Ta-

Tjehenus. Together he and Meruka would make quick amends to rectify the situation, but for now I focused their attention on the task at hand.

We placed the entire delegation under guard at the rear of the army. Scouts were sent to the edges of Ta-Ihu to observe and test their defenses, which were meager. They had obviously not anticipated our army marching against them in such force. Yet our water supplies were now only beginning to arrive and we were parched from a lack of water. If we waited for the supplies to fully water the troops, it would be days, enough time for the Ta-Tjehenus to slither away during the long nights.

We decided that our best hope lay in taking the village quickly and using the plentiful water supply of the oasis and its large lake to water our men. Rekhmireh dispatched an entire division of one thousand men to circle Ta-Ihu from the rear, to cut off any escape route. Once they were positioned, they signaled us with a mirror and we marched on the oasis. I can only imagine the fear in the hearts of the people that day. Such is the folly of men, to assume that all is well, that their day of judgment will never arrive, despite their wrongful behavior. Did the people of Ta-Ihu not know that we were a united land? Did they not realize that they threatened ma'at with their foolish actions?

We were at the very edges of the village itself when Rekhmireh gave the command to charge. With one of the center divisions now deployed to the rear of Ta-Ihu, the two remaining center divisions charged first, spreading out to cover the entire village. Once they were engaged, the flanking divisions would enter the battle. Hor-aha's division was on the left flank. Once the center divisions charged, I whispered a silent prayer to Horus to extend his protection to my son.

The battle to reclaim Ta-Ihu did not last long. Most would have considered it a minor skirmish. So it is that the gods play tricks on mortals. Within minutes our troops swept through the village, their war cries penetrating the air. I watched them from my chair perch as they cut down the few enemy Ta-Tjenhenus that dared oppose us. Then our forces dissipated and I watched our soldiers walking about in the village, dragging their swords and bows and lances, as if they were lost.

Rekhmireh's aide came to retrieve me and when I finally entered the village, no traditional cries of victory greeted me. When I saw Rekhmireh, he was possessed of a sadness in his eyes that I had never before seen. He stood in front of a poor farmer's hut and he stepped aside so that I could enter. When my eyes adjusted to the shadows and the play of Ra's light through its reed stalks, I saw all around me a collection of body parts scattered, of arms and legs, of heads and male members, of children and mothers. Never before, not even upon the terrible killing fields of Dep, had I had the overwhelming desire to vomit at a sight of carnage. In every hut in the village, the same scene was repeated. The Ta-Tjenehus had slowed our approach long enough to slaughter our people and escape, leaving behind only a small group of suicide warriors to defend their illegitimate territory.

I walked out into Ra's full light, too dazed to speak. I cast my head down in shame, shame that men, men who walked the lands just as did I, could act so cruelly, like desert jackals that tore at the flesh of their own kind. Ahpety brought me a goatskin filled with water, but I refused to drink, so fearful was I that I would heave up the contents of my stomach. Throughout the village, clumps of men stood silently. Lone soldiers slumped to the sands and cried, and several vomited along the edges of buildings, brave men who would have readily thrust their swords through another warrior's chest in battle.

As I walked from hut to hut with Rekhmireh, reports began to arrive from unit commanders, listing the casualties of the skirmish. Again, the gods must have had their fun that day, for among the few casualties was Hor-Aha. He led a charge against a group of Ta-Tjehenus who had hidden amongst the stalks of emmer wheat in a field on the outskirts of the village.

I ran to the site of the skirmish and found Hor-Aha laying on his right side, the fletching of a Ta-Tjehenu arrow sticking out of his left shoulder. Meruka was crouched next to him and beside him was his assistant, Sennedjem. Of all matters to enter my thoughts at that moment was the odd observation that the skin of Meruka's bare neck was now wrinkled and hung in gentle folds. Then I saw the rivulets of blood that poured from Hor-aha's wound. I knelt down next to my son and by the mercy of Horus, saw that he was alive. He batted his eyelids at me and managed a wry smile.

"I am sorry, father... I..."

"Be quiet and put this between your teeth!" Meruka said forcefully, taking a small piece of leather from Sennedjem and shoving it into Aha's mouth. "Bear down... I have to remove this cursed arrow."

I watched, dazed, as Meruka pushed hard on the shaft of the arrow until it finally emerged on the back of Aha's arm. Aha bit down until he turned the color of a ripe pomegranate, before all color left his face and he fainted. With the arrowhead now protruding, Meruka broke off the fletching and Sennedjem then pulled on the arrowhead until he extracted the remainder of the shaft.

One of the swordsmen under Hor-aha's command reported that when Hor-aha had seen the slaughter in the village, he instructed his men to search for any Ta-Tjehenus who might be hiding. Hor-aha himself followed several tracks in the sand into the emmer field. He saw Ta-Tjehenus laying among the wheat and, without waiting for his men, he recklessly charged into their midst. By the time his men arrived, Hor-aha had cut down four of the Ta-Tjehenu swordsmen. But, as he turned to rally the rest of his unit, several Ta-Tjehenu archers arose and let loose their fateful volley. Hor-aha lay wounded and two of his men were killed.

Throughout the rest of the day, Meruka and Sennedjem tended to Hor-Aha, cleansing the wound and trying to stem the profuse bleeding. I refused to leave Hor-Aha's side until Meruka took me aside.

"Narmer, it does no good for you to buzz about like a fly. He is your son and the Prince, but he is also a soldier. The best you can do is pray to Horus to act in his behalf and go visit with your troops." Meruka was right.

I met with Rekhmireh, who gave me a quick assessment of the skirmish. Only thirty-four of the village's inhabitants were left alive, out of a number that most estimated at more than six hundred and fifty. There was no way our soldiers could estimate the true number from the condition of the dead. Five of our soldiers were killed and twenty-two injured.

With a heavy heart, I added to the number of dead. After showing the head priest what his allies had done to his own people, I had him executed. His assistants I spared, to spread the word of what the Ta-Tjenehus had done, and of my retribution, to future inhabitants of the village. For those merchants who had stolen from me by withholding taxes, I had one of their hands cut off. Farmers who had aided the enemy had their land confiscated. The task of rebuilding the village, establishing an army outpost and a loyal priesthood I left to Meruka and Rekhmireh.

With evening approaching, I visited Hor-aha. His wound had already become poisoned with pustulence and he thrashed about with a fever. Sennedjem and Panehsy alternated forcing liquids and applying an unguent to the wound. I knew I could do no more than watch and so, carrying a heavy burden, I walked off into the western desert to be alone with my thoughts.

I have heard from stories traders that come to Kem from Babylon, and even Setjet, that they cannot tell the difference between one desert and another, that they are all the same and all to be avoided when possible. Yet, I cannot understand that way of viewing our land, for the differences between the eastern and western deserts are so obvious even a fool would be able to tell them apart. And all but a fool would choose the eastern desert over the western.

I walked away from the camp, over flat sections of deep sand and over tall dunes, only to find more flat sand and even taller dunes, as far as my eye could see. There were no mountains within which I could seek refuge, not one acacia tree to break up the view or provide shade, nothing at all but endless sand. By now, Ra's setting disk cast huge, dark shadows and the temperature began to drop, yet I continued to walk.

Away from the encampment, even the barren western desert soon worked its magic on me. I lived in cities, I visited villages of every description, I heard reports of far-off lands from emissaries and traders. But the desert gives gifts that no other land can give. Solitude. Quiet. Peace. No noise from Mother Nile rushing to Wadj-Wer, no trickles from meandering tributaries, no leaves to rustle in the wind. Just silence. Utter and complete silence.

Soon I was beset by the desert's magic. Each crunch of sand under my feet became a welcome relief from the affairs of state. Men did not curry my favor. The only decision I needed to make was where to place my foot. I climbed a high dune, higher than any I had encountered that evening, and there I sat, removing my dagger belt and my water pouch. As the gentle evening winds picked up and tickled my skin with grains of sand, I sheltered my arms within the tunic I wore.

So I sat, time itself becoming meaningless, as the last sliver of Ra's orb disappeared into the underworld and his silver night disk rose into the sky, full and bright, casting his light onto the undulating forms of the desert landscape. I waited for my ka to absorb the desert's peace, to suck it in and calm me. Instead, my mind would not shake loose the images that confronted it. Before me flashed the gruesome scenes of the dead in Ta-Ihu, jumbled together, tormenting my heart. One image from that day burned my eyes, that of one small hand clutching tightly to an even tinier hand. Two hands, without bodies, laying on the sand, a mother clutching her infant.

I imagined Hor-aha, thrashing on his blanket, of Neith-hotep pacing the floor of our palace in worry, awaiting word of our success and of her son's and husband's safe return, of Anhotek... of Anhotek. My mind raced through scenes of my childhood.

Where was he now, my Anhotek, my teacher and father, the one man who I could count on above all others? Tears filled my eyes as anguish filled my heart.

"Where?" I shouted into the silvery darkness. "Where are you when I need you more than ever?" I held up my fist, shaking it at the bejeweled sky.

"Use your magic! Appear before me!" I screamed. "Or was it all an illusion?" I hung my head down and the tears fell softly onto my ankle. "Where…?" But the words would no longer form. There were no words. Only tears.

I sat thus for a long time, allowing the pain in my heart to pour upon the sands, as Anhotek had done with Mafdet's blood when she was stung by the scorpion. I felt as if every moist part of me had dried and I was nothing more than a desiccated hide. Only then did I feel a lightness overcome my ba, as if it were freed of a weight that I dragged along behind me for so long.

Images of Neith-hotep flew into my heart, illuminating it, lightening for a moment the burdens of Kingship that weighed upon me. And I thought of all the good that Neith-hotep brought to me and to our land. And I thought of Towi, the Two Lands, the lotus and papyrus, the black and the red. And then, for the first time in many years, I again saw the vision of the wondrous Towi that would someday be. The night winds came then, gentle and cool, like Anhotek's soft touch upon my face and I knew then that Horus' wings were spread wide to protect us all.

In that moment, with the shimmering eyes of the gods watching from their perches in the endless night sky, I understood. For the first time, I truly understood. To feel the breath of our loved ones from the next world, to experience the ka of the gods mixing with our own, to illuminate one's heart with the love of family, that is the Divine, the egg of creation, the purity of ma'at. All else, all the rituals and buildings, priesthood and ceremonies were tools, a means to an end. Anhotek knew this, and that night, when he visited me in the western desert, he taught me that lesson, the most valuable of all. We are not only of the gods, but also part of them.

With my ka centered, I stood and breathed in the sen-sen breaths and felt myself fill with Horus' loving spirit. I knelt upon the cool sands and together we prayed, I for

Hor-Aha and he for the future of Towi.

# SCROLL TWENTY-FIVE

*Horus*

It is hard to be this old, to be held captive by a body that no longer quickly responds to your command, if at all, to be possessed of a heart that frequently does not remember a familiar name, nor even what it did earlier that day. Was it not only yesterday that I leaped over enemies, ducked the avenging arc of their swords, rolled away and then quickly thrust my sword through them? I laugh at that image now, for my flabby middle can hardly obey any other command but to shuffle to the table for meals. Thanks be to the gods for also dulling our senses as we age, so that we may at least laugh at ourselves in our infirmity.

Dare I even complain? Despite my frustrations, I am yet alive at fifty-six years. I sit erect and still have my teeth, while most of my countrymen walk stooped over from carrying their heavy burdens by time they are half my age. How many of the elderly must eat only cooked cereal or have their loved ones chew their foods like they were infants again, all because they had no choice but to eat sandy breads and fruits their whole lives that mercilessly grind down their teeth like the worn stones that grind emmer wheat?

It is not the infirmities of the body, or even the heart that are most difficult to tolerate, it is those of the ka. I dwell on my complaints because my ka is unsettled, restive, pressed on every side, in every moment, by the demands of Kem. I sit atop a pyramid of power, few able to make decisions in my stead, none able to decide matters that only the King may rule upon. I look around me and see no one, none others to whom I can turn. My dearest Neith-hotep has journeyed to the next life. Meruka no doubt now ministers to her there. Ahpety no longer serves me, for he wanders in and out of the dreams that precede death itself. These are the times when I pray to Horus to escort me on my next journey, to reward my trials by reuniting me with my lover and my friends. Oh, Kem, how I love and hate you!

"He has arrived," Weneg called to me softly, interrupting my thoughts. He was already bowing and backing away by time I noticed him. How his reverence sometimes irritates me! From the time I ascended to the throne until I reached the age of fifty, Ahpety served me dutifully, but with the familiarity of a brother. To be served by a youngster who thinks me a god is more difficult than I would have ever imagined.

I walked to the mud-brick wall that ran around the edge of the portico. Ra's disk was halfway through his journey and the dust from the constant construction of Inabu-hedj sat like a fog over the land surrounding the palace. Through the haze, I could see the armada of ships making their way toward us, oars out, the drummers beating a cadence to which the soldiers could pull in unison.

Hor-aha would be aboard the first ship to slip into the stone piers that now jutted out from the banks of the busy river in front of the palace. I looked down, over our lush gardens, bursting with the colors of plants gathered from many lands, and the many pools that watered them, all lovingly planned by Neith-hotep. An army of servants tended to the plants, silently pruning and watering. I wondered what the mood of Hor-aha's soldiers would be.

Somber? Angry? And what would I say to Hor-aha, the son that I so loved?

The lead boat shipped its oars, and as it came alongside the pier, I watched Hor-Aha jump from its prow. He was thirty-two, already in his declining years, and I could not help but notice the slight paunch that had slowly begun to accumulate around his midsection. Yet his upper body was still strong and muscular. He wore only his hemp kilt and a leather belt that helped to hide his middle. As soon as he came upon land, he gave a few orders and turned toward the palace, his shoulders slumped.

"Father," he said as soon as he had entered my quarters and clasped my arms in his. "I... I do not know what to say." He hung his head down in shame.

"First, tell me what happened," I said. He seemed crushed by the weight of recent events. "I have only heard reports," I added, pointing for him to sit in the chair opposite me. As he slid into the chair, the scar in his shoulder from the battle of Ta-Ihu puckered.

"It was..." he began, then changed the direction of his remarks. "First, I accept responsibility for what happened, for if... if not for my actions none of this would have occurred." He wrung his hands as he told his tale.

"We were patrolling along the southern border with Lower Ta-Sety when we heard of raids on our villages to our east. For days we pursued the marauders until we came upon a village that was freshly raided. We pursued the attackers, but they fled far across the border."

"And you pursued them there?" I asked, already suspecting the answer. Aha hung his head and nodded.

"Yes, we did. Wer-ka counseled against it, but... I... it had been so maddening trying to get the raiders to stand and fight. I did not want to miss the opportunity to confront them."

"So, you chased them into Ta-Sety territory... without sending emissaries or... or making peace with their local Kings."

"Yes. It was..."

"How many soldiers did you lose?" I asked, dreading

Aha's answer.

"Four..." he began to say, then cleared the frogs that had seized his throat. "Four hundred and sixty."

I closed my eyes then, wishing that I could have kept Aha's answer from reaching my heart.

"It was a trick. They lured us deeper and deeper until we marched through a valley and then they launched themselves against us from all sides. We were helpless. It... it was a slaughter."

I sat quietly for many minutes, thinking how best to handle Hor-Aha's folly. "And, how do you intend to deal with this, my son?" I asked. "How will you recover from this mistake?" It was if I had slapped him across the face, throwing the matter back into his hands. A flood of memories overcame me, memories of the many times Neith-hotep and I had rescued him from his mistakes, all too often at the expense of his own learning.

He placed his hands on the arms of the chair and tightly gripped them. Suddenly, he brought up both his fists and slammed them down. "Damn it!" he shouted. "I am sick of it! My own quickness to action is to blame!" He sat back in his chair, frustrated, and turned his head to look toward Mother Nile. I knew that to speak then would be useless. Aha drummed the fingers of his left hand on the arm of the chair and his right hand held up his chin.

"What am I to do, father?" he asked with such consternation I wanted to get up and hold him.

"What does your heart tell you to do?" I asked. He looked away in anger.

"How am I to know? You are the King!"

"And you will soon be King. But now you act like a dog with its tail between its legs. What you have broken only you will fix."

"King? I, King? I do not believe that will soon happen, father. I wish you good health... you know I do. You have already lived longer than all your friends, longer than my mother. It may come to pass that I never wear the double-crown."

"Hor-aha, my son, I ask a favor of you," I responded,

using the calming voice that Anhotek had taught me so many times through his example. "Open your ears, for I will speak to you from my heart." I waited until he slowly lifted his eyes to me.

"I speak to you as your father, but also as the King of Kem who trains his successor. I am already old and will not see many more Wepet-renpet celebrations." Aha looked away from me and I again waited for his gaze to return.

"Every leader has his burdens and his gifts. I had to carry the burden of Scorpion's ill nature upon my shoulders. His weakness as a father bred within me the strength of patience... patience that... thanks be to Horus, Anhotek further cultivated.

"It is an irony of the gods that you have never known a day without your father's love. Your burden is the very opposite of mine, for my love for you has bred an impatience. Perhaps that is why the gods have granted me a long life... and have taunted you with my good fortune." I smiled at him, hoping my words would settle gently in his heart. The muscles of his neck appeared to relax.

"I lost some of my friends in that battle," he finally said, so softly the words sounded like they oozed from a wounded heart. "They fought to their deaths defending me."

"A leader makes decisions every day that affect people's lives," I said, holding up my hands. "You lost more than four hundred men in this skirmish. When famine last had its grip upon our land, I issued orders to limit rations from our granaries and a hundred times that number perished before the next harvest. In the Battle of Unification, I lost more than three thousand men... and we won that battle!"

Finally, I could see that my words had penetrated Aha's skin. He breathed deeply and sighed. "You are right, father. But, it still leaves me at a loss for what to do."

"Here is what I suggest, and I would say this to you, or Meruka if he were alive, or to Wer-ka tomorrow. You have made a mistake. Examine your heart. Determine what you did wrong. Allow Ra's light to shine on your darkest, most secret weaknesses. Have Ny-Ankh write down these discoveries on the papyrus scrolls he keeps of your life. Ask those whom you trust for their advice, without prejudice that you are the Prince of all Kem. Then, in one month's time, come to me with what you have found and with two... perhaps even three plans for how you will handle it. We will discuss them. But hear me now when I say that I will not tell you what to do. I will give you my counsel, but not my command."

Aha stared at me then with a look that was difficult to decipher. If he was angry at the suddenness with which I plunged him into the uncertainty of greater leadership, he did not entirely show it. If he felt love toward me for the confidence I showed in him, his expression did not fully reflect that either. Instead, he nodded his head with the recognition that our relationship had, in that brief time together, fundamentally changed. And in that shift, I saw a glimmer of the future King of Kem.

As soon as Hor-aha left my chambers, Sennedjem entered, wearing a clean tunic. Upon his ample chest he wore the gold medallion of the Vizier and the gold armband as shaman to the Royal Court. Upon his shaved head he wore his white shaman's cap, the effect of which was to make his large nose appear even larger.

"I must speak with you, my King," he said as soon as he entered.

"Make it brief, for I am tired." Yet, as tired as I felt, Sennedjem, only five years younger than me, looked even wearier. For the hundredth time I had to remind myself that I had supported Meruka's choice of Sennedjem as his eventual replacement. Together we agreed that it would be easier for Hor-aha to appoint the younger Ny-ankh as Vizier and chief shaman when he ascended to the throne if my Vizier was already advanced in years.

"I understand," he said bowing slightly. "Yet what I have to say may not be brief. It is a matter of utmost importance."

I sighed. "Go on," I said, waving my hand, "but I must get up. My knees are stiff from sitting."

Sennedjem reached up to help me rise, but one

disapproving glance from me was all it took to make him reconsider. He cast his glance away from me.

"It concerns Hor-aha," Sennedjem began nervously, his gaze following me as I hobbled around. "There is much talk in the Court... in the priesthood... about this latest... about the recent setback for Kem." I looked out over Mother Nile, wanting her calming influence to settle over me. Instead the line of war ships waiting for their chance to offload their cargo of wounded or weary soldiers unsettled me.

"Go on," I said, for despite the difficulties I had in adjusting to Sennedjem's manner over the years, he had proven himself a worthy counsel. "But please get to the point quickly."

Sennedjem wavered before speaking, as if searching for a way to lessen the impact of his words. But after hesitating, he decided better of his approach and blurted it out. "I think it would be wise to elevate Setnakht to a position in the Court."

As soon as the words left his mouth I whipped my head around. "Never again make such a foolish suggestion!" I spat out. Sennedjem trembled before me and an uncomfortable silence sat between us.

"I... I am sorry," I finally muttered, realizing my folly. Unlike Anhotek and Meruka, who knew me since childhood, Sennedjem was too easily intimidated. I walked back to my chair and sat down with a groan. "Tell me why you counsel me thus."

"I... I am not suggesting that Setnakht... what I mean to say is that..." It took several such starts for Sennedjem to reclaim his wits.

"My counsel is based on what is best for Kem, my King," he finally said. "Setnakht is your only other living heir. He is a bright and lively child." Sennedjem went on singing the boy's praises, as my mind wandered to the end of Akhet, a full year after Neith-hotep's death when, during a time of utter grief and despair, when my ka was lonely beyond imagining, I traveled back to my boyhood home, to the palace in Tjeni, to walk its hallways and gardens and reacquaint myself with the dry river valleys and mountains in the eastern desert that I so loved and missed. In my melancholy, Tawaret, now a mature, shapely woman, and always so eager to please, had spent a few nights in my bed. Her long black hair had not lost its radiance, her eyes their allure, nor her ba any of its enthusiasm. And during our time together I initially felt my weariness lift and my ka lighter than it had been since Neith-hotep's death. But, after those few days I regained my senses and felt flooded by guilt. I left hurriedly from Tjeni, making sure that Tawaret would always be well provided.

"He is but a baby..." I protested, "...too young for a position in the Court... or anywhere else for that matter."

"He is nearly ten years old already, my King, older than you were when Anhotek began to prepare you for rule." Sennedjem waited for his words to take effect. "I am not suggesting that he take Hor-aha's place. Not at all. I am only suggesting that he be given a Court title... that he be given the opportunity to receive military training, that he be tutored in diplomacy, just... just in case."

I could not even imagine Setnakht at ten years of age. The only time I had seen him was just after he was born, at his naming ceremony at the Temple in Nekhen, when I dared not even look at his mother, Tawaret, such was my embarrassment at my weakness. Yet she acted kindly toward me even then. To think of him approaching manhood caused my heart to weigh heavy in my body.

"I will think about your counsel," I finally said to Sennedjem, more to dismiss him than to actually give it the full consideration it deserved. He hesitated, wringing his hands together, wanting to say more. Then he thought better of it and bowed low to the ground and made to leave.

"One other matter," I called to him and he turned around to face me. "Make ready for me to travel to the east bank. I wish to be alone with my thoughts."

"When?" Sennedjem asked.

"Now," I answered. "Right now." He bowed again and made haste to leave.

By early evening I arrived with my entourage at the

foot of the brown mountains in the desert due east of Inabu-hedj. They were not the many-colored desert mountains of my boyhood home, but over the years I had become accustomed to them and even preferred some of their quiet places. The King's Guard set up their tents around mine and soon the servants had prepared an entirely satisfying meal. By then I was exhausted from the day's events and retired to my tent.

I remember Anhotek complaining to me often as he grew older that the sleep of the aged is cursed. As I added years I knew exactly what he meant, for rarely would I be blessed with a night through which I slept completely and soundly. Sometimes I would awake a few hours after I fell asleep. Most nights I would stay asleep until the hours before Ra's disk appeared, then awake with my heart racing, to watch him light up Kem with his orb.

This night I awoke well before Ra appeared and slipped on my tunic quietly. Weneg, bless his young heart, slept soundly on his back, snoring lightly. I pulled back the flap of our tent and walked out into the cool night. The two sentries nearest my tent nodded at me and I approached them by the light of the fire they tended.

"I leave now for a day on the mountain," I whispered, pointing to the peak that towered above us. "Instruct no one to come for me, unless I do not appear at dark, even an hour or two after." They acknowledged my command with their right forearms across their chests. I picked up my water skin, slowly stuffed a leather bag with cheese, dates and bread and shuffled from the camp as the morning desert winds began to blow and the colors of the sky began to take on the gentle pink and orange of day.

In an hour, despite my infirmities, I had climbed halfway up the mountain to greet Ra's disk. I removed my bag and drank from the water skin, then spread my arms wide to greet Ra at the very moment he entered our world. I watched the tiniest sliver of his golden orb peek out from the low-lying mountains that faced me toward the east. I have heard that there are those in Towi who have never greeted Ra in the morning, who have lived their whole lives without seeing his orb newly born and golden and huge in the sky. The priests claim this is an affront to Ra, but I say differently. To see Ra rebirthed is a blessing beyond blessings, one not meant to grace all people of our land, or any other.

I quickly removed my tunic top and spread it on the ground next to me and raised my arms again in tribute to Ra. Who can describe the feeling of his warm rays caressing one's body, enveloping it in the heat of his love? There I stood, accepting Ra's blessing until his flaming disk revealed itself fully in the sky. I breathed in deeply the meditative sen-sen breaths, breathed in the warmth of his glow, and soon I felt transported into the realm of the gods.

In this altogether wondrous state, I sat down upon my tunic, crossed my legs and meditated, as Anhotek had taught me to do. I breathed sen-sen slowly, purposefully, my inner eyes watching the currents of my breath enter my nostrils and swirl within my lungs, before exiting again. I chanted silently in my innermost heart, chanted the special, holy words that Anhotek had revealed to me. I felt myself rise, although I still sat securely nestled in the comfort of the mountain's sand, my back against a smooth rock. I rose and floated toward the edge of the precipice that was below me. I stepped out, as I had done so long ago, when my visions of Kem were fresh in my heart. I stepped out, spread my falcon wings and soared.

The wind rushing by my ears was the only sound I heard. Soon even that ceased and the tranquility of the desert enveloped me. My heart welcomed its stillness.

I soared away, over the barren eastern desert and to the south, to Lower and Upper Ta-Sety, to Meruka's lush homelands, then back to the deserts of Lower Ta-Sety, to the valley where Hor-aha had tragically lost his men in battle. A narrow thread of green appeared to me then and I homed into its familiar embrace as a pigeon does to its roost.

I followed Mother Nile along its fertile valleys, past beautiful temples that had been built under my reign, past hundreds of granaries that had saved my people from starvation, past the glorious cities of Nekhen and Nekheb and Tjeni, all grown larger and more prosperous with trade, along Wat-Hor with its strings of caravans passing each other, laden with all manner of goods, and to Inabu-hedj, its white walls gleaming along Mother Nile's banks. I saw Kem united, prosperous, its people proud, ma'at strong, and it was good.

None of what had transpired in my reign could have happened without Anhotek and as I visioned his sweet face I immediately felt his presence under my wings. His ka lifted me up and gently pointed me back to Tjeni, my birthplace, then south to Nekhen, where I hovered with him to relive my rebirth as Narmer and the ceremony that joined my ka forever with Neith-hotep's, may she be blessed for all eternity.

Ra's light penetrated my skin, bearing with it rich memories of my beloved, made bittersweet by the passage of time. In a rush I recalled the poem I wrote to her. It had been ten years since I last recited it, upon Neith-hotep's deathbed, as she lay stricken with the illness that eats the flesh from within. As I sang its verses, I changed its words to reflect my innermost feelings.

> Ten years it is since I last saw you, my sister,
> And I am feeling ill and old.
> My limbs are heavy, I forget my body.
> When the shamans come, no remedies cure me,
> Even the priests know not the cure.
> Old age is the name for my disease,
> And only your name can put me back on my feet.
> The coming and going of our prayers to each other
> Is what revives my heart.
> More beneficial to me than any remedies you are, my sister.
> More important are you to me than any medical papyrus.
> My salvation will be when we are together once again.
> When I see you again, then I will feel well!
> When you open your eyes to me, my limbs will feel alive again.

When you speak, then I will be strong.

When we embrace, you will drive away all evil from me.

You have been gone for too long, my love.

Thus it was that love, the love of a man and a woman and the love of a father and son, were borne on Ra's rays and comforted my ka. It took me a lifetime to understand it, but as I sat on that mountain, I breathed in Horus' ultimate secret.

How do we know when the truth has been visited upon us? How can we be so sure that the morsel of knowledge we feel we have been given is not merely a deception? I remember asking that of Anhotek after my fitful vision dreams in Ta-Sety when I was but a child. You will know, he told me. With truth you always know.

And so it was on that day, that when I began to flutter my eyelids, when my ka once again settled back into my body and my visioning was over, after Anhotek and Neith-hotep helped me to see that the answers I sought already dwelled within my heart, at that moment I heard a sharp noise in the air, a piercing cry that filled the sky and echoed in the valley below. I opened my eyes and looked up and saw a mighty falcon flying in front of Ra's disk.

# SCROLL TWENTY-SIX

*For But One Moment...*

It haunts me still, on troubled nights like this, when I feel so desperately alone and pace the mud-brick floor for hours. There are times when I can recall the feeling of the liquid warmth caressing my forming skin, now dried and wrinkled. From within that blinding darkness I remember absolute contentment, a peace I've not known since. The sounds were soft and soothing, as if Mother Nile's ripples gently lapped at the swollen stems of the reeds that line its banks. I tumbled, contented, seeking with unformed eyes my own cushioned comfort. I think back to that time, days without beginning or end, strung together as if time had stood still, eternal bliss.

After those first blissful months within my mother's womb, I sensed Scorpion's presence, like Mother Nile's raging torrents during Akhet. I felt the walls that contained me draw tighter. The sadness inside my ka overwhelmed me, yet even now I am not certain whose sadness it was, mine or hers. Soon I shall know, but I suspect the answer already. Am I not my mother's son?

By your loving hands, Anhotek, I was guided from

darkness to light. But by then, like stone in mortar, my destiny had already been cast. By the end my mother knew she was but an actor in a tragic play. Love, loathing, anticipation, fear, happiness, sadness, all parts of the same whole. She loved me, she nourished me, and she loathed the part of me that was him. That was it, was it not? In the end, she could not bear witness to Scorpion's spirit flowing through my ka. She departed, before she ever saw my flesh, before she felt the unbearable pain of seeing even a small part of his ka hidden behind my eyes.

In the twilight of sleeplessness tonight, I again read our picture words, Anhotek, our story, the story of Kem. I run my gnarled fingers over the papyrus scrolls to summon your presence. For but one moment again in this life with you, or with my sweet Neith-hotep, I would gladly surrender my ka to Anubis. But he would make no such deal, for he patiently awaits its imminent arrival.

"How did you know, Anhotek, or… or did you?" I lean forward in my chair to hear your answer, but you only sit silently nowadays staring at me, waiting.

"I seek to… to understand how these things happened. Were you aware of your own greatness? They talk of you even now. The priests, they whisper your name, dear teacher, as if you were still…"

My eyesight is nearly gone. Anhotek comes to visit now and again. He tells me he will bring Neith-hotep and I think that would be very good, for I miss her dearly. It has been a while since I have spoken with her or felt her sweet breath upon mine as together, nestled in each other's arms, we would fall asleep. Or was that, too, a dream? No, she lived, for she was sent to me by Horus, for us to love each other and to create another life to love.

She must be away, busy with the affairs of Kem, checking on the progress of a new temple or officiating in my stead at some impossibly boring event. I can almost see her busily running from here to there, her servants throwing up their hands in frustration trying to keep up with her.

"We did well together, did we not, Anhotek? Oh, you need not answer, for I will speak for us and say that we did.

I am content. Yes, yes, very content."

"Hello, father! I have brought Djer with me!" a voice calls loudly in my ear, before hugging me tightly. I think Hor-Aha has brought something for me, so I lean forward to peer at it. I am surprised by my own reflection.

"Djer... this is your grandfather, the great King Narmer." I feel the man with the familiar voice take my hands and place them on the face of the boy who stands in front of me. The boy whimpers and struggles to run away.

"No, no! Do not cry, Hor-Aha. Are you hurt? Look, Anhotek sits over there to apply a balm to your wound." Then, suddenly, my reflection disappears, replaced again by the murky stillness.

The fog, it comes and goes, familiar, but still frightening. It rolls in each day, over Mother Nile, to where I sit, in Tjeni or Inabu-hedj, I am no longer sure which. It hovers, thin and wispy, at first. Then, in the stillness of night, it thickens and confuses.

"Please, Anhotek, tell Neith-hotep I wish to enjoy her company. There is so much to celebrate. Kem is now one. Our son, he... he grows taller every day. I saw him, today I think. Yes, it was him... or... no, no it was Meni I saw. Yes, Meni! The one who was stung by the scorpion.

"Do you remember him, my dear Anhotek? You do. I can see your smile. Do you recall how you used to hold him, to tell him your stories of creation, to dream with him the dreams of a great Kem, to... to lightly stroke his hair as he basked in Ra's light? He misses that.

"Come, Anhotek. Our story is over. Our work here is done. Horus waits. Take my hand. Let us fly to him now... let us soar together."

# Afterward

Narmer, also known as Menes, lived approximately 3150 B.C. He is buried in Abydos, in a tomb discovered by Gunter Dreyer of the German Archaeological Institute, one of my mentors for this trilogy.

King Narmer was a revered figure throughout Egypt's long dynastic tradition. However, the historical record is scant.

For those interested in learning more about Narmer and the earliest dynastic periods I recommend two scholarly books by one of my mentors for this project, Toby A. H. Wilkinson of Cambridge University, England.

Genesis of the Pharaohs, Thames & Hudson, 2003.

Early Dynastic Egypt, Routledge, 1999.

For an expanded list of references, as well as the latest archaeological discoveries about Narmer, Meryt-Neith and Qa'a, please visit Les' website: www.lesterpicker.com

Les spent nearly ten years researching and then writing his First Dynasty trilogy, consisting of The First Pharaoh, The Dagger of Isis and the upcoming Qa'a.

# THE FIRST PHARAOH READER'S GUIDE

1. The First Pharaoh is set in approximately 3,150 BC. By then Egypt was already an advanced civilization. What aspects of early ancient Egypt culture surprised you?
2. By 3,150 BC the Egyptian legal system already afforded women certain rights and privileges, such as the right to initiate divorce proceedings, inheritance rights and the right to own a business. Does this surprise you?
3. King Narmer was revered by every subsequent King and Pharaoh (a term that originated later) and worshipped as a deity in some instances. What about King Narmer's personality and accomplishments made him so revered?
4. How would you characterize the relationship between King Narmer and Neith-Hotep? Which aspects did you enjoy most? Which aspects did you enjoy least?
5. The relationship between Meni and his father, King Scorpion, was a complex one. Do you feel that King Scorpion loved his son? Do you feel that Menes ways of coping with his father's disapproval were appropriate?
6. Anhotek served as a father-figure for the young Meni. What aspects of their relationship were notable to you?
7. Could Egypt have achieved its future greatness

without Unification?

8. Ancient Egyptian medicine was far advanced by 3,150 BC, but still primitive compared with modern medicine. What aspects of medical practices impressed you and what aspects negatively impressed you?

9. What impact did King Narmer's epilepsy have upon his character?

10. Should Anhotek have done more to mediate the conflict between Menes and King Scorpion?

11. Compare and contrast Ihy's strengths and weaknesses with Anhotek's.

12. How did Mersyankh influence King Narmer's eventual character?

13. How did the ancient Egyptians' adherence to ma'at influence their development as a culture?

14. Was the push for Unification more attributable to King Narmer or Anhotek?

15. Some scholars have suggested that ancient Egypt was originally peopled by black tribes from northern Sudan. In any event, the interactions between Egypt and the cultures to its south were already advanced by 3,150 BC. How does that influence show up in Meruka's character?

16. Egypt society was open to other cultures, albeit on a limited basis due to their geography. How did you respond to Anhotek's and Meni's interactions with the distinctly Semitic Me'ka'el and El-Or?

17. Some Egyptologists believe that ancient Egyptian civilization significantly influenced the formative years of Judaism. Are you aware of any customs, beliefs, ceremonies or practices that are similar in both ancient Egypt and in Judaism?

18. How did the description of the Battle for Unification affect you? Did the goriness of ancient hand-to-hand combat make an impression? Did the characters' response to the realities of battle surprise you?

19. Did King Narmer do a good job preparing his son for leadership?

20. "Come, Anhotek. Our story is over. Our work here is done. Horus waits. Take my hand. Let us fly to him

now... let us soar together." King Narmer on his death bed says these words to his long-dead vizier, Anhotek. Was King Narmer's work truly done? Was Anhotek's?

21. The link between the King/Pharaoh and Horus is a strong and pervasive one throughout the novel and throughout Egyptian Dynastic rule. Like Native American beliefs, the falcon is a strong totem. How did it serve King Narmer throughout his life? Was it a benefit or a curse?

# ABOUT THE AUTHOR

Les Picker has more than 600 writing and photo credits in National Geographic Society publications, Better Homes & Gardens, Forbes, Time, Inc. Publications, Money, Fortune Small Business, Bloomberg Personal Finance, National Parks Magazine, and dozens of other publications. He is a former newspaper reporter, photographer and editor. For three years Les was a columnist for Oceans Magazine and for four years was Editor-In-Chief for a national environmental magazine. Les is a member of the American Society of Journalists and Authors (ASJA), Nikon Professional Services (NPS) and Hasselblad Professionals.

For four years, Les was a weekly columnist for The Baltimore Sun and continues as a freelance feature travel writer. For three years, Les was a regular commentator on National Public Radio's Marketplace, carried on 260 stations nationwide.

Les has an earned doctorate in ecology from the University of Maine, was a faculty member at the University of Delaware and an adjunct faculty at The Johns Hopkins University. His writing website is www.lesterpicker.com. His photography work can be found at www.lesterpickerphoto.com. Les was the winner of the prestigious 2011 Canada Northern Lights Award for Best

Travel Photography.

His novels include:

***The First Pharaoh*** (Book One of The First Dynasty series). The story of the uniting of Upper and Lower Egypt into a dynastic tradition that lasted for 3,000 years.

***The Dagger of Isis*** (Book Two of The First Dynasty series). Traces the life and times, loves, war and Royal Court intrigue of Meryt-Neith, the first female Pharaoh.

***Qa'a*** (Book Three of The First Dynasty series). The turbulent time of the last King of the First Dynasty and the difficult transition to the Second Dynasty.

***The Underground.*** How does a woman solve the mystery of a murdered mother and a doting father?

***Sargent Mountain.*** A happily married woman deals with the death of her husband… and her discovery of "the other woman."

Les can be contacted through his website or at: lespicker@gmail.com. You can follow him on Facebook and on Twitter: http://twitter.com/lespicker

Printed in Great Britain
by Amazon.co.uk, Ltd.,
Marston Gate.